2-2024

TRUST
the
STARS

Center Point
Large Print

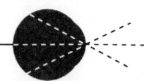

**This Large Print Book carries the
Seal of Approval of N.A.V.H.**

TRUST
the
STARS

TRICIA GOYER

CENTER POINT LARGE PRINT
THORNDIKE, MAINE

This Center Point Large Print edition
is published in the year 2024 by arrangement with
WhiteFire Publishing.

The text of this Large Print edition is unabridged.
In other aspects, this book may vary
from the original edition.
Printed in the United States of America
on permanent paper sourced using
environmentally responsible foresting methods.
Set in 16-point Times New Roman type.

ISBN: 978-1-63808-993-3

The Library of Congress has cataloged this record
under Library of Congress Control Number: 2023946183

The heavens declare the glory of God;
the skies proclaim the work of his hands.
Day after day they pour forth speech;
night after night, they reveal knowledge.
They have no speech. They use no words;
no sound is heard from them.
Yet their voice goes out into all the earth,
their words to the ends of the world.
In the heavens God has pitched a tent for the sun.

~ Psalm 19:1-4

PROLOGUE

Vatican City, Rome, Italy
18 October 1943

Alessandra Appiani walked with a quickened pace toward the front door of the Vatican, her footsteps echoing on the marble floor and the fateful words echoing through her mind. *The Nazis have come for you just as you always knew they would.*

Just beyond the door spread St. Peter's Square with the ellipse-shaped colonnades topped by a balustrade on which one hundred and forty figures of saints stood. Yet not one of those saints could protect her today. In the heart of God's holy city, foreboding filled the air. She'd arrived back just hours ago, thankful to find her four children safe after Italy's surrender to the Allied powers, yet her husband Christian, her love, was missing. Summoned to the door to receive a telegram, Alessandra guessed the news concerned him.

Dear Lord Jesus, give me the wisdom to follow your ways so that I might serve you and the people you have given me. Guide my steps. Strengthen my weary heart. Help me not to fail your call. Use me to give of myself just as you gave. May your will rise above my own this moment and every one of my days.

The prayer came naturally to Alessandra, as it had for the last twenty years. It had been her mother, God rest her soul, who had urged the young Alessandra to submit herself entirely to God. *While others point to our position as one of honor, you must see yourself as a servant of the people and our Lord,* Queen Eliana insisted. Yet today, the prayer meant something different than it had for the last two decades. What *was* the Lord's way amid war? Would she be able to discern it even in this?

Finding the Lord's way guided her daily choices. Whether Alessandra was in the Vatican's safety or their city's horrors, she sought to find the good and do the good. On one side, the grandeur of the Vatican itself—with its towering columns and ornate facades—was a testament to the power and majesty of the Catholic Church. On the other side, crowded and chaotic streets filled with the sounds and smells of a city under siege.

The Nazi occupation had brought a sense of darkness and fear to Rome. Soldiers patrolled the streets, their boots ringing out on the cobblestones. But despite the fear and uncertainty, there was also a sense of defiance in the air. The people of Rome refused to be cowed by the Nazi presence. They went about their business, determined to live as best they could—or at least that's how many wanted to appear.

Alessandra smoothed her hands over the front of her linen blazer, attempting to stride with confident steps. *Remember, act as if you have nothing to hide.*

Years ago, even when war was only a rumor, she had attempted to follow the Lord's way. But in these times, it was a daily choice to do anything to make a difference.

Just a thirty-minute walk from the Vatican was the ghetto of Rome. For 400 years, the four cramped blocks around the Porticus Octavia had been home to Roman Jews. Over the years of the war, Alessandra had traveled there a few times a week. The sick had been tended to. The poor, fed. But she soon realized more had to be done when, twenty-two days ago, the leader of the SS and the Gestapo in Rome, Herbert Kappler, demanded that the Jewish community give him 50 kilograms of gold or 200 families would be deported. And even though the demand had been met, that had done nothing to protect the innocent Jews.

As she turned down the last hallway, moving toward the front entrance, Alessandra's thoughts flashed to the young girl, no older than four or five, who had wrapped her arms around Alessandra's neck so tightly as she picked her up. The girl in her arms had been small and fragile, like a porcelain doll. Her dark hair was matted, and her eyes were wide with fear. Alessandra couldn't imagine what she had been through, what horrors she'd witnessed in her young life. All she knew was that this child needed her help, just as the others had before her.

"It will be all right. We will keep you safe. Have you ever wanted to visit the mountains? These mountains are higher than you could ever imagine," Alessandra had soothed in a sing-song voice.

Alessandra had pulled Miriam close, a surge of protectiveness and love rushing through her. Yet even as she'd carried the child to the safe house just this morning, it haunted her that she could do nothing for her husband. Rumor had it that Christian was under house arrest in Bavaria. Her heart ached, knowing she and her children were safe, but her husband was not.

While conventional wisdom said safety for herself was to stay within the protected walls of the Vatican, something deep within Alessandra's gut told her differently. *True safety is walking in your will, my Lord. Help my steps not to falter.* If the Lord directed her to leave her security for the sake of her husband's life, there would be no question. Love would compel her. Yet she also knew that leaving the Vatican would most likely be walking into a lair of wolves. *Oh, my Lord, keep me strong.*

Up ahead, a young priest stood at the door, holding it slightly ajar. Although a young man, worry lines creased Father Marco's face. His dark brown eyes, usually full of warmth and compassion, radiated fear. His lips were thin and downturned. At her approach, they parted slightly as if prepared to issue a warning. Then, as if steeling himself to face the enemy outside the door, Father Marco straightened. Erect, he set his jaw as if he were made of marble like the floor he stood rooted upon. Even though a warm breeze flowed through the crack, a chill traveled down Alessandra's spine.

"A request has been sent that someone wishes to see me?" She attempted to keep her voice firm. Though she'd always considered herself a capable woman, today, it took everything she had not to crumble under the weight of worry. She forced her shoulders back as she paused before the priest.

As if just brought to life, the muscles in his face pulsed. His mouth clenched. "There are two Nazis who demand your audience." The priest held the door steady.

Her fingertips touched the hollow of her throat above her jeweled necklace. "Two?"

"It is a soldier and an officer with a message to deliver. I insisted you'd just arrived and were weary from travel. I requested that the officer come back tomorrow. Or maybe the day after."

"And still he waits?"

"He states it's urgent—a matter of life and death."

"Does this have to do with Christian?" Alessandra clasped her hands together at the mention of her husband's name. The highest members of the Nazi party had been trying to put a noose around her husband's neck for months. Even though he'd been a faithful party member for over a decade, they now questioned his decisions and motives. And with her brother-in-law's recent death . . . did they believe Christian played a part in silencing those faithful to the Fuhrer? That she did?

"I do not know if it concerns your husband or not. The Germans did not say."

"Yet still, a matter of life and death?" She narrowed her gaze and nodded toward the door. "I will speak to them."

"But, Princess . . ." His fingers wrapped tighter around the door handle. "You are under our protection. You are safe."

"And it is not my job to stay safe, is it?" She motioned to him again to open the door. She didn't know what the future held, but she had to have faith. Faith that God would protect her just as He'd protected the young girl she'd passed into another's capable arms. Trust that God would guide their unique journeys.

With slow movements, the priest swung open

the door, allowing Alessandra to see the Nazi officer before her and the soldier at his side.

The officer stood erect with his hands clasped behind his back. "Can you come with us, Princess? This is an urgent matter concerning your husband. Your presence is requested at our local offices."

Instead of answering the officer, Alessandra turned to Father Marco. "Will you tend to my children and tell them I will be away for the rest of the day?"

He responded with the slightest of nods.

She thought of retrieving her purse but remembered the special papers sewn in its lining. No, that would never do. Then, hoping to appear as if she had no concerns about their request, she exited the Vatican and set her eyes on the waiting car.

The streets around the Vatican were filled with vendors and peddlers, yet few wares were laid out on makeshift tables and blankets. The vendors' journey to the city's center was more ritual than work these days since there was so little to be had.

As the bells of St. Peter's rang across the city, Alessandra knew she stood on the precipice of darkness and light. The work of caring for others—and of the silent resistance and rebellion within the walls of the Vatican—had taken her mind off of the greater danger to herself and other members of the royal family. Yet didn't the Nazis happily strike down anyone in power—especially those whose loyalties were questioned by the Nazi elite?

Alessandra approached the waiting car, refusing to peer into the eyes of evil lest she crumble. She slid into the backseat of the waiting sedan and folded her trembling hands on her lap.

As the engine sparked to life, she refused to look back at the holy church—their refuge in times of trouble. Knowing her children would be waiting for her return tonight caused an ache to grow in the pit of her stomach. *Please, God, I do not know if I am strong enough.*

She sucked in a shuddering breath and squared her shoulders as she prepared for the biggest test of her life. Alessandra could only hope she had the strength to stay the course, neither crumble nor confess. And as her eyes fluttered closed for the briefest second, one thought gave her peace.

She could have faith that another was safe when all seemed lost. Even now, the young girl Miriam was in good hands—like the others Alessandra had helped before her. It was now Alessandra's turn to trust that this world's glimmers of light and goodness could hold out, even under the suffocating cover of darkness.

CHAPTER ONE

Alloria
Present Day

Louis Castillo adjusted the lapel of his tuxedo as he peered into the mirror and blew out a low breath. His warped reflection hinted at the mirror's age. Still, one could expect no less from the medieval town of Las Massana tucked high in the Pyrenees Mountains. He forced a smile, hoping it was believable. The last thing he desired was the pity of festival-goers. Yet they knew, as he did, his heartbreak. What good was being an heir to the throne if one didn't have someone to share life with, someone to love?

Since morning, a crowd had been gathering on the cobblestone outside the window. The aroma of delicious food from the open-air vendors took him back to his youth. As a boy, he'd enjoyed racing up and down the street, stopping at any table, and choosing his favorite foods before racing off again. Those times were some of the few when he'd tasted freedom.

Years later, that sense of freedom still had a bigger draw than the food. He also knew that he hadn't been as free as he imagined. At every festival of his youth, every vendor had been vetted, and Louis's bodyguards had watched his every move. Yet, as a boy, he'd relished the festival days in which he could make his own choices, choose his food, and race around with abandon as if he weren't the crown prince of Alloria.

A banner proclaiming the *Narciso Yepes International Festival* outside the castle window flapped in the breeze. How fitting that Louis would play his violin tonight in honor of the Spanish guitarist whose most famous song, "Romance," was later believed to be an arrangement rather than the guitarist's original work—since published versions of the guitar composition existed before Yepe's birth. Louis also felt very much a fraud when it came to romance, mainly due to the upcoming wedding of Lady Constance Arauz, the woman he'd hoped to spend his life with—a woman who, in a few days, would marry another.

"Not Enough Prince to Catch the Princess," one tabloid had read. The sting of those words spread like venom through his heart. *Not enough, Prince. Not enough.*

The nippy October breeze blew through the open window, urging him to focus on the evening's events. He'd been up half the night planning his escape from this wedding, this continent. If he didn't find a place to breathe, to think, he'd never be able to fulfill his royal duties and host the upcoming grand events.

At the turn of the year, an elaborate festival would celebrate his father's Silver Jubilee, marking King Alfonso's twenty-fifth year of being the reigning monarch of Alloria. Plans had been in the works for years, and until six months ago, Louis had planned to attend with Lady Constance at his side. And now? Louis would face the crowds alone just as he'd do tonight, hoping his smile wouldn't give away the shards of his broken heart.

Louis leaned forward and ran a finger around his collar, wishing he could unbutton the constraints. Then he scowled, noting the sound of footsteps on the tile.

His assistant and bodyguard, Sergio, strode into the suite with a single white flower on a silver platter. "Is the collar too tight? Pinching your neck, sir?" Sergio cocked one eyebrow, yet his eyes were fixed on Louis's face, not his shirt collar.

Louis let out another hard sigh and closed his eyes. "Just trying to breathe, Sergio. Just trying to breathe." He opened them, refusing to look in the face of his bodyguard, who'd become a close friend in the decade of his service. Louis didn't need to see sympathy there.

"I bear a gift from Princess Regina." Sergio pinched the stem between two fingers and lifted it with a flourish. "Your boutonniere." Though

17

twenty years his senior, with gray streaking his temples, there was a humor in the soft wrinkles around his bodyguard's eyes.

Louis fixed his gaze. A simple, single blossom with a double layer of ruffled petals and a perfect black center. His chest tightened at the sight of it. His aunt still treated him as if he were the darling eight-year-old boy he'd been when she'd decided it was her duty to prepare him for the crown after his mother's untimely death.

Ignoring Sergio's teasing glance, Louis nodded to the flower. "An anemone, of course."

One side of Sergio's lip curled in a smile. "Your aunt always has perfect taste. Perhaps to match your tuxedo?"

"We both know the anemone hints at hope for a positive turn of events. My dear aunt's compassion is kind but suffocating." Louis fidgeted with his collar again and then dropped his arms to his sides as his hands curled into soft fists.

Sergio nodded and reached for the collar. "Maybe it is too tight. I brought a spare shirt if—"

"This country's too tight, my man," Louis spoke through clenched teeth. Then he opened his fisted hands and forced them to relax. The last thing Louis needed was the tabloids to pick up on his shortened temper. He hoped none of the press spoke in the language of flowers, like his aunt, and pointed out another reason to pity him.

18

"Are the tickets booked for tomorrow's flight?"

"Tickets booked. Luggage packed. I reserved your room. The only task yet is yours. Have you told her yet?"

The creak of the door sounded just as Sergio finished his sentence, and Louis cringed. With the soft shuffle of his aunt's shoes on the stone floor as she entered the room, his heart jumped as if he'd just been caught with his hand in the cookie jar.

"Told me what yet?" Princess Regina Castillo strode into the room in a red velvet gown that trailed the floor. Her gray hair was combed into a neat twist at the base of her neck. She paused, clasping her hands before her, and watched in approval as Sergio pinned the boutonniere to Louis's lapel.

Louis smiled and extended a welcome hand in his aunt's direction. After Sergio finished, Louis nodded his approval. "I was hoping to see you before the concert, Aunt." He took three long strides to her, taking her hand in his own. "I dare to say there isn't a woman in Alloria who will rival your beauty." He lifted her emerald-garnished hand to his lips and placed the lightest kiss upon her paper-thin skin.

A hint of a smile touched his aunt's lips. "As my mother used to say, '*Más se consigue lamiendo que mordiendo.*' More is achieved by licking than by biting."

"You believe I am trying to win you over with flattery?" Louis widened his eyes as if shocked.

"I do not think so. I know." She slid her hand from his. "And I do hope any bags packed are for the return to Santa Coloma."

"Aunt, you know I cannot attend the wedding."

"You could if you cared more about the country than—"

"Than my heart?"

Regina's shoulders straightened. "Maybe we should discuss this after the concert."

Louis glanced again into the mirror then strode to his violin case. "Yes, we can do that. I will give you a call from the plane."

"You are leaving then?" Her eyes narrowed, and Louis looked away. He hated displeasing her, always had.

He walked to the door, his violin case in his grasp. Sergio moved ahead of him to open the door.

"Louis?" His aunt's voice called after him.

He paused his steps but refused to turn. "Yes, Aunt?"

The silence expanded between them until she finally cleared her throat. "What are you playing tonight?"

With the tight tone of Aunt Regina's voice, Louis knew he wouldn't play the light, uplifting song he'd prepared. To do so would deny the ache building up like a wall of violent waves mounting in his chest. To do so would be to become what he most detested: unflustered, rigid, unemotional.

The memory of his father's tearless face at his wife's funeral filled Louis's mind. *Why must we always stay strong?* He'd wanted to cry even as a boy. *Aren't we real people—people who hurt, who face heartbreak?* The castle could crumble around them, and Aunt Regina's face would display the same calm, unworried look lest the people dare discover that the royals were an actual family filled with personalities and problems.

Louis cleared his throat. "Tchaikovsky, Violin Concerto. Second movement." He turned, expecting to see the familiar flat expression.

Instead, Aunt Regina's eyebrows peaked and then lowered. "Do you wish to make everyone weep? And what of those who play after you?"

"Shall I always think of others only?"

Aunt Regina's gaze narrowed. "Must you wear your heart on your sleeve?" Then, just as quickly, the anger disappeared. Instead, compassion filled her face, again surprising him. She stepped forward and touched his sleeve, offering a soft squeeze on his arm as she used to do when he was a boy. Had she ever been heartbroken and ridiculed for it? So little he knew of his aunt's life before she'd taken charge of him.

Louis's shoulders softened, and his resolve started to slip. Sergio shuffled beside him, alerting Louis of the time and warning him against Regina's magnetic pull toward her wishes.

He readjusted the handle of his violin case in his hand. "What good are emotions if one hides them? Would you rather have me like Father?" he dared to whisper.

"Of course not, but I can already imagine the headlines—"

"*Prince Louis Loses at Love Yet Again?*" he interrupted, voice raised an octave.

"I was thinking, *Runaway Prince.*" She sighed, changing the topic from the music to his escape. "And where are you off to this time?"

"Do you have to ask?" Even as he said the words, the memory of the sun rising over the African savannah warmed him.

"There are other places to tend a wounded heart. The beaches of the Riviera, perhaps. My friend Lourdes has a granddaughter—"

"And *this* is the problem. All the right women, with all the right credentials, have dozens of suitors. Why choose a prince from a small country like Alloria when there are more eligible bachelors like Viscount Althorp Louis Spencer?"

"He's not even royalty," Aunt Regina scoffed, wrinkling her nose.

"In this world, Aunt, the nephew of Princess Diana means more than the prince of a little-known place like Alloria. This is why I need to

22

go somewhere where no one knows me. Where people see me as *me* and not as the crown."

And with that, Louis left the room, preparing to make the crowd weep with his song. Then tonight, at least, he wouldn't have to cry alone.

CHAPTER TWO

Kibera Slums, Nairobi, Kenya

Olivia Garza held the child tighter to her chest as she followed the ebony-skinned guard who walked with authority ahead of her. It had taken some convincing to get Kioko to lead her away from the others, but she refused to take a no. The thin, brown-skinned girl in her arms couldn't be any older than three. It was into Olivia's arms that this girl's mother placed her before collapsing and breathing her last. Believing she could be the girl's mother wasn't realistic. Even though Olivia prided herself on thinking outside the box and working hard to make the impossible possible, this could never be.

Who'd ever allow a single woman who balanced a part-time job in the inner city and co-produced a popular YouTube documentary series—in secret—to adopt a child internationally? Never mind that her mother had done very little mothering. Olivia had no idea what being a mother would look like—or even being a girlfriend. She'd made it her mission to let no man become anything closer than a friend. Relationships asked too much and, from what she'd seen, caused too much pain. And it's not like she had time for a relationship anyway.

Most nights back in Little Rock, she sat alone in her apartment, staring at the glowing screen of her laptop. Even when the city outside grew quiet, her mind raced with edits, deliverables, and deadlines.

With the release of each new episode, she'd watch the views climb. The growing popularity of her documentary was like a dream come true. Her series had become a sensation, with millions of views and countless fans worldwide. Still, it also felt like a tornado tearing through her life. It sucked up her time and tangled her emotions. Her work had the power to lift her and take her to new heights and the potential to leave her shattered in its wake. After all, what if her audience didn't like the person behind the voice, behind the stories? What if they abandoned her just like her mother did—proving the real her wasn't worth sticking around for?

When she was just a voice on the screen sharing the stories of people who bore the same flaws and failures as her mother, Olivia found it easier to open up about her turbulent childhood. She delved deep into understanding fears, hurts, addictions, and even the best of intentions of others. This journey allowed Olivia to view her mother—a single parent with a Jekyll and Hyde disposition—with a new lens of compassion and understanding. Her mom, ever so caring in one moment, would be consumed by a dysfunctional relationship the next, thrusting both of them into peril. When the viewers saw the real Olivia, the one shaped by these experiences, what would they think? Perhaps it was safer to stay in the shadows, to remain a mystery.

With every new episode came new pressures. And yet, she still had to keep her identity a secret. She couldn't let anyone in her day-to-day life know she was responsible for the series' success. While the message was a spark that could set the world ablaze, at times, as the messenger, she felt like a mere flame flickering in the wind.

Despite the exhaustion and fear, Olivia felt a sense of pride and purpose. She was making a difference, telling stories that needed to be told. And soon, it would all come to a head when she filmed her big reveal. As strange as it was, her mother had been happy and whole here—the summer of her eighteenth year, when the entire world had stretched before her with possibilities.

The girl wriggled in Olivia's arms, returning her to the present. Olivia often wondered why her mother went to Kenya. Each query about the trip got a new answer. College could wait. She needed to break free from her controlling mother. She wanted to see the world, to matter, to prove she wasn't a failure. When a family friend offered a spot to work in the slums for the summer with a service group overseas, she took it. It was there she met Olivia's dad and became pregnant. Olivia pondered how it might've been different if her grandparents saw the pregnancy as a challenge, but not a shame. The divide it caused was clear. Her mother left, deciding to raise Olivia alone rather than face scorn.

Two steps ahead of Olivia, Kioko, who'd lived his whole life in the Kibera slums and worked for the same organization she'd come with, led her through mazes of small alleys. Olivia knew she'd never figure out how to get out of here without him. The biggest slum in the world, nearly three million people lived in mud and tin shacks about the size of her apartment bedroom, averaging eight or more people in each dwelling.

Olivia wrinkled her nose as the sewer stench rose from the open ditch she walked beside. Around her, women and children sat in doorways of small shacks. The wind picked up slightly, tossing crumpled-up newspaper about her feet. Other debris bounced over flattened cardboard boxes. Broken glass, cigarette butts, and rusty bits of metal floated in the sewer sludge. She tried not to peer inside the darkened doorways but often heard coughing or low voices talking.

In the distance, a rock-and-roll beat played. Up ahead, the sounds of tin scraping against tin filled her ears as she watched metal sheets being hoisted onto one of the roofs by two tall, skinny young men.

As she neared the young men, Olivia dared to meet their gazes. They were just teens doing men's work. Back home, guys that age would drive cars they couldn't afford and stir up trouble along the inner-city streets. Back home, young men were claiming dominance rather than fighting for survival. In either case, the future didn't look bright for any of them.

The child in her arms squirmed and whimpered. Olivia stroked the dense canopy of the girl's tightly coiled curls. Finally, one of the young men opened his mouth as if he were to speak to her as she moved past. Kioko shook his head and cleared his throat. The young man clamped his mouth shut and turned back to his work.

Olivia had no doubt he would have asked for money if it hadn't been for Kioko's presence. The crumbled American dollars she stuffed into her pockets this morning would have made the difference between those young men eating tonight or going to bed hungry. Still, she'd given away the last of her bills hours ago.

More than that, she didn't have time to slow down, let alone stop. She had less than thirty minutes to surrender this sweet child to an orphanage director's hands and return to where their van had parked. The shadows were already lengthening, proving that the sun would soon be setting, and then it wouldn't be safe for any white person in the slums—not even with a guard. It also would not be safe for her team waiting near the van, preparing to shoot one short clip for the day—the last segment of her story before the big reveal.

Motor oil and cooking smells, mixed with the aroma of beer, assaulted her as she walked past a small workshop where a huddle of men reclined and drank. With a small leap, she crossed a ditch then hurried toward the opening of the wood and clay structure set to the back. It was larger than most, yet the ceiling was still low. Olivia had to bend down to avoid bumping it against the plastered wood as she followed Kioko into the building.

Children's laughter filled her chest with warmth. When Olivia's eyes adjusted to the dim light, she saw the little ones lined up with small tin pans and eager smiles in expectation of dinner. At the head of two lines, older women stirred large pots of porridge, the children's evening meal. Olivia recognized the aroma of the mush. It smelled similar to cornbread but appeared more like watery oatmeal. Even though the children would only get one scoop, it was more than many would have tonight. She smiled, seeing the room's cleanliness and the children's bright faces. If she had to leave this little girl, at least this was a good place where she'd be well cared for.

Following Kioko to the building's rear, Olivia watched a woman enter the spacious room through the back door. She wore a bright head covering, and her long dress was clean but faded. The woman's eyes widened joyfully, and she smiled, showing off brilliant white teeth.

"Now, who might this be?" the woman—no older than Olivia—said with a thick accent. She spoke more to Kioko than Olivia, even as she extended her arms toward the child.

The small girl sat up straighter in Olivia's arms. Then without hesitation, she leaned toward the orphanage director. In one fluid motion, the woman took the girl from Olivia and curled her against her chest. The girl's eyelashes fluttered as if she were fighting sluggishness. Then she snuggled under the woman's chin just as she'd done in Olivia's arms.

"They call her Promise." Kioko's voice was low as he scanned the faces of the dozens of other children who now looked their way, curious about their visitors—especially the white-skinned one.

Olivia stepped closer to the woman and brushed the girl's arm with her fingertips. "Her mother passed away not long ago. No one knows about her . . . family." A pang hit Olivia's heart as she said those words.

The woman nodded once. "Well, she is my daughter now; glory be to God. That is why you've come, yes?"

"Kioko has great trust in you. He also told me

that when I get home, I can wire money to him, and he will come—"

"Yes, yes." The woman waved a hand as if brushing off Olivia's words. "Some visitors give, some do not. It matters not; the Lord always provides. He has ne'er failed me or my children. Not once."

Olivia nodded, took in the girl's face again, and turned to Kioko.

He cleared his throat. "We must hurry. Darkness comes soon."

He needn't provide more of a warning. Olivia looked into the woman's eyes, and peace radiated there. Hundreds of children to care for with only the generosity of others to fill their tummies, and then a new sister tonight. Who knew? Maybe Promise wouldn't be the only one dropped off before morning. And still peace.

"Thank you." Olivia brushed a strand of long dark hair back from her shoulder. Even though she'd only known the girl for a few hours, her arms felt empty, and a longing to belong to someone filled her chest, surprising her. With a farewell grin, she tried to dismiss that yearning.

She moved toward the door with Kioko by her side, yet before exiting, the woman's voice rose behind her. "There is a promise coming for you, too, Olivia. You will not have to face another year alone."

Olivia's heart flipped, and she paused her steps.

She shifted her gaze over her shoulder, meeting the penetrating eyes of the older woman. The soft glow the open window painted her silhouette in a golden hue. Kioko nudged Olivia gently to go. Instead, Olivia took a step closer to the woman.

"I've seen many things in my time, Olivia," the woman continued, her voice gentle yet unwavering. "Trust in the path ahead and the mysteries it holds."

How does she know my name?

Olivia swallowed hard, searching for words. The weight of her loneliness had been a heavy burden, and the prospect of hope felt both exhilarating and terrifying. "Thank you," she whispered, her voice barely audible.

"Come. We must hurry. The others wait," Kioko urged, motioning her forward.

And then Olivia remembered the real reason she was here—to tell a story about this place and the people. About the joys and heartbreak, both of which she now better understood.

CHAPTER THREE

Kibera Slums, Nairobi, Kenya

As they stepped outside, it was visibly darker than when they'd entered the building. The sun hung low in the sky, casting a warm, reddish glow over the men and women, faces streaked with dirt and fatigue. They shuffled along in the labyrinth of tin-roofed shacks that comprised the largest slum in the city. Their steps were weary but purposeful, each stride carrying them closer to the respite they longed for.

Children darted between the adults, their laughter ringing through the air, a vibrant symphony of youth and innocence. They chased one another down the cramped passageways, kicking up dust in their wake, their bare feet pounding against the hard-packed soil. Their energy seemed boundless, a stark contrast to the exhaustion that weighed on the shoulders of their elders.

The tantalizing aroma of food wafted through the air, a mingling of spices and the unmistakable scent of cooking fires. Families gathered around makeshift stoves, crouching low to stir pots filled with thin stews and vegetables, the spoons

33

scraping against the metal in a rhythmic dance. Smoke rose lazily from the fires, curling into the dimming sky.

Kioko moved ahead with quickened steps, and it took everything within Olivia to keep up. Now and then, her feet slipped on mud and debris, yet she managed to stay just a few steps behind him.

Ten minutes later, beads of sweat covered her forehead as they exited the narrow passageway and entered the pot-holed parking lot. Olivia's steps faltered. The equipment was being loaded into the van instead of the camera arrangement she had requested.

"Why are they packing up? No, they can't pack up," Olivia said more to herself than Kioko.

Her pace quickened in time with the mounting tension within her. The tightening knot in her chest constricted, leaving no room for breath, each step amplifying the unease that gripped her heart.

"What are you guys doing? I told you I'd be right back," she called as she hurried toward her crew in a near jog. "You know we don't have an inch of wiggle room. Unless we're saying in Nairobi tomorrow—"

"Not a chance." Rebecca slid out of the vehicle's front seat, clipboard in hand. Her fiery red hair cascaded in soft waves down her back, catching the sunlight and glowing like embers. Her striking features, from her porcelain skin

34

dotted with a smattering of freckles to her vibrant green eyes, often turned heads. But right now, her determined expression showcased a purpose and radiated confidence. "You're not going to bag out on your day on the Masa Mara." A smile tipped up one side of Rebecca's lips, and she pointed a pen toward Olivia's chest. "I only agreed to come if you took one day off to experience the real Kenya, remember?"

"But—"

Rebecca inched nearer and shook her head. "You don't need to worry. We already got the B-roll. We just need to record your Kibera talk, and Roberto will merge it with the video. It's not like they'll see you on video anyway. We just need your voice."

Olivia crossed her arms over her chest, willing the wild beating of her heart to calm. She wanted to argue, to tell Rebecca that's not how she did things, but noting the fading light, she didn't have a choice.

Craning her neck, Olivia looked past Rebecca toward the front seat, attempting to see her red leather journal. "Have you seen my notes?"

Rebecca placed a soft hand on her shoulder. "Girl, you know you don't even look at those notes. Just get over there and speak from your heart, like you've always done."

The same quivers in Olivia's stomach she'd had on their first recording came again. No matter how often she did this, it didn't get easier. With slow steps, she moved in the direction of her cameraman.

With a steady hand, Roberto extended the tripod's legs. The ground beneath the tripod was uneven, and he adjusted the legs with precision, finding balance in the imperfection.

Olivia moved in front of the camera as she'd done dozens of times before, but somehow it felt different. Kioko had directed them to the dying mother upon their arrival this morning. They'd hired him as a bodyguard over the last few weeks as Olivia had worked with a local organization to care for some of the neediest in Kibera. And while Kioko did protect her, he also took her away from the feeding kitchens, into the people's homes, into their lives. It's just what she needed—to connect with this part of her mother's story. To remember that before her mother had become brutal and callous, she'd had a tender, giving heart once.

With the camera mounted securely atop the tripod, Roberto peered through the viewfinder. He squinted as he adjusted the focus and framed the shot.

From the depths of his bag, Roberto produced the lapel mic, its wire thin and coiled like a snake. He threaded it through his fingers, untangling the knots and kinks acquired in transit. Then he pinned the small black clip onto her shirt and handed her the battery pack, which Olivia tucked into the back pocket of her jeans. Stepping back to his camera, Roberto nodded when it was time to start.

"Here, on the edge of the Kibera slums, lies a story untold—a tale of courage, despair, and the search for something more. A 'something more' that was sadly never found.

"It's a story that has drawn me, following the footsteps of the woman who gave me life," Olivia spoke, ignoring the small crowd that had gathered. Instead, she peered into the black circle of the lens. But she didn't see it. She saw her mother's face—thin and pale. Her mother's gaze those last few years was distant, as if she was just a body going through the motions with only a sliver of a soul left inside.

"My mother, a woman of privilege, found herself suffocated by the confines of her upper-class existence. She walked through life with a hollow heart, searching for a sense of belonging that eluded her within the gilded cage of her luxurious world.

"While it didn't seem as if my mother lacked anything growing up, she never wanted to follow the pre-written script she was expected to follow. Her mother—my grandmother—believed heading straight to college after school was the only logical next step. But deep down, my mother held dreams of her own. She yearned to break free from her parents' tight grip, to see the world, and maybe prove herself. She learned about an opportunity to join an overseas trip led by a family friend who worked for a service organization. Regardless of her reasons, my mother's steps took her here. She left the familiarity of her life and ventured to Kibera. Little did she know that she was the one in need of help, seeking solace in the raw humanity that Kibera offered.

"As I walk through the narrow, winding alleys of Kibera, I see resilience and strength in the faces of the people who call this place home. They have built a vibrant community out of hardship and adversity, and their determination to survive and thrive is an inspiration.

"I see my mother's spirit reflected in the people of Kibera. Her desire to make a difference, and to find meaning in the chaos of life, led her to this place. Here the veneer of wealth and status was stripped away. Here my mother had something to offer—herself.

"In the end, Kibera was a sanctuary for her, a place where she could be her true self, unburdened by the weight of societal expectations. It was here that she found her purpose.

"As I stand on the edge of Kibera, I now under-stand that my mother's journey wasn't just about helping others and finding herself. Through her story, I have discovered a part of her that lives on in the indomitable spirit of the people of Kibera and in me. Yet—"

Olivia's voice caught. "She couldn't remain here. And just days before her return, she met a man, one handsome and compassionate. Trying to ease her fears about returning to the States, she found herself in his arms. In his bed. And weeks later, a pregnancy test sealed her fate in the United States. She would not return to Kibera— to the people of her heart. The door to the gilded cage slammed shut, locking her in until she was forced to escape or lose her soul . . . only to discover it was already lost."

Olivia's voice trembled, and her hands moved to her face. She rubbed her eyes, surprised they were filled with tears.

She took a moment to compose herself. To catch her breath. To swallow down the lump building in her throat. "The mother I knew was caring once. Compassionate. Kind. Yet I didn't know that mother." The words came slowly. "Knowing this puts my whole childhood into a different focus." The words staggered out.

"And for the first time . . ." Olivia's words were no more than a whisper. "I can forgive."

She lowered her head, knowing this story truly would end in Kenya. And that's what this journey was all about—forgiveness. Over the last few weeks, as they had filmed, Olivia had explained the many needs of Kibera and the numerous organizations that served the people. It would have been easy to get lost in the immensity of it all, but holding sweet Promise in her arms today had reminded her the most important impact is made one person at a time.

"I came to Kibera believing that I'd be lost in the pain of poverty. Yet I discovered that a tiny miracle could cast a different light on the whole place."

Facing the camera, Olivia continued, "I know many of you have walked with me over the past nine months, as I explored the wealthy lives of Southern families, as I talked to young women who'd faced unplanned pregnancies, as I cried with women addicted to drugs and alcohol, and as I listened to the hard-to-understand excuses of women who stayed in abusive relationships. My journey across the South was a deep dive into the heart and soul of its people. I took internship roles that got me into the living rooms of privileged families, assisting their high schoolers in shaping their college dreams on paper. But it wasn't just about academics. It was about their dreams, their hopes."

She paused, breathing to steady herself before continuing. "I also spoke to young women in counseling centers as they navigated the waters of unplanned pregnancies. Their stories were a blend of fear, hope, and fierce resilience. I've sat with, and cried alongside, women entrapped by addiction at homeless shelters. Their struggles were raw and real."

Her eyes grew misty, yet she kept her voice steady. "But the most challenging moments? These came as I spent time in domestic violence shelters. Listening to women recount why they stayed in abusive relationships tested my understanding and empathy. It's been a learning journey, realizing that every individual story is a testament to human strength and vulnerability." Olivia paused and sighed. "My journey can be summed up in one thought: Until we walk in another's shoes, we cannot truly understand. And when we understand, it makes it easier to forgive."

Without a word, Olivia unclipped the lapel mic and handed it back to Roberto. Olivia didn't need Rebecca to tell her they got what they needed. The silence of the small group told her they had.

Olivia's knees softened, and she moved to the van, sitting on the bumper. Those weren't the words she'd written in her journal this morning. Yet this day had changed everything. Though she'd dedicated years to helping others, holding Promise in her arms ignited a maternal spark she'd never experienced. She pondered what it truly meant to have her own family beyond merely assisting other families.

An inexplicable bond formed when Olivia interacted with the little girl, Promise, and the woman at the orphanage. Was this the essence of family? This deep sense of connection and belonging?

How could that be? The girl had only been in her arms for a few hours, and the conversation with the woman had lasted only a few minutes, but it had been enough to seal the two in Olivia's heart.

Holding that small girl in her arms—her loss so fresh—had unshackled the long-hidden words, setting them free like the indomitable spirit of Kibera, rising above its struggles.

Instead of speaking, Rebecca pulled Olivia into a tight embrace. Olivia rested her cheek on her friend's shoulder, allowing the rest of her tears to come. Then, a few minutes later, when the rush of tears had eased, Olivia took a step back and was surprised to discover a sparkle of humor in Rebecca's gaze.

Rebecca cleared her throat and then looked at her damp shoulder. "And this is why you need a boyfriend. I need a stand-in once in a while." She shrugged. "Sure, you can cry on my shoulder, but you need a hero to sweep you off your feet and tell you that you did an amazing job." Rebecca smiled. "Because you did."

After the last camera was packed up, Kioko motioned for Olivia to join the others in the van, then slammed the door and waved them away. It wasn't until they were back on the main road that Olivia realized she hadn't told him goodbye. Hadn't thanked him. Good thing she had his email so she could write to him when she had the chance.

Rebecca sat on the middle bench seat next to Olivia. "I was trying to lighten the mood before—with the boyfriend joke—but that was amazing. I wasn't expecting that." She reached over and placed her hand on Olivia's. "It was that little girl that changed things, wasn't it? Can you imagine such a small thing and now without a mother? You'll have to tell me later what happened."

Her friend's close presence felt comforting even in the stuffy van. Olivia wanted to share what had happened, but it was too hard to put into words. The young girl had depended on her for a time, and when she handed Promise over . . . Well, the moment was like none she'd ever experienced. It was almost as if her life up to this point had led up to her being there. As if two paths were set to intersect in that time and place.

"The orphanage director knew my name," Olivia whispered.

Rebecca peered at her with wide eyes. "Maybe Kioko told her?"

Olivia pressed her lips together. It was no use trying to explain. There had been no chance for Kioko to tell the woman her name. But, more than that, when the woman had looked into her eyes, it was almost as if she peered into Olivia's soul. *There is a promise for you. You will not have to spend the next year alone.*

"I'm not alone," Olivia mumbled, then tucked her dark hair over her shoulder.

"What's going on?" Rebecca leaned closer. "What happened back there? You're talking to yourself now." Rebecca wrapped her arm around Olivia's shoulders and squeezed.

Olivia relaxed slightly, although the tension in her chest grew with every passing mile.

"How can someone make such an impression on you in such a short time?" she dared to ask. It wasn't until the words were out of her mouth that Olivia knew she spoke of both the young girl and the orphanage director.

"It's because God put you there. He loves you. He trusted you, and that mother saw that. She trusted you too."

The van drove down the narrow streets. They passed small businesses packed together in long rows. Buildings stood tall and proud, their concrete facades scarred by time. Hawkers called out, their voices harmonizing with the cacophony of car horns and engines. Their wares, fresh produce, and trinkets spilled from their stalls, vying for the attention of passersby. The aroma of roasting corn and nyama choma wafted through the air, mingling with the city's scent of sweat and diesel.

Life teemed on the sidewalks. A woman, her

44

head wrapped in bright cloth, balanced a basket with grace, her child trailing behind her. A man in a worn suit hurried past her, clutching a brief-case.

People milled around and didn't care that vehicles also shared the roads. Even when their driver honked, men and women took their time moving out of the way. Their voices rose in an ebb and flow outside the van windows, becoming like background static. Yet even those things couldn't capture Olivia's attention. Instead, she tried to wrap her mind around the orphanage director's words.

Rebecca's comment that Olivia was meant to be there—to be the one to pass the young girl into the director's arms—seemed like something out of a movie. Goose bumps rose on Olivia's arms as she thought of it, and strangely, God seemed closer to her in this moment than He had in any church service.

As darkness fell, they encountered stop-and-go traffic on the highway. Even in this setting, people walked along the shoulder as though they were strolling down city streets. The air in the van was warm, and the air conditioner did little good. They lowered the side windows one by one, hoping to catch a breeze. Darkness had fully descended, and the people who walked along the shoulder of the highway crept like living shadows. As the van slowed to a crawl because of the slowed traffic ahead, a woman's voice filtered through the window.

Olivia jumped. A dark face peered in the open window, no more than six inches from Olivia's face. The woman held up a sleeping newborn then hurriedly spoke words Olivia couldn't understand.

Is she giving me her baby too? Olivia pulled back.

"She is asking for food," their driver called with a thick accent. "She needs to eat to make milk to feed her baby. This is what she is saying. Surely she means you no harm."

The van crept forward, and those in the seats pulled out granola bars, apples, and other snacks.

"Here." Olivia produced a foldable tote from her fanny pack and quickly opened it. A dozen hands dropped food and bottled water into the thin canvas bag. Olivia thrust it into the woman's outstretched hand just seconds before the traffic cleared. The van picked up speed again.

"Did you see how tiny that baby was?" Rebecca leaned in, moving her mouth inches from Olivia's ear. "Thank you for doing this. Today was for the viewers, but it was for us too, wasn't it?"

Olivia nodded. Tears filled her eyes, and she took a deep breath. She crossed her arms over her chest and pulled them against her. Olivia leaned her head back against the headrest and released a sigh. So many people. So many needs. So many, well, emotions.

A familiar anger stirred within her, and she tried not to let it take hold. Why were things still this way? There was enough wealth in this world for these problems to be solved. She felt the same frustration whenever she worked in inner-city Little Rock.

So many young people went to bed hungry and fell asleep, hoping they wouldn't be woken up by gunfire or the wail of sirens, as they did so many nights. With the right people and resources, more could be done. Instead, those who had money—the millionaires and movie stars, the rich and the royals—financed their extravagant penthouses and fancy parties instead of putting that money where it could make a difference.

"You have to let it go." Rebecca nestled her head against the headrest, close to Olivia's. "We can only do what we can do. We can't save the world."

"First, how did you know what I was thinking? Second, we can't save the world, but couldn't we all do a little more?"

"Of course, and God will show us when and how, remember?" Rebecca nudged Olivia's rib with her elbow. "Surely you haven't forgotten what we told ourselves before landing in Kenya? God will show us who to love, who to serve, and who to pray for. He will also bring others to extend love to those we can't. We have to trust him with that, Olivia. We never were meant to save this world alone. That's Jesus's job. We're just the vessels for Him to do His work."

Olivia dipped her chin, allowing the weariness to descend over her. Rebecca was correct, but something inside told her to be alert. *God, what is it? If I'm supposed to do something more, can you show me?*

Gestapo Headquarters, Rome, Italy
18 October 1943

The sun was setting on the Tiber, streaking the sky with purple and orange as it dipped below the horizon. Alessandra cast silent prayers as the car drove to a nondescript side street in Rome's San Giovanni quarter, stopping before a three-story building. News had come to her that the Gestapo headquarters had been established here a month ago when the Germans had taken hold of the city. Never had she thought she'd confirm this for herself.

The air was crisp as Alessandra was led from the vehicle, carrying a chill that penetrated her linen suit, piercing her skin. As the officer led her from the car, a second Gestapo officer waited outside the door, his black uniform crisp and menacing. Alessandra paused before him.

The officer's eyes were hard and unyielding, like chips of ice set into his impenetrable face.

"You are Princess Alessandra Appiani?" he asked, his voice like a steel blade cutting through the silence.

Alessandra met his gaze without flinching. "Yes," she replied, her voice steady.

The officer sneered. "Good, I have some questions for you. Come with me."

The officer escorted Alessandra through the heavy wooden doors of the Gestapo headquarters, once a grand villa of marble and gilt, now transformed into a somber and austere stronghold of control. The officer that flanked her showed no emotion, his face impassive beneath his uniform cap.

They walked down a long hallway inside the dimly lit building, their footsteps echoing off the tile. The walls were adorned with dark tapestries, the faces of the weavers' subjects obscured by years of dust and neglect.

Alessandra's escort led her to a small room at the end of the corridor. The door creaked open, revealing a simple wooden table and two chairs. A single, naked bulb dangled from the ceiling, lighting the worn furnishings harshly.

"Please sit, Princess," the officer ordered, gesturing to the chair. Alessandra obeyed.

Lord, give me the strength of a lion inside, yet the calmness of a lamb, she prayed and perched on the edge of the chair, straight-backed and unyielding.

The officer circled the table, studying her with an unnerving intensity. "What do you know about the resistance?" he demanded.

Alessandra looked at him, her fixed regard unwavering. "I know nothing," she said, her voice low and firm as she had practiced in the mirror. Just as her mother had taught her to do before any important royal function or event.

The officer sat in his chair, slamming his hand on the table. The sound echoed like a gunshot through the small room. "Lies," he spat. "You were seen talking to known resistance members. Tell me what you know."

"I am from the royal family. I speak to all people. I care for *all* people," Alessandra's voice rose in volume. She cleared her throat and dared to narrow her gaze. "I was informed you have information about my husband. If this is not the case, then I will need to ask to be returned—"

"Silence!" The shout split from the man's lips, and red splotches journeyed from his neck to his cheeks.

The officer leaned in, his face inches from hers. His breath was warm on her face. "You will tell me about the transports."

Alessandra looked into his cold gray eyes, careful to keep her own expression resolute.

"I have heard about the transports of art being removed from—"

"I am not talking about art."

She offered the slightest shrug. "Then I have no answers."

He leaned back and swiped two fingers around his collar. If Alessandra wasn't mistaken, she noted the slightest tremble in his hand. "And why did you not flee with your father to the south? Unless you have a greater mission here?"

She sucked in a quick breath through her nostrils, finding the right words. "The king is for the government. The princess is for the people. And unless you have news of my husband, I have nothing to tell you," she said, her voice steady and defiant.

The officer stared at her then stood, his chair scraping against the floor. "We will see about that," he said, his voice a graveled growl as murky and foreboding as the shadows that clung to the corners of the room. "It may take time, princess, but I guarantee you will tell us what we need to know."

CHAPTER FOUR

Nairobi, Kenya
Present Day

*G*od will show us who to love, serve, and pray *for. He will also bring others to extend love to those we can't."*

Olivia nodded at Rebecca's words. She must have drifted off because Rebecca was shaking her leg as their van parked in front of their small hotel. "Hey, sleeping beauty, we're here."

Wiping her moist chin, Olivia stirred to wakefulness. Even though she knew she couldn't have slept for more than thirty minutes, her mind was groggy, as if she'd just awakened in the middle of the night.

The hotel was nestled on the side street, a quiet haven amid the clamor of Nairobi. A wrought-iron gate, black and weathered, stood guard at the entrance. Flowers, vibrant and bold, greeted the guests. The walls, white and cracked with age, provided a haven of escape.

Staggering into the small room she shared with Rebecca, Olivia collapsed into the narrow twin bed. She'd just settled her head onto a pillow when her phone announced a video call. Then she remembered what day it was. Sarah-Grace's wedding. It hadn't been a coincidence that she'd chosen this of all weeks for their trip. Always a bridesmaid, never a bride. Olivia couldn't do it again. Not that she wanted a relationship herself. She'd rather not deal with all the fluff, frill, and expense when real needs existed.

As Rebecca announced she was taking a shower, a call came in, leaving Olivia torn about whether to answer it. Her mind was emotionally drained. Pulling on the last of her emotional reserves, Olivia answered it. Within a few seconds, two women's faces filled the screen—one old enough to be her grandmother and the other just a teen. Both dark skinned with broad smiles.

Trying to hide her true feelings, Olivia forced a strained smile. "Miss Jan, Trinity. Hello!" She waved. "Are you there? Is the dress on?"

"What, now, Olivia? I can't hear you." Miss Jan tilted her head as if that would help her hear better. The older African American woman's smile was a balm for Olivia's weary soul. Miss Jan's eyes, deep pools of warm coffee, held the wisdom of years. They were the eyes of a woman who had listened, understood, and guided countless young souls through the storms of life. Miss Jan had been Olivia's school counselor years ago. When Olivia had taken a part-time job serving teens in inner-city Little Rock, Miss Jan had been the first one to volunteer to help her.

"She asked if the dress was on." Trinity's

voice rose as she called out to Miss Jan, then she returned to Olivia. "You told us to call you once Miss Sarah-Grace was ready. It's funny that you'll see her all done up from over there in Africa before her husband, and he's just in the next room."

Shifting her position, she lay across her bed then kicked off her dirty tennis shoes. "Yes, I want to see."

The picture shifted as Trinity walked across the room. Even though Olivia couldn't see Trinity's face, she recognized her giggle. "You must like weddings if you wanted us to call you while you're over there," Trinity said.

Olivia smirked. "Of course. And it's a little-known fact that I've caught the bouquet no less than seven times."

"Oh, that's gotta be something lucky. Your turn next!" Miss Jan's voice called even though she was no longer in view.

Taking a deep breath, she noticed a blur of white—the bride. Sarah-Grace was one of their most dedicated volunteers. Who else would organize a banquet to take place just a few months after her wedding?

Until this trip came up, Olivia had agreed to be a bridesmaid. Sarah-Grace and the other volunteers assumed Olivia was dedicated to a mission trip. They were oblivious that she was the driving force behind the evocative documentary *In My*

Mother's Steps. Only her core team and Rebecca were privy to this secret.

Olivia had always prioritized honesty, so she never intended to deceive anyone. When she and Rebecca embarked on their filming project, Olivia believed that using only her voice and not revealing her face could more genuinely convey her mother's narrative. Once the first video went live and gained traction, Olivia braced herself for the inevitable recognition. She assumed someone—perhaps Miss Jan, one of the many volunteers, or the young women—would point out the connection. But no one did.

The teens mainly watched content on TikTok, which wasn't where Olivia posted her videos. Miss Jan, deeply involved with her family, rarely watched television. Sarah-Grace was preoccupied with wedding plans. If any of the other volunteers did happen upon the video and identified Olivia's unique voice, they kept it to themselves. Olivia always expected someone to connect the dots, but that moment never came.

Sarah-Grace had understood, of course. She'd even joked, "Go. You're needed there. Besides, my mother's spending way too much on flowers, and it'll save you from having to give the 'put-money-where-it-really-matters' lecture."

Trinity paused and readjusted the phone's camera to capture Sarah-Grace standing in her wedding dress. "Okay, here she is. Miss Sarah-Grace, say 'Hi!' "

The bride stood like a vision of grace and purity, her simple white dress a testament to the beauty found in the unadorned. The fabric appeared as light as air itself.

Catching her off guard, Olivia sucked in a breath. Her friend looked beautiful, like something out of a magazine. "Sarah-Grace, oh my goodness. I have never seen such a beautiful bride."

Sarah-Grace's skin was porcelain against the ivory sweetheart neckline and lace-covered cap sleeves. The bride's reddish blonde curls were pinned up, framing her face. A simple tiara adorned the top of her head.

"Stunning. You are truly stunning."

"Thank you. I *feel* like a princess. But more than that, I can't believe I'm marrying the man of my dreams."

The words caused a pinch in Olivia's heart, but she ignored it.

"You deserve it. You're a perfect match." Olivia leaned up on her elbows. "Turn around so I can see the back." Instead of a veil, a panel of sheer lace looped down from each of Sarah-Grace's shoulders then fell to the floor. Olivia sucked in a breath. "You look just like a princess ready for the ball."

Happiness, tinged with regret, filled Olivia.

Had she made a mistake by skipping her friend's wedding? As quickly as those thoughts filled her mind, Promise came to mind. Where would the young girl be if she and Kioko hadn't come upon that dying mother at just the right time? Olivia had heard the horror stories of what happened to orphaned children who weren't immediately taken into orphanages run by loving caregivers.

The camera swung away from the bride, and Miss Jan appeared on the screen. "We won't keep you. You look as if you haven't slept in days."

Olivia chuckled. "Thank you, Miss Jan. I have had a little trouble sleeping." She didn't have the heart to tell her friend that the burdens of her heart affected her more than lack of sleep. In addition to working with young women, Olivia also had a large online audience to serve.

As Olivia delved deeper into sharing the tales from her mother's life, the engagement on her platform grew. Every narrative, every memory of her mother's seemingly long yet fleeting journey, resonated deeply with her audience. Her openness about the broken chapters of her mother's life touched many, making them feel a kinship with her. In return, her inbox filled with their heartrending stories, painting a tapestry of shared human experiences.

Many people enjoyed Olivia's interviews, but something odd stood out. Even with all those viewers, no one from TV or newspapers tried to learn who she was. You'd think the news folks would be curious about her. Maybe that was the idea. Without showing her name and face, Olivia became like everyone else. Her story felt like it could be anyone's.

There were weeks Olivia had to ignore the messages, sure that one more story would cause her heart to crumble. Then, feeling guilty for not writing back, she'd stay up late on multiple days to catch up.

It was hard to imagine she would return to her apartment in Little Rock in a few days, pouring strong coffee into a cracked mug. She'd sip her coffee and dive into the waves of heartbreak that flowed through her inbox. Each email, a cry for help or a tale of despair, would wrap its tendrils around her heart, squeezing tighter with every word she read.

Like they always did, her fingers would fly across the keys as she crafted words of comfort and encouragement. And as she answered each email, the city outside her apartment window would stay still with the darkening night. As much as Olivia loved helping others, it never seemed enough.

From the sounds of it, music was starting. Instead of the wedding march, Sarah-Grace had chosen "Coming Home" by Leon Bridges. An ache stirred in Olivia's heart. Coming home had never been something she'd looked forward to for most of her life. She'd lived in Little Rock for almost ten years, but even so, that didn't seem like home.

"Hello? Hello. Jan." Laughter spilled from Olivia's lips as she watched Jan wave at someone. An unexpected ache settled over her heart. Miss Jan seemed like home in a way. That realization brought a new lightness to her heart that hadn't been there for days.

Finally, Miss Jan glanced down and noticed their video call was still connected. Jan's eyes widened. "Oh look, you're still there."

"I'm still here."

"What was that? It's getting too loud in here." Jan moved the phone, and Olivia got an image of her ear.

Olivia couldn't help but laugh again, joy filling her with the antics of her seventy-year-old friend. "I said you look beautiful, Miss Jan." Even though she hadn't said it, Miss Jan did look beautiful.

"I'm sorry, Olivia. If you're talking, I can't hear you."

The image bounced around, and Olivia got glimpses of the pillars of flowers and men and women dressed up in their finest. That's one thing Sarah-Grace had insisted on—that the event be semi-formal—just like the fundraiser she was organizing for the *Character Club*. Which was another event Olivia wouldn't mind missing.

She'd rather walk through sludge in the slums of Nairobi than in heels anywhere. She forever turned her ankle if she rose even as much as an inch off the ground. Self-imposed human torture if she'd ever seen it.

"Okay, that's better." From the looks of the mirror behind her, it appeared Jan had retreated to the quiet of the bathroom. Quiet except for the occasional flushing of a toilet.

"We told you we'd call you from the wedding, and it's nice, real nice. It'll be getting started in just a few minutes, but since I have you on this video, I need to tell you. Liv, we have a big problem. I know I shouldn't bother you on your trip, but it's something we need to talk about."

"Didn't think you'd add 'dramatic suspense' to the wedding program," Olivia quipped, trying to keep the mood light. However, the tension in her gut grew as she saw the worry creeping into Miss Jan's face. This may not be a laughing matter.

Miss Jan sighed. "The wedding will start any minute, so I'll tell you quickly. There was an electrical fire in the basement of the church. Everything we bought for this year's program are gone. And it's doubtful that the insurance will cover any of it."

"All the things?" Olivia opened her mouth, unsure if she heard her friend right. She shook her head in denial. Her mind raced to all the months they'd spent on fundraisers and seeking out supporters so they could buy the projector for their meetings, their mentor workbooks, and even the crockpots for their cooking classes. "What are we going to do?"

"Sarah-Grace is organizing the banquet. We'll have to explain that we'll need more funds than we thought. We'll pray that folks are generous, won't we?"

"Does Sarah-Grace know about the fire? About the need for more money? We'll have to talk to her about how the banquet plans are going when I get back."

For the third year, she was leading their support group, or *Character Club* as Miss Jan called it, for teen girls in the inner city. Word had gotten out about their positive impact on the community. As soon as she got back, Olivia would start making calls.

"That girl's head is so up in the clouds. I don't know if she knows or not." Miss Jan clucked her tongue. "It is her wedding day . . ."

"Yes, but if you have a chance to ask about the plans for the banquet . . ." Olivia wasn't sure if Miss Jan heard her because, at the same time, Trinity's voice was calling, "C'mon. It's starting. Are you going to be walking up the aisle with the bride?"

"Got to go. I wanted you to know, Olivia. But I also know that God has a plan. He made a promise to us, remember? Everything is just going to work out." And with that, Miss Jan hung up the phone, leaving Olivia staring at an empty screen.

God has a plan. God made a promise. Was it a coincidence that she'd heard those words multiple times this evening? The thing was that only losses happened today, no gains. *Lord, I don't know what's happening, but I'm scared to face it all. Please help me so I don't have to face all this alone.*

Rome, Italy
Two Weeks Earlier, 1943

The air was thick, with the scent of soup simmering in the restaurant kitchen and the murmur of conversation. Most places had closed when the Germans had arrived two weeks ago, but Alessandra was thankful this small café was still open. She'd asked her husband Christian to join her here. No one would think much of the princess—the second oldest child of the King of Italy—and her husband enjoying lunch together. Especially not since Christian, who was German-born, had been a member of the Nationalist Socialists movement since the earliest days.

That was before most of Adolf Hitler's supporters understood what *der Führer* was up to. And these days? Christian stayed close to the Nazi elite. Not because he believed in their cause but rather to learn the Germans' plans to keep his family safe. Yet Alessandra was starting to think that soon even that would no longer be enough.

Just beyond the windowpane, Nazi soldiers marched with mechanical precision through the cobblestone streets. Their presence cast an ominous shadow over the Eternal City. Ancient Romans believed Rome would go on no matter what happened to the world or how many empires rose or fell. Yet how could her city withstand this?

The Germans filled Rome's hallowed streets, casting a dark pall over the city's indestructible spirit. The soldiers' black boots thumped on the cobblestone, their iron hearts beating to the rhythm of their orders. They'd come for the Jewish families, who were now huddled helpless and terrified on the sidewalks—lambs awaiting slaughter.

The soldiers, like wolves, with eyes cold and deadly, had no pity for the old, sick, or young. Soldiers grabbed men, women, and children by their arms, pulling them toward the trucks awaiting transport. Like the bleating of sheep, family members cried out in fear and confusion. In the scene, a nightmare came to life. The soldiers' actions were cold and merciless, like the winter winds blowing across the Alps.

Tears pricked her eyes, and Alessandra told herself to stay calm—to think of a way to help the

Jewish children. Where she could not overwhelm the Germans in power, she could do so with her intelligence and her courage.

She forced herself to turn away from the window and instead look at the marble-top table, studying the pattern and blinking back tears. How many Jewish families would be removed, leaving empty streets and quiet homes? And why? Because the Jews would not conform. Because they could not be bought with wealth or intimidated by power. The hatred of Jews had been around for generations, and somehow hostility toward God's chosen people grew in Hitler's mind until they became the source of all problems.

Yet, for every evil, good can still be done. Alessandra's mother had taught her as much since she was a child. If only she could discover that good now.

Across from Alessandra, Christian cleared his throat, drawing her attention. His eyes were dark and unyielding, reflecting the world outside the window.

"You mustn't," he said, his voice low and steady. "If you try to help them, you risk everything. Our family. Our lives."

Christian's German accent was as thick as the soldiers on the streets outside.

"I cannot stand by and watch them be taken, especially the children," Alessandra whispered, her words barely audible above the hum of the café. "I must do something."

Christian clenched his fists on the tabletop. The tendons in his hands stood out like cords against his skin. "You are one person, *cara mia*. You cannot save them all. And if you try, you will only bring more pain and suffering upon those you love. Upon *yourself*."

Her gaze flickered to the window, the glass a cold barrier between her and the world outside. The shadows of the people being led away, their faces etched with fear, danced across the pane.

"I cannot ignore their suffering." Alessandra's voice was barely more than a breath. "If I turn away now and do nothing, then what? Who will be left to stand against this darkness?"

Christian reached across the table, covering her hand with his. The warmth of his touch contrasted with the chill in her heart. "You cannot bear the world's weight on your shoulders, my love. You must choose your battles. If not, you will be consumed by the darkness you seek to defeat."

She searched his eyes for strength, but a storm raged within.

What if it was our children? she wanted to ask. *Wouldn't you want someone to help them—save them?*

Instead of asking, Alessandra pulled her hand back and lifted the cup, her hand shaking slightly. The porcelain was cool against her lips, and she could feel the heat of the liquid inside. She had been hoping for a comforting sip of tea, but there was no tea in Rome. Instead, the drink was bitter, like the taste of disappointment.

Alessandra tried to swallow it, keeping her emotions in check. She did not want to show weakness in front of Christian.

She took another sip, the bitter taste still lingering on her tongue—a reminder of life's harsh realities and the sacrifices she had to make.

Alessandra focused on the face of the man sitting across from her, pretending she wasn't already determining her next steps.

Outside, older men shouldered children and skirted around the Jews. They quickened their faltering steps, but they could not move quickly enough to hide the truth from the children's gawking. Women clutched parcels of food, eyes downcast. *Not enough food. Never enough.* Yet it was all they had. And at least they had their lives. At least they were not the ones being dragged away.

Christian reached across the table and took her hand, breaking her trance. "You should come with me."

"You're leaving?"

"I need answers. Only then will I understand what may be done to keep my family safe. This is only the beginning of what's to come for Rome. The Fuhrer requires more shipments."

"Please tell me you speak of art."

"Not art."

She pulled her hands to her lap, her fists clenching tight.

"This is the Jews' home, too." Her voice was no more than a whisper. "And so many are just children."

He ran a hand down his face. "Nothing I say will stop what you have on your mind, will it?"

She didn't answer. She didn't need to. The plan was coming together bit by bit. *Oh, Lord, please give me the courage to follow through.*

CHAPTER FIVE

Nyota Skyline Lodge, Kenya
Present Day

Louis stepped into the sports restaurant at Nyota Skyline Lodge with Sergio. This time of year, there was no fire in the open hearth. Yet, he was greeted by a warmth that seeped into his bones. This balm eased the tension of the last few months of performing royal duties: state dinners and charity events, walkabouts, and interviews. The events were fine. Instead, the problem was doing them all with a smile as the news of his former girlfriend's engagement and the upcoming wedding was on every news source.

The hum of conversation washed over Louis, mostly from groups of tourists who'd spent the day sightseeing and viewing the protected animals of the game preserve. The symphony of laughter brought a smile to Louis's lips and caused a deep ache.

The wooden tables, sturdy and unpretentious, stood like sentinels throughout the room, every one an island of refuge for those seeking solace in the company of others. Sergio pointed to a table. Louis settled into a chair, the worn leather molding around him as if waiting for his arrival.

The glow of a television screen adorned the wall, and a cheer rose as one of the Kenyan players made a goal. Other than Sergio, there were very few people with whom he could relax and be himself. As heir to the throne, Louis had to question any new relationship, deciding if each person wanted to get to know him or was more focused on what Louis's position could offer.

The aroma of food, rich and comforting, filled the air. While Louis's stomach rumbled, his attention turned to the laptop on the table across from them. An older couple had their browser opened to YouTube. Louis recognized the music for the opening credits of *In My Mother's Steps*. He raised his eyebrows then turned to meet his friend's gaze.

"Even here." Sergio sighed. "It looks like you found a few more people who are as obsessed with that show as you are."

"If you would watch it, you'd understand. The narrator—you don't see her face—but something about her is hauntingly beautiful. She goes to these places and interviews people, really listening to their stories. You can hear the heartbreak in her words." *Heartbreak I wish I could ease,* Louis thought, though he didn't say those words aloud.

"At the end of every episode, she shares about her mother's life," Louis continued. "Her mother was from an upper-class family. She didn't like being told what to do—no college degree or marriage for her. So she came to Africa—Kenya, actually—to work with a service organization. When she got pregnant and returned home there was even more conflict. She ran away with her daughter and got in with the wrong people, spiraling far from the type of upbringing she had. The saddest thing is that she could have asked for help. Instead, she attempted to raise her daughter alone."

"Attempted?" Sergio stroked his chin. "That doesn't sound good."

"When she talks about her mom—" Emotion caught in Louis's throat. "It's almost like you can hear that scared little girl in her voice." He smiled. "Scared but trying to be brave."

"And that appeals to you?" Sergio asked.

A waiter placed two chilled bottles of water before them. Instead of interrupting, the waiter stood erect, allowing them to finish their conversation.

Louis nodded to the waiter once, acknowledging his presence, then focused again on Sergio. "I can't stop thinking about her. It's the only thing that's given me peace after Constance ended our relationship. Just knowing there is someone who isn't afraid to share her real emotions, struggles, and pain. Well, that gives me hope."

"Isn't afraid?" a soft chuckle escaped Sergio's

lips. "How can you say she's not afraid? She doesn't show her face."

"She's going to show her face," said the elderly man sitting at the next table. "She mentioned it in the video, just released. She's on her last stop, right here in Kenya. A series of videos will be shot in the Kibera slums—"

"She's in Kibera?" Louis straightened in his seat.

Sergio shook his head. "Don't even think of it. We just got here. We're not heading to Nairobi."

"But if she's there—"

"This mystery woman doesn't want to be found, remember?" Sergio smirked and lowered his voice. "Not even by a prince."

Louis looked at the menu. Of course, he wouldn't head to the Kibera slums searching for a mystery woman—would he? He focused on the waiter. "I'll have the pilau, but have it delivered to my room."

"Yes, sir." The waiter turned to Sergio.

"I'll have the same. And I guess I'll have it in the room too."

"Stay. I'll go straight there, I promise. Extra security has already been set up."

Sergio looked at the game on the television. "I will be up right after my meal."

Fifteen minutes later, Louis stood at the veranda's edge, his gaze fixed on the horizon. His thoughts strayed thousands of miles away to the last perfect day he'd spent with Constance. They'd taken a weekend trip to Paris. After dinner, he'd held her in his arms as the warm spring air carried the scent of roses. As they sat on a bench in Belleville Park gazing up at the Eiffel Tower's glimmering lights, she invited him to her room.

"Don't you think it's time?" Constance had asked, kissing his neck.

"You know I would love to, and someday . . . after the wedding."

His arms had been around her, and she'd stiffened, pulling back from his embrace.

"What's wrong?" he'd asked, even though he'd known the answer. Constance attended church several times a month, but she struggled with her faith. It was another tradition she felt limited them as a couple. Louis had told himself he would iron it out after they married, but the wounded look in her eyes that night said that wouldn't be the case.

"I am not sure we're a good fit," Constance had said, her voice soft yet determined. Then she stood and crossed her arms over her chest, turning her back to the glimmering lights of the Eiffel Tower and looking beyond him as if she saw a different future there.

"What do you mean?"

"I do care for you deeply, Louis. But the life you live, I cannot fit into that mold."

"We can make it work. You don't have to change entirely," he implored, reaching for her hand.

"You don't see, do you? Your world, filled with tradition and duty, suffocates me."

Louis hadn't known how to answer that because there was no answer. Even though he only sometimes appreciated the traditions that came with his role, he understood them. He also knew his relationship with God was more than just tradition. It was his life, as his mother had taught him. And if Constance couldn't see that, then maybe she was right. It was time to allow things to end.

The weight of their shared history hung between them as they returned to their hotel and separate rooms, yet it wasn't enough to keep them together. And it was only two weeks after that night when Louis had seen the photos of Constance with her new love. Even now, the memory of that first headline caused Louis's heart to ache. *That was then; this is now. Lord, I don't want to spend my life alone.* His mind returned to the documentary. *Bring me someone like that—someone with a seeking heart. Someone for me to love who also loves you.*

A knock at the door told Louis his dinner had arrived. He ate it as the sun dipped low, the sky filling with hues of orange and pink, casting long shadows across the African landscape. The wind

73

whispered through the trees, but he no longer felt as hungry as when they arrived. Even here, in his favorite place, he felt unsettled. After eating less than half his meal, Louis covered the tray and returned to the veranda.

"I need to believe in your plan, Lord," he murmured into the night, questioning how any good could emerge from the situation. Back in Europe, the weight of royal obligations shaped his life. As a prince, the constant pressures of tradition and duty loomed large. Every move he made was in the shadow of past monarchs. Perhaps, for once, he yearned for a respite from always placing the kingdom first.

In the wilds of Africa, freedom whispered to him like the rustle of leaves, yet it was a freedom he'd never be able to obtain. It wasn't that Louis wished to walk away from being royal. Being royal wasn't the problem. Finding someone who would love him for himself, not a title, was.

Louis leaned against the railing, scanning the horizon as if searching for something beyond his reach. An approaching vehicle broke through his reverie. He watched it enter the gates of the lodge. As the vehicle came to a stop and its occupants emerged, Louis noticed the unique assortment of luggage and equipment that accompanied them.

Even though he couldn't make out their conversation, he could tell by their accents they were Americans. Staff from the lodge carried their luggage to the lobby. Louis's interest was piqued when he spotted tripods and bags. *A movie or television show?*

The new guests moved about unloading, and the rhythm of their actions revealed a practiced familiarity with each other. Then, as if his whispered prayer had been brought to life, a voice floated up to him. The cadence in the woman's voice was a melody that stirred something deep within his chest. He turned his gaze toward her, her figure standing just beneath the veranda, a phone pressed to her ear.

"I just got into cell service. So sorry I didn't give you a proper goodbye." She laughed. The world seemed to pause, and the sounds of the other arriving guests faded into the background as Louis focused on the woman's voice. "Thanks, Kioko, and I have something else to ask too. I wonder if you had an account I could wire money to. I—"

The conversation of another van full of guests arriving rose and drowned out the woman's words. He thought she said something about making a promise, but what she said didn't matter. *I know that voice.*

Louis's heart pounded as he struggled to reconcile the woman's voice in the documentary with the one who stood before him.

Yes, it's her. Louis leaned over the railing and noted the tilt of her head and the curve of her lips as she spoke. The cadence of her speech was the same. The man from the dining room had been right. She was here. Not just in Africa. The woman from the documentary was standing just below him and was beautiful. Petite with dark brown hair pulled up in an easy ponytail. She wore jeans and a pullover fleece jacket, yet she seemed to have a sense of purpose even as she stood and talked on the phone. It wasn't the relaxed stance of someone on vacation but rather a woman on a mission. Was the older man right? Had she come to shoot the end of the documentary where she revealed herself?

Louis smiled briefly. Just an hour earlier, he'd wanted that—desired to know who she was. Yet now? A defensiveness rose in him—a feeling of protectiveness. To reveal her true self would be to open herself up to the attacks of others. He knew what it was like to be in the public eye. No matter what he did, there would be someone who disagreed with it. Someone who wielded words that pierced as sharp as any sword.

He considered calling down a welcome for a moment, but the woman finished her phone call and hurried inside to join the others before he had the chance.

In the distance, the sun dipped lower in the sky, and he knew that the arrival of these filmmakers had to be more than a coincidence. Louis took a deep breath, the scent of the African soil filling his lungs. He had to find a way to meet and spend time with her. He wanted to get to know her but, strangely, protect her too. She'd put her life on hold to walk in her mother's steps, and why? So she could release the bitterness she'd been storing up. So she could plan a future without feeling held back by the past.

And maybe it's a future with me.

The words came to Louis's mind before he could stop them. It was foolishness, he knew, but then again . . . she was here. Louis didn't know what tomorrow would bring, but the fact that this woman was here tonight gave him more hope than he'd had in a long time.

CHAPTER SIX

The chattering of monkeys from outside the tent matched the nagging in Olivia's heart. The large shelter was one of many situated at the lodge at the edge of the Masai Mara animal preserve. It was big enough for two beds and a small trunk to store one's things. It even included a bathroom with plumbing.

There was nothing like sleeping outside with just the canvas to keep yourself from the elements. During the middle of the night, the sounds of the monkeys filled the air, and the occasional roars of lions reminded Olivia that she was not in civilization anymore.

She and Rebecca were also warned to keep the zipper locked because the monkeys liked to get into people's things, and the monkeys knew how to unzip. Upon arrival at the lodge, the yellow blouse hanging from one of the trees indicated that someone hadn't heeded the warning in previous days.

The chatter of monkeys hadn't been the only thing that had kept Olivia tossing and turning. She'd thought of Promise. Was the young girl all right? Did she miss her mother? More than that, Olivia worried about the young girl's future. She had met the teens who'd spent their whole lives living in the Kibera slums. Although different, Olivia knew what it felt like to look at the future and see no way out. Her mother's death had led to an exit point, but it didn't feel that way.

Olivia also worried about revealing herself to her audience. They knew her voice, her story, but what would they think of *her?* She'd poured out so many feelings and emotions as she'd told her stories—but that's because no one had known it was her. Now, in a couple of days, they would.

Then to add to those worries, Rebecca—the strong one—had taken ill. Olivia settled on the side of Rebecca's bed, wondering if she should wake her. Of all the days for Rebecca to be decommissioned. Olivia brushed a strand of blonde hair back from her friend's face.

Rebecca stirred, squinting open one eye.

"Hey, you. Feeling better?"

During the last two days, Olivia hadn't had time to worry about the electrical fire in Little Rock or that all the supplies for their teen program had been lost. Worries about that would have to wait until a different time.

Yesterday morning, Rebecca had awoken in extreme pain from an infected tooth. Rebecca's whole side of her face had been swollen. Thankfully, Kioko had known of a good dentist who'd pulled the tooth. That had taken all of the morning. Then, they rode in a bumpy van down dusty roads through the Kenyan countryside to their lodge near the Masai Mara wildlife preserve for the rest of the day.

The road from Nairobi to the Masai Mara had been long and dusty, with the sun beating mercilessly on the savannah. The jeep bounced along the rough terrain, kicking up clouds of red dirt behind it. Inside, the passengers had been jostled about like loose coins in a pocket.

Their driver was a seasoned guide, his weathered face creased with lines. He'd easily navigated the twists and turns of the road, scanning the horizon for signs of wildlife. Sadly, there was little for him to point out. He'd told them things would be different once they went through the gates of the Masai Mara on their safari day.

While Rebecca slept, Olivia peered out the window, her eyes wide with anticipation. But the only wildlife she saw were clusters of thin cattle guarded by Masai men who stood tall and proud on the savannah, their brightly colored robes bil-lowing in the breeze—like warriors from another time, their bodies lean and muscular.

Watching their van drive by, the Masai men seemed to sense their admiration, standing a little taller, their eyes shining with pride. The guide had told her they were the last of their kind—the guardians of a way of life passed down through generations.

Last night, the pain meds had helped Rebecca

to drift off. Still, Olivia had awakened numerous times to Rebecca's low moans mixed with the sounds of wild animals outside the tall, log walls that wrapped around the perimeter of the lodge compound.

With a grimace of effort, Rebecca rose into a half-sitting position. Olivia knelt on the floor beside her friend. "How are you feeling?"

A low moan released, and Rebecca touched her swollen face. "My tooth feels a bit better. Antibiotics are helping," she mumbled.

Olivia rose and turned on the single electric light in the tent's center, which cast shadows of the poles and herself against the walls. Since they'd arrived earlier, Olivia felt they were being watched. Or, more specifically, she was being watched. Of course, everyone outside the tent could read the story by the shifting shadows cast upon the fabric. An unsettling chill crept through Olivia's bones.

Even though it was warm inside the tent, she rubbed her arms against the rising goose bumps. "I'm so glad the antibiotics are helping. It would be sad if you missed our last full day here in Kenya."

Rebecca tried lifting herself onto one elbow but crumpled back into bed. "I feel like my face is a punching bag. I can't—"

"No, no, no." Olivia pressed her hand against her forehead. "Don't say you can't go. You're the one who wanted to do this so badly. I would have stayed in Kibera."

"I went on a safari last time. You . . ."

"Stayed back and worked, I know. And maybe this is a sign I should stay here with you. Or maybe we should head back." The memory of holding Promise tightly against her chest caused a longing within her heart that Olivia hadn't expected. She would also love a chance to talk to the orphan director. When talking to Kikyo last night, she should have asked how the woman had known Olivia's name. Also, what had the director meant by her words? *There is a promise coming for you, too, Olivia. You will not have to face another year alone.*

"No." The word shot from Rebecca's mouth, causing her to wince. "You have to go," she mumbled again, sounding as if her mouth was full of gravel.

Olivia lifted her chin in mock defiance. "My mother didn't go on a safari."

"Enjoy one last day." Rebecca offered a weak smile, and warmth filled Olivia's chest. "The reveal will be hard. After this . . . the media."

Olivia cocked her head and eyed her friend with a curious expression. "Wow, you sure do know how to argue, especially for someone whose face looks like it's been kicked by a mule."

Rebecca wrinkled her nose. "Yes, then?" She touched her face and winced.

Olivia sighed. "Yes, I'll go, but I never expected to feel so bad about leaving Kibera. Even after all we did, there are so many more needs."

Sadness filled Rebecca's green eyes, and tears blurred Olivia's. *If only I could do more.*

Olivia didn't say the words aloud, but the feeling was always there—a boulder in the pit of her gut. After all, if she didn't, who would care for the least of these? Maybe Rebecca didn't understand because she'd never known the feeling of having nothing.

As a child, Olivia had once attended a backyard Bible club and had heard that God answered prayers. Even when Olivia knew little about God, she often prayed that He'd send someone to bring food or drop off money to pay a light bill.

Being on the other side, Olivia knew what a difference kind people had made in her life. Time and time again, they'd shown up, and because of that, Olivia's faith had grown. The love of people had helped her to believe in the love of God. More than anything, she wanted to do the same for others.

The squawks of monkeys outside the tent increased, and Rebecca pointed up to the canvas tent top. "Listen."

Olivia lifted an eyebrow. "I'm waiting for someone to break into 'The Lion Sleeps Tonight.'"

Rebecca pointed to the tent flap. "It's morning, breakfast time."

Olivia stood. "And you?"

"All set up," Rebecca mumbled. "Send in a tray." Rebecca waved her hand, shooing Olivia away. "Get going, you."

"And, yet again, here I am alone."

"Maybe a handsome tribesman will win your heart?" Rebecca smiled then winced.

"Ha, ha. That would be something. I don't need forever love, but companionship would be nice."

Rebecca lifted her eyebrows in question. "Lower your standards, maybe?"

"Fat chance. I need to find Mr. Save-the-World, or I'm not interested. I'm not the type of girl to live in a subdivision, drive a nice car, and prepare snacks for two kids and a dog." Olivia lifted her hands in surrender. "But don't worry, I'll go, and I'll be amazed." Olivia stifled a laugh. "By the animals, of course."

Rebecca winced in pain as she held back a laugh. Even though Rebecca was a trooper, Olivia knew her friend needed time to rest, which meant Olivia heading out on the safari would be the best option for both of them.

Olivia slid a light jacket over her T-shirt, excited about the promised animal encounters for the first time. When was the last time anything had amazed her?

Once, a therapist had told Olivia that she'd

put up a wall around her heart to protect herself against all the hard things she'd faced in her childhood. The wall came in handy as an adult, primarily when she worked with so many people in need. Yet, too often, that wall caused peace and happiness to bounce off too. As she zipped the jacket, Olivia told herself to enjoy the day without worrying about the many things out of her control.

Lord, you know what I need. I want to make a difference, a real difference. I'd also like to experience joy.

Olivia grabbed her camera, phone, and portable charger. A bit of self-care would do her good. She'd been working day and night for two weeks straight. She needed to refresh her soul. She needed to witness God's creation and remember His rule over this world.

With a final wave to Rebecca, Olivia unfastened the lock and unzipped the tent. She stepped out into the cool morning, letting the canvas tent flap close behind her. The wind whispered through the trees, carrying with it the scent of the earth. The early morning was dark and quiet. The sun had yet to rise, but the merging sunrise tinged the light gray sky.

Within the walls of the complex, tall light posts illuminated the compound, highlighting other guests emerging from similar tents. A few people greeted the morning on the balconies of the five-star lodge. Olivia wanted to think about something different than how much one of those rooms cost a night. The clerk had mentioned at check-in that the best rooms had views of the protected reserve. Nearly every day, guests could see elephants, giraffes, and lions. Olivia was thankful they at least got monkeys.

Olivia scanned the trees above as she walked, looking for any new items the monkeys had collected. She wasn't disappointed. A white bra hung by one strap and a red one next. A chuckle slipped from her lips.

"You have to share your secret." A man's voice with a strong European accent interrupted her thoughts. "That smile is brighter than light flooding over the savannah, and I just have to know why."

Olivia turned toward a tall figure. With a straight-back walk, he matched her stride as if they were already friends. Instead of being alarmed, Olivia found herself intrigued. Even though he didn't wear a name tag, she wondered if he worked at the lodge. Maybe it was his job to make the guests feel more comfortable. Yes, that had to be it.

"I wish I had something witty or interesting, but I was thinking about the monkeys. They seem to like, uh, women's things." She paused for a moment and pointed.

The man followed her gaze, and surprised

laughter spilled from his lips. "I see. Yes, that would make one smile now, wouldn't it? Savage creatures, I tell you."

Now it was her turn to laugh.

Olivia continued toward the lodge, heat rising to her cheeks. The man walked with a gentle gait next to her, and goose bumps rose on her arms. He had to be at least six inches taller than her five-foot-three-inch frame, but he matched her stride so comfortably that it seemed they'd walked together a hundred times before.

"Did you just get here? To the lodge, I mean," she asked. She'd given him the perfect opportunity to tell her if he was an employee.

"Yes, last night. I'm a guest, but this nearly feels like a second home. My father—well, this is one of his favorite places. He brought me here as a child. Things of late have been stressful, uh, at work. I made a rash decision to come. Something about the roar of a lion waking me from my sleep reminds me that there's a natural world out there that exists beyond tasks and duties." His steps slowed then stopped, and Olivia did the same.

"And you?" She was so captivated by the intensity of his blue-eyed gaze that she resisted the urge to take a step back, to escape from the heat rushing through her body at his closeness.

The man's clean-shaven face highlighted his chiseled jaw. A small dimple rested on his cheekbone even when he wasn't smiling. Olivia willed the thumping of her heart to slow. It was a simple conversation, nothing more. She wasn't the type of woman who drew the attention of guys like this.

She resumed her steps again, and he did the same beside her. "It's my first time in this part of Kenya. We've been in Nairobi, in the Kibera slums, for the last two weeks." She sighed. "I need a reminder that beauty exists and that it's okay to take the occasional deep breath." She hoped the words sounded convincing.

They neared the lodge, and both of them paused again. Olivia turned to him, unsure what to do or say but confident that she didn't want their conversation to end.

"Do you have plans for the day?" the words spilled out, and Olivia's eyes widened, surprising herself. *What am I doing?* Yet simultaneously, she hated the thought of not seeing this guy again. She didn't want this moment—whatever it was—to end.

The man tilted his head toward her. "I picked up a novel at the airport. I considered finding a hammock and diving into it."

Olivia nibbled her lower lip. *Be brave, ask him . . .*

An awkward moment passed, and she quickly breathed. "Listen, my friend was supposed to go on a safari with me, but she's sick." She pointed a thumb in the direction of their tent. "I signed up

with a group, and I don't know any of the others
. . . uh, not that I know you either, but if you're
free, you're welcome to join us, join me. The
ticket is already paid for. I'd hate to see it go to
waste."

He eyed her curiously, yet his gaze was full
of warmth. Tilting his head, the man stroked his
chin. His smile grew, and a matching dimple
appeared on the opposite cheek. "It would be a
good economic decision for the ticket to be put to
good use. And I suppose my novel can wait until
tomorrow."

Movement from the doorway of the lodge
caught his attention. Two men and a woman
talked. Olivia wasn't sure if this man knew who
they were, but he'd shifted his weight from side
to side, intense discomfort.

He turned so his back faced the door of the
lodge. "I assume you're going to breakfast?"

"Yes, they're supposed to have a wonderful
buffet. Do you want to join me?" Heat rose to her
cheeks at her boldness, and his smile brightened
even more.

"I've already eaten, but I would love to join you
on the safari. What time will you be leaving?"

Olivia glanced at her watch. "Thirty minutes.
We—I—uh, I'm supposed to find the white van
out front."

"Splendid. I will be there. It will give me
a moment to gather my things." Then with a

twinkle in his eye, he leaned closer. "Only one thing: Who, may I ask, invited me?"

"Oh, I'm Olivia . . . from Little Rock."

"Very good. And I'm Louis . . . from *Alloria la Vella*. It's a pleasure to meet you, Olivia from Little Rock. Thanks for inviting me. I sense today will be wonderful."

It wasn't until the man, Louis, was twenty feet away that Olivia realized she was still holding her breath. She released it then placed her palm on her forehead.

"Stupid, stupid," Olivia whispered. She should know better than to engage in such a way with a stranger. Even though he appeared safe, most serial killers did.

Maybe he wasn't a serial killer, but was he safe? Olivia crossed her arms over her chest, knowing one thing: he was charming. Way too charming. Time and time again, she'd seen her mother get swept away by these types of men who, with the promise of love, only brought hurt.

At least she and Louis were going to be with a group today. She couldn't imagine anything terrible happening when they were with a driver and other guests.

Straightening her shoulders, Olivia walked up the steps to the lodge as if every nerve in her body wasn't tied up in knots. *It's an ordinary day to make a new friend.*

Olivia shook her head. *This is not ordinary,*

and, man, I'd love someone like that as more than a friend.

The fragrant fresh bread and bacon aroma met her as she entered the lodge. The dark floor shone as though freshly laid. A pair of long tables laden with food extended before her. To her left, guests sat at dining tables, talking and sharing breakfast.

Olivia hesitated just inside the entrance, her hand reaching for her belly. A half-hour prior, it had rumbled its discontent, urging her to satiate it. Now it twisted within her, and her appetite had vanished.

A sudden flutter, akin to the dance of butterflies, leaped from her stomach to her chest as she grasped the notion of spending the day with a stranger—a striking one, no less. She took a plate from the modest pile, serving herself a portion of fruit and a cup of yogurt. The day ahead on the safari would be lengthy, with many hours to elapse before the anticipated sack lunch. She had to eat something.

Olivia had scarcely settled down with her breakfast and had yet to take a bite when she pulled out her cell phone and typed in a search Alloria la Vella.

Alloria la Vella is the capital of Alloria, a principality in the Pyrenees mountains between France and Spain.

She hadn't known Alloria existed. Olivia

clicked on one of the photos. An aerial winter scene displaying high mountain peaks, white with snow, filled the screen. Golden lights, shining from stone buildings, brightened the valley between the peaks, appearing as a golden waterfall between the mountains.

She clicked on the next photo. A spring or summer image of a similar view showed a mix of modern buildings and stone medieval-type structures set among green rolling hills. The high mountains surrounded the small city like protective walls. It looked like something from a fairytale book or movie. Did real people live in places like this?

This handsome, charming man lived in paradise. *Perfect.* Her heart was already flip-flopping, and they'd spoken to each for no more than five minutes.

Just think of him as a friend and nothing more, she urged herself while at the same time counting down the minutes until it was time to leave. She finished her fruit and yogurt and then researched more about Alloria, which was believed to be founded by Charlemagne. Although fewer than one-hundred thousand people live in the country, tens of millions of tourists visit every year.

Olivia's stomach constricted as she continued reading. The absence of customs duties and taxes rendered Alloria a significant international retail trade nucleus. Despite its modest size, the nation thrived in wealth and tourism—two things she loathed.

Yet, here she was, lodged in one of the finest establishments in the region and about to embark on a safari. Without Rebecca's insistence and her footing the bill, Olivia would never have squandered money on such opulence. She shuddered to consider the number of meals that could have been purchased for children in Kibera with the sum Rebecca had expended on a single night's stay.

Olivia slid her plate away, resolving to seize the day without letting those thoughts weigh her down. Regardless of how her interactions with her newfound companion unfolded, she would witness nature in a manner she had never experienced before—a way most people never had the chance to. She needed to view this day as a gift.

For one day, she could set aside the troubles looming in Little Rock, her friend's dental issues, and even thoughts of sweet Promise. Olivia would ignore that she'd soon reveal her true self to the world. Instead, she'd let the splendor of God's creation restore her spirit today. At the very least, Olivia would attempt to. And she'd enjoy the companionship of a handsome man who caused butterflies to dance in her stomach.

CHAPTER SEVEN

Louis had nearly forgotten that today was the day of Constance's wedding until they entered the lodge's glass-walled suite overlooking the Mara River and spotted the morose look on Sergio's face.

The aroma of coffee mixed with the sweet scent of the orchids displayed on the front entry table. Sergio glanced up from the computer in his lap.

Thankfully Louis's bodyguard understood why Louis had skipped the wedding and traveled to Africa instead. He needed space for his heart to mend, his mind to still, and his body to relax from the constant demands of his schedule.

The expansive suite was his favorite at the lodge. Although modern, its design included local stone and Kenyan cedar. Beyond his private bedroom was a wraparound deck with an infinity pool. If he'd come across any woman other than Olivia, Louis would have suggested they eat a catered lunch and spend time poolside watching the hippos in the river and the other animals beyond. This suite wouldn't have impressed Olivia from Little Rock. That she'd mentioned his safari ticket was paid for and that breakfast was included with their stay told him a lot about her. She wasn't used to luxury.

Of course, he knew that. Last night after hearing Olivia's voice, he'd rewatched his favorite episodes of *In My Mother's Steps*.

Through the flickering images on the screen, Louis had glimpsed Olivia's world and learned much about her. Of course, he hadn't known who she was before last night, and most of the world still didn't know. It amazed him that she'd come to this lodge of all places on this day and had invited him to join her on a safari. It was almost as if God had orchestrated a divine dance, leading them to each other at this moment.

Through the documentary, Louis heard the tremble of pain in her voice as she spoke with those who shared her mother's addictions and struggles. He'd heard her stifled sobs as she'd stood at the gravesite where her mother lay, a victim of suicide.

As he watched week after week, Louis had gotten to know a woman fiercely determined to confront the demons of her past. Olivia seemed unafraid to delve into the darkest corners of her mother's life, peel back layers of pain and sorrow, and understand the woman who had given her life.

But when she'd stood before him today, Louis had also seen a woman who was fragile and vulnerable. Even with a smile, the ache in Olivia's eyes had been palpable, cutting deep into his soul. Even though he'd just met her,

Louis felt a fierce protectiveness for her, a desire to shield her from any more hurt.

Olivia was the opposite of Constance, whose interests had only gone skin deep. Constance wouldn't have been interested in any bag that cost less than ten thousand Euros. And even when Constance visited his family's royal residence, she'd looked at it to remodel more than to appreciate his family's heritage.

For the first time since Constance broke things off, Louis realized her extravagant tastes would have brought conflict if their relationship had continued. While his family enjoyed a privileged position in Alloria, their wealth was not comparable to that of Europe's other royal families.

Sergio lounged playfully in a leather chair, his laptop flooded with tabs about the wedding. "I really thought she was the one. Our karaoke nights were legendary!" He exaggerated a heavy sigh and theatrically wiped away a nonexistent tear as he switched tabs. "I'm mainly here for the dress reveal. Constance did have a knack for turning heads with her style." He peeked over the screen, flashing a mischievous grin at Louis. "Being your bodyguard meant our date locations were not exactly my choice. Remember that time we ended up at that spy-themed dinner?"

Louis leaned back, amused. "Ah, Sergio, always the protector but never the romantic lead.

Perhaps if you had more romance in your life, you wouldn't be so enthralled by my escapades."

Sergio shot him a playful glare, "Oh please, Louis. I'm sacrificing my love life for the greater good of the kingdom!" He paused for comedic effect before adding, "Besides, you think I don't want romance? My mother reminds me daily about wanting grandchildren. 'Sergio,' she says, 'I'm not getting any younger!' But here I am, safeguarding you and attending spy-themed dinners!"

Sergio offered a wry smile as he readjusted the laptop on his lap.

Sergio had been Louis's bodyguard for over a decade, and he'd never failed to be there when Louis needed him. Sergio's appearance was unassuming, but he exuded calm confidence that put Louis at ease. He wore jeans and a simple T-shirt, a departure from his usual tailored suits, but in Africa, they could relax. They were far from the prying eyes of the media, and it was a welcome respite from the constant attention they received in Europe.

Louis watched as Sergio sipped his coffee, savoring the rich aroma. The way Sergio held the mug with a firm grip, peering over the edge of it as he swallowed, proved he was always aware of his surroundings. It was a small gesture, but it spoke volumes about Sergio's training and experience.

Sergio was more than just a bodyguard. He was a trusted confidant, a friend who had seen Louis through some of his darkest moments. Sergio's steady presence had comforted Louis when he needed it most.

"*Most* of the dates." Louis smirked. "You joined us for only a few of the mountain hikes or paddles across the lakes."

"I'm not as young as I used to be."

Louis moved toward the coffee cart that had arrived in his suite while he'd been out for an early morning walk. He poured himself a cup of coffee and added one cube of sugar, stirring. "Which is why I'm surprised you're awake. I'd assumed you'd be sleeping." He sat on the black and white striped couch, reminiscent of a zebra's pelt, and then pulled a gray velvet pillow onto his lap.

"And that troubles you?"

"Well, truthfully, now I must tell you my plans instead of apologizing later for my disappearance."

"Your plans? As of last night, your plans included reading in a hammock with the view of giraffes."

"This is better than a novel. *She* is better."

"*Who* is it this time? Did you extend an invitation to one of the women on your aunt's 'most eligible bachelorette list'?"

Louis sipped his coffee, enjoying the warmth

as it traveled down his throat. Relishing the impatient look on Sergio's face as he waited for an answer. "Just the opposite. I met someone in the courtyard this morning, and she invited me to go on a safari with her."

"What do you mean she invited you on a safari? You said yes to a woman you do not know?"

Louis took another sip. *But I do know her.* But he wouldn't tell Sergio that, not yet anyway.

"I do not believe it needs an explanation. She invited me, and I agreed. She is no threat."

Sergio lifted an eyebrow. "The fact that you state that makes her even more so." He glanced at his gold watch. "We don't have time to do a background check. I will have to join you—"

"No." The word shot out of Louis's mouth. He firmly set his coffee cup on the table, and coffee sloshed over the side. "You are not invited."

"Please tell me this is a joke. You cannot be serious. I already have received a call from your father." Sergio closed his laptop and placed it on a side table beside his chair.

"And?"

"He is angry we did not follow the complete security protocol. Months of preparation must happen before travel abroad is allowed."

"Allowed?" Louis stood. "I'm growing weary of that word. How foolish of me to want to travel on vacation on a whim. To go on a safari on a whim." He moved to his suitcase and extracted

his leather camera case. "Besides, I will return this evening, and no one need know."

Sergio threw up his hands. "So, off with my head." He pressed his head against the soft, white throw draped over the back of his chair. He rubbed his brow, extracting a heavy sigh. "What do you even know about this woman?"

"Her name's Olivia, and she's from Little Rock. I think that's in Oklahoma."

Sergio released a low moan and ran his hand through his salt-and-pepper hair. "Arkansas, but close."

"I also know she says what's on her mind, which is refreshing." Louis couldn't help but smile. "She even pointed out lady's undergarments put up in trees by the monkeys." That comment had endeared this woman to Louis. Everyone he knew had been so careful with their words all his life. It sometimes made him feel like he had relationships with robots, not people. Horror of horror for someone to do or say the wrong thing.

Sergio scowled. "So she doesn't know who you are."

"I wouldn't be so excited about the day if she did."

"This has me worried."

"You know, as well as I, that my life is not in danger. And if my father discovers that I ditched you, I will take full responsibility."

"Do you think I am worried about your life?"

Sergio shook his head. "I can see that dopey smile, my man. It's your heart that I fear for."

"Yes, well, that would never do, would it?" Louis didn't want to let Sergio know his genuine fear. As he'd walked with Olivia, Louis had spotted someone he believed he recognized. Pacific Noah was one of the top celebrity reporters in Kenya. The man talking to the lodge manager looked like Pacific, but Louis hadn't moved closer to confirm.

It would be like Pacific to attempt to make a splash on the international media scene with a story about a depressed prince hiding away in Africa, refusing to leave his suite. This was another reason Louis needed to get away for the day—to get out into nature and away from Pacific and his search for a story at the lodge.

Louis released the breath he'd been holding and stepped out onto the balcony. Unlike the other lodge rooms or the tents in the courtyard, his balcony gave him a view over the lodge's high walls into the Masai Mara and the wildlife that overflowed the savannah. Though dawn had not fully broken, anticipation bubbled with the thoughts of seeing the wonder of this place through Olivia's eyes. Yes, he had high hopes for this day.

CHAPTER EIGHT

Olivia glanced at her watch, her heart pounding. She didn't want to be late. She hurried to the waiting van, eyes scanning the small groups. Foreign tourists chattered excitedly among themselves.

She positioned herself farthest away from the van's door, hoping to make it easier for Louis to spot her. She couldn't shake the worry that he might not come. What if he had just been trying to be friendly and had no real intention of meeting her?

Her fears were compounded when the driver opened the side door and motioned for them to climb in. Louis still hadn't arrived. A wave of disappointment washed over her.

Olivia tried to push her doubts aside as she approached the van. Had she honestly expected him to come? Still, she couldn't help feeling a twinge of sadness at the thought that he might not show.

One by one, the driver checked the names of the guests with those on his roster.

"Olivia and Rebecca?" The guide looked at Olivia.

"My name is Olivia Garza, and my friend couldn't make it, so—"

"I'm here." Louis's voice came out of nowhere. Olivia turned to watch him approach, his eyes fixed on hers. Her knees trembled, and she straightened her back. *He came.*

His blond hair was hidden under a baseball cap pulled down over his brows. An expensive-looking leather satchel hung over his shoulder. From its bulkiness, Olivia guessed he'd brought his camera.

Louis stood next to her, smelling like sandalwood and bergamot. Two of her favorite scents. Her heart flipped, and she willed it to calm.

"And you are . . ." The driver looked at the paperwork in his hand. " . . . not Rebecca."

"Wonderful observation." Laughter spilled from Louis's lips, and he reached forward and grasped the man's shoulder. "I can already see this will be a magnificent day." With a slight squeeze, he released the shoulder. "I am taking Rebecca's place. If you'd simply like to put down Louis." He cleared his throat.

The driver narrowed his gaze. Then his eyes widened, and his face brightened. "Louis." He cleared his throat. "Louis, not Rebecca. Yes, I will take note."

A barely noticeable nod of Louis's caused the driver's eyes to sparkle, and Olivia wondered if the driver noticed *the big tipper* displayed in her new friend's dashing smile.

103

The driver bowed his head and stepped back from the open door. "Pleased to have you join our adventure, sir. This day is one none of us will ever forget. None of us."

"Wonderful." Louis clapped his hands together. "Olivia and I just met, and I hope the savannah will help me make a great first impression." He took a step back to allow Olivia to go first.

Her hand grasped the cool metal of the door grip as she climbed into the van. "Thank you. How courteous."

The van had tall sides and an open roof. Olivia sat in the second row from the back, near the window. Even though there were numerous available seats, Louis settled beside her. He scooted down in his seat and lowered his hat over his brows.

She laughed. "It's still dark out. Are you afraid the sun will come up that quickly and shine in your eyes?"

"It's quite a habit, isn't it?" He pulled it up a little higher so she could see his dark blond eyebrows and intense blue eyes. "People always mistake me for Brad Pitt." He winked at her. "I simply hope to save you the trouble of protecting me from their photo requests. It does get rather tedious."

Olivia secured the seat belt. "In that case, I don't mind your hat, especially since I haven't had time to practice my *jiu-jitsu* in a while."

Louis's laughter filled the van, and Olivia settled deeper into her seat. The van started and left the lodge's walled compound, pulling onto a paved road. As they approached the edge of the game preserve, the landscape began to change. Tall grasses swayed in the breeze, and acacia trees dotted the horizon. The air was thick with the scent of the wild, a heady mixture of dust, grass, and animal musk.

The sun had climbed a little higher on the horizon, casting a golden glow upon the dusty road. The van rumbled along, kicking up small clouds of red dirt. They traveled a few miles, passing through dry savannah and sparse acacia trees. Eventually, they arrived at a small village where the low, round houses stood like ant hills on the horizon.

The houses were constructed of clay, baked in the relentless sun, with flat roofs. Tall pens made of branches and brush nestled between the homes, serving as enclosures for livestock. The village people moved about their daily tasks, their red clothing contrasting against the dusty landscape. Both men and women wore long red sheaths that hung to their knees, while some adorned themselves with red capes draped over their shoulders.

The van drove slowly through the village, its occupants taking in the sights and sounds of this foreign place. The Masai people moved abo' doing their daily work with their distinctive red clothing and shaved heads. Few of the locals looked up as the van passed by.

"For centuries, the Masai have relied on their herds of cattle, sheep, and goats to sustain their way of life, moving across the vast savannahs of East Africa in search of grazing land and water sources," Louis explained, his voice gentle, as if he were her personal tour guide. "They've maintained their cultural identity and traditions despite droughts, disease, and conflict with other tribes."

Olivia thought of the young men she'd seen in the slums. "Can the young people afford to stay here? Do they stay?"

"Many leave to find work. The youth go to urban areas," Louis explained.

"And end up in slums like Kibera?"

Louis nodded. "Sadly, yes."

Up ahead, a large brick and wood structure with a pointed roof signaled their arrival at the game reserve. The sign above the entrance read Masai Mara National Reserve, Sekenani Gate.

Metal gates blocked the entrance, and a line of vans was already waiting. Guards wearing camouflage outfits, carrying guns, walked up and down the line of vans.

Clusters of Masai women circled the parked vehicles. They carried carved giraffes, colored beaded necklaces, wood-carved face masks, and other items. The women waved the items toward the passengers sitting in the vans, and a flurry of activity resulted any time cash bills were handed out the window. Multiple hands reached for the bills while tossing handcrafts into the vehicle windows.

Olivia gasped, pointing to the commotion. "They're so desperate to sell their things. How can they even keep track of who's selling what?"

"They sort it out, and any sale benefits them all. Tourism has been down lately, and they need the money for food. For survival. Selling one of their items can be the difference between their children having dinner tonight or not."

Olivia reached for her fanny pack. "I've already bought a few things, but getting a few more items will help . . ." Her voice trailed off as she pulled out a twenty-dollar bill from her wallet.

Yet instead of pulling into the line behind the other vans, the driver drove around to a second gate and motioned to one of the guards. The guard approached, and the driver spoke to him in low tones. Then, to her surprise, the guard walked around the van toward the side door.

Olivia's heart pounded. Were they in trouble? Had they done something wrong? Beside her, Louis removed his baseball cap. He ran his fingers through his hair, letting it fall softly onto his forehead. The guard opened the side door and scanned the passengers, and then his gaze settled on Olivia and Louis. With a small salute in their direction, he closed the van door and waved the driver through the second gate, leaving the other vans behind.

Rubbing her chin in confusion, Olivia turned to Louis. "Was that guard looking at us . . . at you? Do they think we're a famous movie star couple or something?" The wind blew through the open top, bringing the aroma of fresh air and wild grasses. Olivia brushed away the strands of hair that blew into her face as she fixed her eyes on Louis's handsome profile.

"I told you I often get mistaken for Brad Pitt. And you could pass for Mila Kunis."

"If I were Mila, I'd be with Ashton, not you." She smirked. "Surely that can't be it."

Louis shrugged. "I don't know. Maybe one of the passengers has VIP status and paid for special treatment."

Olivia eyed the other passengers. "But who?"

"That's the thing, Olivia from Little Rock. Those types of people often don't want to be noticed. They want to fit in. They wish to be unseen."

"Good to know, but I feel bad. I was going to buy some handcrafts." She glanced back over her shoulder, watching the gates disappear behind them, and then she slipped the twenty-dollar bill back into her wallet.

"Don't worry about that. I'm sure an even

bigger crowd of sellers will be waiting when we exit." He flashed her a smile, highlighting his dimples. "But I appreciate your concern. I don't see such compassion every day, especially in my, uh, job."

"It must be hard—the work you're in." She eyed him, waiting for an answer. *Who are you, Louis?* She wanted to ask. But something held her back. If Olivia started asking him questions, he'd likely do the same with her. So far, she hadn't told anyone about the documentary and pushed thoughts of the reveal out of her mind. *I'll worry about that tomorrow.*

He chuckled. "You have no idea how challenging my job can be at times. It's truly all-encompassing."

Up ahead, the sun crested the horizon, drawing her attention away from Louis's words. Shafts of orange and pink light lit the sky, stretching over grassy plains. Rolling hills stretched in every direction, and golden grasses waved in the breeze. Scattered here around the savannah, bare thorn trees rose. Twisted branches spread like gnarled fingers, a symbol of resilience in the untamed beauty of the savannah.

But the landscape's beauty paled compared to the animals that filled the land, appearing like an illustration from a children's Bible storybook. Clusters of antelope ran and jumped with babies at their sides. Small deer moved in herds, leaping in smooth waves nearly as one. Birds flew up from the ground, filling the sky with streams of color rising. They rose in a spiral and then drifted down again.

"I can hardly believe I never made the time to come out here this early, all the times I've been to Africa," Louis said wistfully.

"You were just waiting for someone to invite you," Olivia teased. The corners of her mouth curled up in what she hoped was a playful grin.

She sucked in a deep breath. The crisp and pure air seemed as new as creation—the breeze so gentle and sweet, like the breath of God.

Louis faced her, and her heart skipped a beat as his eyes sparkled with what appeared to be affection. *Surely not. I'm just imagining things.*

Her gaze flickered between Louis and the breathtaking view outside the window. The scene's beauty was not lost on her, yet the man beside her equally consumed Olivia's mind.

"I was waiting for an invitation." His words sounded more like a statement than a question.

"Yes, you were," she whispered, her voice barely above a breath. "And this is amazing. I—I don't even know what to say."

Louis's eyes fixed on her, and the air between them grew thick with unspoken emotions. "You don't have to say anything," he murmured, husky. "Just being here with you is enough."

Her heart swelled warmly, and Olivia told

herself not to get caught up in his gaze. This wasn't real—couldn't be real. Louis acted as if he knew her. Yet that was impossible. Unless . . .

She wrinkled her nose and rubbed her brow. Had Louis watched her documentary? Did he recognize her voice? *Impossible.* They were in Africa, and he was from Alloria. What would someone from a popular Pyrenees destination be doing watching the documentary of a nobody from Little Rock?

Then again, why would he act so familiar, as if he knew her? *He's acting as if he already cares.*

Did it matter? She could almost hear Rebecca's reprimand. *"Stop trying to figure everything out, Olivia, and enjoy the moment."* It was the type of advice Rebecca would give and precisely what Olivia wanted to do—enjoy this time with Louis without thoughts or questions about what tomorrow would bring.

Olivia took in the wonder outside the window. A throaty laugh escaped. "Look at this," she said, her voice filled with wonder. "This is paradise."

"Yes, quite stunning," Louis said, his eyes on her. He reached over and grasped her hand. He offered a gentle squeeze and then released it. "Thank you for inviting me. There's no place I'd rather be."

The world before them was Eden. Abundant Eden. Previously, when Olivia had thought about going on a safari, she'd imagined they'd see a few animals. But this was nothing like she'd pictured. Stretched in every direction, multiple herds of wildlife danced in ebbs and flows. She considered pulling out her phone to take photos but didn't want to miss being part of this natural world. And also being connected to this handsome man beside her. He was part of the glory of this place too.

"This has to be a dream. The whole thing. Even you." The words came out before she could stop them. Heat rose to her face, and she dipped her chin. "I'm sorry. I sound so . . ."

"Amazed." He leaned closer and offered unrestrained laughter. "It's a wonderful thing to witness. And what's not to be amazed about?" He stood to get a better look at the wildlife, and she did the same.

The top of the van reached her chest, and she leaned against the sides of the open top. The warm air enveloped her, and Olivia's hair flowed behind her as if joining in nature's dance.

She elbowed him. "Would you do me a favor?"

"Yes, of course."

"You brought a camera, didn't you? Can you take some photos of this?" She swept her hand toward the scene before them. "I only have my cell phone, and I know it won't do this place justice."

"I'm an amateur, but I'll try." Louis pulled his camera from its case and hung the strap around

112

his neck. Then he changed the lens. Click, click, click went the shutter. They rarely spoke except for oohs and ahhs at the beautiful display before them. Even though the other tourists were photographing the wildlife and talking, their movements and voices faded in the distance. Though surrounded by people, it seemed like their world alone.

"I suppose this is why it is important to come early," he offered. "The animals are most active in the cool of the day."

Despite her tense stomach muscles, she nodded and attempted to think of something witty or insightful, perhaps comparing Louis to a graceful gazelle or an agile cheetah who snuck into her day, but her words tangled in her throat. This man unnerved her. He was handsome, yes. And then there was his accent. Words rolled off his tongue with a beautiful cadence. More than that, he moved with such grace.

"It was worth the missed sleep." It was all she could manage and so insufficient.

A small gazelle darted at the edge of its herd. Seeing the van, it hopped in their direction. As if teasing, the gazelle turned and bounced back with such intensity that the entire herd was alerted.

About fifty gazelles took off, their movements synchronized as if following an invisible leader. Their agile bodies bounded powerfully across the grassy landscape. Then the creatures hopped over a small rise in the terrain, one by one disappearing out of sight.

Olivia grinned. "I think that little gazelle roused everyone up to give us a good show." She couldn't help but giggle. "That had to be one of the most adorable things I've ever seen."

"I agree." Louis's voice was husky. *Click.* Olivia turned to see the camera pointed toward her.

"You're supposed to be photographing the wildlife."

"I can't help myself. I've been on a safari dozens of times, but never with someone like you. This truly is delightful."

Delightful? "Of all the things. No one's ever used that word about me." She shrugged. "Maybe the vacationing Olivia is more fun than even I knew."

The rumble of the van's engine, and the vibration under her feet, kept her grounded, reminding her this was not a dream.

Rome, Italy
5 October 1943

A beam of light, which dared to filter through the broken window, did little to help Alessandra make out the face of the huddled forms before her. One of the young priests told her where to find the young mother and her daughter hidden among other rescued Jews.

"It's all right. Do not be scared. I have been sent to offer help." Alessandra kept her tone calm and her words gentle. "I know you have prayed, and I'm here. They say you asked for help for your little one?"

Even with those words, Rachel did not answer. Alessandra's lower lip trembled with the rise and fall of the mother's breath and the soft snores of the sleeping child. *Could I do it—hand over my child to another?*

Another minute passed, and Alessandra's eyes adjusted to the dim light. Rachel—no older than twenty-five—huddled in the corner, tightly holding onto her daughter. Eight-year-old Leah looked not much older than five, her body so thin and frail from lack of nutrition.

"We have found a way of escape for your daughter," Alessandra finally offered.

"My daughter alone?" The woman's voice was soft, curious.

Alessandra released a sigh of relief, thankful the woman had spoken. The time ticked by. They didn't have much time. "It's the best we can do. I am sorry."

"It is an answer to prayer. You are correct," the woman's words trembled as she spoke. In the light of the window, Alessandra could now make out the woman's sad smile.

Crowded around the mother and daughter, the other hidden Jewish women sat silent. Alessandra noted tears in many of their eyes. *Do they think of children lost?* Yet their furrowed brows and tight lips told Alessandra they lacked trust. She didn't blame them. These survivors had been forcibly rounded up and loaded onto a train car, with no idea where they were being taken or what would happen to them.

Brave partisans had stopped the train, rescued these women—and the young girl—and hid them away in a safe location. Or at least safe for now.

Alessandra closed her eyes and tried blocking out the train wheels clacking against the tracks not two hundred yards from the underground storage room. The Nazis had yet to discover this refuge, but Alessandra had seen numerous patrols within the train yard even as she'd made her way here. Urgency caused her to change her tone and speak with authority.

"If you want to save your daughter's life, trust me. I am your only hope. I—" Leah whimpered, interrupting Alessandra's words.

Without a word, Rachel lifted her child. The color drained from her face, yet she set her jaw firmly with resolve.

The young girl's eyes fluttered open, and tears pooled, threatening to break free.

"It's okay, sweetheart," Alessandra whispered,

pulling the girl close. "You'll be okay. You have to be brave. We both have to be brave."

Alessandra stood and offered Rachel one parting glance. "May God be with you." The words caught. "Always with you."

Without another word, Alessandra turned and hurried the way she'd come.

Lord, give me the wisdom and guidance to understand how to help. May this child always know of her mother's love. And, Lord, bless this mother who was strong enough to release her only daughter into my arms.

CHAPTER NINE

Masai Mara National Reserve, Kenya
Present Day

The sun hung brightly over the savannah, and the air had a tangible calm as if the entire landscape stilled under the golden rays. The sun's stare was unbroken by clouds, transforming the yellow grass into a shimmering sea. Strips of shade stretched out from the slender acacia trees. Small groups of animals took refuge under them. The van rumbled on, and only a bird's distant cry rose occasionally over them.

As the van jolted over a bump in the road, Olivia stumbled, her balance thrown off. Just as Olivia was sure she was going to tumble to the van floor, two hands wrapped around her. Louis pulled her against his side, his arms encircling her with a gentle strength.

She allowed herself to be held there, lost in the sensation of his warmth and steady heartbeat. She felt safe and protected as if nothing could harm her.

Then she righted herself, pulling away from him with a soft smile.

"Wow, that was close. Thank you." She placed her hands against the opening of the van's top. "I'm all right now."

Louis held on just a moment longer. "All good then?"

"Yes, thank you for saving me." She turned and motioned to his camera. "It's good you had on that strap."

"I would have dropped it to save you." His hair danced against his forehead, and she realized he'd ditched his baseball cap.

"And lose my photos?" She shook her head. "I'd rather have skinned knees."

Louis leaned his forearms against the top of the van as they rumbled along. "Well, both you and the photos are safe. At least for the time. But we better be more diligent about watching for potholes."

"I'd rather risk my neck than miss out on this." She grinned at the waving grass that spread as far as she could see.

"So true. Just smashing. It's a scene I always enjoy. I'm glad this game reserve is here. Just think, all of Africa must have looked like this a few hundred years ago. I trust my Creator even more when seeing the natural world closer to how He designed it. If He can create such beauty in animals, it gives me hope for my life."

Warmth filled Olivia's heart. One minute ago, she would have believed nothing could top this moment, but Louis's words did just that. *So he's a man of faith, too.* How in all the world did she happen to run into the one perfect guy on the planet? There had to be something wrong with him. Other than the fact that he lived on the other side of the world, in a country she had never heard of before today.

"Such beautiful design." She sighed. "And just think—God knew we'd experience this together."

His brow furrowed slightly. "I wasn't looking forward to this day. It's been a black cloud on my calendar for a while. Novel or not, I probably would have wallowed in self-pity, but then I ran into you, Olivia from Little Rock. What a gift."

Olivia wanted to ask him to explain this dark cloud. Instead, she again pointed ahead, and he started shooting more photos.

Impala, springbok, and gazelle grazed together. Olivia tried to hold back a squeal as a warthog ran across the road, followed by four piglets with tails sticking up straight in the air.

But the memory of Louis's arms around her still lingered, and she couldn't help but wonder if there was something more between them. The way he held her and the tenderness in his eyes suggested he felt a connection too. As they continued their journey through the savannah, she found herself stealing glances at him, her heart beating a little faster each time their eyes met.

In the distance, a hill was covered with black dots, and as their van continued, Olivia's eyes widened. A lone zebra walked along the roadway.

"A zebra!" she squeaked. "Growing up, I had a zebra stuffed animal. It's the one thing that stayed with me for a long time."

"Oh, yes, you are excited about a zebra now." The driver laughed as he called back over his shoulder. "But before the day is through, I guarantee you will be saying, 'Dumb zebras, get out of the road!'"

Olivia was captivated by the surroundings, finding it hard to believe that anyone could become desensitized to such beauty. Nonetheless, with his daily exposure to the landscape and tourists, the driver must have had his reasons.

"Can you imagine this being your job?" she asked.

Louis shrugged. "It's not as easy as it seems. I've heard from some of these drivers. Tourists can be a handful, the animals aren't pets, and don't get me started on the unpredictable weather. But most concerning is that these drivers sometimes face real dangers."

Olivia turned to him, eyebrows raised, "What do you mean?"

"Even though this place is heavily guarded, poachers can still be problematic. And if a guide happens upon poachers, it's dangerous. Poaching is a serious crime, and the last thing a poacher wants is to be caught."

"You know a lot about Kenya."

"My father brought me here when I was

younger. After I grew up, I started coming alone. There's something special about this place. I feel alive here. The important things back home, such as work matters or my father's expectations, are far away." He ran a hand down his chin and then glanced over at her. "I hope I'm not rambling."

"No, not at all." She tucked a strand of dark hair behind her ear. "What else do you know about Kenya, about this reserve?" It was easier to ask him questions than to be asked what she was doing in this country.

"No matter how often you come, you'll never see the same scene twice. I know that being here is a privilege. I'll not take it for granted."

"But is it hazardous? It's so peaceful, so calm right now."

"One thing you want to watch out for is the cheetah. The flat, open terrain is perfect for their hunting style. Look for them on elevated mounds. They scan the plains looking for the weak and injured."

She laughed. "Does that include us?"

"If we stay inside the van, we'll be all right."

She held up her hand. "Wait, aren't we supposed to have a picnic lunch . . . outside?"

Louis shrugged. "We need to have a bit of excitement now and then, don't we?"

Olivia softly punched his shoulder. "Not that type of excitement, thank you very much."

Hours passed as they enjoyed the scenery before

them. The sun rose higher over the savannah, and the animals were spotted less frequently. Some tourists continued to stand, talking to each other in words that Olivia didn't understand.

Louis and Olivia sat. There was a comfortable silence between them as the van rolled along, rocking them gently.

"Do you know the name of those creatures with long horns?" Olivia pointed toward a herd of large tan animals up ahead. "They look like a mix between a cow and a deer, right?"

"Those are Eland antelope. They are quite husky beasts."

From what Olivia remembered of the nature videos she'd been drawn to in school, she thought the savannah would be more violent. Hunt or be hunted. Unlike creatures in the zoo, hindered by the walls and chain-linked fences, these animals moved within and around each other with less fear than she imagined.

A breeze moved over the savannah, stirring dust from the dirt road. A lone tree stood along the side of the road, tall and stately.

"I wonder why there aren't many trees," Olivia said.

"Marauding elephants. They have stripped tracts of land—the beasts." He smiled.

She thought of the elephants in the Little Rock Zoo back home. She couldn't imagine them marauding and pulling up trees. Though large, they seemed shriveled and weak from their captivity. Thinking of them made her heart ache.

"That would be so amazing to see a wild elephant today. It would make my whole year."

"Seeing an elephant would make your year?" He chuckled. "Is that all it takes?"

"Why, yes. Honestly, until this moment, I didn't realize how amazing it would be to see these animals in their natural habitat. The crazy thing is, I almost gave it all up to be with my friend, Rebecca. When she refused, I tried convincing her to let me return to Kibera for the day. Both seemed like a better option than doing something touristy alone. I may have chickened out if I hadn't invited you. So, thank you."

"I'm the one who needs to offer thanks," he said, his voice tinged with gratitude and something more profound. His eyes locked onto hers, sparkling with a warmth that sent shivers down Olivia's spine. "This is much more thrilling than reading a novel."

Olivia's cheeks flushed, and she couldn't help but smile at his playful wink. The air crackled with unexpected electricity between them. She longed to hold onto this moment forever, to let it weave itself into the fabric of her being.

"And I hope that you see your elephant, Olivia. I'd give you such a gift if I could." The way he said her name made her feel like the protagonist of a grand love story, and her heart danced at the sound of it on his lips.

Today was a dream. A chapter ripped from the pages of a fairy tale. But tomorrow, reality would come crashing back. Tomorrow they'd film Olivia's reveal just as the first rays of dawn stretched over the African plains. Then, after they were through, they'd head to the airport, arriving just in time to catch their evening flight home to the States.

Olivia hadn't even known Louis for a whole day. Still, the thought of leaving him, of saying goodbye, tugged at her heartstrings with an ache she couldn't ignore.

With a heavy sigh, Olivia silently vowed to cherish every remaining moment. She would savor Louis's gaze, his hand brushing against hers, and his voice that spoke with such tenderness. Tomorrow would come, but for now, they had the beauty of this place and the excitement of getting to know each other.

Suddenly the van stopped, and the driver pointed. A hundred feet from the road, an antelope carcass lay surrounded by small jackals and giant vultures with large brown wings. Each wing appeared longer than Olivia was tall.

A shiver of discomfort raced down Olivia's spine as the vultures squeaked and squawked over the carcass. Out of all the things she'd seen so far today, the vultures' hideous faces and the way they plucked at the creature's flesh disturbed her the most.

The driver turned off the engine and parked the van. After using the CB radio on his dash to report what they'd found to other drivers, he walked to the back of the van, motioning to something outside the window. Each person stood to get a better view.

"Two lionesses brought him down. See? Yes, they have their fill now."

Just up the hill beside a small tree, two female lions lounged under the shade of its branches. Olivia would have missed them.

"Those lions just allow the other animals to eat their fill?" Olivia asked as she watched in amazement as five small jackals darted back and forth, grabbing pieces of the animal carcass and running away. The vultures fought for their portions. They squawked and waved their wings at the jackals as if to frighten them, but they seemed unfazed.

"Are the lions going to go after the other animals?" a woman sitting near the front of the van asked with a thick German accent.

"Those lionesses have full stomachs, yes? They are in retreat. In rest," the driver responded. "After a night of hunting, they need to nap with stomachs full of their breakfast."

The driver pointed into the air. "I hope these will not be the only lions we see today. Since we were the first through the gates, we are the informants to tell the others where to look. There are many roads to take within the reserve, and as guides, we each go our ways and then report to the others. Keep your eyes fixed near large rocks and low shrubs, where the soil is coolest. As the sun sets this afternoon, we may see them rise . . . and that is quite the show."

Olivia's curiosity about why their caravan was the first through the gate resurfaced. Still, she didn't want to pull her gaze from the scene to ask. She'd leave her questions for later.

After everyone took their share of photos, the van moved on, and Olivia and Louis sat. Louis's arm, tan and muscled, relaxed over the back of her van seat. Pretending to be looking out at the herds on the hillside, Olivia took the opportunity to study Louis's face better. Light freckles dotted his skin, including a scattered pattern over the bridge of his nose. Louis's blond hair ruffled in the wind, and his dark lashes blinked once, then twice.

Look away. Look at the savannah. Search for the lions in the shade. It's much safer. She couldn't let her heart get caught up in this man. She'd come for work, nothing more.

Encompassing their vehicle, the expansive plains unfurled with only subtle rises disrupting its stark flatness. As they rounded the bend, Olivia spotted a herd of buffalo with large, curved horns. Beyond that, wildebeests with shorter horns and shaggy hair covered the hills.

She gasped and pointed. "Look, the buffalo have the birds on their back, just like in the movies."

"They're not pretty. Not graceful. They certainly are not flashy. Yet they are symbiotic with the oxpeckers, who eat ticks, fleas, and other bugs."

"They seem so gentle."

"Not with humans. They don't give a warning before they charge," Louis warned.

"It sounds like you know this from experience?"

"My father once allowed me to bring a friend on our trip. I must have been eleven or twelve. We did everything we were told not to do. We got into trouble numerous times. I am surprised we survived." He pointed toward the wildebeests. "Those things stampede straight ahead at top speed. A tree saved us. I'm not certain how Willie and I managed to scale it. I wish someone would have caught it on video."

Olivia laughed, imagining the sight of two boys being chased by the ugly wildebeests. The best part was Louis's wide eyes and goofy grin as he shared the memory. Olivia couldn't help herself. She lifted her phone and took a quick photo of his expression. She'd only taken one picture of the day. His face, with that silly look, was the one she wanted to capture.

How had she ended up in this enchanting place, sharing this fleeting but undeniably unique connection with Louis? It felt as if God had conspired to bring them together. Of all the times and places, they'd found each other, two lonely souls seeking solace and companionship.

The realization both thrilled and terrified Olivia. She'd grown accustomed to solitude, believing her heart was destined to remain untouched. But now, in Louis's presence, a spark had been ignited. She couldn't ignore the magnetic pull she felt toward him.

Olivia hesitated. She didn't want to build castles in the air, to let her hopes soar too high only to crash in disappointment. Life had taught her to be cautious. If she'd learned anything from her mother, it was that if things seemed too good to be true, they probably were.

Still, as Olivia looked into Louis's eyes, she couldn't deny the longing that welled up within. It whispered of possibilities, of love's sweet embrace. With a bittersweet smile, Olivia pushed aside anxious thoughts. She'd allow herself to believe, if only for a little while, that love had a way of finding its way into the most unlikely hearts.

A part of her whispered that perhaps this encounter was a divine gift, a reminder that she didn't have to spend her life alone, that her heart could be drawn to another. It seemed God himself had orchestrated their meeting, threading the delicate strands of their lives together for this very moment. But why?

Would God bring Louis today only to have her lose him tomorrow? What could be the purpose of them finding each other? Olivia released a sigh. Perhaps she wouldn't discover the truth for decades. Or maybe she'd never know.

Alloria
Present Day

The room was dimly lit, the curtains drawn, as Regina Castillo sat in her favorite armchair. She glanced at her hands on the armrest, weathered and aged. They didn't seem like her hands. The years had slipped away like sand in an hourglass.

For years she told herself the present crises required more attention than the past stories, yet there was no excuse. She couldn't let another decade pass without their family's true story coming to light. *Better we control how the story is told rather than the press.* Heaven knew they could make a mess of things. Still, something inside urged Regina to wait. What was six months anyway?

Regina released a breath. She needed that time, especially since she wanted to tell Louis the truth before the story broke. She'd planned on telling him last year, and then Constance broke his heart. Her nephew had been walking through the previous six months as if in a fog. She just hoped his time in Africa would clear his head. She also prayed he'd stop running from the pain and allow the Lord to heal his heart.

Her press secretary, a young man with an air of ambition, stood by her side, his pen poised above a notepad.

"Hold the story, William," Regina said in a voice that carried the weight of her years. "I don't want to overshadow the king's jubilee. It would cast a shadow over his celebration, and that's the last thing I want."

William furrowed his brow, the pen still suspended in midair. "But Your Royal Highness, this story could be a turning point, especially with the media's focus on Prince Louis's broken heart. We need something worth rejoicing about—not the fact that the heir to the throne is yet again unlucky in love."

Regina sighed, her eyes wandering to the framed photograph of herself and her brother, the king, taken years ago after his coronation. She reached out and traced the outline of her younger self with a shaky finger.

"I know, William," she said, her voice tinged with nostalgia. "But this jubilee is a milestone for our country, a time for unity and celebration. It's not about heroes of our past, no matter how noble they were. It's about honoring the king's reign and everything he has done for our people."

William's eyes darted between the older woman and the photograph. "I understand, ma'am, but why hesitate? This story could solidify your nephew's legacy. Who wouldn't want to celebrate such a story?"

A flicker of emotion danced in the older woman's heart. She took a deep breath, gathering her thoughts before responding. "It's not about Louis's legacy. His time will come. This jubilee is for our current king—a testament to the enduring strength of our nation. I don't want personal affairs to overshadow that."

Regina cleared her throat and allowed the weight of her words to hang in the air. William finally lowered his pen, understanding the depth of her conviction.

"I see, ma'am." His voice softened. "I'll hold the story for the sake of the jubilee. You must be aware that there may come a time when the press discovers the truth. It will just take a diligent person to come across the right information for all to be revealed."

A faint smile touched Regina's lips, and she nodded. "Thank you, William. I am well aware of that fact. For now, I'm willing to take that risk." Her eyes met his. "Your loyalty and understanding mean more to me than you know. Let's ensure this jubilee remains a moment of joy for our family and people."

With a nod, William folded his notepad. "Thank you, ma'am."

And only after he left the room did Regina look at the waiting text message and the image displayed. She smiled, seeing the joy on her nephew's face as he stood in the safari van overlooking the savannah. The young woman at his side was dark-haired and beautiful, with an innocence that caused Regina's heart to warm. She owed a debt of gratitude to Sergio. In all her years, Regina never had crossed paths with a bodyguard who showcased such a remarkable blend of resourcefulness and unwavering dedication.

"Good for you, Louis," she mumbled to herself. And the fact she'd received this photo was a good sign. Sergio only sent her happy reports. That must mean Louis's bodyguard must like the young woman.

Regina pressed the number, but Sergio didn't answer. So instead, she texted a message.

Background check?

Within a minute, the text reply came.

Already done. Olivia Garza is twenty-five years old and from the States. Mother deceased. Father unknown. Works with underprivileged youth. In Kenya, filming a documentary. The closest relative is a research assistant at the Archaeological Museum of Naples. No huge red flags.

Regina's eyes widened. She straightened in her chair. After reading Sergio's text twice, Regina pushed her intercom, buzzing the press office.

"William, on second thought, I have an idea. Have you ever thought about telling our story in a documentary?"

CHAPTER TEN

Masai Mara National Reserve, Kenya

L ouis settled into his seat with the rocking of the vehicle beneath him. He was just about to ask Olivia to tell him more about her life in Little Rock when she jumped to her feet. With Olivia's sharp intake of breath at the sight of a small cluster of elephants in the distance, followed by her joyful exhale, there was no place Louis would rather be on this planet.

Olivia squealed as she clapped her hands together.

"Did you see that? Three elephants! Not one but three."

He rose. "Bravo! There you have it."

She turned to him. Dark brown eyes, the shade of chocolate, were framed with lashes fluttering excitedly. Louis resisted the urge to sweep her up in a congratulatory hug. Instead, he offered a high-five, which she accepted.

"Your year is now made, correct?" *I know mine is.*

He'd never experienced a day like this. While the beauty of the morning had been delightful, the woman at his side took his breath away. He had been captivated by Olivia's story as he'd watched the documentary. He'd grown to care for the unseen woman as he'd listened to her voice, sharing the vulnerable parts of her story. But to see her, and to know she was just as endearing in person, made Louis feel like he was the world's luckiest man.

As much as he wanted to continue watching her—and experiencing her joy—he had a job to do. He lifted his camera and fixed his eye on the viewfinder, focusing on the lumbering forms in the distance.

"Best day ever," she exclaimed with unbridled joy. She turned to face him once more, her eyes sparkling with delight. "And you are correct," she continued, a soft smile gracing her lips. "This made my year."

Louis couldn't help but be captivated by her radiant happiness. Her energy was contagious, and he was drawn to her like a moth to a flame. As he met her gaze, he sensed an inexplicable connection between them.

Their eyes met, and a warmth surged, kindling a flame deep within. The world around Louis faded as the intensity of their connection grew. *Dear Lord, help me. I'm falling too fast.* Then again, he'd been getting to know her for months already, hadn't he?

A gentle breeze played with her hair, causing it to cascade around her face. The pink that rose on her cheeks deepened. Louis took a hesitant step forward, closing the already narrow distance between them. The rhythm of his pounding heart matched the rapid flutter of butterflies in his stomach.

His hand wavered as he reached for hers, their fingers weaving together. The feeling was both exhilarating and reassuring. Within Olivia's gaze, he found a hint of promise. Suddenly, his future seemed a little brighter.

The sound of the engine winding down snapped Louis back to reality. Olivia withdrew her hands and settled back into her seat. A pang of longing hit Louis as he followed suit.

With most of the wildlife behind them, the driver pulled to a dirt pull-out under a giant baobab tree. Before opening the side door, the driver stood on the van's roof and scanned the horizon with binoculars, looking for predators.

After five minutes, he stepped down and nodded. "Yes, yes. This is a good place to have lunch. You eat, and I will watch." The driver laughed, throwing back his head. "This way, we will ensure that we are not the ones who are lunch today."

Louis turned to see the color draining from Olivia's face. He tried not to laugh and wrapped an arm around Olivia's shoulders. "It's safe. The driver just looked around and saw nothing that could harm us. He does this every day, remember?"

"I remember that carcass from earlier." She pressed her hand to her neck to protect her throat. "I don't feel like being a buffet lunch today." She winced.

A smile tugged at Louis's lips, but he tried to hide it. Olivia was cute even when she was afraid. How was that possible?

Olivia's jaw tightened, and she scanned the area around the van. He needed her to think of anything else to put that image of the antelope carcass out of her mind.

"Do you recognize that tree?" He pointed to the tall tree that flattened on top and stretched into the sky. "It is common in African mythology. It's called the Tree of Life. That's a good sign, right?"

"Sure, the Tree of Life. But let's sit closest to the van, all right? I know predators pick off the animals hanging on the edges." She scooted as if to get up, and he let his arm drop from her shoulders.

"Survival to those who can leap into the van the soonest." He nodded. "I like that."

But instead of standing, Olivia remained seated. She tilted her head slightly. "Part of me worries about becoming lunch, but even deeper, there is a feeling that I'm safe with you, Louis." Her lips parted slightly as if the words even surprised her. "And you have to know I don't say that lightly."

He watched as the fear that had once clouded

her eyes gradually faded, replaced by a glimmer of hope and trust. At that moment, he felt a surge of joy deep within his heart, pleased to witness the transformation before him.

Louis pressed his lips together. *Should I tell Olivia I know who she is? Know how much those words mean?* He decided against it, knowing she'd reveal all when the time was right.

Her smile spoke volumes, whispering of vulnerability and resilience intertwined. It was a fragile offering, as if she were tentatively extending a piece of her soul to him. And he, in turn, cherished the privilege of being the recipient of that rare and delicate gift.

The sun was descending, casting longer shadows across the landscape. Clouds began to dominate the sky, occasionally parting to allow beams of light to pierce through like spotlights on a stage.

Louis found solace in Olivia's company. Her genuine nature and engaging conversation made him forget about the role he often had to play. Today, with her, he felt like just Louis, not the prince the world expected him to be.

Her presence had been a welcome distraction from Constance's wedding. The media was likely buzzing, not just about the wedding, but also about his conspicuous absence. Everywhere else, he would have been bombarded with reminders: news stories, photos, and discussions about Constance leaving him for a more enticing prospect. Almost everyone he knew, plus count-less others who followed the tabloids, were aware of this heartbreak.

Yet after this day on the savannah, with Olivia at his side, Louis was beginning to look beyond this disgrace. Maybe he could have a promising future. Perhaps he wouldn't always have to be the jilted prince.

Louis wanted to know more about this woman. In the hours they'd spent together, he had determined she was considerate and kind, intel-ligent and witty. He was already planning when he could see her again. Louis couldn't imagine this friendship ending when the van parked tonight and they went their separate ways.

They emerged from the van, and the driver pulled blankets and picnic baskets from the back. Louis took one of the blankets from the pile then winked at Olivia. Instead of spreading it out under the shade of the tree, he spread it under the shadow of the van, right next to the door.

The driver removed wrapped food packages from a cooler, handing one to each guest. They opened their paper-wrapped lunches to find apple, papaya, tomato, and cucumber slices. The bright colors of watermelon and mango chunks shone against the sun's rays. Fresh bread, chicken salad, and homemade chutney completed the meal.

"This looks so amazing," Olivia said, not shy

about digging in. She handed Louis a paper plate and began to scoop up food. He tried to hide his smile as he thought of the other girls he'd dated who would have most likely chosen a few pieces of fruit and would have claimed they were full— yet another thing to add to his list. As the day passed, his mental list of what he appreciated about Olivia grew.

They ate in comfortable silence, and after taking a long drink from his water bottle, Louis turned his attention to the dark-haired beauty beside him.

"Why are you doing that . . . again?" she asked, wiping her napkin at the edge of her mouth.

"Pardon?"

"You know. Looking at me like that. Do I have something in my teeth?"

"I'm sorry. I don't mean to stare. I'm just thankful for this day."

"Yes, me too."

"And maybe I'd like to know a little about you." Even as he said the words, Louis told himself not to push. *There's a reason she hasn't revealed herself in the documentary.* Her mother's complicated story was one she was coming to terms with.

"What do you want to know?" She took a large bite of her sandwich and looked at him with her eyes full of questions. Her brow furrowed.

Yet maybe she trusts me. Would that be too much to ask?

"So, Olivia from Little Rock, I know you're here for humanitarian efforts, but what do you do for work?"

She brushed a strand of hair from her forehead. "I co-lead a teen girl support group called the Character Club. We're in inner-city Little Rock."

"Teen support?" Louis thought back to the documentary episodes where Olivia had interviewed young moms—trying to understand what it had been like for her mother to face an unplanned pregnancy. *Of course, it makes sense why she's chosen this as her job.*

"We meet weekly, have dinner, bring in speakers, and stay involved in their lives. About thirty come, but a core group of eight or so." Olivia shrugged. "There are many obstacles— poverty, abuse, teen pregnancy, and low high school graduation rate. Then there's the funding of it all. One of our best volunteers, Sarah-Grace, helps with that. Sometimes it seems too big of a problem to face, but Miss Jan—my co-leader— and I tell ourselves that if they make just one better choice that week because of something they've learned, then we're making a difference."

"Of course you are, Olivia. That's amazing. It seems as if it could consume so much of your time." *Such passion and purpose.* "And you're

142

helping with a different organization here in Kenya?"

"Yes." She glanced away, watching a bird swooping above the savannah grasses. "There's a lot to do in Kibera. Have you been there?"

"I have." He couldn't tell her he'd visited the edge of the slums with one of Kenya's highest-ranking cabinet members. They'd been discussing Alloria's relief efforts to help the unemployed youth. "There are so many needy people, especially children."

Olivia plucked a strand of savannah grass and twirled it around her finger, sighing. "There's this orphanage called *Fruitful* with more than two-hundred children from toddlers to teens. One brave woman, with a few helpers, cares for these children with the help of others. She teaches them to dance and perform. She trains them to make jewelry from the garbage. These children, who have no one, soon have each other, and together their skills bring enough money for their food and different needs.

"I was there at the beginning of last week. The bricked walls of the room were too small to contain all their energy and joy." Her smile broadened, and her hair danced around her face as the wind rose again. "Most of the children are AIDS orphans. Some children have AIDS themselves, but without money for doctors, there's no way to know who is infected. The director and her helpers care for the children as much as possible."

"I imagine it was hard leaving that." Louis placed his hand on hers, and she nodded.

"Yes, it's truly maddening. Some have immense wealth and influence, while others struggle with the basics. I work hard to keep my heart open, but it's challenging when I see those with abundance often overlooking those in need. They dwell in their grand homes—their castles—while many lack even a simple roof over their heads."

Louis tried not to wince even though her words were like a stab to his heart. While one part of him wanted to defend himself and those in his circle, most people gave far less than they could. An uneasiness overcame him as he imagined Olivia discovering his home—a castle.

Louis nodded as she talked, making a mental note to ask later for more details about this orphanage. Indeed, he could speak with his father about doing more.

The groups finished eating and packed up their things. Olivia leaned against the side of the van with her weight on one foot. She was so casual, so confident, with her arms crossed over her chest. The warm sun overhead showcased bits of red highlights in her dark hair, and the smile on her face hinted at true contentment.

Once the driver reloaded the supplies and the

group settled into their familiar seats, Olivia's words continued.

"As I was sitting in *Fruitful* on our first day, a small girl no older than three approached me. For the briefest moment, I wondered if holding a child with AIDS was safe. But as I looked into her eyes, it no longer mattered. She was motherless, and she craved a mother's love, even for a moment. And so I wrapped her up in my arms and prayed."

Olivia stopped there, but Louis could see from her gaze that there was more. Something else she hadn't told him—something she'd experienced. Maybe a story about another child?

She opened her mouth and then closed it again.

"You have something else, too, don't you?" Louis dared to ask.

"Something else happened." Olivia put her head back against the headrest. "At the end of the week, we were on the other side of the slums. One of the teachers we'd met invited us to a sewing school for women that she had just started. We were on the way there when we heard a child crying. When I paused, I saw a little girl sitting by what I thought was a pile of trash in the alley. The director, other volunteers, and one of the guards wanted to go ahead. The other guard knew I wanted to stay and help the girl. Kioko told me he'd stay with me. He said that sometimes people used children as traps for robbery, but he knew that girl would haunt me if I at least didn't try."

Tears rimmed her eyes, and Louis took Olivia's hand.

"When we approached, I realized it wasn't a pile of trash that the toddler sat by, but a woman . . . her mother." Olivia's lower lip trembled. "She said something to Kioko then motioned to me."

Emotion filled Louis's throat, and he attempted to swallow it away. "It's all right if you don't want to tell me. If it's too hard."

"No, no. I want to tell you. Though I don't know why." Olivia's brow furrowed. "Somehow, as hard as it had been in that moment, what I'd experienced was beautiful too." She offered a shy grin. "I hope I'm making sense."

"Yes, of course."

"The frail woman talked to Kioko. Her voice was barely a whisper. Then with the last strength, she tried to hand her daughter to me. She wanted me to care for her." Olivia brushed her hair from her forehead and then wiped away a tear. "Out of everyone, I was there at that moment. And as if sensing that her mother was gone, the little girl climbed onto my lap. She wrapped her arms around my neck as if she didn't want to let go."

"And the girl, where is she now?"

"Kioko knew of another orphanage—one close to where we were. He called the other guard and told them of our mission—to take the girl there.

It was getting dark, and they told us to hurry." She bit her lip as if lost in her thoughts.

"And you took her there?"

"Yes. The woman there was so kind. I knew the girl would be in good hands. Still . . ." She let her voice trail off.

He squeezed her hand. "Still?"

"I wonder if it was enough. The mother gave her daughter to me. Even though I'm not prepared to be a mother, and I don't even know if it's possible to adopt . . . I wonder, you know?"

Olivia returned the squeeze, holding his hand like a lifeline. "And the orphanage worker was so kind. She had such hopeful words for me." She met his gaze, and Louis was confident he could get lost in those depths. "She said such kind things, and now I'm here with you." Her voice was no more than a whisper. "It's like a gift."

Was he the gift? He hoped so.

Louis attempted to clear the emotion from his throat. He had to do something to help. "Unbelievable. Really. I did not know someone like you was out there in this world, Olivia. And I have to say I'm ready to write a check. I'd love to get the information for the orphanage when we return to the lodge—actually, both orphanages."

Laughter spilled from her lips. "That's not why I told you."

"I know, but how could I not hear that story and want to help? It must be rewarding."

Olivia scrunched her nose. "Yes, well, there are those who disagree. According to a friend who does my taxes, I barely make enough to scrape by. And according to my former roommate, I get too involved and try to do too much at the expense of myself."

Louis's heart went out to her. He was ready to be back at the lodge. He pictured inviting Olivia to dinner and talking under the stars on the open patio. Yes, the deck in the general lodge area would work. After hearing Olivia share her heart, he was sure she wouldn't appreciate his expansive suite. His gut tightened. And what would happen when she discovered his status? That was a conversation he'd have to handle with care. He liked to believe he was a different type of prince, but his track record would prove otherwise.

She's right. I've been so self-absorbed in my duties and troubles that I haven't taken the time to discover the needs of others and find more ways to help.

They came across another herd of zebras, and dozens blocked the road. The driver approached and honked, but the zebras were slow to move.

A grin filled Olivia's face. "Move, dumb zebras, move." Laughter at her comment filled the van.

"Yes, see. I told you." The driver pointed into the air. "Every time, this happens, I promise."

"Remarkable. And I just thought we'd be lucky if we saw a few baboons." Olivia chuckled. "And we haven't even seen one of those yet."

"Unless you count me." Louis gave his best baboon impersonation. Olivia rolled her eyes.

He laughed and then winked. "I am certain you did not come to Africa to find a friend, but I want to keep in touch."

"I'd like that." She yawned then settled her head back on the seat. The corners of Louis's mouth lifted slightly as her eyelids closed. He'd do anything to spend more time with this woman. Anything.

Gestapo Headquarters, Rome, Italy
19 October 1943

Alessandra's quivering hands smoothed her blouse as the night weighed heavily on her shoulders. Moonlight from the high window bathed the rectangular cell in a cold shade of gray. She leaned against the rough stone wall as fear clung to her like a second skin, its grip unyielding. Christian had feared she'd end up here. Why hadn't she listened? Then again, she thought of Leah and the other children. Each one should be out of Italy by now. And soon, if travel went well, they'd find their way to the high Pyrenees mountains, where safe homes awaited each one.

Her gaze fell upon the narrow cot, its coarse blankets beckoning her weary body. Alessandra closed her eyes, yet her mind flooded with images of her four children, their faces etched with worry and longing. At least they were safe at the Vatican.

She slumped onto the cot, sighing. She longed for their home like a bittersweet melody. She missed the days when they'd been a happy family with her children's laughter and her husband's touch. Even when Christian had insisted that she and the children find refuge in the Vatican, he had believed his friendships with the Nazi elite would ensure his safety. Obviously, that wasn't the case.

Alessandra must have fallen asleep, for she awoke to a sunlit room. The voices of the guards, low and menacing, sliced through the silence. She strained to catch snippets of their conversation, piccing together the fragments of her fate. Every word uttered carried a chilling weight and threatened to consume her fragile hope.

The clinking of keys echoed down the corridor, a chilling reminder of her captivity. She smoothed her hair as best as possible and stepped forward as the guard approached.

"This way, Princess," he sneered, leading her out of the cell and guiding her down the hall. Thirst thickened her tongue, and her stomach growled, but Alessandra would not make a request. Instead, she wiped the sleep from her eyes and straightened her shoulders as she walked into the small office thick with the smell of sweat, fear, and despair.

The officer who'd been there yesterday sat in the same chair. His hair was neatly brushed, and he appeared rested.

At least one of us is. Alessandra refused to show any sign of weakness and strode into the room just as confident as she had the day prior.

The officer eyed her and motioned for her to sit. Only when she had did he speak.

"So it seems I cannot take you to your husband after all." He sighed as if the news troubled him, yet she knew better. The officer's eyes were not fixed on her face but the large diamond on her finger.

Alessandra clenched her fist, suddenly understanding. "Surely there has to be a way?" She adjusted the ring on her hand.

He looked at her with a cold, emotionless gaze.

"I need to see my husband." Alessandra kept her voice steady.

The officer leaned back in his chair. "And why should I let you see him?" he asked, his tone clipped and dismissive.

She pulled the ring from her finger and stretched it in his direction.

Without hesitation, he took it from her hand. The officer looked at the ring momentarily, then back at her. "I'm not interested in your trinkets," he said, his voice hardening. "Your husband is a criminal and will be punished accordingly."

Alessandra's heart sank. "Please." She attempted to hide the desperation creeping into her voice. "He's done nothing wrong. Please, just let him go."

The officer's expression softened slightly, and for a moment, she thought he might relent. But then he shook his head.

"I'm sorry," he said, his voice terse. "There's nothing I can do." With a grim smile, he tucked the ring into his pocket and motioned for the guard to take her away.

CHAPTER ELEVEN

Masai Mara National Reserve, Kenya
Present Day

The jeep rocking over the dirt roads had lulled Olivia to sleep. The tender touch of a hand brushing a strand of her hair from her face stirred her to wakefulness.

"Olivia, we're almost back."

The accent reminded her where she was and who she was with. Olivia's eyes opened wide. She sat up and wiped her face. Heat rose to her cheeks. She'd fallen asleep against Louis's shoulder. "I didn't drool on you, did I?"

Louis cocked one eyebrow and patted his shoulder. "Just a little damp. Nothing a quick run of a dryer cannot fix."

Olivia grimaced. "I'm so sorry." She rubbed the back of her neck.

Louis chuckled. "No need to apologize." His lips turned up in a half-smile highlighting his dimples. "It was rather nice. Reminds me of times visiting my aunt's quarters. I feel comfortable there in a way I can't explain. More often than not, I find myself dozing in front of her fire or out on her patio. I'm glad you were comfortable enough to drift off." His hand covered hers. "I hope we can do this again."

Aunt's quarters? She supposed they used a different word for *home* where he came from.

"Do this again?" She sat up straighter. "You mean meet up to explore the savannah and take far too many photos of zebras?"

"Or maybe just meet to chat. I like to travel. Next time, I can show you my favorite cafés in Paris."

A disbelieving chuckle escaped Olivia's lips, but as she met his sincere gaze, her laughter dissolved into a mix of surprise and intrigue. His eyes held a glimmer of mischief and determination, creating an undeniable allure that pulled at her heartstrings. The air thickened with unspoken emotions, and Olivia felt a flutter of anticipation in the center of her stomach.

"Paris?" she repeated, her voice laced with a hint of wistfulness. "Well, that's not on my agenda this year." She paused, searching his face for any sign of jest. "The only time I leave the States is on a work trip. I'm not much of a vacationer."

As the words left her lips, she couldn't help but feel a pang of regret. The thought of exploring the romantic streets of Paris with Louis, hand in hand, felt like a missed opportunity she hadn't even considered until now. Her gaze flickered downward momentarily.

He continued to study her, his gaze unwavering and intense. Olivia's heart raced as she tried deciphering the meaning behind his penetrating stare. Was he disappointed? Did he believe she was pushing him away just as they got to know each other?

"Yes, I see," he finally spoke, his voice gentle yet tinged with vulnerability. "Well, I'm thankful to have this time with you on the day you chose adventure over work." He shifted slightly in his seat, a subtle movement that brought them physically closer. "And I am sorry I did not think of it, but I am happy to repay the cost of my excursion."

Olivia's breath caught, her eyes widening. The gesture he offered was unexpected, and it stirred a swirl of conflicting emotions. On the one hand, she appreciated his thoughtfulness behind his offer. Then again, that's not what she meant.

With the growing viewership and her monetized YouTube page, her finances were more stable than ever. It's just that she didn't see herself as that type of person—someone who could live a life of leisure and explore Paris with a handsome man. Olivia's brow furrowed. Then again, why couldn't she be? Spending time with someone like Louis was special.

Is it all right to open my heart? To enjoy life?

Her gaze met his again, and she felt an unspoken connection between them, an invisible thread that tugged at her heart. It was a moment of truth, an opportunity to explore the unknown and step out of her comfort zone. Paris might not have been part of her plans, but maybe this unexpected turn of events was meant to lead her down a path she'd always secretly longed for.

She took a deep breath, her voice soft yet filled with determination. "You know what? Maybe I could use a vacation this year after all. Perhaps Paris is exactly what I need." Her words hung in the air, anticipation and uncertainty merging into a heartbeat.

Their eyes locked, and in that electrifying moment, Olivia couldn't help but wonder if this unexpected twist of fate was the start of a grand adventure. Recording and releasing her documentary allowed her to face her pain, discover her anger concerning her mother's choices, and heal. And while she believed the whole journey would give her peace with the past, maybe it also prepared her for the future.

She grinned, having more hope for her future than she'd possibly ever had. "You don't have to pay me back. Rebecca would be highly offended. She's always trying to set me up on dates, and she'll be thrilled to know who joined me. Not that I am calling this a date . . ." Olivia brushed a strand of hair from her shoulder.

"I don't mind if you call it a date. I swore to give up on dates earlier this year, but I'll have to reconsider if they're this delightful."

"Give them up?" She studied his handsome

156

face, sure he was joking. "There has to be a story behind that. Is your father keeping you that busy with work?"

"That and the fact that the woman I had set my affections on started dating another. I'm a fool. Too hopeful. Either that or dense. But today was the perfect day to meet you. Yes, if this is what dating could be like, I'm all in."

Although he said the words with a playful tone, there was sadness in his gaze. Maybe that sadness had to do with that dark cloud he'd mentioned.

"Was something happening today?" Olivia tilted her head, ignoring that their lodge was just ahead and this wonderful day with Louis would soon end.

"Her wedding day. Which is another reason I fled to Africa." He stroked a hand down his cheek. "Now you truly understand what a sorry sap I am."

"I think it's sweet. I can't imagine someone caring for me like that . . . heartbroken to the point of leaving the country. I've never met your type in Little Rock."

"I'm not sure what you mean by 'my type.' But if we can't meet in Paris, maybe—"

A flurry of movement outside the van caught her attention. Strobes of light from camera flashes disoriented her, and the shouting of voices of a crowd situated outside the gates of their lodge sent her heart pounding. Olivia leaned forward in her seat as their driver cried out in dismay.

A crowd of photographers rushed into the roadway, and the driver slammed on his brakes. Flashing lights assaulted the van. Olivia curled against Louis as if to hide from the lights, the commotion, the shouts. She closed her eyes as Louis's arm went around her, pulling her tightly against him. His hot breath drifted across her hair. Then he leaned down and spoke close to her ear. "It'll be all right, Olivia. Look, the driver's going to get us through this."

She opened her eyes then sat up slightly. The gates to the lodge were opening, yet tall Masai men wearing red clothes blocked the crowd while motioning the driver to enter. Rolling down his window, the driver waved his arm, directing the mass of photographers out of his way.

When they didn't move, he laid on his horn and slowly continued driving forward. Olivia winced and covered her ears. The crowd with the cameras shouted questions, but Olivia couldn't make them out over the sounds of the horn.

"What's happening?" Olivia's voice called out to Louis and the driver. The worried cries of the other passengers filled the air, and their excited voices equally confused her.

With one swift motion, Louis removed his arm around her and sat. "I should have known." His words emerged as a growl, and his fists balled in frustration. He rushed to the front of the van and slipped into the passenger's seat. "Go, go. They'll move. Just drive ahead."

With the crowd parting, the driver shouted something Olivia didn't understand and gunned the van. A cry escaped Olivia's lips. She was sure they were about to plow down the crowd that stood in their way. Like the parting of the Red Sea, the men and women scrambled to the sides of the road, yet they continued snapping photos and calling out questions.

As if from a scene out of a movie, the large wooden gates of the lodge opened. Only as the gates closed behind them and the van moved toward the front of the lodge did Olivia release her breath.

She stood and hurried down the aisle of the van, plopping into the seat just behind the driver, then fixed her gaze on Louis. *How does he know what's happening? What's going on? Who is he?*

"Where should I take you, Prince Louis?" the driver asked.

Prince Louis?

"To the front of the lodge should do." Louis ran his hand through his hair. "I should've known. Why can't they just give me some peace?"

Louis murmured under his breath, his words barely discernible to Olivia. He then swiveled in his seat, directing his gaze to another tourist. "Any clue how they figured it out?"

"No, sir. Someone from the lodge must have

159

leaked information about your arrival." The older man with salt-and-pepper hair held up his cell phone. "Our service has been down all day. There is no way I could have known what was waiting."

The revelation hit Olivia like a tidal wave with an intensity that left her breathless. The man who had mingled seamlessly with the German tourists spoke with a British accent that mirrored Louis's.

A sense of unease settled over Olivia as she observed the handsome, older man. His tan complexion and air of familiarity raised more questions than answers. The world around her seemed to blur, spinning in a disorienting whirl-wind.

Doubt seeped into Olivia's thoughts, planting seeds of suspicion and uncertainty. *Am I part of a reality TV show? Was this all a carefully orchestrated set-up?*

The weight of doubt pressed upon her. Her fingers trembled, but as her gaze looked between Louis and the enigmatic older man, her heart remained caught in a turbulent dance of hope and despair.

Olivia pressed her hand to her forehead and leaned forward in her seat. *The perfect day. The perfect guy.* It was as if someone was trying to set her up. Olivia's stomach lurched, and nausea rolled in waves.

The driver parked the van and exited to open

the side door, allowing the other tourists to disembark. Olivia sat motionless while those behind her shuffled in their seats, gathering their things. Her eyes fixed on Louis, seated in the passenger's seat—the man she thought she'd been getting to know.

"What's going on?" Her voice came out no more than a whisper. She glanced from the other tourist seated behind her to Louis. Both stayed in their seats. "You two know each other? No, seriously, what's going on?"

Louis released a heavy sigh as if trying to determine his words.

"Just tell me the truth," she spouted. Her hands trembled. This had to be some type of nightmare. The hope-filled emotions of the day crashed around her. She pointed from Louis to the man. "You know each other, but you've acted as if you didn't all day."

Louis turned in his seat, facing her, his eyes wide with desperation. "I didn't know what to do. Sergio was here when I arrived. I'm unsure how he managed it . . . but it wasn't the plan. It was supposed to be our day, I promise."

Sergio?

"You acted all day as if you knew no one in this van. But you did." Olivia's nostrils flared, and she pressed her lips into a tight line. "What's going on? How come you haven't answered my question? If you had a friend in the van, why

161

didn't you say so?" Her gaze narrowed. "Why would you lie to me and act as if—"

As the weight of the day's revelations settled upon Olivia, a new thought infiltrated her—an idea even more shocking than the realization that they had unknowingly spent the entire day with someone Louis knew. Her voice quivered with curiosity and apprehension, her heart pounding. "Louis, who are those people out there, and who are you? And why did our driver call you *Prince?*"

The air around them grew heavy with tension as if the truth carried an unbearable weight. Louis's eyes met hers briefly before he lowered his gaze, his features etched with guilt and sorrow. His silence spoke volumes, and Olivia's heart sank with each passing moment.

A tumultuous storm of emotions raged within her—confusion, betrayal, and the ache of heartbreak. She couldn't comprehend how the man she had spent the day with, who had captivated her with his charm and warmth, could be harboring such secrets. The cracks in their blossoming connection suddenly widened, threatening to shatter the fragile foundation upon which it stood.

The other passengers, now brimming with excitement, disembarked from the van, their voices mingling with the swirling thoughts in Olivia's mind. Their joyous chatter contrasted with the heavy silence that enveloped Louis and Olivia.

Louis took a deep breath, his fingers nervously rubbing his brow. He opened his mouth, and for a fleeting moment, hope flickered in Olivia's eyes. But the following pause stretched, and her hope withered away, replaced by a sense of impending heartache.

"Olivia, listen," Louis finally spoke, his voice tinged with regret and desperation. "I can explain."

His words hung in the air, and Olivia's heart trembled. She longed for answers, for the truth to unravel the tangled web of emotions. Yet, part of her feared what his explanation might reveal.

"Explain? Explain what? Just answer the question." Olivia pointed to the driver. "Did he call you *Prince Louis?* What does that mean? Please tell me you're not a prince . . . of Alloria. This is a joke, right?"

She placed a hand over her stomach, willing herself to calm. She'd opened her heart. She'd shared her stories. She'd even shared about Promise.

Not only did she pour out her heart, but Louis was also the type of person she spoke against. And obviously, for good reason.

"You have been lying to me. All this, today, is a lie."

More than anything, Olivia wished that all of

them would laugh and tell her they'd come up with this scheme when she'd been asleep. That they'd just pretended to know each other as a joke. Instead, Louis moved to the seat across from her, motioning to Sergio to give them some privacy.

"Olivia, I was going to tell you. When we got back, I was going to find a way."

She turned and peered out the window, attempting to get her emotions under control. Outside, two additional men strode out from the lodge and stood at attention outside the van. Yet they didn't move. Instead, they stood erect as if waiting for a signal before opening the door.

"This is not what I wanted to happen. I didn't want you to find out this way. We didn't have time to plan things out. You asked me to join you, and I found a way . . . I had no idea I'd be discovered so soon. Or that my bodyguard, Sergio, would find a way to join the safari. I was surprised to find him in the van when I arrived." Louis shrugged. "I can't say I blame him, though. My father can be difficult to deal with if he learns of situations when one does not follow the protocol."

Olivia's temples throbbed with the weight of unanswered questions. She pressed her fingertips to her forehead. The pain pulsed in rhythm with her racing thoughts, converging in the center of her head. "Louis, what's going on?" She looked away, turning her focus back outside the window.

Louis gently grasped her trembling hand. She considered pulling away. Instead, her hand tightly held his.

"Look at me," he pleaded softly, his voice filled with a tenderness that tugged at her heartstrings. "Please, Olivia."

Reluctantly, Olivia let her eyes open. The vulnerability in Louis's gaze took her by surprise.

He held her look, his fingers tenderly brushing the back of her hand, silently urging her to trust him through the storm of doubts. "Olivia," he whispered, his voice barely audible above the tumultuous storm of emotions. "I wish I could shield you from all this pain, from the truth."

She pulled in a breath and held it, waiting.

"My name is Louis Castillo. Prince Louis of Alloria. I haven't lied. I came here to escape all that's happening back home. And I'm also not lying when I tell you that today is one of the most wonderful days I've had in a long time."

She jerked her hand away from his. "You're a prince? A real-life, William and Harry type of prince?"

With an amused smile, Louis met her incredulous gaze. "In the flesh, although I must admit, my polo skills aren't quite up to par with William's, and my hair's faring a bit better than Harry's," he quipped, his charm as irresistible as his easy humor.

A mischievous twinkle danced in Louis's eyes, his playful words meant to charm and captivate. But for Olivia, the echoes of past heartbreak reverberated through her mind. The smiles of those who had promised to save her mother, to love and protect her, flashed like fleeting cards in a game of chance. The warmth that once enveloped Olivia's heart became a searing heat, scorching her.

Olivia's instincts screamed for her to run and flee. Every smile and every promise had been tainted by deceit, leaving her mother broken and discarded by those who had claimed to care.

Lies—those were the foundation upon which every interaction had been built. A warning alarm pulsed in her mind, urging her to protect herself from the waiting heartbreak.

As the van walls seemed to close around her, Olivia pushed herself to her feet, her head spinning as she rushed toward the door. "I need air," she managed to gasp out, her voice strained and laced with distress and sorrow. One of the men outside swiftly opened the door for her. Olivia stumbled out, the ground beneath her feet feeling unsteady. Bent over, hands on her knees, Olivia fought to regain her balance. Her breathing grew ragged as she tried to steady herself.

In an instant, strong arms enveloped her shoulders. *Louis.* He guided her toward a nearby set of wooden steps, and she allowed herself to be led.

Sinking onto the steps, Olivia didn't have the strength to fight against Louis. She closed her eyes and felt his gentle hand on her back.

Olivia took a deep, shuddering breath. Her trembling hand reached to wipe away a stray tear that escaped her closed eyelids. As the ache in her heart threatened to consume her, she leaned into Louis, hoping against hope that somehow, amidst the heartbreak, a sliver of hope would emerge.

"Get her a drink of water." Louis's voice broke through the fog.

She opened her eyes to see that the tall wooden gates to the lodge had been shut. Still, the sounds of the commotion beyond the gates pushed through.

Their van driver gave her a passing glance and a compassionate smile before climbing into the vehicle and driving away. Louis's bodyguard had slipped away too, yet Louis remained at her side.

She wanted to tell him to go away. Instead, something kept the words locked inside.

He settled down on the wooden step beside her. "I didn't mean for this to be such a shock. I do apologize. I just assume everyone recognizes me. As soon as we headed off, I realized you didn't know who I was."

She scooted farther away on the polished mahogany step, putting space between them. The light blue sky was darkening to navy blue as afternoon slid into the evening. The air smelled of the fragrant flowers that grew on bushes near the railing of the steps and of barbecued meat and smoke. Her stomach growled, but she ignored it. Had it just been five hours ago when she'd eaten a delicious picnic lunch next to Louis, believing it was the perfect day? It wasn't the dream she'd thought it to be. Instead, it was more like a nightmare.

One of the Masai men approached with a water bottle, but she waved him away. She forced herself to look at Louis, wondering how he would explain. Rather than the charming look that he'd worn moments before, regret etched his face.

"It was so nice to experience someone wanting to get to know me for *me*. I am so sorry I allowed myself to be caught up in the day. And for not revealing myself sooner."

Olivia released a low moan as Louis's words settled into her heart. "I told myself to ignore the warning signs that all of this seemed too good to be true. I should have trusted my gut." Olivia stood and placed her hands on her hips. With every ounce of willpower, she pushed down the hope she'd allowed to surface, shoving it into its rightful place behind a wall of mistrust.

A deep sigh escaped her, and she glanced into his eyes. "I enjoyed spending time with you, Louis. Even though I made a fool of myself. I'm sorry it has to end with such a quick goodbye." She stalked away as the laughter from the monkeys in the trees reverberated around her.

"Olivia, please, can we talk this through? Can you give me a chance?" He rose to follow her.

She shook her head and quickened her steps. "Please, just leave me alone," she shouted over her shoulder. "If you care at all, Louis, let me be."

Hurrying away from the lodge, she dashed through the courtyard toward her tent. But catching sight of it, tears blurred her vision. *How will I ever explain today to Rebecca?* She wasn't Cinderella, and no happily-ever-after would come out of this.

With a swift motion, she unzipped the tent. She was not her mother. She knew better. While she might have been deceived once, she was no fool. She had witnessed the aftermath of relationships built on deceit. Wasn't her journey following her mother's footsteps all about understanding and choosing a different path?

Her fists clenched in frustration. The day had been magical. Overwhelmingly so. And she'd been swept up in it.

CHAPTER TWELVE

Nyota Skyline Lodge, Kenya

The tent smelled of chicken noodle soup and hot chocolate; both were sitting on a tray before Rebecca as Olivia entered.

Rebecca sat crossed-legged on the cot with her Bible open in front of her. She held her pen within her teeth and looked up eagerly as Olivia entered. Rebecca's eyes widened, and her eyebrows folded. Then she removed the pen and dropped it onto the cot. "Whoa, who died?"

Olivia stepped through the tent door flap with a huff. She attempted to relax her clenched jaw and quickly wiped away the tears that had managed to break through. "My soul. My pride. My heart. You name it. Dead."

Swinging her legs to the side of the bed, Rebecca leaned forward, her eyes widened. "I don't understand," she said, her voice tinged with confusion and worry. "It was a simple safari."

Rebecca opened her arms and offered a hug, but Olivia shook her head. That one act of comfort would break down the dam she'd built to hold back her tears. Instead, with a trembling hand, Olivia held up her palm, gesturing for Rebecca to keep her distance. She needed to find her footing, to hold herself together just a little longer.

A surge of frustration rose within Olivia. She pointed her finger into the air. "There was nothing simple about that safari," she exclaimed, her voice laced with anguish. "I promise you that. It was the best day of my life . . . and the worst too."

Olivia's shoulders trembled. Walls erected around her heart with each breath. She couldn't let Louis in. She couldn't make the same mistakes.

Rebecca's eyes brimmed with empathy, then her mouth opened as if a new realization had dawned. "Wait." Rebecca closed her Bible and pushed it out of the way. "Did you meet someone?" She patted the cot beside her, urging Olivia to sit.

"Yes, I met someone." Olivia settled beside Rebecca, her hands spread open on the scratchy blanket. A smile came despite Olivia's best efforts, sending a blow to her heart. "And it's not just any guy. He's a prince."

Rebecca's gaze filled with curiosity and concern. "Like a *prince,* prince?"

Olivia's heart clenched, knowing the deception inflicted upon her mother—the lies, the stolen trust, and the gradual unraveling of her mother's world until nothing was left. Not even the will to carry on.

A surge of unease coursed through Olivia's veins, overshadowing her fleeting joy. "Yes,

171

although I didn't know that at first," she continued, her voice laced with sorrow. "We had the most amazing day together. I laughed and smiled so much that my cheeks hurt." Her voice trailed off. "For the first time in a long while, I believed I could fall in love."

As Olivia spoke, the sting of betrayal seeped into her words. The memory of her mother's suffering cast a shadow over her heart.

She furrowed her brow. "He was—is—amazing," she struggled to say. "For the first time, I considered allowing myself to hope. But when we returned to the lodge, the paparazzi were waiting for us. Dozens of them, all with cameras."

As Rebecca rose from her seat, stretching her arms wide, Olivia's mind replayed the image of her own mother's suffering. This time, Olivia allowed Rebecca to pull her into a hug, and it was clear that Rebecca was trying to be supportive while simultaneously in awe of what she was hearing.

"This sounds like a movie," Rebecca gasped, settling back onto her cot. "Seriously, you spent the day with a prince?"

"A real-life prince from a country I've never heard of. Alloria." Her appetite for answers grew, yet it was overshadowed by the lingering fear of more lies and shattered trust. "By the way, are you going to eat that?" Olivia pointed to the soup in a feeble attempt to distract herself from the pain that gnawed at her soul.

"How can you eat at a time like this?" Rebecca tucked a strand of her dark hair behind her ear. "Let me get this right. You finally met *the guy* but must forget about him because he's rich and royal?"

As Rebecca waited for her answer, Olivia picked up the bowl and spoon and took a big bite. The soup, despite its lukewarm temperature, tasted good. And it was comforting. She needed comfort right now.

"He's a prince, yes. There's a whole lot more to that. He didn't tell me. He had the whole day to share the truth." Pain shot through her heart, and she took another bite from the soup as if it was a balm to her soul. "He *lied* to me." The soup lodged in her throat, and Olivia swallowed it down. "I've seen what lies can do." Her voice lowered. "How they destroy."

Rebecca was no longer listening. Instead, she scrolled through her phone.

"Wait, are you looking him up?" The answer came when Louis's face appeared on Rebecca's phone screen.

"Prince of Alloria, Louis Castillo, age twenty-seven." Rebecca's eyebrows lifted in approval. "Yes, he's royal, all right. And it says here, one of the top ten bachelors of the world."

Olivia placed the bowl of soup back onto the

tray. Her chin fell to her chest, and she shook her head. "It doesn't matter how eligible he is. He lied to me. Deceived me. No one can find out about this."

"Oh, it's going to get out." Rebecca typed something into her phone. A small gasp escaped Rebecca's lips. With a wince, she turned her phone so that Olivia could again see her screen.

Olivia's mouth dropped as she spotted herself front and center of a popular tabloid website. *That's me. That's . . . us.*

She was seated in the safari van, leaning against Louis's chest, hiding from the onslaught of photos. Louis's arm was around her, and the tender look on his face caused her eyes to well and her heart to ache. A longing to see him again mixed with the pain of his lies and the horror of the invasion of the paparazzi.

"Ugh. They have no right to do that. How can they just take my photo and share it with the world like that?"

"What do you mean, *ugh?* This photo and how he's protecting you is the most romantic thing I've ever seen." Rebecca sighed and placed a hand over her heart. "And didn't you just tell me it was the best day of your life?"

"That was before I realized he is royalty and privileged. And he hid that from me. He withheld that from me, and every moment of this day was based on a lie. He said his name was Louis, yet he forgot the rest. Louis, the future king of Alloria."

Taking a calming breath, Rebecca gave Olivia a pointed look. "Olivia, try to see it from his perspective. He's a prince. He'd want some semblance of normalcy—a small sliver of anonymity."

Her best friend was taking his side? Olivia opened her mouth to argue, but Rebecca held up her hand. "No, hear me out. It's like when you meet *anyone* new. You don't give them your whole life story in the first hour, right? You hold back a little. Take it slow. Let the layers peel back naturally over time."

Olivia crossed her arms over her chest and jutted out her chin. "It's obvious you grew up with a counselor for a dad. I swear, you've got this knack for knocking down my arguments with the finesse of a seasoned therapist."

"Well, you must admit it's come handy with the documentary." Her friend's eyes locked onto hers, part unwavering firmness and part tender concern. "And let's be honest, you haven't been an open book," Rebecca continued. "There's still so much Louis doesn't know about why *you're* here."

Olivia pressed her lips tight.

"It's just like that safari you were just on—uncharted territory and the thrill of discovery. Breathtaking views and even the occasional bumps in the road."

175

"This is more than a bump. It's a crater."

"Only if you let it be." Rebecca looked at the screen. "And I'll tell you something else. You are his type."

"His type?" Olivia leaned in closer for a better look at Rebecca's phone.

Rebecca used her thumb to scroll down the screen. Image after image of Louis scrolled by with petite, dark-haired beauties at his side.

Olivia covered her face with her hands. "I feel like such a fool. I never just live for the moment; the one time I do, *this* happens. I humiliate myself."

"But I don't understand. What do you mean *humiliate?* You said you felt more comfortable with Louis than you had with anyone. Your cheeks hurt because he made you smile, remember? And what about, 'For the first time, I thought I was capable of falling in love.' "

"Key word *falling* . . . as in flat on my face." Heat rose to Olivia's cheeks. She fanned herself and moved to the tent flap opening it to let in a breeze.

The noises outside the tent were a symphony of untamed life. The soft rustle of leaves from the acacia trees carried on the gentle evening breeze. In the distance, the rhythmic chorus of crickets provided a constant backdrop.

Occasional echoes of territorial disputes among the mighty lions that prowled the savannah met her ears. Their mighty roars caused a shiver to race down her spine. How would she sleep tonight knowing those animals were just on the other side of the tall wooden fence? How would she sleep remembering Louis's arm around her shoulders? She'd never expected to be so close to the king of the jungle . . . or the someday-king of a nation. Africa was full of wonder.

Africa. The documentary. The reveal.

Not once, during her time with Louis, had Olivia thought about the documentary. Tomorrow was meant to be the culmination, the grand finale where she'd finally unveil her face to the world. It was a promise she'd made to her loyal viewers. But now, faced with the reality of her connection with Louis, she knew that the long-awaited reveal couldn't happen.

Olivia's heart pounded. She shot to her feet. "I can't record tomorrow." Her voice was tinged with a hint of desperation. "We're not going to be able to do the reveal."

Rebecca's lips puckered in concern as she set down her phone. "But it's the last episode," she whispered. "You've been building up to this moment. You have to do it."

"I can't." Olivia gestured toward the image of herself and Louis that still adorned Rebecca's phone screen. "Don't you see? What will this look like to the world? People will believe that it was all a contrived set-up, that I did it for attention.

The entire purpose of following in my mother's footsteps will be lost. Instead, everything will be centered around me and Prince Louis."

As the gravity of Olivia's words sank in, the color drained from Rebecca's face. "You're right. It can't happen." Rebecca pressed her hand to her forehead. "Your viewers are going to be so disappointed."

It was the last thing Olivia wanted to hear.

Rebecca lifted the phone again, gazing at the photo. Then she glanced at Olivia out of the corner of her eyes. "It can't happen . . . yet. But maybe the story hasn't reached the end." She sat up straighter. "What if you give Louis a chance? What if this is part of the story?"

Olivia shook her head, defiance and self-preservation coursing through her veins. "Why would I do that? My life is already intense without adding royal complications. And why invest energy in a romance that will ultimately lead nowhere?"

Rebecca waved her phone in Olivia's direction. "Come on. Look at this. Look at him," she implored. "You have to give it a try."

Tension gripped Olivia's chest, squeezing the air from her lungs. She retreated to her cot, and she turned her back to Rebecca. With her face buried in her hands, an image emerged in her mind—a memory she'd suppressed for years. A piece of her mother's story that had remained untold. It was a memory she had consciously hidden, fearing the complications it would bring to her already intricate narrative.

She'd been only a young child, perhaps five or six years old. Sitting in a car beside her mother and gazing at a grand, imposing house. It was a part of their history, a chapter of her mother's life that had been carefully omitted from the documentary. Olivia had guarded this memory, convincing herself that its omission was for the sake of simplicity, for keeping her story focused on the core characters.

But now, as the weight of the past bore down on her, Olivia realized it was more than simplicity. It was the fear of being consumed by a world where appearances and judgments reigned supreme.

"You don't understand," she confessed, her voice trembling with anger and resolve. "I can't live as if the most important things in life are what we wear, who we're with, or what people think of us."

"And that's what Louis is about, is it?" Rebecca asked. "You've figured this out after only one day?" She sighed. "Or is it something else?"

Something else? Leave it to Rebecca not to drop the subject.

Still, the memory narrowed in Olivia's mind, focusing on the image of her grandparents standing in the doorway of their opulent mansion. Her mother stood before them, tears streaming down her face, seeking solace and acceptance. But instead of embracing her, her grandparents coldly retreated into the safety of their privilege, shutting the door on her mother's pain.

Anger pulsed through Olivia's heart, threatening to consume her as it had done many times before. She pushed the memory aside, banishing it to the recesses of her mind. She knew all too well the danger of letting that resentment overpower her, clouding her judgment and tainting her relationships.

Throughout her life, she had surrounded herself with those she could help, those who saw beyond social status and accepted her for who she was. It was a refuge, a haven away from the suffocating expectations of her world.

As her mind delved deeper into her memories, Olivia realized each painful experience her mother had endured had left an indelible mark on her own approach to love and relationships. Her grandparents' disdainful rejection reverberated within her, a constant reminder of the heartache and disappointment that lurked beneath the surface of privilege and reputation.

"Couldn't let the riff-raff ruin their reputation, could they?" a bitter voice whispered within Olivia. With a determined strength, she pushed the image out of her mind, refusing to succumb to the anger.

The documentary had been Olivia's way

of seeking understanding, of delving into her mother's plight, of forgiving her mother and moving forward. It was a journey she had embarked upon to heal her wounds and find solace within herself. The allure of Louis, and the complications that came with him, threatened to unravel the progress she'd made.

"I can't get caught up in the royal drama. My life will not become an episode of *The Princess Diaries*."

"Uh, sorry. That reference doesn't work." Rebecca rubbed her swollen cheek. "*The Princess Diaries* was a movie, not a television show. There were no episodes. And you didn't discover that you are a princess. Instead, you were swept off your feet by a prince. That is more similar to *The Prince and I*, which is a fitting title for today."

Olivia adjusted herself to face her friend. "This is not funny. It's a cruel fate that the one guy I've been moderately interested in is in direct line to the throne of a European country."

With a playful gleam in her eye, Rebecca grinned. "Oh, come on. I've been telling you where there's drama, there's an audience, but falling for European royalty? You've really out-done yourself this time. Next, you'll tell me he's secretly a superhero too."

"Believe me, the last thing I want is to get sucked into a media circus. I've worked hard to build my credibility, and I'm not about to gamble it away on some cheap viewer-bait tactics." Olivia crossed her arms over her chest. "I want people to tune in because they trust me, not because they hope to witness some royal scandal unfold."

Rebecca gently patted Olivia's arm. "Honey, you need to stop worrying what others will think. And you need to consider *not* closing the door on this—on him. Sleep on it. Maybe what seems like a tragedy is a gift. Everything happens for a reason, right?" Rebecca pointed to her swollen face. "I'd like to think getting a tooth pulled in Africa led to something good." She sighed. "Don't do what you always do—block your heart from those who want to love you. Promise me you'll think about this?"

Olivia nodded, acknowledging her friend's plea. Yet deep within her, she couldn't make that promise. How could she believe that any good could come from this situation? The thought of her face being thrust into the spotlight, exposed to the prying eyes of the world, was the last thing she desired. It had taken her months before she agreed to reveal her face in the final episode of her documentary. Why would she open herself up to the judgment of the world and scrutiny that came with dating a prince—no matter how wonderful he was?

CHAPTER THIRTEEN

Buchenwald Concentration Camp, Germany
28 October 1943

The cold wind cut through the thin coat of Alessandra's coarse dress and plain coat as she sat huddled in the back seat of the black sedan—her hands bound and her heart heavy with despair. Once filled with vibrant colors outside the car window, the landscape now appeared muted and lifeless, mirroring her spirit. After spending nearly a week in the Gestapo headquarters in Rome, she'd been flown to Berlin. And after a fitful sleep in a tiny prison cell, she'd spent half a day being driven northeast near Weimar.

The vehicle stopped at a gate, and the heavy iron and wooden doors swung open with a creak. *Buchenwald.* She'd heard rumors of this place of horrors. Yet even more than thoughts of what awaited were concerns for her family. How much did her children know, or even her parents? They no doubt sought answers and had come up empty. Just as she'd had no answers about Christian. Her children were safe in the Vatican, and her parents—the king and queen—had fled to Southern Italy to safety, yet would the Nazis

183

use her arrest to draw them out of protection?

The car drove past rows of barracks and a sizable parade ground where thin men—thousands of them—stood erect in the biting wind. Striped uniforms hung on their bodies. Alessandra forced herself to look away, knowing one more fissure to her fractured heart could cause it to break in two completely.

As the sedan parked, armed guards barked orders, their stern faces etched with a cold detachment that chilled Alessandra to the bone. She stumbled out of the car, her legs weak from hours of confinement, and was quickly ushered toward a small barrack behind a tall wall.

A guard pushed her into the one-room enclosure. The door closed behind her. The dim room enveloped Alessandra, leaving her momentarily disoriented. Her eyes strained to adjust to the gray light filtering through the barred windows. The room consisted of a bed and a table. Movement from the direction of a small table caused her to jump. A man sat there—a Nazi officer.

"Please, I don't wish to frighten you." The officer stood and clasped his hands behind his back. He approached with slow steps.

Everything within Alessandra told her to cower, but then, her mother's gentle instructions filled her mind. As a child, Alessandra would rather stay home with the staff than attend royal functions. All the attention—and having to know just what to do and what to say—had made her wish to run and hide. But Mother had taught her differently. *You not only stand for yourself, Alessandra, but you also stand for our people. You represent our family, our throne. If the people can't look to you for strength, who can they turn to?*

When she didn't respond, the officer continued. "I know this is not what you're used to, but I assure you, your arrangement is far better than most."

Alessandra stood tall, scanning the small room. Alessandra's lungs tightened. When was the last time she'd been completely alone? Never. As a child, there'd always been someone to tend to her. As a married woman and mother, her days had been filled with caring for her husband and children. She blew out a slow breath, willing herself not to panic. "Correct. A better arrangement would be with my husband, my children."

The officer, adorned with the symbols of oppression, stood and approached, eyeing her cautiously. "I cannot promise freedom, but I will do my utmost to ensure your comfort as far as it is within my power."

"Comfort?" She fixed her eyes on him, keeping her voice gentle. If she spread her arms wide, she could nearly touch each side of the sleeping area. It was open to a sitting area with a table and two chairs. It was the right size for one person. "How can one find solace in such a place? Surrounded by barbed wire and suffering souls?" Her words quivered like a fragile bird's wings, struggling to flee amidst a storm of pain.

His expression softened, and a flicker of empathy emerged in his hardened features. "I may wear this uniform, but I refuse to let it consume my soul entirely. Each day, as I witness the depths of human suffering, I find solace in the small acts of kindness I can offer. It is a thin line I walk between duty and compassion."

His words caused a crack in the wall of hate she'd built up over the days of her captivity. A tear escaped her weary eyes, her heart aching for the contradiction. "But why? Why do you care? Why do you respect me?"

"I respect you because, despite the circumstances, you have retained your strength and dignity." He paused, briefly glancing away. "More than that, this is not our first meeting."

She stared at him, torn between her instinct to despise him and her reluctant recognition of his flawed nobility. Alessandra searched his face. After her marriage, she'd lived in Berlin for nearly as many years as she had in Rome. Was he someone she knew? A friend of Christian's, perhaps?

"You do not remember me, but I was a guard at the Opera House for many years. Before the war, of course. And during all those years, I was never allowed inside, as if the likes of me were not welcome in such a fine place."

"And you saw me there?"

"I did. You always offered a kind word and smile." He nodded as if reliving the memory. "More than that, my mother clips every news article she can find about the royal family. She was quite pleased when the great-grandson of Queen Victoria married an Italian princess."

And what would she think of Christian now being held by the Nazis? And me also?

Instead of asking, Alessandra forced a smile, rubbing the chill on her arms. "I haven't been to Berlin for many years. The Opera House was a beautiful place. I heard it received damage during the bombings." She shivered and looked at one of the stiff-backed chairs. "Do you mind if I sit?"

"No, of course not."

The officer pulled out a chair for her, and she sat. Then he took the opposite chair, eyeing her as if they were friends having coffee instead of a captor and his prisoner.

"I've never stepped inside the Opera House. But there was a special birthday—"

"Goering invited Christian and me," she injected. "As his guests on his special day."

"Can you tell me about it?"

Alessandra's gaze shifted to the window as the last traces of daylight faded. Directly in view was a shared courtyard, an area where moments of reprieve might have been found if not for the looming stone block wall on its far side. This massive barrier, with its rough-hewn blocks, kept her in solitary confinement, separate from the main camp. The stark contrast between the courtyard's limited freedom and the towering wall symbolized her seclusion. Beyond the wall were the other barracks, their activities and sounds just out of reach. Yet she didn't long for that world. Her thoughts were anchored firmly on a particular memory: the evening of January 12, 1936.

"My breath caught as I stepped out of the automobile and looked up at the State Opera House." Even though weariness overwhelmed her, Alessandra attempted to keep her voice steady. "The entrances were lined with a dozen footmen in crimson liveries carrying lanterns on poles, adding to the pomp and circumstance of the event. My husband, Prince Christian of Hesse, grasped my hand. We entered, speechless at the splendor before us."

The officer nodded as she spoke, urging her on.

"General Hermann Goering, German Minister of Aviation and Premier of Prussia was cele-brating his forty-third birthday with a spectacular celebration," she continued. "As the night wore on, the atmosphere grew more and more festive. The room was filled with laughter and music, and the champagne flowed freely. It was clear General Goering could feel the warmth of the alcohol spreading through his veins, and he started to loosen up. He laughed and joked with his guests, regaling them with stories from his time in the military and his experiences in the Luftwaffe.

"At one point, he even took to the stage himself, grabbing a microphone and belting out a rousing rendition of a popular German folk song. The crowd cheered him on."

Her words felt like poison to her lips. Pain pierced her heart. She had cheered with them. Goering had been a friend. Of course, that was a decade ago. Neither she nor Christian had known the darkness of the Nazi leader's heart then. "As we entered the ballroom, he welcomed us. Then we were shown to our shared box with Goering's wife and their children."

The officer's chin dropped. "You sat in Goering's box?"

"Yes, and for one unforgettable night, I let myself be dazzled by the splendor, knowing it was the largest party Berlin had seen since the Kaiser left."

The man sighed as if her words nourished his soul. She eyed him, and the officer's eyes sparkled briefly, reflecting the images conjured by her words. From the delight on his face, it was as if he could almost hear the symphony of laughter, the clinking of glasses, and the enchanting melodies that filled the air.

A bad taste rose in her mouth, and she couldn't end her story there. "The more I looked around, the more uneasy I became," Alessandra continued. "I could feel all eyes on me. I felt a twinge of melancholy for the familiar surroundings of my own Italy. Married to this German prince and seated with Goering, I knew my actions were being observed and judged." Alessandra paused, touching her fingertips to her lips. "The music, laughter, and the aroma of flowers didn't ease the knowing. The stage was filled with ballet dancers, but everyone in that room was more interested in my every move."

Why am I confessing such things?

The officer narrowed his gaze. This was not the story he wanted to hear.

She took a deep breath and released it, continuing before she lost her nerve. "But I don't have to worry about that now, do I?" Alessandra sighed.

The officer rose without a word. As he reached the door, he paused and turned.

"There are other political prisoners within the courtyard," he revealed. "You are free to walk around outside. I know this is not where you wish to be, but it is the best I could offer."

His words hung in the air, suspended between them, like a fragile bridge of temporary respite.

Alessandra absorbed the information, her mind simultaneously calculating the possibilities and dangers of such newfound freedom. It was far from an ideal existence, yet the prospect of open space and fresh air whispered of a fleeting liberation.

The officer paused, his gaze lingering upon her as if awaiting gratitude or acknowledgment.

"Thank you for making me aware," Alessandra responded with a swift nod. "And please send my regards to your mother."

A brief, unexpected tremor of emotion flashed across the officer's face, a flicker akin to embarrassment or vulnerability. It was a fleeting glimpse beneath the rigid facade—a momentary crack in the armor that separated them.

CHAPTER FOURTEEN

Jomo Kenyatta International Airport
Nairobi, Kenya
Present Day

Olivia's backpack hung heavily on her shoulders, its weight bearing down as if burdened with her worries. With each step she took along the bustling walkway leading to her gate at the Jomo Kenyatta International Airport in Nairobi, her progress seemed sluggish, slowed by her physical and emotional load.

Announcements blared over the speakers, with footsteps shuffling along and the occasional clang of luggage rolling across the polished floor. The scent of jet fuel lingered in the air, intermingling with a faint aroma of coffee wafting from a nearby café. It was a familiar fragrance that usually comforted her . . . but not today.

As the clamor of voices echoed through the airport terminal, Olivia scanned the crowd, taking in the kaleidoscope of faces passing by. At least she didn't see anyone from the press. Her shoulders eased a bit as she noticed the vibrant colors of traditional garments some travelers wore, a stark contrast to the muted tones of her clothing.

Her fingers fumbled absentmindedly with the strap of her backpack. She tried to focus on the laughter and camaraderie shared with her team over the last few weeks, but they were like faded photographs in an old album. The clearest memories were the ones spent with Louis the day prior. As much as she longed to be angry with him, he was right. She wouldn't have given him a moment of her time if she'd known he was a prince.

Deep within, a knot formed in Olivia's stomach. It clenched tightly, constricting her breath. *Am I doing the right thing by not giving Louis a chance?* Her decision bore down on her like a vice. Not that it mattered. She'd soon be boarding a plane for America, leaving Louis far behind.

Even though her team had planned on filming the last episode—with her big reveal—this morning, Olivia had canceled that. Instead, she'd filmed a short clip. Not knowing what to say, she'd followed Rebecca's advice.

"These days in Kenya stirred up more than I could have imagined," she said for the video. *"While I've learned so much about my mother's story, I'm discovering my own. And for now, this story isn't over."*

She hoped it was intriguing enough to keep her viewers interested yet vague enough that anything she came up with for the final episode would make sense. Until then, Olivia would wait for the media to forget about Prince Louis's safari date. She guessed Louis would move on in a month or two, and the press would find someone else to hound. Then, no one would connect her with the prince when she released the reveal. At least, that was her hope.

Voices floated around her in languages she didn't understand—not that she wanted to concentrate on them anyway. She needed to escape, forget, and move forward. This flight would be the first step.

She took a deep breath. A hollow ache filled her. Her mind told her to run from feelings for Louis and not allow herself to be pulled in. Her heart, though, didn't get the memo.

Almost like walking through a dream, she found the B2 gate with a flight to Amsterdam. From there, she and Rebecca would travel to Atlanta. She moved down a row of seats in the waiting area and sat, noting the woman sitting across from her. The young businesswoman wore a black and white checkered dress with a red jacket. Even though a computer was open on her lap, the woman flipped through the newspaper pages.

A soft gasp escaped Olivia's lips when she saw her face on the front page. It was a photo of yesterday's picnic. Her head was tilted back slightly in laughter, and Louis's loving gaze was fixed upon her. Loving was the only way to describe it. The tender look in his eyes and his enraptured smile melted her heart, yet at the same time, she wanted to vomit.

A Judas had emerged from somewhere within the merry band of safari adventurers. They'd taken the image of her and Louis, a single moment frozen in time, plucked from a greater whole, and splashed it across the media. The violation was a real pain that cut through Olivia's heart like a cold, merciless blade.

Yesterday, she'd lived immersed in the bubbling joy of being with Louis, oblivious to the world's prying eyes. Today, it felt like she'd been stripped bare, showering unknowingly behind a glass wall with the world on the other side, watching, judging.

A knot of dread tightened her stomach, constricting her breath. She let the backpack slide from her shoulder and thud onto the gleaming white tile floor. She fixed her gaze on the floor, hoping it would swallow her whole.

Would they recognize her? As inconspicuously as she could, Olivia removed her sunglasses from the case in the side pocket of her backpack and slid them onto her nose, leaning back in her seat. She felt like a fool, but it was better than being mobbed. Or was that taking it too far? She didn't know how this royal celebrity stuff worked.

Footsteps approached, and a form stood before her. Olivia's shoulders tensed. Finally, she dared to look up. Relief flooded her when Rebecca came into her view.

Rebecca smirked. "As if those glasses are going to hide your identity." The attention of those closest to her and Olivia followed Rebecca as she sat down and dropped her pink backpack onto the floor with a flourish. Within seconds, the other passengers turned away as if they'd realized another loud American was causing the stir.

"Will you chill with the comments?" Olivia spoke through clenched teeth.

"As if you have a chance of being unnoticed? Do you know the circulation of that newspaper alone?" Rebecca pointed her chin toward the newspaper in the hands of the woman sitting across the aisle.

Olivia shrugged. "Honestly, I don't want to know." She scooted lower into her seat.

"The *Daily Nation* has 4.3 million readers a day. I googled it," Rebecca said in a low tone. "And that's just one newspaper. I scanned the newsstand on the way over and picked up a few for souvenirs." She patted her backpack. "Mostly the ones in languages I didn't understand. How cool is that?"

"What is wrong with these people?" Olivia mumbled. "Can't they go back to reporting on Kate Middleton stepping out in coral for the first garden party of the year?"

"Fashion may be queen, but romance is king for

newspapers. Especially for a prince who's been unlucky in love." Rebecca chuckled and ribbed Olivia with her elbow. "Do you like that? I just made it up. Pretty good, huh?"

Rebecca spread her arms wide, and Olivia sent up a quiet prayer for the plane to board early. As far as she remembered, they weren't seated together.

"Did you read the headline?" Rebecca whispered, leaning close. *"Prince Louis's Sun Kissed Safari.* Another one read, *Wild Romance?* I like that one best."

"I just want to forget it all. Forget the day happened."

Rebecca lifted an eyebrow and nodded. "Oh, okay, you do that." Then she took a bag of crackers from her backpack.

"How can you eat at a time like this?" Olivia wanted to spout, just like Rebecca had asked her. Rebecca wasn't the one in crisis. If Olivia wanted this to disappear, she'd have to let it go, despite her friend. The good news was that another story would fill that front page tomorrow. By then, she'd be home and back to her everyday life. Then she could put the whole thing behind her.

Olivia pulled out her phone and opened her email. She needed to get her mind off the newspaper directly across from her with her face plastered on it. Or, more importantly, with Louis's face and handsome smile. He did have the kindest eyes. Her lips curled slightly as she remembered how he'd teased about drool on his shoulder after she'd dozed off. Thinking of their ride in the van now, it made sense why they'd been allowed into the Masai Mara Reserve first. The driver and the guard knew about their elite passenger. Did they all think of her as a fool?

The elderly gentleman beside Olivia was clad in the vibrant hues of a running suit. His eyes, aged but still sparkling with vitality, glanced in her direction. A kind smile graced his lips. Olivia reciprocated his smile. The soft murmurs from Rebecca, however, combined with the faint clicks from her phone screen, soon captured Olivia's attention.

"Rebecca, please," Olivia implored, her voice a mere whisper. Her gaze slid downward, her phone becoming a convenient hideaway. "Let's not continue this discussion."

The older man's head tilted in Olivia's direction, his question hanging in the air. "What topic, may I ask?"

A fiery heat blazed up Olivia's cheeks as she gently tipped her sunglasses, giving him an apologetic glance. "I was just conversing with my friend here." A brief thumb jerk toward Rebecca dimmed the light in his eyes.

"Do I recognize you?" he asked, his gaze piercing. "Your face . . . it seems familiar."

Olivia shook her head, swiftly readjusting her glasses as a shield. "No, no. I assure you, you don't. My face . . . well, it's just one of those that people often find familiar."

Rebecca's muffled voice rose again, her words swallowed by the crunch of a chip. She leaned forward, her eyes squinting as if trying to decipher the newspaper sprawled across the aisle. Olivia found solace in that Rebecca hadn't yet resorted to pulling out her collection from her bag.

Ignoring them both, Olivia retreated into the sanctuary of her phone screen. She immersed herself in unread emails, attempting to cleanse her mind of yesterday's events. She skimmed two e-newsletters from authors she followed, then deleted them. And then realized she had no idea what either had said.

"Remember what we'd been praying before we came—for God to show us who to love, serve, and pray for?" Rebecca's voice interrupted her thoughts.

Three hundred forty-five emails still to go, and no motivation. "Yes, of course."

"I was thinking about it and, well, I never really thought it meant *love*, love."

"That isn't funny."

"I'm not joking. You can't brush this off like something amazing didn't just happen yesterday." She lifted her phone and waved it in the air. "I've seen the photos of you two together. Sparks are an understatement."

"Yes, well, just forget you ever saw those. I got caught up in the day. Who wouldn't? It was so amazing. So beautiful . . . all the animals. The experience of a lifetime."

Rebecca nodded. "Yeah, I didn't see any animals in the photos posted on the *Daily Chat*."

"The last thing I need is love. And especially not love with someone like . . ." Olivia looked away. *Someone kind and funny. Someone who was interesting to talk to and listened as I spoke.*

But also someone who'd lied to her and made her look like a fool. Someone who thrust her into an unwanted spotlight, scrutinized under the world's microscope. A man who lived a life of privilege likely oblivious to the struggles of everyday people like those she worked with in Little Rock.

Olivia returned to her emails, searching for a response from Sarah-Grace regarding their upcoming fundraising banquet. "The girl's head is in the clouds," Miss Jan had remarked. While Olivia understood that Sarah-Grace was on her honeymoon and might not prioritize answering emails right away, she still felt anxious. After all, the fundraising banquet was only a month and a half away. For some reason, though, those concerns seemed less pressing than they had before.

After serving in one of the largest slums in the world, worries about finding extra money to replace everything they'd lost was hardly the same level of crisis as the slums. Promise's sweet face filled Olivia's mind. She almost could feel the young girl wrapped up in her arms.

How was Promise now? Olivia made a mental note to reach out to Kioko about transferring funds to help care for the girl. Then, after deleting ten spam emails, Olivia found an important one.

Dear Aunt Liz stood out like a beacon amid the sea of faces Olivia called family. The moniker "Aunt" was more of an endearment than a statement of blood ties, yet she was as close to kin as Olivia had ever known after her mother's death.

A woman of wisdom and grace, Liz had dedicated her life to being an archivist. This role demanded meticulous care and a deep reverence for the past. Her realm was the still, silent corridors of history. Liz's companions were the whispering echoes of the bygone eras in the parchment she delicately preserved.

Liz breathed life into the old and the forgotten as a book conservator. Her deft hands were skilled at coaxing faded words back into existence, preserving their stories and wisdom for future generations. With a magnifying glass held perpetually in one hand and a paintbrush in the other, she painstakingly erased years of neglect from timeworn pages. The kind of life Liz lived was, to Olivia, a meaningful life, a life that mattered. It was a life worth aspiring for.

Hey Bean-bug,

Sharon told me you were in Africa. I can't wait to hear more about your trip. I am in Naples, which sounds more exciting than it is since I spend most of my days inside archives and back rooms. (My poor, aching back.) At least the to-go lunches are decent.

There is so much history here, being so close to Pompeii. But there's something new that the museum received just a few months before I arrived. We think you can help us, but first, let me explain.

You're not going to believe what we've found. It's the journal of a princess held in Buchenwald concentration camp. Yes, you read that right—an actual princess. I'm not going to tell you which country she was from. Please trust me on this. I don't want you researching this woman until you hear me out. I've only translated a few pages, but they are fascinating. They mostly share about her life with her husband, Christian, who was in the German royal family.

A private party has approached us about creating a documentary about this woman's life. The budget is small, and this patron suggested perhaps a recent college graduate would be interested. And when I told our patron that my niece had a Media Studies and Communications degree, she asked me to reach out.

I'm going to need help with this one. And I don't mind begging for it. As you know, museums need more funding. This project could open up doors for us.

If you're interested, I can email a PDF. If you could read the translated pages, maybe you could help us figure out how to best write this woman's story. Her voice matters. People need hope, and who better to provide it than a royal who wrote about one of the darkest times in man's history?

So, that's that. I want to say, "I understand if you can't help," but I'm praying you can. If this goes well, I'll be trusted with more important historical documents. More than that, it will be an honor to serve our patron. Bean-bug, what do you think?

All the best,
Aunt Liz

"Hey." Olivia nudged Rebecca's arm, sitting straighter in her hard plastic seat. An announcement of a delayed flight blared overhead, and she had to speak louder to get Rebecca's attention. "You have to read this." She handed her phone to Rebecca.

Rebecca read through the email with a mix of interest and puzzlement. "Who's Liz again?"

"My aunt, sort of. She is the younger sister of my last foster mom. I still talk to Sharon occasionally, but Liz and I are closer friends. Liz is the one who encouraged me to go to college. She encouraged me to travel. She always listened when I had a crazy dream to share."

Rebecca tapped her lower lip with her finger. "She's the one who sends you postcards—" An announcement blared, cutting off Rebecca's words.

The soothing melody of the man's voice over the intercom, the unique rhythm of the African accent, was bittersweet music to Olivia's ears. She lingered on it, knowing it would soon become another memory, another fragment of Africa that she would tuck away in her heart.

The prospect of home, with its mundane routines and familiar comforts, tugged at her. It was the known, the safe, the everyday life that she was used to. A slight ache crept into her heart, a root of longing that anchored her to this foreign land. Promise, the child who'd wormed her way into Olivia's heart, now orphaned, was here. Louis, the man who had stirred emotions within her she'd never known before, he, too, was here. She thought he was, at least. It was a strange realization that the geography of one man could matter so much to her. Had he already flown back to his own country, his princely duties beckoning him?

Olivia typed out a quick response. "Really? A mysterious royal tale? I'm all ears for this fresh take." She showed her response to Rebecca.

Her friend chuckled. "Good one, but with our recent royal saga, that princess tale is practically yesterday's news." Rebecca winked. "But what did she mean about spending her days in archives and back rooms?"

"Liz is a book conservator. She preserves books and papers, often working in the basements of museums," Olivia answered.

"I guess that's not so bad, especially if she gets to work in places like Naples."

"Naples sounds okay, but lately, I've been thinking about wanting to see Paris." The words came out without thinking, and Louis's voice filtered through her thoughts. *Next time, I can show you my favorite cafés in Paris.* Goose bumps rose on her arms, and she rubbed them away.

Rebecca cast her a side glance. "Are you cold? I have a light sweatshirt in my backpack you could wear."

"No, I'm not cold." How could Olivia

explain? "It's just that my life no longer seems like my life. First, uh, I met someone royally interesting. Now my aunt's emailing me about an old journal from a princess she wants me to look at. I leave the country only to find myself caught up in international affairs at a royal level."

International affairs. That wasn't a phrase Olivia used often. And it wasn't correct either. *International affair.* As in, singular. The other one was over.

Olivia grabbed her backpack, tucking her phone into the front pocket. Heaving her backpack onto her shoulder, she sighed, mumbling to herself. "You'd think finding a Prince Charming would be a dream, but right now, I'd trade him for an Average Joe in a heartbeat."

Buchenwald Concentration Camp
November 1943

The thin shafts of sunlight entered Alessandra's cell through the barred window, splaying across the simple wooden table where she sat alone. Before her, a brown paper package sat unopened. When had someone entered? How had she slept through it? A shiver ran down her spine.

Alessandra breathed deeply then wrinkled her nose at the faint, metallic odor of death that hung in the air, a sinister reminder of her fate.

Her fingertips traced the edges of the package's rough exterior. Did she dare hope for a Bible? She gingerly opened it.

Instead, a worn leather journal with a single ink pen was tucked inside. She could make out a tiny note from beneath the paper wrap, written in blocked letters: "A gift from my mother."

Alessandra thought of the conversation with the officer. Somehow he'd slipped in and left the gift before she'd awakened.

Outside her cell, voices rose. Through the window, she observed other political prisoners exiting their cells, congregating in a shared courtyard. She desperately wanted to be with them, to recapture that lost sense of community, but she remained planted in her seat.

The journal called to her. A sense of urgency pumped through her body. Who knew if she'd ever leave this place. Was this gift an omen of what was to come?

A thousand untold stories weighed down on Alessandra like the pen in her hands. Taking another deep breath, she picked up the pen and started writing. Even if she didn't make it, maybe her words would.

* * * * *

I do not know who will read this or if it will ever be found, but something inside me urges me to tell my story. One may question why a princess would end up in a Nazi camp. It's one of love.

Love brought me here. But I am getting ahead of myself.

My name is Princess Alessandra Appiani, and my father is the king of Italy. Or at least, as far as I know, he is still king. This story could start in a hundred different directions. I could speak of my simple childhood—simple for my status. I could write about my parents and brother and sister. I could share my heart bound to my country, my Italia. Instead, this story must begin with the man I love. It is because of love that I find myself where I am. If you are reading this knowing who I am and why I am imprisoned, it may shock you that I fell in love with a German. Yet I will be the first to confess that it was not a German who captured my heart; it was Christian. And Christian just happened to be born under the German flag.

I met my Christian at an exhibit of paintings in Rome. Of course, I knew of the German prince before our meeting, but I was shocked by how bright and kind he was. He was pleased I spoke his language so well. He did not know then that I was a linguist and could speak most European languages fluently, which has served me well over the years. Christian loved art and architecture, not one to be lured by power and politics. He enjoyed the simple things of life, and while we both knew our place among the royals, we could be ordinary people together.

We married in a medieval castle, and some first wondered if we could marry. I am Roman Catholic, and Christian is a Lutheran. Father worried the Vatican would not give its consent. Still, when Christian wrote a written declaration that he would renounce all claims to the throne and make no effort to convert me, permission was granted.

To think my Christian would renounce all claims to the throne for me.

The first years of our marriage were beautiful. We spent most of our time in Rome, yet the happenings in Germany stretched into our world. As the Prince of Hesse, Christian joined the Nazi Party in 1933 with the appointment of Adolf Hitler as Chancellor. Of course, no one knew then what plans Hitler had for Germany or the Nazi Party.

Fear grips me as I write this, yet what can they do to me that they haven't already done? Christian and I were followed for years, and our deeds were recorded. We have been threatened. Our children's lives have been at stake. And now I am a prisoner with little hope of freedom.

Still, a true leader does what is right even when no one else does. Christian taught me that. More importantly, I have done as I should before my Lord. Loved as He did: with sacrifice.

I am locked away in confinement at a Nazi

death camp, yet my heart is free. Christian and I did all we could to save the lives of those we felt the duty to protect. Even though the idea was mine, Christian saw to many details. I know their freedom is worth my imprisonment—from the first delivery made until the last. Yet, I worry that those I love now must pay for our convictions. Lord, please keep my children safe! Let them not suffer for my deeds or those of my husband.

Buchenwald Concentration Camp, November 1943

I dreamt about Christian last night. Our marriage was a happy one. We enjoyed horseback, tennis, yachting, and traveling by car. Our home was a small villa designed by Christian and built on the grounds of my father's country residence. We spent more time in Italy than in Germany because it suited my health better. That didn't mean we were unaware of the political happenings in Germany, especially regarding Chancellor Adolf Hitler.

In the beginning, Christian joined the socialist movement because refusing would be more of a disruption to our happy life. Of course, at the time, we could not even fathom where that political leaning would take us. To see where I am now—the prisoner I have become—would be unthinkable. Worse is not knowing my husband's fate. A Nazi officer told me that

Christian was arrested, and they would only release him to me. I know it was a trick to get me to leave the safety of the Vatican, where I had taken my children.

Living in love and starting a family, I did not allow too many worried thoughts to fill my mind until September 1937, when our Prime Minister Mussolini announced his unshakable support for Hitler. My father's alarm was enough for us both, especially when Mussolini spent six months embellishing Rome for a visit by the Fuhrer, putting a seal on their axis.

While Hitler was civil enough at the court banquet during his visit, I and others who understood German overheard him urging Mussolini to get rid of the monarchy, which he considered a useless drag on the regime. When I shared these words with my father, he became another person for the sake of his throne. He became the puppet of evil men, breaking my heart. But what does one do when fearing losing one's throne or life to madness? And, yes, I am well aware that even these few sentences I write here are enough to give me a death sentence. But to me, my verdict has already been sealed.

I should have known from the curses I heard from Hitler's mouth during that first visit that this would be my fate—no matter my husband's position and ties to the Nazi party. We were fools to believe that if we simply kept our level heads, we'd be able to stay one step ahead. I trusted my husband, so I did my best to remain uninvolved. Yet how can one stay uninvolved when caught in a raging fire with the pillars and the roof of your world crumbling around you?

My dear Christian. It is my love for him that brought me to this place. After having nearly twenty years with him as my husband, I would not trade a day with him for my freedom. Because they knew of my love, they lured me out of safety into the wolf's den. Yet, if I had stayed, I would have always wondered if I could have saved the life of my loved one.

* * * * *

CHAPTER FIFTEEN

Nyota Skyline Lodge, Kenya
Present Day

Louis paced the balcony overlooking the savannah, although his mind was far from the blue sky, the waving grasses, and the herds of animals in the distance. His mind was only on her, on Olivia. In his mind's eye, he pictured her petite frame, olive skin, and long black hair. Her pixie face reminded Louis of a Disney princess, yet her spunk told him she wouldn't wait for a prince to save her.

He scoffed. *Pity the cartoon prince who shows up to rescue that one.* Yet that spunkiness intrigued him too. To be royal, one must learn how to stand up for oneself.

He rubbed his brow, shocked at where his thoughts were already taking him. Was he already picturing Olivia as his wife? After one day? Maybe that was taking it too far. Or was it?

His gut ached, remembering the horrified expression on her face when she discovered he was a prince. He would have received a better reaction if he'd told her he was a bank robber. It made no sense. What could be so unappealing about being royal? The royal life wasn't easy, but he enjoyed being a public servant. As his father had taught him, his words, actions, and decisions mattered.

"I've messed everything up. I'm the greatest fool. I have to find a way to redeem myself."

Louis directed his words to Sergio, who lounged at the outdoor dining table. With the wide-brimmed hat, sunglasses, and a fruit smoothie, Sergio looked like he was enjoying their time in Africa. Yet Sergio's heart wasn't the one shredded into a million pieces.

Sergio lifted his glass and took a long drink from the straw. "Things went well until we got back to the lodge. The two of you looked like a natural fit."

Louis narrowed his gaze and pointed at his bodyguard. "And you were not supposed to be there. I told you I did not want you to come."

"Yes, well, I answer to your father and not you. If something had happened, I could have been imprisoned for life."

Louis took two steps forward on the gleaming wood deck, smelling a whiff of Sergio's cologne mixed with the aroma of the African Amaryllis in a vase on the table—a symbol of love, beauty, and determination, just like Olivia. When he'd returned from his mid-morning walk to see the new blooms decorating their suite, Louis took it as a confirmation that he couldn't let this woman go—not so quickly.

Lunch had been laid out for them, and sitting next to his plate was a black leather portfolio with the gold embossed crest of Alloria on the cover, just as it was every day.

Louis sat at the table across from Sergio. He took a bite from a croissant and then took a sip from his coffee. He opened the portfolio, attempting to focus on the paperwork. Work had found him. Another part of Sergio's job was to see that it did.

"What is so urgent today?" he asked, even though it was clear the papers inside involved details for his father's jubilee.

"Seating charts for the first dinner and details for the ball kicking off the celebration."

Louis poured himself a glass of water from the silver pitcher. After months of dedicated practice with the orchestra, his fingers still vibrated from the strings of his violin. "This event is three months away."

"All the details from the three years of planning are here. The dinner kicks off the four-day holiday weekend, followed by the jubilee parade the next day, and this is just the first of many events. These things need to be solidified now."

Louis briefly glanced at the chart. Heads of state, important dignitaries, and celebrity guests. So much of the same. "Yes, this is fine."

Sergio opened another folder to pull out a small stack of papers, but Louis held up his finger. With the jubilee months away, Louis had difficulty focusing on it, especially with all the tussling in his heart. He pictured Olivia's betrayed gaze.

"Not now, my man. Can we do this later? Tomorrow morning, I promise. Humor me, please."

With a nod, Sergio pushed the papers and envelope to the side and leaned back in his chair. With a half smile, he took a croissant and spread fresh butter on top. His proffered nod encouraged Louis to proceed.

"Serg, if you had asked me a few days ago about the most beautiful sight in the world, I would have mentioned acacia trees silhouetted against a savannah sunset. Or maybe herds along the floodplains."

Sergio lifted one eyebrow as he listened. "But something else has captured your attention. Or should I say someone else?"

"I know I have said this before, but I've never met someone like her. Olivia is so comfortable in her skin, yet there is so much innocence and wonder in her gaze."

Louis pushed aside his plate, the memory of the spunk in her brown eyes as she pointed to the bras the monkeys had dragged into the trees bringing the softest laughter to his lips. He rose and strode to the edge of the balcony. He couldn't hold back his smile. He tipped his head backward and allowed the warm African sun to warm his face.

The memory of Olivia's head resting on his shoulder as the jeep had carried them back to the lodge warmed his thoughts. His heart gave an extra thump. Just as quickly, a dull ache settled in his gut because Olivia was gone. He'd messed up. She ran. He let her go.

Sergio's laughter broke through. "I have never seen you quite so enraptured."

"And I have never known a feeling like this." He placed his hand over the pit of his gut, then moved it over his heart, spreading his fingers wide. Warmth infused his body.

"I almost feel guilty to have that moment with her—her first day on the Masai Mara. It is similar to the delight of watching my niece and nephew open presents on Christmas, only better. There's nothing like seeing the beauty of God's creation in her eyes."

Her gaze also had pain, perhaps from a significant loss or a greater longing. He wasn't sure. She'd shared a little about her work, but he wanted to know more. What hardship in one's past would propel them so desperately into helping others?

On the drive back, he'd wanted to ask, but she'd already shared so much. Louis hadn't wanted to scare her and watch her dart away like a frightened gazelle. Then again, that happened because he hadn't been truthful with her. Could things have been different if he had confessed his royal title and his lot in life from the start? Or would she have pushed him away and not given him a chance?

Louis turned and rested against the deck's railing. In the distance, the chattering of monkeys, followed by the distant roar of a lion, sounded. He paused and stroked his chin. His senses were working overtime, and the aromas of the savannah grasses and a distant river added to the mixed emotions. *I'll never see the savannah the same for as long as I live.*

Sergio slowly ate his breakfast, acting as if nothing had changed, as if Louis's world hadn't wholly tilted on its axis.

Louis paced again as if he were a caged lion, unable to pursue what his heart desired. "I wish things could have ended differently. She was so angry after she got out of the van. I need to make it right with her."

"Well, from the words I heard from her mouth, you embody everything she's against. As much as I hate to say this, you must let her go—delightful girl or not. She has already headed back to Arkansas."

A new thought entered his mind. Louis stood straighter as shivers danced along his spine. He snapped his fingers. "That's it. I'm going to Little Rock. I will stay there for a while and get to know her. I have no vital duties for a few months, do I? I will go to Arkansas and show Olivia I'm more than my title."

Sergio slid his sunglasses from his nose, panic in his gaze. "Excuse me. Did you just say that you are going to Little Rock?"

Louis stroked his chin. "Have you ever been to the States?"

"I haven't, but I won't entertain the thought. You going to Little Rock, of all places, makes no sense."

"This makes complete sense."

"No, it doesn't make sense. But I've seen that look in your eyes before. I'm lounging on a deck overlooking the savannah and listening to monkeys' chatter. You decided to come here, and we're here. Nothing I say will change your mind, will it?"

"Absolutely not."

"Well, I suppose there is only one thing to say. You can't go alone."

"Of course, I can. I'm a grown man."

"You're also the heir to a throne. There is more at stake here than your heart."

"But should I deny my heart for the sake of the family I was born into? It's not as if I've ever had a choice about anything. But this . . . this I will choose."

Sergio pushed his plate to the side. He crossed his arms over his chest and narrowed his gaze. "Is that so? When are you going to tell your aunt?"

Aunt Regina. She, of all people, will have something to say about this.

Louis cringed, picturing the displeasure on her face. Since he was a small child, he'd lived to please his aunt. She'd cared for him when he'd felt lost and alone. Could she see that he was fumbling now just as he had then?

Louis plopped into the chair and laced his hands on his lap, determined to do what he knew he must. "I suppose I will be the one to tell her. Can we catch a flight home tonight? Surely we can make that happen."

"We? You mean me." Sergio sighed, removed his napkin from his lap, tossed it on the table, and nodded. "*Surely*. Yes, I will be the one to make all the miracles happen." He cleared his throat. "Oh, how I wish I could be a fly on the wall for that conversation."

CHAPTER SIXTEEN

Little Rock, Arkansas

Olivia awoke to the sound of the neighbor's television, traffic from Interstate 30, and the constant drip of a leaky faucet, and she immediately relaxed and settled deeper into her bed. She was home. As soon as she started to relax, though, the memory of the crowd of reporters outside the lodge sent her upright. With a groan, she pushed strands of dark hair away from her face and released a soft moan.

She was home, but it wasn't the same. Her face had been splashed across the front pages of magazines and newspapers worldwide. While on her flights, she'd dared to hope that maybe the news hadn't reached the States, specifically Little Rock. After all, she hadn't even known there was the country of Alloria, let alone a handsome prince who was heir to the throne. Maybe this type of news didn't matter in her state.

When they'd landed and she turned off the airplane mode, her phone started pinging endlessly. Text messages, voicemail notifications—thankfully, they were all from people she knew who had seen the photos. She never had gotten into social media—or posted private information online—so no one from the press had figured out who she was or where she lived. And the news headlines reflected that. *Prince Louis's Mystery Woman Disappears, Leaving Him Alone and Heartbroken.*

The accompanying photo showed Louis walking through the lodge courtyard with his hands in his pockets, his shoulders slumped, and a forlorn look on his face. So different from the joyous smile and bright eyes she'd seen during the safari. Her heart ached, but what choice did she have? As much as she enjoyed Louis, spending time with him could only lead to no good.

She should have stuck to her resolve. She should have remembered what she'd learned from her mother—that giving one's heart to a handsome, charming man always leads to no good.

When Olivia arrived home yesterday, she'd gone straight to bed. Even though weariness overwhelmed her, she had stayed up for hours, crying on her mattress until no tears were left. She'd told herself it was jet lag, but it was more than that. It was the shock of Louis's deception. It was the memory of Promise's mother dying. It was missing the feel of Promise in her arms and Louis's smile. It was the fact that she could open her heart to Louis if she hadn't been raised as she had.

She also felt shock and pain from the journal pages she'd read—words penned during World War II that were as fresh and heartbreaking as if the woman still lived.

Olivia had sent a short note to Liz telling her she'd love to be involved in the project. It would give her something to do while she waited to finish her documentary. It felt good to know that she would be helping her aunt with a project that mattered.

By the time Olivia landed in Amsterdam to change flights, an email had been waiting from Liz.

Bean-bug,

I'm so excited to get your help! There is so much I want to tell you, but for once, I will limit the sharing. (And so sorry for all those times I spilled the beans when telling you about your Christmas gifts. How many years did you miss the surprise of Christmas morning? At least four that I know of.)

Anyway, because I want you to start thinking about how we can best share this story, I'm sending you transcripts of the pages that we've completed. Don't shoot me, but these journal entries are not in order. Our princess wrote in her journal within Buchenwald, and as you can imagine, the conditions were horrible. We're still trying to figure out where the journal was in the years between when it was written and found. That's a mystery all in itself.

Some pages are missing. Others are stuck together. If the pages arc stuck, we have ways to get to the text inside, but it's an expensive process. And I'm still trying to get approval for that.

These words will be hard to read, but what a discovery! Oh, and remember, please do not share her words with anyone. We want it to make the greatest impact when her story is revealed.

All the best,
Aunt Liz

Olivia hadn't wasted any time before reading the journal pages. She'd read them on the flight, attempting not to worry the other passengers with her tears. If her heart hadn't been aching enough already, the princess's words hit her.

What had happened to her husband, Christian? To her children? What happened to her? Did she survive? Liz had been right—Olivia wanted to Google it, but she promised not to until Liz allowed it.

Thankfully, Olivia had taken a few days off to readjust to being home, so she could stay in bed all day. Knowing she wouldn't get anything productive done, given her despondent feelings, Olivia pulled up the PDF from Liz with the translated pages. She turned to the ones that hit her to the core.

* * * * *

The scent of the ovens does not leave me. Although no one speaks of it, we all know why the odor is strong. A fellow prisoner declared that what is happening beyond our tall wall of isolation is the practice of hell. I pray daily for the souls of those who breathe their last under the bootheel of these devils.

The heartache of destruction, all because God considered the Jews his chosen people. The Nazis believe they deserve what another has been given. Still, they will never receive honor and wealth by force, devastation, or death. For a season, yes. But for a lifetime? No. For eternity? Never. Knowing they will face a Judge who knows what they've done is my only consolation.

I do not envy the freedom and power of those in Nazi command. I would rather be locked in chains than climb the skeletal forms of another to make myself higher. Envy told them they were something they were not. Greed declares they are entitled to what is not rightfully theirs.

The Germans forget that they, too, are but flesh and blood. They forget who God is. They forget they deserve nothing, and so they fight for everything. The Lord's way is the way of peace, of sacrifice, of love.

I have told these things to my children, just as I was taught. The greater honor we are given, the greater ability to serve—to give of oneself. Yet, can I teach anything now? I write in these pages wondering if someone, anyone, will hear.

* * * * *

Goose bumps rose on Olivia's arms as she read the last line, just as she had done yesterday when she'd read the words upon the airplane. The hair on the back of her neck stood on end. Reading these words neared a sacred moment. This princess knew God and trusted in His justice. That beauty was even greater than the pain of her shared experiences.

Me. I'm reading. I hear you. Olivia tried to imagine going from a palace to a concentration camp. As she did, she tried to keep Louis out of her mind. There was enough hurt going on inside without thoughts of him. He was a part of her recent past. The media would get weary of the lack of story, and things would soon be as they were before she'd met him. That was at least one resolution she could look forward to, right?

Alloria
Present Day

Louis was on his feet when the knock sounded at the door. Even though he'd arrived home just last night, he'd had no time to rest. From the first light of dawn, he'd risen and planned, knowing the conversation would happen that day. Nevertheless, he admitted he was surprised it was here so soon.

How quickly word spreads, especially when it comes to mutiny. He smirked.

His aunt rarely visited him in his private chambers. They often met in the common areas. Louis also was familiar with her apartments on the royal grounds, where she had lived since childhood. Yet the knock had come.

He glanced around the apartment, ensuring everything was in place, even though he knew it would be. Even though he'd dropped his jacket and suitcase just inside the door when he'd arrived home, no evidence of either showed. Staff had seen to that.

Instead, blue and cream cushions sat perfectly arranged on the brown leather sofas. A family photo—not flowers—was displayed on the wooden, angled coffee table. The cream linen drapes had been opened, welcoming sunbeams to warm the room. Despite the familiarity, this was not where he wanted to be.

He opened the door to discover his aunt with a scowl and schedule in hand. Louis stepped back as if that would protect him from the scolding.

"What is this I hear about you going to America? Of all things." Aunt Regina strode uninvited into the room wearing a yellow dress the color of sunflowers—sunflowers, the symbol of unwavering faith and loyalty.

She paused as she reached the sofa—the brown leather giving a masculine feel to the room that his mother had once filled with everything floral—then paused, noting the difference, and faced him.

Louis closed the door, strode to her, and waved a hand. "Please, Aunt. Have a seat."

Aunt Regina did so, perched on the edge as if ready to pounce on him at any moment.

Louis took a high-back chair, recently re-covered in navy blue, sitting across from her. "You were made aware of my upcoming trip?"

"Louis." The word came out as a soft hiss. "I was hoping I'd come and hear this was a mis-understanding." She placed the papers on the table before her. "I asked Sergio for a printout of your schedule. There is no room for such a trip."

"He brought me the same printout, and it's in my office." Louis nodded and smiled. The one thing his aunt had difficulty standing up to was his smile.

Aunt Regina's shoulders relaxed like he'd just

228

waved a magic wand in her direction. She took a deep breath and released it. Her forced smile stayed in place as she unfolded her hands and folded them again.

"You know you cannot be spared for even a day. The jubilee events are the most important in our country's recent history. You play a part in every aspect. There are suits you need to be fitted for and menus to sample. Not to mention, your sister is hosting a dinner for Lady Constance and her new husband. The media took note of your absence at her wedding. We need to prove that there are no hard feelings. Her father is one of the top businessmen—"

"There are no hard feelings, Aunt," he interrupted. "Yet, I know Catina. The thing she hates most is hosting dinner parties, which is another reason I cannot attend. Another royal puppet has a life no longer her own." His words came out curter than he intended. He forced himself to relax and leaned forward, resting his elbows on his knees, hoping to remind his aunt that he was not her enemy here, simply her nephew whom she adored.

As if catching on to his ploy, Aunt Regina stood. "Which is the real reason why you're not attending, isn't it? To prove you're not a royal puppet?"

"Something like that."

His aunt nodded. "I will not speak for your

sister, but I want to address your plans. Don't you see how you deceive yourself, Louis? You desire to be your person yet quickly appreciate every convenience. Did you not just arrive home by private plane at your father's expense?"

Louis grimaced. She'd heard that too. He made a mental note to arrange different transportation for his trip to the States.

"I could walk away from Father's purse strings if I found the right person. Or maybe the right cause." He added the second part quickly, hoping not to set Olivia in his aunt's sights next.

"The right person?" Aunt Regina turned to him. "I saw the photos, just like everyone else. Care to tell me about this mystery woman?" If he wasn't mistaken, his aunt's features softened.

"Yes, of course. How about we ring for lunch? Would you like to take it to my dining room? I don't believe you've seen it since the remodel."

Aunt Regina nodded, and Louis was confident he noted tears rimming her eyelids. "It looks so different. So modern, with clean lines, yet not cold. Your mother would approve."

"I appreciate that, Aunt." He approached and touched her arm. "Lunch then?"

"Yes, of course."

Louis couldn't remember when he had a more delightful meal with his aunt. Just the two of them, without an agenda. Aunt Regina left the papers she'd brought on the coffee table. Worries about him going to Arkansas went unsaid. Instead, his aunt listened with rapt attention as Louis told her about Olivia and the day he'd spent with her.

"I'll admit, she seems delightful. So unpretentious. And I did always find it amusing to see the monkeys' choice of, um, let's say, *decorations*. I believe those undergarments are the easiest to hang from trees." Laughter slipped through his aunt's lips, and Louis smiled. He couldn't remember the last time his aunt had laughed like that.

"Louis, I have a different agenda than the one I carried into this room." Aunt Regina tilted her head and examined him. "I haven't seen you this alive in ages. I'd almost forgotten how things used to be before . . ."

The room quieted at Aunt Regina's words. They both understood their lives had been defined before and after his mother's death.

"What do you propose I do?" Louis dared to ask.

"Leave this place," Aunt Regina urged, her voice brimming with a raw intensity. "Go anywhere that allows you to follow your heart." Her words hung in the air, carrying a weight of longing and unspoken dreams.

Louis, taken aback by his aunt's fervor, felt a surge of emotions stir within him. His eyebrows

231

lifted in surprise, his heart yearning for the freedom she spoke of. Yet, a tinge of apprehension clouded his thoughts, burdening him with the weight of his responsibilities.

"But what about all my duties?"

Aunt Regina's eyes held a flicker of empathy, a glimmer of understanding. She spoke, her words resonating with a mix of wisdom and vulnerability. "Don't fall to their demands, their suffocating schedules," she implored, her voice laced with a hint of regret. It was clear she too had experienced the shackles of duty, and now she yearned for Louis to break free from their clutches.

"Don't sacrifice your true self for the sake of the crown, Louis," Aunt Regina began, her voice gentle yet commanding, echoing the many sacrifices she'd made over the years. "There are moments when I too feel chained to our duties, bound by tradition," she confided softly, the tone revealing a vulnerability Louis had never witnessed before.

He looked at his plate, the untouched delicacies suddenly losing their allure. Aunt Regina's own untouched meal seemed a reflection of his inner turmoil.

"Once, there was someone who held my heart," Aunt Regina continued, her voice layered with shades of bygone days and quiet lament. Louis recalled a faint memory of an old newspaper clipping, hinting at his aunt's forbidden affair with a man not of their status.

"He used to call me his 'songbird in a gilded cage,'" she reminisced, a touch of melancholy evident in her voice. "Arnie often challenged me to break free, but the chains of duty were too strong, or perhaps my will was too weak." She sighed deeply, the weight of past choices evident. "Had I chosen differently, I often wonder if we would have been happy together."

Louis glanced at his aunt, his eyes glistening with unshed tears. Then he peered out of the windows at the mountains, the high peaks of the Pyrenees speaking of unmoving strength. His aunt wasn't as strong as she let on. Louis didn't know how to respond, so he silently waited for Aunt Regina to continue. Instead, she moved her fork around her plate as if deciding which bite to take.

When she didn't respond, Louis cleared his throat. "I suppose there is no greater enemy of the crown than one finding their longing outside the palace walls and falling in love—forfeiting duty for one's affections—is there?"

Aunt Regina stilled her hands and eyed him with curiosity.

"I can't walk away from who I am, Aunt, yet is it right to ask anyone to become trapped in the titles and expectations?"

His aunt cut off a small piece of her salmon.

She lifted it to her mouth and then paused. "I suppose you'll never know unless you go. I can let the staff know we will continue as planned and await your return for anything we need from you."

Louis nearly gasped. He had never expected those words from his aunt's mouth. Yet feeling their openness, he dared to ask the question plaguing his mind. "What if I go and Olivia won't have me? Or rather, what if she wants me and not the establishment? She has already made it clear to me what she thinks of that. If I love someone, why would I want to trap them?"

Aunt Regina dabbed the corner of her mouth with the linen napkin. "The right person won't consider it a trap. Oh, how I wish I'd known that then. The right person will be strong enough to bring good change without bowing to the wrong ideals."

"And that type of person is out there?" Louis hoped it was true. Prayed he'd found the one.

"I'm praying she can open her heart to all you represent. Your title is part of you, after all. Since you were born, Louis, I've been praying for God to protect your heart and prepare the right person for this role. She's out there. I know she is. And if you believe Olivia is worth pursuing, you must go to her now. I insist."

CHAPTER SEVENTEEN

Little Rock, Arkansas

Usually chauffeured, Louis relished the rare moments he could drive himself. The freedom, the thrill of navigating unfamiliar roads—it was exhilarating. Who would've thought that simply driving around a new city would give him such a rush?

As Louis wound through the older part of Little Rock, he felt as though he had been transported onto a movie set from the nineteen sixties or seventies. It had an almost eerie, ghost-town vibe. Age-worn brick buildings, their windows clouded over time, stood guard over the sidewalks: Cooper's Auto Parts, Nissi's Cosmic Beauty, Food Giant. Though there was litter scattered across the streets and cars lazily making their way in both directions, there was a clear sign that life still persisted here, even if the place seemed lost in time.

He paused at a stoplight and heard the blaring music even before he saw another car approaching in his side mirror. The vehicle was an older sedan, its body lowered close to the ground and its tinted windows hiding the occupants inside. Music boomed from inside so loudly that the auto trembled to the beat. Goose bumps rose on Louis's arms, and he wondered if he'd made a big mistake. If Sergio could see him now, his bodyguard would have wrung his neck. Louis still couldn't believe Aunt Regina had also agreed that deciding whether he wanted to take his bodyguard would be up to him.

What am I doing here? Is this worth it?

As soon as that last thought entered Louis's mind, he pushed it away. The light turned green, and he continued following the GPS. Yes, Olivia was worth it. The conversations they shared, the laughter, the humor. It had been so different than any other relationship he'd ever had.

Louis enjoyed being treated like an average person. He hadn't realized how much he'd despised the careful approach everyone took when speaking to him until Olivia hadn't. He wanted more of that. He wanted more time with her.

Following the directions, in half a mile, he turned into a parking lot filled with trash. He parked before a large concrete building with high windows. Just under the metal roof, a sign read *Community Center*. On one side a basketball court had the rusty bones of two rims, but the nets had been lost to time, giving the court a sad look that told stories of its glory days. A partially fenced area of overgrown grass stood on the other side. It was a motley congregation of nature left to its own devices. A sight rather different from the manicured greens he was accustomed to back home.

Again it was something he expected to see in an old TV show. While the sidewalks along the road in this part of Little Rock had been empty, a group of teens walked toward the center. More teens congregated around the doors.

A few cars were parked in the lot, and another vehicle pulled up beside him. Butterflies danced within his stomach as Louis turned off the ignition. He'd had meals with presidents and world leaders but never felt so nervous as he did at the thought of seeing Olivia again.

An older Black woman with salt-and-pepper hair carried a large aluminum foil container. He quickly parked the car and jumped out. The parking lot smelled of car exhaust and wet asphalt.

After locking his door, he hurried up to her. Wonderful smells were coming out of the container.

"Excuse me, ma'am, can I carry that for you?"

She paused next to a bike rack. Seeing him, she took a step backward as if startled. "And who are you?" The woman, who looked in her early seventies, eyed him suspiciously as two teen boys walked by wearing baggy hoodies with baseball caps turned backward.

"Hey, Miss Jan," they both said with a wave.

She faced the young men with a broad smile then turned back and lifted an eyebrow at Louis as if she hadn't heard his offer to carry the food. Louis considered the reasons for the woman's hesitancy. Perhaps she believed he was there to bring her harm or worried he'd leave with the meal.

"I would be happy to carry that inside for you," he repeated louder. His stomach growled. Louis reached toward the large pan of food, but still, she hesitated.

Miss Jan eyed him, looking at his shoes, then at his clothes, and finally resting her gaze on what he hoped was a friendly smile. "Are you selling something, young man? Because we don't have any money."

"Oh no, I'm not. I am here to see Olivia. Olivia Garza. I am . . . a friend, and I saw online that this meeting was open to the public."

"I know Olivia's friends." Then Jan's dark eyes widened. "Did you meet her in Kenya?"

"Yes, actually, I did." He grinned bigger now.

"You sound like you're from Europe."

"Guilty as charged."

Miss Jan pulled her head back slightly, startled. "And you came *here* to see *her?*"

"Yes, I did. I hope that's no problem."

"No problem at all." Miss Jan thrust the pan into his hands. "But we need to get inside quickly."

"Is there a reason for the rush?"

"I'd say so," Miss Jan called over her shoulder, moving toward the door. "She's a runner."

"A runner?" Louis followed Miss Jan inside.

"If Olivia sees you, she may leave." Miss Jan clicked her tongue. "You'd think you were some escaped criminal, given how she evaded my question about if she'd met anyone."

Louis followed the older woman inside, and she pointed to a row of white plastic tables. "Put the food over there, and then we need to talk. I want to know what's happening and why you came to Little Rock to see my Olivia."

The scream of a police siren sounded outside, followed by voices shouting. Miss Jan didn't miss a step. They walked past a sign-in register and moved down a long hall with dingy tile and fluorescent lights overhead. A door on the right was open, but the light was off. It was a preschool classroom.

Along the hall walls, motivational posters hung. "Be the change you want to see in the world," one read. "Whatever your hand finds to do, do it with all your might. Ecclesiastes 9:10," read another. Louis considered what it would be like if such things hung on the wall within their royal residence back home. A smile curled on his lips as he imagined his aunt's reaction to seeing one in the great hall hung under the oil paintings of former kings and queens of Alloria.

Miss Jan led him to the far door, used a key to open it, and turned on a light. She motioned him inside, and after he entered, she shut the door behind him.

"Who are you, and what's going on?" Her words were direct, as was her gaze.

"I am a friend of Olivia's. We met in Kenya."

"Did you meet doing service work?"

"No, on the safari. It was quite lovely. We—"

Miss Jan held up her hand. "And you came all the way here to see a *friend?* Please tell me you're here for a meeting and it worked for you to come by."

She needed to read the headlines more closely.

Louis eyed the woman, trying to determine how to get her to trust him without having to tell her exactly who he was. He swallowed hard, attempting to find the words. Was it just a few weeks ago that he'd discussed oil trade with South America at a cabinet meeting without breaking a sweat? Today the steady gaze of this woman left him wholly flustered.

"I am sorry I showed up like this. I just flew in today and hoped it would be a nice surprise for Olivia. I was in Kenya on holiday when I met Olivia. You know as well as I do that I wouldn't have come to see her if I didn't wish for more than friendship. But for now, that is what we have, and I hope she finds my presence tonight a nice surprise."

At his explanation, a smile widened on Miss Jan's face, and she nodded once. "All right then, I guess you can stay." Then she turned and pointed to a blue plastic bin on one of the shelves. "If you can use your muscles, that will be great. It's our plates and things for tonight's dinner."

Louis reached for the tub, which was lighter than he expected. Back home, plates were carried on silver trays by dozens of servants.

He followed Miss Jan back to the central area. He was halfway down the hall when a woman's laughter sounded. He tilted his head in recognition, and his heart quickened as her voice carried toward him.

"I promise you, even in the Kibera slums, the teachers at the school dressed neatly," Olivia chuckled, her laughter bubbling forth like a joyous melody. "I'm unsure how they could press their shirts and make them so white." Her amusement filled the air, enveloping them in a moment of shared mirth. "I felt like such a slacker when I showed up in my jeans and sweatshirt."

As Louis entered the room, his senses heightened, and a rush of emotions consumed him. His mouth grew dry, and a wave of heat coursed through his chest, spreading like wildfire. His hands tingled with nervousness and anticipation as if every nerve ending within him had been awakened.

Miss Jan, carrying a tray of food, paused beside

a table, and Louis carefully placed the large plastic bin on the floor. He scanned the room until he spotted Olivia, who sat with her back facing him. She was engaged in conversation with a group of teenage girls surrounding her. Their laughter and chatter filled the space, creating an atmosphere of youthful energy and camaraderie.

At that moment, two teens caught sight of Louis and nudged each other, their excitement palpable. One of them couldn't contain her enthusiasm and called out, "Is that Channing Tatum?" The words hung in the air, a mix of curiosity and awe.

Louis couldn't help but smile, his heart fluttering at the unexpected comparison. He raised his hand in a friendly wave, acknowledging their excitement. With cautious steps, he moved forward, anticipation swirling within him. However, as Olivia's back straightened, a sudden tension filled the air, casting a shadow over his excitement.

"I'm not Channing," Louis began, his voice gentle and warm, hoping to ease the unexpected tension. "But that's quite a compliment. My name is—"

"Louis," Olivia interrupted her voice sharp and tinged with anger. Her words struck him like a sudden gust of wind, knocking the air out of his lungs. His heart sank, heavy with the weight of doubt and uncertainty. Had he just made a terrible mistake? The warmth that had filled his chest moments ago now turned icy, spreading a chill through his veins.

Louis searched Olivia's face for a glimpse of understanding, a flicker of forgiveness. All he found was a mask of confusion and hurt. He longed to explain himself, to bridge the divide that had unexpectedly formed between them. Words failed him, and he stood there, hushed by the realization that he might have jeopardized something precious.

As the room fell into a heavy silence, the unspoken emotions between Louis and Olivia hung in the air like an unanswered question. The promise of connection and the hope of building something meaningful now trembled on a delicate thread—their future uncertain.

CHAPTER EIGHTEEN

The European accent was just as swoon worthy as Olivia remembered. Without thinking, she rose and turned. "Louis. What are you doing here?" She hadn't meant her voice to sound so harsh, but the way Louis's smile faded drew attention to the sharp tone of her voice.

Her gaze darted around the meeting room, settling on the open door, expecting the flash of cameras and the shouting of paparazzi. It was bad enough that only a few hours ago, the media had discovered her first name and the town where she used to live, posting it online. Olivia hoped it would stop at that. Thankfully, Miss Jan and her friends in Little Rock did not keep up media tabloids.

Even though she had only told a few people about her documentary, numerous people had worked on the project. If anyone let it slip that the person behind the documentary was the same one photographed with Prince Louis, then the last year of her work would come to nothing. Olivia wanted the slow path to forgiving her mother to be what drew viewers so that perhaps they, too, could learn to forgive. The wrong type of media attention could make it a spectacle, not a journey to self-discovery.

Olivia took in Louis's button-up shirt and slacks. Rather than dress shoes, red and white Converse tennis shoes covered his feet. She hid a smile. For his effort to dress down, she had to give him an A.

When he walked toward her, though, there was nothing casual about him. Louis still had a presence she'd admired, as if he had command of the room. "You can take the prince out of the castle, but you can't take the castle out of the prince," she mumbled.

"What did you say?" one of the teen girls, Leandra, said with a toss of her black braids.

"Oh, nothing." Olivia clasped her hands before her, telling herself to be calm and reminding herself she *was* mad at him for deceiving her. But he'd come all this way—halfway around the world—to see her. Didn't that count for something?

While a few volunteers had messaged her, seeing photos of her with Louis, none of the teens had figured it out. Olivia breathed a sigh of relief that none of the girls in her group paid much attention to national newspapers or magazines. They knew she'd met someone handsome and charming in Africa, but she'd made all the volunteers promise not to share precisely who the stranger was. If it had been posted on TikTok, Olivia's day out with a prince would have been discovered in less than a minute.

Olivia forced a smile, trying to act as if Louis's arrival hadn't wholly uprooted her world. She could never let these teens in on how much his presence rattled her, or she'd never hear the end of it.

Louis paused before her, a twinkle in his eyes.

"What did you say? Somethin' about a castle?" Leandra repeated.

Olivia crossed her arms over her chest and attempted to act annoyed that he'd come all this way. At the sight of his smile, which highlighted both dimples, it was a lost cause.

"I said, 'What a surprise,' but I should say, 'Welcome to Little Rock.' What was it, Louis? You didn't see enough of the wildlife? You had to check out my wild teens?" she joked.

The young women around her broke out into animal sounds as if playing along. Trinity was the loudest, with the sound of a monkey calling out.

Louis nodded and waved to the young women. Olivia was pretty sure she saw Leandra swoon.

"I was intrigued," he said. "After hearing about your program and all the wonderful choices these teens are making, I had to see it myself."

He approached and reached out a hand to the young woman closest to him. "Hello, my name is Louis. Happy to make your acquaintance."

Trinity reached out her hand. Louis took it in his. He slowly lifted it to his lips, softly kissing

246

her dark skin. A loud howl rose from the other girls, and in a moment Olivia's suppressed attraction resurfaced.

Her heart flitted like a butterfly in a whirlwind of emotions. Louis's treatment of her girls tugged at her heartstrings. She couldn't deny the gentle tide of care and admiration.

Just as quickly, doubt entered her mind. Olivia's elation faded, leaving a bittersweet ache. Was this charming display real or a ploy to woo her?

Olivia shook her head as if attempting to toss away the warm feelings, but her heart remained entangled in his web of emotions. She couldn't let him draw her in so quickly. She couldn't be so easily deceived.

Did Louis think his princely gestures would easily win her heart? He didn't realize he had ignited a flame that both warmed and frightened her.

"Will you kiss my hand too?" Leandra called out.

Then, as if he greeted a row of princesses who'd just arrived at a ball, Louis went down the line and kissed each hand. You'd think they'd just been kissed by their idol, rapper Travis Scott, by all the giggles and shrill laughs going on.

Hearing the commotion, Miss Jan approached. "I don't know what's happening here, but dinner's getting cold. Olivia, will you pray?"

Olivia shifted, glancing at Louis. A pleased smile lifted his lips as he lowered his head. Heat rose to her cheeks, and Olivia felt like a frog was caught in her throat. Every head was lowered, but Miss Jan glanced up and caught her eye. Some of the teens began to snicker.

"Olivia?" Miss Jan asked.

"Oh, yes, of course." She said a quick prayer, and as soon as the amen was out of her mouth, the young women rushed to the table and lined up.

"Chicken spaghetti, salad, and brownies. There's plenty for everyone," Miss Jan called after them. "Don't be shy."

A fluttery feeling filled her stomach with Louis standing beside her, but Olivia had to eat something. She'd cleaned out most of her food before leaving for Africa, and she hadn't been shopping yet, so she'd been living on cups of soup and stale crackers for days.

"Hungry?" she asked Louis as the line started to dwindle. He stood beside her, eyes wide, taking it all in.

"Famished." Louis rubbed his stomach as if coming out of a trance. "That smells quite delightful. I've always wanted to try real, American fare." He followed her to the end of the line.

Olivia's laughter filled the air. "Real, American fare. You've got that right." Her arm extended, encompassing the humble surroundings of the inner-city community center. "You can't get more American than eating on paper plates."

With a graceful gesture, Olivia signaled for Louis to go ahead and join the line. Her heart skipped a beat as he moved forward, his presence electrifying the air around them. Every step he took stirred emotions within her that she had tried to keep at bay.

Louis, eager to experience the unfamiliar, scooped up a serving of chicken spaghetti and plopped it onto his plate. The plate tilted precariously, threatening to send the contents sliding off. Panic flashed across his face, and with quick reflexes, he swiftly set down the serving spoon and rescued the plate from disaster. The relief over him was tangible, as if a small victory had been won.

Olivia couldn't help but chuckle, her laughter a mixture of fondness and lightheartedness. "Please tell me this isn't the first time you've used a paper plate," she quipped, a glimmer of teasing in her eyes. Her defense wavered in the presence of his endearing innocence. *He's here.* The reality sank in like a warm embrace. *Louis is here.*

A sheepish smile played on Louis's lips. "This is indeed a first."

She smiled at that confession. Louis's unfamiliarity with paper plates stirred an unexpected warmth in his willingness to leave his gilded cage. To be honest, to be vulnerable, and to be here with her.

The fragile thread that had connected them so unexpectedly now trembled with the weight of uncharted possibilities. As their eyes locked, a silent understanding passed between them. Louis was doing this for her—to show Olivia she was worth pursuing, even in this foreign place.

"I wish I could tell you otherwise, but this experience is new. I cannot wait to tell my dear aunt about it. She's always wanted to come to the States. She sent me with her regards."

Olivia's eyebrows lifted—*Princess Regina of Alloria.* Even though Olivia told herself not to, she had looked up some things about Alloria and its royal line. *Sister of King Alfonso, who's been on the throne for nearly twenty-five years. Prince Louis, oldest child and heir.* Louis also had a younger sister.

Trinity, who stood beside Louis in line, eyed him and wrinkled her nose. "But you eat at people's houses, don't you? Or at graduations? What about barbecues? Haven't you ever been at an event and been handed a piece of cake on a paper plate?"

Louis cast Trinity a playful smile. "My father's in government—or rather international relations. Even though I've traveled the world, the opportunity to eat from a paper plate hasn't presented itself before today."

"Or maybe it's because your father wanted to make sure no one in those places was trying to poison you." Trinity's dark eyes widened. "I saw that in a movie once."

"And you're not afraid to eat our food?" Leandra shot Miss Jan a playful look. "Maybe Miss Jan is a spy against . . . where did you say you came from again?" Leandra sidled up to Louis.

"I didn't say, but it's a small country called Alloria, and I don't fear Miss Jan or anyone else here. And it is quite amusing that this *is* my first time eating on a paper plate at an event."

"My, aren't we special then?" Miss Jan gave a low whistle as she placed a piece of garlic bread on his chicken spaghetti. "And don't forget to get a napkin before you sit. You'll be extra excited. They're paper too."

CHAPTER NINETEEN

By the time dinner concluded, eighteen teen-age girls sat around the long plastic tables. Their usual boisterous banter and loud jokes were replaced by a quieter, more reserved demeanor, undoubtedly due to Louis's presence.

Louis approached Olivia with a sheepish look as they cleaned up after dinner. Miss Jan hurried over without hesitation to ensure she was in on whatever Louis had to say.

"It often takes me longer to 'get a clue,' as the young people like to say." Louis quirked his eyebrow. "But is this meeting only for young women and women leadership?"

Olivia held back her smile. She could not allow him to charm her. "First, I don't know any young people who still use 'get a clue.' At least in our country. Second, yes, usually. But sometimes we have male speakers—"

"But don't think you're going anywhere. It's okay that you stay." Miss Jan pointed and wagged her finger. "I insist. I want to talk with you, young man." She leveled her gaze. "If that's all right."

"Yes, of course." Louis grasped his hands behind his back and rocked back on his feet and forward again. Olivia could tell he was trying to be nonchalant, but she wasn't fooled. He was nervous. And by the severe look on Miss Jan's face, she wouldn't let him off easily.

A wide smile quickly followed Miss Jan's stern look. "Don't you worry, son. I won't bite. But before we talk, we have a game to play."

Louis helped Olivia and Miss Jan rearrange the tables to create a bigger space for the evening game Miss Jan had prepared. As Olivia stacked chairs to get them out of the way, she tried to grasp that Louis was here.

What had brought him all this way? Earlier, during their conversation about last-minute details, Miss Jan had sensed a change in Olivia and inquired if she'd met someone. Olivia had opened up about her moments with Louis in Africa. While Miss Jan expressed her reservations about Louis not being entirely honest at their first meeting, she hadn't entirely written him off either. Of course, Olivia hadn't admitted to her friend that Louis was a prince.

"There's a reason why people do what they do," Miss Jan had said over the phone. "And from what you've told me, it seems like that poor man has had his heart broken more than once. Worse than that, his hurting soul is displayed to the world. If I faced that, I'd also want to hide that part of my life. But of course, that's just me talking."

As she watched him scoot tables out of the way,

the walls around Olivia's heart lowered. Could he have done something different, better, than hiding the truth of who he was? Yes. But Olivia could have done the same. *He doesn't know the whole me, either.* Most people were unaware of all the pain and loss she had inside. There were things she hadn't even told Miss Jan during the four years they'd worked together. Then there was the documentary. Few people knew about that, especially that Olivia was the creator, the voyager, and the voice behind *In My Mother's Steps.*

"Okay, everyone!" Miss Jan clapped her hands. "I need you all to line up into two rows, ten in each. Olivia, I want you at the head of the first line. Trinity, can you be at the front of the second?"

Trinity nodded. Even though she was petite like Olivia, she attempted to stand tall, walking as if she owned the place. Yet, as Olivia looked closer, something seemed different about Trinity. While she displayed the same outgoing, spunky attitude, Trinity was paler than usual, and she had picked at her dinner.

Olivia started a line, and Louis was the first in her line, followed by eight more teen girls.

The others moved to make a second line. "We ain't gonna do no running, are we, Miss Jan?" Trinity placed a hand over her stomach. "That chicken spaghetti ain't sitting so well."

"No running, Trinity. You barely have to move in this game." Miss Jan moved to one of the tables where a pump of hand sanitizer sat. She walked down the line squirting the liquid into each person's hands. Everyone rubbed in the sanitizer, and Miss Jan nodded, satisfied.

"We're going to play Electric Wire. Now, I need everyone to grasp hands." Miss Jan moved to the end of each line and placed a dollar bill on the ground. "This is the game. When I say go, Olivia and Trinity will start by squeezing the hand of the person beside them. We must see which team goes the fastest and picks up the dollar first." Miss Jan pulled more dollars out of her pocket. "If you're on the fastest team, you'll get to pocket all this money. There are a few bucks for each of the winners. You can buy a Coke or somethin' later."

Louis stretched out his hand to her. "Come on, Olivia. We have to do this. I need my first big win in America, yes?"

She placed her hand in his, and electricity shot up her arm. *Miss Jan, did you have to pick this of all games?* The warmth and softness of his hand melted the walls around her heart a little more.

Olivia's heartbeat quickened. His eyes fixed on hers. She could be swallowed up into the blue if he let her. He offered the softest smile and stroked the back of her hand with his thumb.

Fireworks, and it wasn't even close to the Fourth of July.

It wasn't until squeals erupted around them that Olivia realized that Miss Jan had shouted, "Go!" She had missed it.

Olivia gasped. She squeezed Louis's hand quickly, but it was too late. By the time he squeezed the hand of the young woman standing next to him, the other team had already managed to squeeze hands down the line and pick up the dollar.

Moans erupted from those on Olivia's team while squeals and laughter sounded from the winners. Miss Jan's laughter carried over both groups as she passed out dollar bills to the winners.

"I just knew I'd see sparks flying in this game," Miss Jan called. "I guess that's why they call it electricity."

Heat rose to Olivia's cheeks, and she attempted to release Louis's hand, but he held on. She looked at him and saw both humor and care in his gaze.

"I'm sorry I made us lose. I'm even more sorry that I didn't confess the whole truth to you when we were in Africa. Will you forgive me, Olivia?"

"Well, let's talk about that later, all right?" She pulled her hand from his. "This is not the time. Not the place."

Louis nodded, then placed his hand on her

shoulder and gave it a gentle squeeze. Sparks shot from his fingertips, racing down her arms and spine. Warmth filled Olivia, followed by anger. Nineteen sets of eyes were on them, and the noise in the room stilled as all the young women—and Miss Jan—watched their interaction.

Please, stop touching me, she wanted to say. She didn't like the attention, the spotlight. Yet, at the same time, the words didn't come. Olivia enjoyed the tenderness of his touch and the fact he'd come all this way to see her.

"Why don't we get on with the next part of the night?" Olivia finally said, forcing a smile and taking a step back. Then, as if everything she and Miss Jan had planned for this meeting had been erased, Olivia had no idea what was next. She looked at Miss Jan and lifted her eyebrows. "And I must still be dealing with jet lag because I have no idea what is coming up." She circled her head with her hand. "It's gone, just gone."

More laughter and hoots filled the room, and a tall young woman, Elly, with white-blonde hair, stepped closer. "I don't think it's the jet lag that has you like this, Miss Olivia. Look at you. I've never seen your cheeks so pink."

"All right, let's not give Olivia a hard time." Miss Jan moved to her purse and tote bag that she'd set on one of the tables. "Tonight, we will write thank-you notes to those who run the Community Center. They're letting us meet here for a few months until we can figure out something else—and at no charge. Isn't that nice?"

Miss Jan pulled a box of thank-you cards from the tote bag. "Olivia, why don't you and the ladies sit here and write the cards?" She cleared her throat and looked at Louis. "I will use this opportunity to talk to your young man."

My young man? Olivia wanted to argue—to tell Miss Jan that he was just a friend—someone she'd met and had never planned on seeing again. But the words didn't emerge.

Instead, she simply nodded and motioned to the young women. "Let's set up two tables end to end. Writing thank you cards is a nice idea, and this is a skill you'll have for life." Yet even as she said those words, she could sense Louis's attention. Even though she wasn't looking at him, she knew he was watching, smiling. As Olivia sat, she rubbed away the goose bumps that grew on her arms, hoping she could teach the teens how to write a thank you card. Her stomach filled with butterflies, and she dared to let down even more of her guard.

Louis came for me . . .

He really came.

Louis approached the table and pulled out the folding chair, sitting across from the older woman.

Miss Jan lifted her chin and peered at him through the bottom half of her glasses. "Did

258

you believe you could just come here and sweep Olivia off her feet?"

Well, she's not wasting any time. He sat up straighter, hoping to be clear minded enough to gain her approval. It mattered, and they both knew it.

"No, ma'am. If I could sweep Olivia off her feet that easily, she wouldn't be the woman I thought she was."

Miss Jan narrowed her eyes. "She's important to us. We need her."

"Yes, and I have plans to stay a while."

"Is that possible?" Miss Jan scratched her temple. "Don't you have work wherever you come from?"

"I do have work, and I plan to do it virtually. I will have meetings with staff, uh, employees. There's a big event coming, and they desire my input, although I have no doubt they would do well handling everything without me."

"And you care about Olivia? Really care?"

Louis rested his elbows on the table, folded his hands, and leaned forward. How could he share his heart without sounding like a fool? After all, they'd only spent one day together. One perfect, beautiful day. He swallowed the emotion building in his throat. "I know it seems like a crazy idea to come all this way to spend more time with a woman I just met once. But don't you know that Olivia isn't like anyone else?"

Miss Jan patted the place over her heart. "I hold her right here. You know you're right."

Tapping his chest with two fingers, Louis nodded. "I want to get to know her better. I didn't do things right last time. I wasn't truthful. I'd like to try again." He rubbed his chin, feeling his eyebrows fold in. "Do you think she'll let me?"

"She's a smart girl, but she also carries a lot of pain. She hasn't told me everything, but I know some things . . ." Miss Jan's voice trailed off. "It's easier for her to push away than let in someone. I'm hoping she won't knock you to the curb. We'll both have to see, won't we?" Miss Jan reached forward and patted his hand. "I have hope. Don't you be afraid to hope too."

Warmth filled his chest as he looked into this woman's dark-eyed gaze. She spoke with such confidence and compassion. He wondered if he'd ever get to where he felt that comfortable in his skin.

"I'm willing to hope. But I have to admit I have a feeling that Olivia's not the only one who I have to win over. Those young women have been watching me all night. I wonder if they'll give me a thumbs up or down."

Miss Jan's gaze flickered between him and the teens writing thank-you cards. He respected how she guided them to be kind and thankful despite the likelihood that they witnessed violence and crime daily.

"I think thumbs up, except for a few." She shrugged. "But some of those ladies don't trust most men." She opened her mouth as if she wanted to say more, then closed it again. "I won't tell their stories, but I'm sure you understand."

He nodded. Would he ever have the chance to hear those stories unfiltered? While he knew the plight of the less fortunate, he rarely got a real-life glimpse like this. Even when he'd visited lower-income areas before, local organizations often did their best to spiff things up. Not to mention bodyguards always surrounded him.

As eye-opening as it was to drive into this area and spend time with these young women, there was still much to see and understand. He knew Olivia could tell him more.

The idea excited him. He clasped his hands on his lap, forcing himself to sit still, reminding himself that he and Olivia would have more time to talk. And he hoped he'd have time to get to know some of the young women better too. Looking at them, he wished he could find a solution. To expand their view of the world. To help them rise and thrive in their unique ways.

"They are wonderful young ladies. There's so much personality in this room," he commented.

Miss Jan chuckled. "That's a kind way to say it. This is a hard place to grow up in. Each has struggles, but we love them, you know?"

He thought about Miss Jan's words. "It must

be hard living in this type of area. Have you ever considered finding good boarding schools to attend so they can get out of this environment?"

Miss Jan shook her head. "That would take a lot of schools—and funds, which we don't have—and I'm not certain it would help. As depressing as things look to us, this is their community. More than that, Jesus tells us in Mark, chapter seven, that it's not what's on the outside that's the problem. It's inside."

From the look in her eyes, Louis sensed she had more to share. He sat patiently, nodding in encouragement. "Go on."

"No matter where they go, they'll have themselves." Miss Jan pointed to her chest. "Wherever I go, I have myself, too." She chuckled. "That's been a problem at times."

The laughter of the teens beside them rose, and Miss Jan waited for it to fade before she went on. "It won't help if we assist them in getting into a better environment if they still have their ol' sin problem going with them. Instead, we do better work when we help them make positive changes from the inside out, which only happen with Jesus. Then wherever they go, there He is."

He nodded slowly, processing her words. Then his fingers brushed against the stubble on his chin. "I needed to hear that."

They finished the thank-you cards, and a cacophony of moving chairs, shuffling bodies, and hushed murmurs rose around Louis. He glanced over and saw Olivia's eyes on his. Even in the middle of the noisy moment, the soothing balm of Miss Jan's words found a home in the depths of his soul.

Louis smiled, hoping to ease the delicate furrows of Olivia's brow. The bright eyes he'd witnessed in Kenya were now clouded with worry. He yearned to cup her face in his hands and ease away her fears, telling her that they'd figure it all out. Miss Jan was right. They needed to remember that any hope of change had to start from the inside out. And everything inside Louis told him that God had brought Olivia into his life for a reason.

His gaze returned to Miss Jan, a beacon of strength and grace—her laughter a testament to a life of gusto. A small smile began to unfurl on her lips, lifting her smooth, dark cheeks. The sight brought a warmth to his heart that he couldn't quite explain.

"I don't *think*. I *know* I needed to hear that." Louis's voice quivered, and he cleared his throat.

Miss Jan pointed her finger heavenwards, reminding him of his childhood governess. Yet this woman spoke to him not as a prince or child needing guidance but as a fellow sojourner in the life of faith. Miss Jan was a few steps ahead.

"I just say what I feel my Father God is stirring in my heart," she confessed.

A sense of belonging washed over him, the feeling of being seen as just Louis—not a prince or future king, but a man seeking connection and authenticity. He didn't know if Miss Jan was aware of his royal lineage. She didn't act like it. Still, he felt in his bones that she would scold him, whip his ego into submission if he ever strayed from the path of righteousness— regardless of his royal title.

Louis admired that and respected it. He yearned for more of that honesty, that candor he rarely encountered within the high walls of his palace. The number of times he had experienced such sincerity could be counted on one hand. This time with Miss Jan was a precious gem to be treasured.

Louis looked back at Olivia, a silent vow passing between them. He was not just a royal figure but a man open to understanding, growth, and, most importantly, truth. And in the company of Olivia and Miss Jan, he was finding the space to be just that.

So much of his life—and the lives of those around him—were like golden jeweled goblets. They appeared shiny outside, yet no one dared to reveal the inner workings. It's as if everyone he knew walked around with their goblets held high, attempting to impress others while most likely hurting from poisons hidden within. How freeing it would be to live for a time just being himself and allowing unguarded exchanges like this to happen. To have intimate and essential conversations without others worrying that their opinions could have royal repercussions.

Amid the low hum of conversation and the clatter of the tubs of dinner supplies being packed up, a subtle signal from one of the teenagers drew their attention. A young woman with reddish curls raised her hand and waved it. A furtive glance passed between her and Miss Jan.

With an air of quiet grace, Miss Jan began to rise, her hand bracing the white plastic table. Her chair scraped gently on the floor, signaling a peaceful end to the conversation.

Louis watched her, struck by the respect and attention she commanded without uttering a single word. Slowly, he mirrored Miss Jan, pushing back his chair.

"Thank you for this." He placed a hand over his heart and tipped his head toward her.

"I'm glad you're here, but don't expect it to be easy. Any of it." Miss Jan shook her head. "God tells us to love one another, and when times get hard, fall back to that. Ask God to show you what love is at that moment, then do it. As hard as it is, do it. Jesus will take care of the rest." Then with one more pat on Louis's hand, Miss Jan straightened.

A boulder grew in the pit of Louis's stomach. Miss Jan was right. This was going to take a lot of work. Getting Olivia to trust him would be the first step. Would she give him a second chance? He fiddled with the top button of his shirt. "To think how to love another, in any situation, are wise words. I will take them to heart. Thank you."

With one last smile, Miss Jan walked over to the table of girls to dismiss them and to pray. Louis sat once again and shot up his desperate prayer. *I'm out of my league here. My title and charm won't help. Lord, guide the real me to touch the real her—deep in our hearts and souls where it counts.*

Louis paused. Words he didn't want to add to his prayer were stirring in his mind and calling to be let free. He released them despite the pain coursing through his heart. *Bring something good out of this—out of us—even if I don't get the girl in the end.*

An ache filled him at the thought of walking away without the opportunity to see if something could come out of their relationship. *And help me not give up too quickly, no matter how my ego is crushed.*

He thought of his aunt, and her lost love. He'd give it his all, even if his heart were broken. He couldn't imagine living decades with thoughts of, "What if?"

And as Olivia's eyes met him from across the room yet again—filled with fear and hope—

peace settled over him. Being here was worth it. Olivia was worth it.

* * * * *

Buchenwald Concentration Camp
Date Unknown

I thought I had seen true horror during the Great War when I traveled to the war hospitals with my mother. To see death at such a young age caused me to look to our Lord, for indeed, there had to be a good heaven for such suffering souls. The nurses and doctors fought against death in the hospitals, but at Buchenwald, death has full reign. Death haunts. Death stalks. Yet the not knowing haunts me even more.

I do not know if I will ever see my husband or children again. Perhaps they are already lost. I am not confident about which would be worse—knowing that their lives were cut short or seeing that they face such fearful times without me holding them close. What if I had stayed? Would we all be safe now? Was my act of sacrifice for nothing?

Lord, where are you in all this? Where?

* * * * *

CHAPTER TWENTY

Little Rock, Arkansas
Present Day

Olivia sat cross-legged on her sofa as the warm sun streamed in, falling on the piles of notes and paperwork on the coffee table before her. A mug of cold coffee also sat on the table next to the vanilla-bean candle she'd lit to hide the stench of the dumpster beside her apartment complex. *Just like where Louis lives, I'm sure.* She smirked.

Olivia glanced at the clock, unsure why she agreed to meet him for lunch. When he'd asked her for a lunch date after the meeting, she'd put him off for a few days, making the excuse of getting caught up on work. She'd expected Louis to get tired of waiting and leave. In fact, for the last three days, every time she received a text notification, she was confident it would be a message from him alerting her that he'd flown back to Alloria. Instead, at 8:00 a.m., she'd received a text stating that he looked forward to seeing her today.

Even though Olivia tried to get work done, it was useless. She'd also tried contacting Sarah-Grace for an update about their fundraising banquet. How long were honeymoons supposed to last? Too long for Olivia's peace of mind.

But even that wasn't the main thing she thought of. She couldn't reconcile that the amazing man she'd met—who turned out to be a monarch apparent, the heir—had come all this way to spend time with her. It just didn't make sense.

The hours ticked by until noon, and her emotions swayed between excitement and dread. Olivia knew she'd have to tell Louis that being more than friends wouldn't work. His role and lifestyle went against everything she believed in. He lived a privileged life in the spotlight, and she preferred to be behind the scenes. The idea of facing paparazzi anytime, day or night, the media chronicling every part of her comings and goings, gossip columnists digging into her past—it was her worst nightmare.

As Olivia considered that, the final episode of her documentary came to mind, and with it came a wave of conflicting emotions. She'd started this journey to reveal her true identity, but now doubts gnawed at her.

She'd met Louis unexpectedly, but the more time she spent with him, the more she realized that maybe the purpose of their meeting was to stop her from revealing herself. It would garner attention if she went ahead with the original plan and revealed her identity in the documentary. But it would be fleeting attention focused solely on her and her past. Was that what she truly wanted?

As she thought about it, another idea took shape. She could film the final episode, completing the journey she had embarked upon. Still, instead of revealing herself, she could tell her audience that she had changed her mind. By staying hidden, viewers would have the chance to see themselves in the story. They could delve into their problematic pasts, find strength and inspiration, and connect with the universal themes her documentary sought to explore.

Olivia scribbled notes, her pen dancing across the paper. She liked the idea of giving others the space to reflect and to find themselves within her story. It would be a gift to her viewers that went beyond her journey. By staying true to the core message of her documentary, she could help others find solace and hope in their own lives.

At that moment, Olivia knew what she had to do. With renewed determination, she set aside her original plans. She embraced the idea of staying hidden, allowing her documentary to speak for itself.

As Olivia prepared the script for the final episode, a sense of peace settled over her. After jotting down a rough draft, Olivia opened her laptop to see if Liz had sent her any updates about the journal or her princess. She'd just opened the email program when her phone rang. Rebecca's name flashed on the caller ID.

Although they'd briefly chatted over the last few days, Olivia had always made an excuse to get off the phone. She'd yet to tell Rebecca that Louis had come or that she'd put off seeing him. Olivia knew she'd get tongue-lashing if Rebecca found out.

Olivia had questions about Louis's motivation for coming to see her, and until she knew the truth, she wouldn't let her heart open a crack. Was he here for her, or did he just like the idea of her? Someone outside his social rank. Someone new and exciting.

"Hello?" Olivia answered the phone, attempting to make her voice sound light.

"I know you're busy trying to catch up in life, but I can't stop thinking about it."

Oh no, here we go. She will tell me how I should have been nicer to the prince.

"About?"

"Has your aunt told you any more about the woman who wrote the journals?" Rebecca's words rushed out as if she were afraid Olivia would have another excuse as to why she couldn't talk.

Olivia breathed out a sigh of relief. "I was just opening my email to check. Liz told me she would send me more information once they finished the translation. From a note she sent yesterday, it seems some people question whether these are the princess's words. They are looking at handwriting samples, although my aunt believes that may not help much. The writing is small and fills every inch of the page. The tiny writing could have a factor in the formation of letters."

"You're talking as if you know more about her than what your aunt has told you."

Olivia bit her lower lip. Should she confess that her curiosity had gotten the best of her? Even though Olivia hadn't wanted to reveal any details, they were too easy to find. Putting "princess, concentration camp, WWII" into her search engine yielded only one result. Olivia knew this had to be her: *Alessandra Appiani, Princess of Italy.*

"A princess inside a concentration camp isn't something one hears about daily. A quick online search can pull up some interesting facts."

"And what did you find? I want to understand how this isn't a story everyone knows. Can you imagine Kate Middleton put into a situation like that?"

Olivia glanced at her watch again, seeing that she only had fifteen minutes until Louis would arrive to pick her up. Her stomach flipped, and she rose and moved to her bathroom to do something with her hair.

"You can't compare Princess Alessandra with Kate Middleton. Alessandra's father was a private person. He shunned most publicity. He was a figurehead but avoided interfering with the government. The king let Mussolini take over, appearing in public only when not given a choice."

"Alessandra's father was king, but he let someone else run his country?"

Olivia set her phone on the counter and put it on speakerphone. "I have to admit I fell down the rabbit hole of research. Even though everyone knows about Hitler, few know about Mussolini. I had no idea he was a journalist and newspaper editor before he founded the Fascist party in Italy."

"Words have power," Rebecca quipped.

Olivia brushed out her hair, then applied mascara and a tinted lip gloss, calling it good. "Yes, well, as much as I'd love to tell you how Mussolini ordered his men to kill everyone who opposed him, I have a lunch thing I must run to."

"Okay, enjoy your lunch, but call me tonight. I have a feeling you're hiding something from me."

"Me, hiding something?" Olivia chuckled. "But, yes, I'll call you tonight."

When she hung up her phone, the reality of what was happening next hit her. She'd be seeing Louis in just a few minutes. Part of her wanted to cancel, but the other part wanted to see him again despite her long, mental list of why things wouldn't work. Even though so much had gone wrong in her life, their one day in Kenya had proven that good could still happen. She just hoped she could stand firm against the prince's charms.

Trying to ignore the butterflies dancing in her stomach, Olivia grabbed her purse. She stepped onto the landing between apartments, locking her front door behind her. She lived on the second floor of a complex that had seen better days—not that it had ever been fancy.

Rebecca had insisted that Olivia find a better place in a safer part of town, but Olivia liked it here. A few young women in their support group lived in the same building. She'd even gotten involved with a kids' after-school program, helping a few times a month. Miss Jan agreed that her connection with the younger kids would make them more willing to join the Character Club when they became teens.

When a white SUV pulled into the parking lot, Olivia had just reached the bottom step. Gleaming in the sunlight and new to the lot, the vehicle undoubtedly belonged to Louis, who'd insisted on picking her up. Even though she couldn't see clearly into the tinted windows, she waved and watched as it parked. As soon as the vehicle turned off, Louis stepped out. His blond hair had been recently trimmed, and he wore khaki slacks and a white buttoned-up shirt. One of his arms held something behind his back, and he waved with the other, striding up and stopping before her.

For days Olivia had told herself she'd use this lunch to explain why she couldn't be involved with someone like him, but as he stood before her, she found herself lost in the depths of his blue eyes. He was so handsome, kind, and thoughtful. Her heart turned to Jell-O in her chest.

"Hey," she managed to say and then cringed as an image of her mother came to mind, memories of her flirting with her newest mark. At least, her mother had considered them her marks. Ultimately, her mother always ended up used and tossed to the side. Olivia straightened her shoulders and placed her hands on her hips as she gazed at him. "I could have driven myself, you know." She pointed to the vehicle. "Nice ride."

His face fell slightly at her response, but the smile remained. "At least the steering wheel is on the right side, unlike when I visit London."

He motioned to the SUV and then moved ahead to open the door for her. His shirt sleeves were rolled up, and the veins and wiry muscles inside his arms popped with distinction. She remembered the strength of his body sup-porting her as she leaned against him in the van on the safari. She'd allowed herself to be pulled in by his charisma then. *Stay strong, Olivia.*

As they left the apartment complex, he drove

them toward Interstate 30, away from the inner city. She could have guessed that. If Louis had wanted to find the classy restaurants, they would not have been in this part of town.

"How has work been going?" His smile brightened as he guided the SUV onto the highway.

"Good, I guess. I've gotten some things done." She shrugged. "I was just rethinking some of my plans."

Olivia bit her lip, and for the briefest moment, she considered telling Louis about the documentary. Maybe it would make it easier to explain why they couldn't date—why she needed to stay out of the spotlight.

"Miss Jan told me the other night that when it comes to change, we must look at our hearts even more than our circumstances. If our heart is focused on God, He will be there no matter what changes come."

"That sounds like something she'd say." Olivia sighed. "And she's right, of course."

A stirring within caught Olivia by surprise. She'd been so sure things would not work with Louis that she realized she hadn't thought to pray about it. Or had she?

Before leaving for Kenya, she and Rebecca had prayed over the phone more than once. They prayed for divine appointments. They'd prayed that God would show them who to love, who to serve, and who to pray for. Promise was an obvious answer to that prayer, but could Louis be too?

Lord, did you bring Louis into my life so that I can care and pray for him? She imagined back in Alloria that many people could have ulterior motives for friendship. Could God have put Louis into her life so she could show him God's love? Hope alighted in Olivia's heart at that thought.

She watched him drive with what she hoped was concealed interest—the way one arm relaxed on the armrest, the fingers of his other hand gripping the steering wheel, the firm profile. She saw it now—from this angle, he did resemble Channing Tatum. She smiled when she remembered when they drove to the gates of Masai Mara.

"Inside joke?" He glanced over at her.

She pressed her lips tight, attempting to hide her smile. "It's not a joke. I remember how you wore that hat and those glasses in the van. Now I know why. You didn't want to be recognized."

"Not that it mattered. Word still got out."

"Does it always?"

"Always what?"

"Get out?"

He pointed to the glove box. "Truthfully, my glasses and hat are in there. I'm less likely to be recognized here than in Kenya. That lodge became a second home, especially after . . . a great loss in our family."

She nodded, wondering if she should ask more

about his family's loss then deciding against it. She had to remind herself not to get too close to Louis. It would be better for her to keep everything on a surface level. "I'm so sorry," she managed to say.

"Thank you, Olivia. I appreciate that. I'd love to share more at another time if you'd like, but for now, I must take you to the best taco spot."

"Tacos?"

His face brightened, and golden hair fell across his forehead. "It's been my mission. Tacos are one of my favorite foods, and they aren't done well where I live. I've tried four places here in Little Rock."

"Four places? In just a few days?" She couldn't help but laugh.

He shrugged. "I told you, I like tacos. But . . ." He let his voice trail off. "I hope you don't mind. The best ones, well, they sell them out of a food truck. It is near Riverfront Park. We can eat at one of those outdoor tables and maybe walk along the river."

"I won't mind. That sounds perfect." Brick by brick, the wall she'd erected around her heart crumbled. She couldn't think of a more perfect date if she tried.

They found a place to park in downtown Little Rock. Olivia always loved the historic brick buildings, quaint cafés, and yellow trolleys that moved up and down the streets with the ring of a bell. Louis led her to a taco truck, which she'd never noticed. He suggested they order the steak street tacos with onions and cilantro. He also ordered a side of chips and queso to share.

After a prayer of thanks for their meal, Olivia took a bite. Dozens of flavors burst in her mouth. The meat had the perfect spice and homemade corn tortillas. The spicy taco sauce added just the right punch, and the fresh onions and cilantro added even more flavor.

Olivia dabbed her mouth with a napkin. "You were right. These are amazing. How did you find this place?"

"I asked an older lady at the grocery store. I could tell by the ingredients in her cart she was making homemade Mexican food. Since I thought it too forward to invite myself to dinner, I asked where to go for the best tacos. She recommended this place, and I'm glad she did."

They finished the rest of their meal in near silence, simply enjoying the food and each other's presence. After eating, Louis threw away all their trash, pulled two small white packages from his front pants pocket, and handed one to her.

"A wet wipe. Brilliant." She grinned. "You thought of everything."

"Nothing but the best for you." He winked, sending electricity racing through her limbs.

With a wave of his hand, Louis motioned to the

Riverwalk parallel to the Arkansas River. "Care to join me?"

"I'd be glad to join you, sir," she said, rising then falling into step beside him.

As they walked, Louis's fingers brushed against hers. She thought it had been an accident until his hand moved closer, grasping hers. They walked hand-in-hand, watching a lone barge move down the Arkansas River and listening to the thump, thump, thump of the vehicles going over the bridge overhead.

They talked about Arkansas, and she shared how she'd moved there six years ago in an attempt to start a new life. Memories of Africa, especially the safari, followed.

"I've also been praying for Promise," Louis confessed. He placed his free hand over his heart. "Something about that story—knowing that little girl is out there—won't leave my mind."

Pausing her steps, Olivia turned toward him. "That means a lot. You have no idea . . ." Emotion caught in her throat, and she pressed her back against the railing along the trail.

What else have you been praying about? Us? The tenderness in his gaze answered her question, although she'd already known it deep inside herself. Her heart doubled in size at his closeness.

Louis faced her and took a step forward. His eyes became hooded. He looked at her lips, and she sucked in a breath. He wanted to kiss her. Olivia's lips parted, but she didn't know what to say. Could he feel the heat radiating off her? Could he sense her attraction too?

He leaned forward slightly but quickly stepped back and crossed his arms over his chest as if trying to put a physical barrier between them. "Listen, Olivia. I have to get this out there. I am attracted to you. I wouldn't have come here if I weren't serious about wanting to get to know you better. But I need to be smart. I know how to charm women. But this time, I'm considering how I can lo—uh—*care* in every situation. As much as I want to kiss you now—" He cleared his throat. "I feel the more caring thing to do is to give you time. To give *us* time."

Olivia blew out a quick breath. "You . . . you are frustrating. I want to be angry at you, but it's hard." She playfully stomped her foot. Somehow he knew just how to take down her guard. She respected him even more because he wanted to kiss her but didn't.

Louis frowned. "That doesn't make sense. Why do you want to be angry at me?"

"Because then it would be easy just to forget this whole thing—our mutual attraction. There, I said it. I'm attracted to you, too. But I know who you are, which is frightening—knowing that your life and mine would also be in the limelight. But when I'm with you, there's no place I'd rather be."

Louis reached forward and took both hands in hers, rubbing the backs of her hands with his thumbs, sending tingles up her arms. "Have you ever been in love before? Was your heart broken? Is that what scares you?"

"No, not even close. I've never allowed myself to give even a piece of my heart to a guy."

His eyes widened with curiosity.

"It wasn't my heart that was broken—not directly. But I saw my mother's heart crushed again and again. She gave so many pieces away then was gone." Emotion caught in Olivia's throat. She couldn't share more. Not with him. Not now. She'd only shared the truth about her mother's death with Rebecca. And even though the death certificate said something else, Olivia knew her mother's cause of death was a trampled heart.

Do you see that it still haunts me? She wanted to ask him, but Olivia straightened and nodded toward the direction they'd come from. "How about we head back? There's a place a few blocks away that makes homemade ice cream with crazy flavors like vanilla lavender. Want to try it?"

Instead of moving in that direction, Louis wove his fingers between hers then lifted her hands to his lips, placing the softest kiss on her knuckles one by one. Her eyes widened, and a rush of adrenaline surged through her. Then he released her fingers and pulled her into a gentle hug as if she were a precious piece of porcelain.

Olivia put her arms around his neck and rested her full length against him. Her skin heated at the closeness, and excited and fearful emotions raced through her. A great weight of loneliness lifted in his arms—an emptiness she hadn't realized existed until Louis's tenderness seeped into the empty hole within.

And when Olivia was sure her knees would give out, Louis kissed her forehead tenderly. Then he released his grasp from around her waist. She did the same, and Louis stepped back, peering down at her with a smile. "Flower ice cream sounds perfect. Lead the way."

* * * * *

Buchenwald Concentration Camp
Date Unknown

Even though I pray for my children without ceasing, my body longs to be in my husband's arms. From the start, no one expected us to be attracted to each other. He was ten years older and from the German royal house. I was a young woman who often felt as uncomfortable as my father in affluent circles. Yet there was something from our first conversation that interested me. Christian saw me. Seated next to each other at an official function, I had a hard time turning to give attention to the older woman on my other side. Once I started speaking to Christian, I wanted to talk to him alone.

While many people saw Christian as an aloof bachelor, Christian only devoted his time and attention to what mattered. And when I became what mattered, I never felt so loved.

It made no difference that I was Catholic, and he was Protestant. We believed that our true faith was greater than man-made institutions. And we lived nearly a perfect life, especially when children joined our family. Then things changed in Germany, and Christian found himself caught up in the cause. Even though my death is already determined, I will not speak of Christian's choices regarding joining the Nazi party. Those who truly know him know the truth.

When the message was delivered that Christian was arrested and would only be released to me, part of me knew it could be a trap. Even so, it was worth the risk. I could not live in the safety of the Vatican knowing that I could bring him freedom. I do not know if my arrest meant my husband's release. I pray it is so.

I understand that I wouldn't change a thing. Christian was worth the fight. Crossing into another world to be with him was a decision I will never regret. I'd rather have decades of love and loss than never be loved. While the world says we were never a match, my heart disagrees. I am the woman I am today, even in this place, because I dare to believe that God gave me this man to love . . .

* * * * *

CHAPTER TWENTY-ONE

Little Rock, Arkansas
Present Day

One of Olivia's favorite things to do was to eat grilled cheese sandwiches and tomato soup while watching home makeover shows before bed. But tonight, she could hardly stomach food, and her living room felt empty with only her in it. There was no other reason for such a feeling except she knew Louis was in town. Curiosity had her thinking about what he was doing and whether he also recalled their wonderful day together.

I'm in so much trouble here. Even though her mind told her to run, her heart said otherwise. She liked Louis. She really liked him, and as much as she told herself not to let her heart get pulled in, it was no use.

After having their ice cream, Louis had asked about some of her favorite things to do in Little Rock, and he'd been shocked that she hadn't done much. She'd first moved to Little Rock because of her friendship with Rebecca. They'd been in the same small group at their church in Dallas, and Rebecca had moved to Little Rock to finish her degree in Mass Communications and to move back closer to her parents. They'd shared an apartment for a few years until Rebecca moved to Nashville for her dream job. Rebecca had been busy with school, and Olivia was never comfortable exploring independently.

Hearing that, Louis insisted on taking her to a park he'd discovered in North Little Rock with a re-creation of an eighteen eighties-era water-powered grist mill used in the opening scene of the movie *Gone With the Wind*.

Olivia decided she wasn't hungry and put her sandwich and soup into the fridge. She turned off the television, started a load of laundry, and turned to her laptop, hoping work could capture her attention, but it was impossible. She was about to shut down and call it futile when a small chime indicated she'd received an email.

Hey Bean-bug,

Just a short note. I hope you're doing well. I am happy that the handwriting expert has confirmed that our journal writer is who we thought—the princess. And even though I'd told you that I didn't want to reveal too much too soon, you know I've never been one to keep a secret. The author of this journal was Princess Alessandra Appiani, who was arrested and taken to the Buchenwald concentration camp because it was believed she was a spy—even though her father was the king of Italy. She was married to a German noble who was also part of the National Socialist Party, which we all know is the Nazi Party.

Alessandra wasn't in the line of the throne because, at the time, women could not claim the title of queen. Instead, the monarchy went to the male heir, her younger brother. I will look up more information, but that puts a whole twist to the story, doesn't it? Who would have guessed that an actual princess would be held within the walls of a concentration camp?

We are tackling the more readable pages first. The handwriting is so tiny that we must use a magnifying glass to make out some pages.

I hope to have more pages to send soon.

Love,

Aunt Liz

If she didn't know Liz better, Olivia would have believed that getting the first email the day after she'd met Louis was some type of set-up. If she'd heard the story of a "princess in a concentration camp" from Rebecca, she would have believed the story was made up to garner sympathy for Prince Louis. But Aunt Liz likely hadn't even seen the tabloids. She was more interested in antique documents than tabloid gossip.

Olivia would never confess she'd figured out the princess was Alessandra Appiani even before Aunt Liz had told her. She pulled out her notebook with the facts she'd written inside. *Princess Alessandra of Savoy married a German Prince, Christian of Hesse, at Castle Racconigi in 1925. The couple had four children, and she died in Buchenwald Concentration Camp.*

Even though it had been a week since the first email from Liz, Olivia still had a hard time grasping the truth. "There was a real princess who died in a concentration camp," she mumbled. Olivia recalled Rebecca's comment about the princess. It was still hard to believe. How did everyone not know about this?

The rapid thumping of Olivia's heart encouraged her to sit up straighter in the chair. Viewers were going to be fascinated.

Olivia had already requested that Liz search for photos of this family and obtain permission to use them. Now, she looked back at her notes, sliding her finger down the paper to find where she'd left off. Alessandra had met Christian at a formal dinner held by her father, and even though he was Protestant and she was Catholic, they'd found a match in each other. Her father had agreed to the marriage despite their religious differences, and they resided in both Germany and Italy. Yet

Christian was part of the Nazi party. Had he been a dedicated follower of Hitler? Had he aligned himself with Mussolini? Did Christian know of Alessandra's spying against the Nazis? Or had it been a false accusation? Or perhaps Christian had been a spy along with her. The journal pages may reveal answers to these questions. She hoped so. Olivia went back to the email to read the newest translation.

* * * * *

Just as I did with my children, my mother wanted me to live as much of an ordinary life as possible while growing up. My mother saw how status and privilege given to children at a young age created prideful and foolish adults. My siblings and I had chores, and we considered the staff more as family. More shocking were the times when I was reminded of our royal status.

I will always have a memory of my father when he opened parliament. Just a girl in my teens, he was my world. He drove away that day in a crystal chariot drawn by white horses, their harnesses sparkling with jewels. Buglers led the way. But my father's fear of losing all control in the government caused him to relinquish that control to the one man who most abused it.

* * * * *

A chill ran down Olivia's arms. Hadn't she and Rebecca just been discussing Mussolini? And now she was delving into the writings of someone who'd experienced those very events, whose father had handed over power to a madman. Alessandra had straddled two worlds. Where had she truly belonged?

Olivia set down her pen, wondering about how Louis was raised. Had his parents believed in giving him a normal childhood? She made a mental note to ask—and for the first time, she wanted to. She *wanted* to see him. She was happy that he was here.

Tears filled her eyes, and she clasped her trembling fingers on her lap. She wanted to give him a chance. *I want to see him, to be with him.*

She had no idea what that meant for the future, but how could she turn her back on someone so wonderful? A new peace filled her heart as she read the journal pages.

* * * * *

My father became a puppet in Mussolini's hand. Mussolini wore a top hat each week to meet my father at the Quirinal Palace in Rome, so my father could sign his royal signature to all new laws. As much as I loved my father, he was weak-willed. Did he mourn the mandates he signed? Did he understand his signature sent tens of thousands—anyone who opposed Mussolini—to their deaths? Did he know the flourish of his name on paper would also inadvertently send me away?

From my arrest, I knew my earthly father had no power or control to save me. He was king, but that was not enough. He cannot see to my rescue even if he knows where I have been taken. He is defeated without trying, even if he knows I have been arrested. One cannot simply close one eye and hope to keep evil at bay, but that's what my father is doing. The Nazis are as proficient in their deception as they are in their madness. My father is as penetrable as his crystal carriage, and he knows it.

Earthly hands are tied by the cords of those to whom they bind their allegiance. Whether my father believes that Christian is the good Nazi he proclaims to be or whether he dares to listen to the rumors that Christian and I helped Jews escape certain death, I will never know. My heavenly Father knows my heart and where my true duty lies, where Christian's true duty lies.

My heart aches as I wonder who my children believe me to be. Did they see enough tenderness in our daily interactions for them to hope I would be tender to others? Leaving them in hopes of saving their father was the most challenging choice I ever had to make, and I pray they will stay strong until we meet again. And if we never meet again, I pray that the Lord will guide them to all truth.

* * * * *

Olivia reread the passage, considering the princess's words. *Leaving them in the hope of saving their father . . .* Where did she go? When did she leave her children? And did her actions—at the cost of her freedom—save her husband? Olivia wrote a note to research that later.

Too many emotions fought for prominence in her mind and heart. She still struggled with thoughts of Kibera and a longing for Promise. Happiness from spending time with Louis lightened her heart. And sadness for a princess who saw her father as weak and unable to help her stirred within her. The one who should have had the power had been powerless. But Alessandra was a woman of faith. Had she continued to turn to God in her need? Olivia hoped that more journal entries would prove it to be so. Olivia couldn't imagine facing the darkness of a concentration camp without God. Or to spend a day without him at all.

Lord, are you trying to tell me something? Another thought entered her mind, but she quickly pushed it away. Even though Miss Jan often spoke about everything God was doing in her life, Olivia saw God more as a benevolent caretaker than a caring father. As long as she obeyed Him and stayed on His good side, the more likely things would go well. Olivia liked picturing God with her, yet most of the time, she

293

had to trust that was so. It was as if she imagined him hanging around and then jumping in when things got too overwhelming for her to tackle alone.

So far, since Olivia had become a Christian at sixteen, that view of God had worked fine. But maybe there was more to a relationship with God, as Miss Jan said. And as Louis had professed today, too, when he'd echoed Miss Jan's words: *If our heart is focused on God, He will be there no matter what changes come.* It was a nice thought. If only she believed it.

Olivia reread the note from Liz for the third time and then shut the top of her laptop computer. She had so many questions. *What was it like for an Italian princess to marry a German noble? Had Christian been part of the Nazi party before Alessandra met him? Had she known then what the Nazis were about?*

A deep, mechanical grinding sounded from the other room, interrupting Olivia's thoughts. Within seconds, the pungent odor of burning rubber met her nose. She rushed to the laundry room, lunged forward, and turned off the machine. The grinding stopped, and Olivia froze, gagging on the stench of burning rubber. Was the washing machine on fire? She didn't see any smoke. She waited and eyed the device and then lowered her shoulders in resolve. Releasing a frustrated breath, she moved to the living room and found her phone. After plopping down on the sofa, she clicked the speed dial for Rebecca.

Her friend answered on the first ring. "Yeah, what's up?" The sounds of traffic and horns honking could be heard over the line. Rebecca must be stuck in traffic on her way home from work. Olivia needed to learn how her friend coped with living there. She'd rather worry about being held up whenever she got gas than sit in traffic for hours daily.

Olivia readjusted on the sofa, tucking her feet under her. "What's *broken* is a better question."

"Your heart? Please tell me it's not your heart. Did you see in some tabloid that Louis has already moved on?"

Olivia wrapped her arms tight around a throw pillow. The feel of the plush fabric against her skin was a weak distraction but a distraction nonetheless from the fact she hadn't been truthful with her friend.

"Not my heart, the washing machine."

"Let me guess. You haven't called to get it repaired yet, have you?" Rebecca laughed on the other end of the line. "Maybe one of these days, you'll get a better handle on negotiating. Get that washing machine fixed before hand-washing your clothes in the sink."

Olivia's mind recoiled at the thought of calling a repairman. She saw herself at a tender age, small and insignificant, listening to her mother argue with unseen forces on the other end of the line—drug dealers, debt collectors, and angry family members. Calls that started with slurred greetings quickly descended into shouting matches, all within the fragile walls of their small apartment. The noise would echo through the space, making Olivia feel as if she were trapped inside a haunted house, unable to escape the nightmare.

Even though Olivia didn't mind making calls for work, she put off making any call in which she'd have to seek help, especially if it meant inviting a stranger into her home.

"Okay, I'll call. But a repairman may take a few days to get here. What will I do with all the dirty clothes still in my suitcase?"

"What did you do before?" Rebecca's voice was upbeat. She was never one to allow Olivia to wallow in pity. "There's always the laundromat."

"I love the idea of getting mugged while watching my underwear spin in the gentle cycle," Olivia joked.

Rebecca laughed. "Why do you wash your underwear on the gentle cycle? I toss everything in together."

"Maybe because I can. Can't I have a few luxuries in life? Sorting clothes is one of them." One side of Olivia's mouth rose in a slight smile, and the tension of moments before had eased. "Or at least it used to be."

"Can you invite someone to go with you?

296

Maybe get a hold of Prince Charming?" Rebecca's voice rose over the traffic noise. "Ask him to fly over to experience real, American life. I suppose it doesn't get more American than an inner-city laundromat."

Olivia rose and strode toward her small balcony, looking into the apartment complex. She'd told everyone she wanted to move to the poorer side of town to get to know the people she served. Except for Rebecca, few people knew this lifestyle was the one she was most comfortable with. Joking aside, going to the laundromat didn't bother her. It felt more at home than an upscale mall. If she and her mom had lived in an apartment as lovely as this one, with a working kitchen and door locks, she would have thought they were living like queens.

"Hey, this is my exit," Rebecca hurriedly said. "I'm almost at church for worship practice. I'll check in on your laundry saga tomorrow."

After a quick goodbye, Olivia hung up. Before she could change her mind, she dialed Louis.

"Hello, Olivia."

She pictured Louis's smile on the other end of the phone. "I, uh, have a question to ask you."

"Of course, anything."

She returned to her sofa and settled into it. "My washing machine broke. I thought if you didn't have anything to do tomorrow, we could pick up a pizza and head to the laundromat—"

"That sounds delightful," he said, his voice a blend of amusement and warmth. It was a warmth that made her insides flutter. It was a warmth she was scared of yet yearned for.

"Do you even know what a laundromat is?" she shot back, trying to stifle the tingling sensation his response had elicited. His laughter traveled through the phone and settled in her heart like a memory she wanted to keep.

"I've seen one on television." His voice carried a hint of jest.

She grinned, enjoying the playful exchange. "Then you're in for a treat, but one warning."

"Yes?"

"Unless you want to get mugged, you'd better get some normal clothes. No button-up shirts and slacks. Maybe try to find some jeans and T-shirts. Try to look . . ." She paused, her heart pounding against her rib cage as she cleared her throat. "Not royal."

His chuckle was low and warm. "I'll see what I can do."

"Wonderful. I'll pick you up at your hotel tomorrow. Why don't you give me your address?" She tried to keep her voice steady, but the hint of excitement betrayed her.

There was a brief pause, the silence heavy with unspoken emotions. Then he gave his address. She couldn't help but feel a thrill of anticipation as she wrote it down. This might be a simple errand to a laundromat, but with him, it would be anything but ordinary.

Olivia held onto the phone, listening to his voice, the underlying promise of tomorrow making her heart race. The prospect of their upcoming outing felt surprisingly intimate, and she had to remind herself not to get lost in the fantasy. It was a trip to the laundromat, after all. Just a mundane chore that held the potential for so much more.

CHAPTER TWENTY-TWO

Olivia parked, and the nostalgic street scene reflecting in the window made the laundromat appear like a relic of the past. Louis climbed out of her car, carefully balancing the pizzas as he shut the door. She hefted the bulging laundry bag from the backseat, and together, they strode toward the laundromat's entrance.

The moment they crossed the threshold, an edgy vibe settled around Olivia. She spotted two teenagers in white T-shirts and gold chains, their attention shifting from each other to Louis and herself. One of them quirked an eyebrow at his friend, a predatory gleam in his eye that ignited an uneasy feeling within her. A grip of fear tightened around Olivia's heart, and she immediately regretted choosing this place.

"You know, on second thought," she began, her voice trembling slightly. "I probably have enough laundry to last a few days until my washer gets fixed."

Louis didn't respond to her anxiety. Instead, he held up the pizza boxes, and his voice carried an unexpected confidence. "Hello, guys, hungry?" he asked. "We have pizza."

She paused mid-step, her breath catching as the two teenagers leaned forward with interested expressions.

"Seriously, man? You gonna share?" the taller of the two called out. Their predatory demeanor vanished as smiles replaced the smirks on their faces. They sauntered over, the initial tension dissipating.

Ignoring the half-dangling television overhead, Louis chose a chair underneath it, oblivious to the potential hazard. He settled, back straight, with the pizza box resting securely on his knees, the picture of nonchalance.

Olivia felt a rush of emotions. The sight was surreal, as if he had just erased the lines between their worlds. She marveled at how he remained unruffled despite the precarious television overhead and the initial tension in the room. There was a sense of thrill, a strange kind of allure in how he defused the situation.

She couldn't help the smile that tugged at her lips. Here was a man who didn't just walk into her world but embraced it with open arms. She was scared, excited, and overwhelmed all at once. And despite the broken washing machine, the dangerous neighborhood, and the dangling television, Olivia wouldn't have traded this moment for anything else. The laundromat, with its fluorescent lights and humming washers, suddenly felt like the setting of a romance novel she never knew she was a part of.

With lifted eyebrows, Louis opened the box lid with a flourish as if he was revealing crown jewels. "Pepperoni with extra cheese." The words rolled off his tongue, and the guys eyed him with interest.

"Hey, dude, you're not from around here, are you?" the shorter guy asked, reaching into the box and pulling out a slice. Grease from the pizza trailed down his hand as he lifted it to his mouth.

Louis grinned. "Nope. I'm from the other side of the ocean where getting a pizza like this is impossible."

Olivia smirked, doubting Little Caesars was served in the palace.

Louis grabbed his piece of pizza and paused, glancing up at her. "Olivia, won't you join us?"

"Yeah, sure. Of course." Heat rose to her face when she realized she'd just been staring again. "Let me just get these loads started, okay? Save me a slice."

Busying herself with the task, she loaded the towels, colors, and whites separately, grateful for having pre-sorted the loads at home. Olivia started the laundry, the steady hum of the washing machines providing a comforting rhythm.

When she finally turned to look at Louis, she was taken aback by the sight. Amidst the mundane chaos of the laundromat—chipped folding tables, metal laundry baskets on wheels, overflowing garbage cans, and detergent-splattered tiles, he looked so out of place yet entirely at home.

Engrossed in conversation, Louis seemed

302

oblivious to the world around him. She felt a magnetic pull and found herself moving toward him, sitting beside him and joining their shared moment over a slice of pizza.

The two guys were deeply conversing about expensive tennis shoes, and Louis was right there with them. His genuine interest and engagement were so compelling that they could convince anyone that tennis shoes were his lifelong passion.

In the echo of their laughter and excited chatter, something within her shifted. It was a care for Louis that transcended simple friendship, a depth of feeling she'd never known before. The word *love* whispered in her heart, and she was unable to shake it off. The warmth and tenderness bubbling up within her strongly resembled the love stories she had read.

Louis's concern for others, his genuine engagement, and his warmth were qualities she'd never associated with his status. For a moment, she could envision a life with him.

A woman walked into the laundromat, her arms burdened with laundry bags. A young boy was tagging along, his gaze darting around the unfamiliar place.

"We have one piece of pizza left," Louis called out, lifting the nearly empty box. The boy's eyes lit up, but he looked at the woman for approval. Upon receiving a nod, the boy scampered toward them but paused when he saw the two teenagers.

Louis's act of kindness tugged at Olivia's heart. He wasn't just Louis, a foreign prince. He was Louis, a man who could engage with everyone in genuine conversations, showed kindness to strangers, and made the ordinary seem extraordinary.

"It's okay, little dude. We don't bite. Com'on, it's still warm," the teen called, a grin filling his face.

"Care for a beverage?" Louis moved to the vending machine, paid with crisp bills, and returned with six bottles of water.

"Water? I thought you were gonna get soda, man." One of the teens shook his head in disappointment.

"Sorry, just a habit," Louis said, stepping around the garbage bags of dirty laundry the woman had just brought in.

"Nah, it's all right, man. We good."

As the teenager drank, he commented about the bottled water being a favorite among white women. When he glanced at Olivia, his eyebrows lifted in a playful challenge. "No offense, though."

She smiled in response, her heart warmed by the unexpected camaraderie in this room. "None taken."

Louis stood, throwing away the remnants of their meal and washing his hands at a small sink. He returned to his seat, but this time when he settled beside Olivia, his arm slid around her, his hand squeezing her shoulder gently. The touch was casual but intimate, sparking electricity through her body. She turned her face toward him, aware of their proximity. She found herself yearning for him to stay this close, always.

"Thank you for inviting me," he murmured, his voice low and filled with an intensity that made her heartbeat stutter. His gaze dipped to her lips, and Olivia wondered if this might be when they would share their first kiss amidst the whirring machines and under the watchful eyes of two teenagers and a little boy.

"You're wel—"

Her words were abruptly cut off by the harsh sound of gunshots, a startlingly loud noise that reverberated within her. The shattering of glass was cacophonous, the squeal of tires outside deafening.

She dove to the floor, her heart pounding. Louis quickly reacted, covering her body with his as he shielded her. The second gunshot echoed in the room, a terrifying reminder of their vulnerability. A scream tore from her lips, lost in the ensuing chaos.

As she huddled beneath Louis, feeling the warmth and strength of his body shielding her, the fear was potent.

A man's cry of pain rang out.

Was Louis hit while trying to protect her? *Of*

all Allorian history, the prince could be dead because of me.

More squealing from tires filled the air, and Olivia opened her eyes. Splatters of blood pooled on the tile floor in front of her. "Louis! Louis!" her voice cried his name.

Louis pulled back to sit and helped her to do the same. Cries filled the room—a mother clutching her son. The two teens cried out and cursed.

"Did you get hit?" he asked.

Olivia looked over her body. Blood was on her hands, but it wasn't hers. "I'm fine, but you—"

"That's not my blood. I'm all right." The color drained from Louis's face. He looked at the two teen boys. One boy leaned over the other, his knees resting in the growing circle of blood.

Her stomach lurched. "Was he shot? Was he shot?" the words spouted from Olivia's mouth.

The taller teen leaned over his friend. "Hey, Dante, get up. We need to go, man. Get up!"

Dante moaned and tried to sit up. Looking closer, it seemed he'd been shot in the leg. The amount of blood coming from the wound overwhelmed her.

The cries of the boy rose in the air as his mother raced out the door with her son in her arms and darted toward her car, her laundry forgotten.

As the woman drove away, Olivia pulled out her phone to call the police. She'd just started to dial when Dante's friend knocked the phone out of her hands. "Don't do that, lady. Do you want to get us killed?"

Olivia looked into the eyes of the young man. "What do you mean? I'm calling the police—for help. Who did you think I was calling?"

"Don't you know?" The teen cursed under his breath. "Are you stupid? That's what's going to get us killed."

Dante sat and then struggled to stand. "Yeah, don't call." He moaned. "Help me get out of here. I'm okay. It just nicked my leg."

"It looks like more than a nick," Olivia dared to say.

Louis put his hand on the young man's shoulder. "Listen, we need to get medical attention. This could be more serious. It could have hit an artery—"

"No, man." Dante stood, balancing on one leg. Sweat beaded on his brow. "I've been shot before. This isn't that bad. Barely got me." Then he turned to Olivia. "We can't have the police come. That's why they shot at me. Last night, I saw a friend get murdered. I know who did it. I saw them. They didn't kill me, but they're warning me. I gotta be careful, right, Trey?"

Trey wrapped Dante's arm around his shoulder, and they moved to the door. "Shut up, man. We need to get out of here. You said enough." Then, moving quicker than Olivia expected, they darted out of the building.

The sounds of sirens filled the air. It wasn't her, but someone had called the police. She leaned over and picked up her phone off the floor, weakness flooding her.

Olivia didn't realize how much she was shaking until Louis's arms surrounded her. She sat on the floor with her back against the wall. Louis held her tight and rested his chin on top of her head.

"I can't believe that just happened," she said. "I've worked in this area for years. My mom and I lived on streets just like this. In all that time, I never saw someone get shot right in front of me."

She quieted, thinking about what that teen had said. He didn't want the police involved because he'd be more of a target. She'd heard of that happening. She'd heard similar stories from the teen girls in their program, but the fear in the young man's eyes helped her understand.

"Louis," she breathed out, her voice trembling. The teen's bravado, and the fear of moments ago, all seemed inconsequential compared to the man holding her. "What if you had been injured?"

"I was thinking the same about you," he murmured, his eyes reflecting the fear that had momentarily gripped her heart. "Can we leave? I want to get you out of here to a safe place."

"But you shouldn't be here," she protested, feeling a tight knot of anxiety in her chest. The reality of the danger they had narrowly escaped was sinking in. "It's too dangerous." She sucked in a deep breath, willing herself to stay calm. "You should have security."

"I told my aunt I didn't want it. I want to spend time with you without a bodyguard hovering within six feet of me."

"You shouldn't have said that," she countered.

"Not that they listened," Louis confessed, rubbing his brow. "Though I haven't seen Sergio, there are signs that he's around. An SUV with tinted windows that's always nearby, a slip-up by the hotel front desk staff describing a man who looks just like Sergio. He's here, somewhere."

"So maybe he's here . . ." Olivia began, her voice trailing off as she realized the implications of his words. He'd deliberately rejected security to have some time alone with her. It was reckless and terrified her, but it also touched her deeply.

She looked up at him, her heart swelling with emotions she couldn't quite put a name to. He was making decisions that could put him in danger, but she knew they were made out of deep care for her. That thought was both terrifying and incredibly touching.

The words were barely out of Olivia's mouth when a man with salt-and-pepper hair rushed in the door, stepping over broken glass.

"Look who's here," Louis said. Olivia couldn't tell if it was anger or relief in his voice—maybe a mix of both.

Sergio gasped when he saw the blood on

Louis's pants. "The police are outside," he said as he neared. "Do you need assistance?"

"No, I am fine." Louis moved from the ground to the chair and helped Olivia do the same. Her knees trembled, and Louis held a hand to the small of her back. Was he hoping to strengthen her with his touch or seeking strength?

"We need to go now." Sergio's voice was firm.

Olivia looked back and forth between the two men. "They will probably want us to make a statement."

"I do not have to." For the first time, Louis's voice trembled.

Olivia's head pulled back slightly. She looked at Louis's pale face. Fear flashed in his eyes, although he tried to hide it. He studied the blood on his hands and let out the softest gasp. His hands trembled, and she wondered if this was the type of event that could cause someone to go into shock.

Even with the sounds of sirens outside, Olivia attempted to stay calm and keep Louis's attention on her and not the blood around them. The taste of pepperoni was still in her mouth, yet her stomach felt weighed down as if she'd just eaten bricks.

Her thoughts flashed to not fifteen minutes prior when they'd been laughing and joking with those two young men without any idea of how quickly a simple day at the laundromat could turn into something one would see on *Law and Order*.

"Did you say you don't have to talk to the police?"

"No, I don't. I have diplomatic immunity. It's not as if I saw anything anyway." His voice was flat, and she guessed it was due to fear. *Did Louis think someone would turn on him if he talked to the police?*

"You may have diplomatic immunity, but I don't." She pulled back from him and crossed her arms over her chest. "I need to talk to the police. They need to know what we saw and what we heard."

"But aren't you afraid, Olivia, that they will see you talking to the police and then target you, too?"

The corner of her lip flinched. She was right. He was worried.

"I've done many things that folks don't like in this area, but I've been fine so far." She squared her shoulders. "Justice needs to be served. If that young man witnessed a murder, then he needs to tell who did it."

Louis pushed off the plastic chairs and stood. "And put his family and friends at stake?" Color started to return to Louis's face.

"We need to get going. Louis, my car is around back." Sergio's voice was firm.

Louis turned to her. "I think a simple statement that you didn't see anything will be satisfactory.

We will be waiting for you. You can join us in Sergio's car, and we'll return later for yours."

"No." Olivia's voice snapped like a whip, its harshness piercing the silence in a way that startled even her. "I'll take my car. This is my home, remember? I can handle myself." Her eyes fixed on Sergio's. "Just . . . take care of him, all right? Make sure he's somewhere safe."

Louis seemed to teeter on the edge of a protest. But the determined glint in Sergio's eyes held him back, silencing him. As they vanished into the night, Olivia lingered beside the shattered window, her gaze steadfast on the void they left behind. The warmth that once brimmed in her heart for Louis was now a fractured mess, a mirror reflecting the heartache that had settled deep within her soul.

A uniformed police officer strode into the laundromat just as Olivia exited. She hesitated, ready to engage him in conversation, but was cut short when he gestured toward a cluster of officers huddled by a police car. Her heart beat frantically against her ribs, knees threatening to buckle under the weight of her fear. But she forced down the lump in her throat, drawing upon her last reserves of courage, and slowly, unsteadily, made her way toward the assembly of officers. Her breath hitched as she stepped forward, her mind whirling with emotions. Courage was not the absence of fear but the triumph over it.

Two female officers were engrossed in taking statements from other witnesses, their expressions professional and focused. A male officer spotted Olivia approaching and turned to face her. His hair was shaved close to the scalp, and his thick, bushy eyebrows added a depth of character. Olivia was sure she'd seen him before, perhaps when working with the teens.

He pulled a small notebook and a short pencil from his front shirt pocket, flicking open the notebook in a practiced motion. "Were you inside when the shooting happened?" His tone was gruff but not unkind.

"Yes. I-I was inside doing my laundry," she managed to stutter, her voice just above a whisper. She gestured behind her with a trembling thumb. "My laundry's still inside."

As she repeated her story, a churning mix of emotions washed over her—shock, relief, and an underlying anxiety that seemed to cling to her like the clothes still sitting in the washing machine.

The officer's eyes widened, as if he were trying to decide if he believed her. "You do your laundry in this part of town? You look more like a West Little Rock person to me."

"I live just a few blocks over."

His eyes widened even more, and he wrote something in his notepad.

"I work with the Character Club. I'm the program director."

He clicked his tongue. "Ah, that makes sense. Did you see anything?"

Olivia found herself wrestling with the information she had. She knew their names—Dante and Trey. She was privy to Dante's haunting secret about his best friend's tragic death and Dante's knowledge of the culprit. This could be valuable information for the police. Yet, Louis's words echoed in her mind, warning her of the potential danger she could put them in. The weight of this decision pressed heavily on her conscience, the line between right and wrong blurring in the face of reality.

"There were two teens. One was shot . . ." she began, her voice cracking slightly.

The officer looked away momentarily, his interest waning. "Your name?" he asked with the briskness of someone who'd had this conversation countless times before. Since he didn't press, Olivia didn't either. Instead, she sent up a quick prayer for the two young men.

She told the officer her name, and he scribbled it down, his demeanor remaining impersonal, aloof. She knew too well the stereotype she presented—a privileged white girl playing the role of savior. She wanted to set him straight, to tell him that she grew up in areas even harsher than this.

A bitter taste filled her mouth. She wasn't looking for his approval. But at this moment, his dismissive demeanor stung. Her chest tightened, not with anger, but with a silent, resigned pain.

"And your two friends?" the officer asked. "I saw them leaving in that fancy car."

"They are visiting from out of town. I shouldn't have invited them down here." She shrugged and decided to go along with the officer's view of the situation—that they were just some white people who shouldn't have been on this side of town. It was easier that way. Telling the officer that Louis and Sergio had left because of Louis's diplomatic immunity would bring unwanted attention.

"My friends were pretty shaken up. All we heard was the gunshot and the squeal of the tires. They left. I can pass on your card to them if you'd like them to call you."

"Not needed." He looked back over his shoulder to the two female officers. They were following the trail of blood. One motioned to him, and he nodded in their direction. "All right then. Thank you for talking to us. Can I get your number?" The police officer handed her a small notebook, and she wrote her number next to her name.

Heat rose to her cheeks as she headed inside after the officer took back the notebook. She felt foolish for bringing Louis into this situation and embarrassed for him. Even if he had wanted to stay with her, his choice would always be to flee danger for the sake of the crown.

As she reached the door of the laundromat, she noted a man standing just outside the door. Louis. Olivia resisted the urge to run to him. She approached with quickened steps.

"Are you all right?" he asked, tenderness in his gaze.

"I'm fine. But I thought you left."

"I pulled my prince card and demanded we stay. I'd never forgive myself if anything happened to you, Olivia." His eyes were wider than normal, and fear mixed with worry in his gaze.

"I was just talking with the police. He asked about the two of you. You need to go. Are you all right with meeting me back at my place? It'll take me just a few minutes to get my things. I will dry my clothes at home."

Louis clutched her arm. "You're going back in there? We really should leave."

"Those are my clothes—most of them." She motioned to her jeans and Nashville T-shirt that Rebecca had gotten her last Christmas that read *Boots and Besties*. "I know this outfit is cute, but I think we'll all get tired of it after a few days." She didn't mention both had blood on them, too.

She'd tried to keep her tone light, but Louis didn't crack a smile at her joke.

"Besides, it's safer now than ever." She pointed her thumb in the direction of the glass door. "A half-dozen police officers are standing back there."

"Yes, very well then. We'll meet you soon enough." And with that, he gave her a quick hug and hurried back around the building.

Olivia thought about Louis's response as she walked inside the laundromat, stepping on shattered glass. Her heart warmed that Louis had come back to check on her, but at the same time, she knew Sergio likely would be a regular fixture from now on.

She rubbed the tension headache forming over her eyebrows. She couldn't imagine living a life where a person's every move was monitored. Actually, she could. Most of her mother's boyfriends had done that—but out of possession rather than protection. Her chest tightened at the memories.

As Olivia hurried to the washing machines, a sinking feeling came over her. Feelings of helplessness as the memories of what happened when her mother's possessive boyfriends turned into abusive ones. The same pattern happened over and over. Her mother would find a new boyfriend who seemed too good to be true, but soon he'd show his true colors.

Within a year, things would be so horrific that she and Olivia no longer were safe. Her mom would move them to a new place, trying to escape the wrong decisions and bad people, only to discover they hadn't run nearly far enough.

Sometimes they were joined in the new

location. Other times they were dragged back to the horrors they'd just tried to escape. And when her mom would get far enough away, she'd find someone else, and the cycle would begin again.

Olivia gathered her things, trying to forget the sound of the gunshots and breaking glass. Conflicting feelings battled within her. Had she done the right thing by not giving the officer all the information?

She'd heard the teens at the center say, "Snitches get stitches—and sometimes end up in ditches." Maybe she was a coward—perhaps she and Louis both were. Yet one thing was clear. Louis couldn't fit into her ordinary life, and she also knew that she couldn't fit into his.

Louis and Sergio were waiting when she arrived home, but she made an excuse about needing a nap after the unexpected excitement to send them on their way. Of course, there was no way she could sleep with the memory of the gunfire going through her mind.

Instead, for the rest of the day, Olivia went through the motions. She dried her clothes and used hydrogen peroxide to rub the blood out of the ones she'd been wearing. She was thankful to see an email from Liz to get her mind off what had happened. Maybe in a few days, she'd tell Liz the truth—all of it. Then again, Olivia's struggles didn't compare to being arrested and sent to a concentration camp.

Hey Bean-bug,

I'm sorry it's taken me so long to get back to you. The amount of work is staggering. I hired an assistant, but it didn't work out. But everything will get done when it gets done, I suppose. Translation takes so much focus, and that's hard to do when I have to work on multiple projects. There are always more historical documents that need to be restored, and it's hard to tell my boss I just want to get back to the journal.

Anyway, I was able to translate a little bit more, and I had a co-worker check the copy. The more I read this princess's words, the more I mourn that such an amazing soul could be lost at the hands of a madman. Alessandra had so much to offer the world, yet she died alone. I won't say more than that. I don't want to give the whole story away. Not yet. Read her words, and then I'll tell you what else I've uncovered in this research surrounding her death.

* * * * *

Buchenwald Concentration Camp
Date Unknown

The only thing that saves me from this place is sleep, but how difficult it is to find. When I first came here, I dreamed of the children. They were calling for me, and I tried to find them. I could hear their voices, but I could not see them. My cries woke me.

Now, I dream about my mother. I'm walking the halls of my childhood estate looking for her. A few nights ago, I found her, and she sat at the base of the full set of armor that Father had set up against his office. In my dream, I was young again, and I climbed into her lap, and then she pointed to the armor. "Remember where the fight is," she whispered in my ear.

* * * * *

CHAPTER TWENTY-THREE

Little Rock, Arkansas
Present Day

Louis turned to his side, wishing he could sleep. Every time he closed his eyes, he saw that young man falling, bright red blood pooling around him. When he first arrived, being in Little Rock reminded him of being in Kenya. He felt more connected to the world around him than he did back home. Like the Masai Mara, the fights on these inner-city streets were between life and death. This was no game. This wasn't the TV or backlot sets of those American crime shows he'd liked to watch as a teen.

Sleep was impossible, so Louis rose and shuffled on slippered feet out to the kitchen area for something sweet, hoping to find a packet of hot cocoa. Louis wasn't surprised to see that Sergio also was awake. After what happened at the laundromat, Sergio insisted on moving in with Louis, and they'd switched to a two-bedroom suite. While Louis had conceded to that, he'd put down his foot when it came to Sergio following him everywhere he went, especially when he spent time with Olivia.

Even though the events of that day were

shocking, Louis had been impressed by how Olivia had held herself together. He couldn't think of another woman he knew who would have pulled herself off the ground and continued with the same bravado. Yes, she'd been shaken, but she hadn't been grounded. If Olivia could handle this, she could handle anything they faced in his world.

"Couldn't sleep?" Louis asked Sergio, walking to the cupboard. He smiled when he noticed two packets of hot cocoa left.

"I slept for a little while, but then I was under attack in my dreams," Sergio admitted. "Of course, that dream was better than the one where I had to approach your father's study door, knowing I had to tell him the news."

"News?"

"News that his son and heir was dead. News that all his transition plans were no longer good. News that just as he'd lost his wife, he'd also lost a son before his time."

Louis filled one mug with hot water and put it into the microwave. "It was only a dream, yes?"

That was the wrong thing to say. Anger narrowed Sergio's gaze and furrowed his brow. "I suppose you receive some thrill being here," Sergio spouted. "But the truth is this is not your home. It's not a game. Things could have turned out differently. You have to admit it, Louis. It's time to go home."

"I know this is not a game. I also know spending time with Olivia is worth it. Why can't you accept that fact?" The microwave beeped, but Louis ignored it.

"Accept it? You aren't serious, are you? Everyone knows you must do this because you feel unworthy. Your heart has been broken more than once. You need to prove that someone can still care for you."

"You think this is just about me? Is this just about my ego? You've been around Olivia. You can see she's an amazing person. I've known that since I watched the first documentary. I—"

"And you've told her that?" Sergio interrupted. "She knows you discovered who she was in Kenya, right—even before your chance meeting?"

"Told her?" Louis's words escaped in a whisper. He'd thought about telling her, but fear of losing her had kept those words inside.

Sergio crossed his arms over his chest and jutted out his chin. "Wasn't that what made her so angry the last time, hiding the truth?"

Louis ran a hand through his hair. "But we can also say she hasn't been candid with me. She hasn't brought up the documentary either." The microwave beeped again, but Louis no longer wanted cocoa. He pulled the cup from the microwave and dumped the steaming water into the sink in one fluid motion.

"And why would she? You've already broken

her trust once." Sergio shook his head. "You're worried about Olivia being unable to handle your position, but I'd worry more about your honor as a man. First, you act as if you just happened to run into Olivia when you knew who she was. Then you're here pretending you can be an ordinary guy. *This* Louis might get the girl. But how are you going to keep her when she discovers the truth? I'm here to keep you safe, but I'm also concerned about your heart. If you want Olivia to love the real you, she must know who that is. Know that your life is not your own."

Louis sucked in a breath as if he'd just been sucker punched. Sergio's eyes darted away momentarily, a flicker of guilt crossing his face. Sergio was right. How could Louis expect Olivia to open her heart when she had no idea what she'd be getting into? Hiding the truth had nearly ruined things the first time. As noble as Louis wanted to be, he needed a few days to figure out how to tell Olivia the truth.

Minutes ticked by, with only the noise of the highway outside their hotel filling the space. Finally, Sergio looked at his watch. "I'm starving. We never got a real dinner tonight. A sports bar just down the street is open twenty-four hours. Care to go?"

And just like that, Louis knew this wasn't an issue Sergio would harp about. Louis would have to figure it out himself. Sergio had said what he needed to and how he was returning to his rightful role.

"Give me ten minutes to change."

"Make it five," Sergio said curtly before retreating to his room.

Louis tried to act as if Sergio's words hadn't bothered him, but the realization hit like a tidal wave, crashing against the walls of his heart. Sergio was right. Louis's wounds of past heartbreaks still festered within him. The desperate need to prove himself worthy of love had driven him to this point. Now how was he going to get out of it?

Arriving at the sports bar twenty minutes later, Louis's gaze fell upon the wall-mounted flat-screen TVs, the screens filled with a cacophony of sports events. The volume was muted, replaced by a deafening barrage of blaring music. It was impossible to decipher the outcomes, let alone comprehend the simultaneous chaos unfolding on multiple screens.

The noise and commotion of the room mirrored his heart's disarray. As Louis sat there, lost in the sea of discord, he yearned for clarity. He wouldn't find it here.

The room smelled of grilled steaks, beer, and the spicy sauce on the pile of chicken wings on Sergio's plate. The bright orange sauce on the pyramid of chicken didn't look appealing. Instead, Louis had chosen a salad, although he couldn't eat it. With the tension in his gut, getting anything down would be impossible.

A group of guys walked past in jeans and T-shirts, and their strong cologne assaulted his overwhelmed senses. Louis considered asking Sergio if they could get their food to return to the quiet hotel, but Sergio was eating his chicken wings with gusto and dipping them into some white sauce. At least one of them could have a good night.

"Olivia is an amazing person. But in the end, does it matter?" Sergio asked between bites, picking up the conversation where he'd let up. "She will not fit in your world, the same as you don't fit into hers. You got shot at today, and you know she'll get shot at by everyone who meets her."

"Shot at?" Louis took the lemon wedge from the edge of his glass, squeezed it into the water, and took a sip.

"Not with physical bullets, of course. But you know the gossips. You know the looks that will be cast over dinner tables and across ballrooms. You know the expectations, the tabloids, the media. They will slaughter her. Their words and accusations will shoot straight to her heart. And her blood will be on your hands. If you love her, Louis, you'll keep her out of this. Just look at what happened to poor Meghan Markle. She can never do anything right, according to the English tabloids. If you care for Olivia, it's best if you let her go."

"Let her go? I can't do that. I can't fear the system or the people who believe their opinion matters. I can't walk away from the love of my life."

Louis's stomach tension loosened, but he still had no interest in food. Yes, he did feel love toward her, but he was unsure if the same could be said for her. He thought he saw deep care in her eyes, but could it ever be more than that?

"Just because people point fingers and gossip doesn't mean they're right," Louis continued. "What is the role of the heir to the throne? To give his everything. To rule with wisdom. This is a step of wisdom. Olivia knows more about people and their needs than most of those in positions of power. This is a new world we live in. My role should no longer be about parties, looking good, or getting the right attention from the right people to promote causes. In my book, Olivia is ahead of the game. She is the type of queen who I will need by my side. She sees the world as I need to see it better. I'm not going against what my father desires. I'm giving my father what his country needs. It's Olivia, and it just so happens she has my heart."

Sergio nodded and continued eating. Louis wasn't sure if he was listening or if he believed a word that Louis had said. How many times had

Louis poured out his heart to Sergio? More than he could count. But this was different. Olivia was different. Sergio might not be able to see that now, but Louis hoped he would soon because Louis wasn't planning to go anywhere.

"Yes, she has your heart, but I haven't seen the same interest from her. And you know what it's like—to be more devoted to someone than they are to you, right?"

Louis pushed away his salad, weariness overwhelming him. It was the middle of the night, and he was in a sports bar watching his bodyguard eat saucy, orange-colored chicken. The irony of the situation wasn't lost on him. Sergio's words were his deepest worry. Their relationship was worth fighting for, but was Olivia willing to fight?

Just as Louis offered his credit card to the waitress, his cell phone vibrated with an incoming text message. He sat up straighter. Olivia was the only person he'd given his American cell phone number. His heartbeat quickened.

You up?

Yes. He answered back.

Sergio paused his eating and shook his head.

I'm having a hard time sleeping. Figured you'd be too.

It's like something from a movie, isn't it?

The waitress approached with the receipt. Louis signed it.

I wanted to thank you for coming back to see that I was okay, Olivia texted next.

I wish I'd acted braver. It shook me up.

Me too.

Louis watched his phone, anticipation simmering under the surface as he waited for her next words. Was she just reaching out to ensure he was okay, or was there something more she wanted to share?

I don't want to keep you up, but I almost forgot that I'm volunteering for an after-school program tomorrow. Want to join me?

I don't know what that is, but yes, if it means I can see you.

The smile that grew on Louis's face was involuntary, warming him from the inside.

Be at my house by two.

Sounds perfect.

As Sergio motioned toward the door, Louis nodded and rose to follow. His heart was filled with a lightness he hadn't felt in a while.

See you then, Olivia texted.

See you then, Louis responded, his fingers gliding across the screen.

Stepping out of the noisy restaurant into the peaceful night, Louis was filled with a renewed sense of hope. Olivia's invitation had been more than just a date. It was a promise, an understanding that they both were willing to fight for what was blossoming between them. The challenges they'd faced were daunting, but for the first time, Louis felt a surge of confidence that they could navigate them together. As the door swung closed behind him, he carried with him the warmth of Olivia's words, a beacon of hope in the uncertain path that lay ahead.

CHAPTER TWENTY-FOUR

A line of kids stretched halfway down the block as Olivia walked toward Riverfront Park with Louis. Had it been just a few days since she came here with him to eat tacos? She bet he'd never imagine that they'd be walking together with fourteen third and fourth graders and two teen helpers.

The cooler temperature and gray clouds dotting the sky proved Arkansas wasn't all sunshine and warmth. Olivia hoped the rain would hold off until they returned to the community center. Driving the small bus, especially during rain showers, made her nervous.

Louis's smile grew as the group drew closer to the Riverfront Park area. "Well, we're heading back to our old stomping grounds. I recognized this place."

His intentional drawl caused her to smile. He was dressed in jeans, a Razorback baseball cap, and a flannel shirt with the sleeves rolled up to the elbow. *He fits here.*

Don't go there, Olivia. Just because he dresses the part doesn't mean he belongs.

He walked by her side, strolling along behind the kids. "So, you do this a few times a month?"

"Yes. Do you remember the community center where the Character Club is held?"

He nodded.

"Other volunteers have an after-school program there for kids. They help with homework mostly. They also teach them chess, and they sometimes go on outings. I volunteer to take the kids to the park several times a month. It's up to me to find a friend or two to help." She shrugged. "Today, you're the lucky one."

"Lucky is right." He rubbed his forehead. "But don't you worry you'll lose one?"

"They are usually good about sticking close." Even as she said the words, the children slowed before her. "Traffic jam ahead," she teased, pointing to where they all clustered around a large window.

"What has made them so entranced?"

"It's the Museum of Discovery. The kids have wanted to go."

A young boy with brown curls rushed to her almost as if on cue. "Miss Olivia, can we go there sometime? I heard there's a tornado room. It shakes, is loud, and makes you feel like you're in a real tornado."

"A tornado room?" She paused and grinned as his name came to her. "Charlie, that sounds scary, doesn't it?"

"It sounds cool," a small girl named Emerie said.

Olivia placed a soft hand on each of their shoulders, wishing she'd had something like this as a child. A loving adult who gave her time and attention—the correct type of attention.

"It does sound like fun, doesn't it?" Olivia smiled. "I'll have to look into it. I'm not sure how much a membership would be. We can't do it today, kids."

"What do you mean, membership?" Louis paused by Olivia's side. He lifted his hat slightly and scratched his hair.

"There's a cost for the kids to get in. They probably have a discount for programs like ours, but we don't have that in the budget right now. I will look into it, though."

He glanced inside, leaning close to see beyond his reflection. "Do you mind if I go in and ask a few questions?"

"No, of course not."

Up ahead, some of the children ran around the corner with the two teen helpers trying to keep up. Louis pointed. "Didn't you say that they tend to stay close? Some are proving your statement false." He chuckled.

"Yes, that's a problem." She sighed. "I know they're heading down the hill to the park. I need to catch up." She placed a hand on Louis's arm. "I'm going to run ahead."

"I'll meet you there in a few minutes."

Olivia moved toward the head of the line of

children. She rounded the corner, breathless, then stopped short. The whole group of kids was huddled there.

"Wow, great job, kids. I was worried. I thought you would run ahead."

"But you told us, Miss Olivia, that if we can't see you, we need to stop right where we are and wait. We were waiting for you to show." With bright red hair, Elsie smiled up at her with a gap of two front teeth.

"Yes, that's what I told you. I am so glad you were listening. You know, maybe you can teach some of the older kids about how to listen better."

The small girl's shoulders straightened, and she puffed out her chest with pride.

Olivia looked behind her and saw the last kids rounding the corner without Louis. He must still be inside.

Emerie noticed too, and she pointed. "Oh, Mr. Louis is in trouble. He didn't stay where we could see him," Emerie chanted, wagging her finger.

"Well, he would be in trouble if he was one of the students, but he's one of the adults. He went into the museum for a minute. Now, everyone, pair up with your partner. We're going into the park."

The children paired up and walked down the sidewalks to the park and playground. Just beyond the park, the wide Arkansas River flowed. Both traffic and pedestrian bridges stretched over the water. Olivia always appreciated this nature between the city streets and the water's edge. She thought of her time here with Louis, and her insides warmed at the memory of how he'd kissed her knuckles.

It was only after he'd taken her home that Olivia realized she should have taken Louis to Junction Bridge—a pedestrian bridge—to see all the locks put there by couples to show their unending love for each other. Goose bumps rose on Olivia's arms as she imagined herself and Louis snapping shut a lock together. Would they throw the key into the river to symbolize the lock being secure and permanent? For the first time, that thought didn't frighten her.

The footsteps beside her caught her attention, and Olivia's heartbeat quickened at Louis's approach. Instead of smiling, his eyes widened as he scanned the playground, trying to take it all in.

The children were spread out in all directions, and Olivia noted panic in Louis's eyes. "You seem a little overwhelmed."

He looked from one group of kids to another. They scattered into tunnels and behind climbing rocks. Some played tag, while others climbed a giant metal dome. "How on earth can you keep track of them all?"

"I can't. It's impossible. I use my ears more than my eyes." Olivia adjusted her ponytail and then cupped her ear.

"Your ears?"

"I listen for the shouts or the screams. When one rises in volume, then I know there's a problem I need to help with."

A scream sounded louder than the others, and Olivia noted a crowd of children moving to the slides. Olivia pointed. "See what I mean?"

They walked in that direction, and Louis gasped when he saw the slides on their level sloping sharply downward along a grassy hill, finally stopping far below.

The screams came from children who climbed onto the slide and rushed down, tumbling as they reached the soft grass at the bottom. Laughter carried on the crisp autumn breeze, and Olivia took her sweatshirt from around her waist and slid it on.

Louis stepped beside her, more at ease now that the children were gathered in one general area.

"What did you learn about the museum?" she asked.

His lips tipped up in a smile, and a twinkle appeared in his eyes.

"I was on a mission. I went into the museum, and I talked to the director. I told her about your program and all the wonderful things you do for these kids. I also told her that we could alert the media, that you'd write a press release if she gives you a yearly pass for these kids to go to the museum."

Alert the media? Olivia's eyebrows lifted at his choice of words and his directness. "Wait, you just came out and asked that? Directly?"

"Yes, and she thought it was a wonderful idea. They have a special grant for kids living below the poverty line. So, we're helping them in two ways. We're connecting them with these kids and their families and getting more information about the museum into the public."

"Let me get this straight. You just walked in there without talking to me and asked to talk to the general director. Then you made this offer, which includes me and adding work to my schedule?" It was genius, but Olivia didn't need him to know that. At least not yet. She crossed her arms over her chest and feigned anger.

Louis took a step back. "I'm sorry, Olivia. I should have asked. It seemed like such a great solution. I could help you write the press release, although I do not know what I would do. Maybe I could buy you dinner tonight? To give you more time?" He offered a too-wide smile, looking like a child who hoped he wouldn't be sent to his room.

Laughter spilled from Olivia's mouth. "I'm sorry. That was just too easy. You have to stop taking me so seriously. You're not in trouble." She couldn't help it. She threw her arms around his neck. "I can't believe you did that. Why didn't I think of that?"

"It takes special training, you see." He peered down and rested his forehead on hers. "First, you have to see what you have to offer, and then you have to consider what you need."

She nodded, and his head moved with hers. "Go on."

"Then you have to consider what someone else needs and what you can offer."

"It sounds simple, but it makes sense."

She pulled back slightly, tilting up her chin. "Since I need dinner tonight—to give me time to write this new press release—I'll join you." She sighed. "But it seems you're getting the bad end of the deal. I got a membership. I get dinner, and you get . . ."

"That is easy. The pleasure of your company. The treasure of your smile."

"You sound like a poet—" Cries filled the air, reminding Olivia of where she was. She dropped her arms from Louis's neck, moving them to his strong arms that held her, and looked around to find a group of children sitting underneath a tree, pointing and laughing at her . . . at Louis.

"Olivia and Louis, sitting in a tree, k-i-s-s-i-n-g," the children sang in unison. "First comes love, then comes marriage, then come babies in a baby carriage."

"My, creative little beasts, aren't they?" Louis smirked.

His body felt warm and inviting, and even

though Olivia knew she should let him go, she held on for a moment longer. "Creative? Are you telling me you don't have that chant in Alloria?"

"I can't say that we do," Louis replied, his grin unwavering, a twinkle of amusement in his eyes. He didn't pull away, keeping Olivia nestled in the haven of his arms. The scent of him, a mix of musk and sandalwood, washed over her, reminding her of their closeness, their bodies pressed against each other in a moment of shared vulnerability.

Olivia's heart pounded against her chest, the rhythm matching the pace of Louis's heartbeat, palpable under his flannel. She looked up at him, meeting his gaze. Her breath hitched.

"It's cute, isn't it?" she whispered, her words barely audible over the children's laughter.

The corners of Louis's mouth twitched as he looked down at her, his eyes never leaving hers. "Quite," he replied, his voice equally soft, the smirk on his face slowly transforming into a tender smile. "Although I must say, I wouldn't mind the sequence of events they proposed."

Olivia's cheeks flamed at his words, and she looked away, her grip on his arms tightening. She was sure her heart would burst out of her chest, the magnitude of her feelings for Louis threatening to overwhelm her. She wanted to reply, say something equally romantic, and tease him, but she found herself lost in the moment and him.

Finally, she met his eyes again. "You're a smooth talker, aren't you, Louis?" she said, managing a playful grin despite the flurry of emotions coursing through her.

Louis merely chuckled, the sound resonating through Olivia. "Only for you, Olivia," he whispered, his words creating a romantic symphony in Olivia's heart. It was a song she was beginning to love—a song she was starting to crave.

His face was so close. They would be k-i-s-s-i-n-g if he leaned down just inches more.

"That chant is older than me. I remember singing it as a child, especially when grown-ups got mushy."

"Mushy? That is not a term I have heard before." There was a playful light in Louis's eyes, a flicker of joy that made her stomach flutter. But underneath it, a hint of seriousness.

"It means being sweet on each other." Feeling self-conscious, she stepped back, and Louis released his hold around her waist.

"Yet again, a new idiom."

"How can I explain it? Mushy means soft on the inside with . . ." Olivia bit her lower lip. " . . . with feelings for each other."

"Does it mean I am your boyfriend?"

"Well, it can mean that—"

"I like the idea of being your boyfriend," Louis interrupted.

"I don't know how that would work. With you

being . . ." She let her voice trail off lest anyone overhear his royal status.

Louis wrapped his arms around Olivia's waist again, interrupting her. "Wait, are you breaking up with me?"

"No," she said, shaking her head, her voice barely above a whisper. She tried to smile, but her lips trembled. "It's just . . . you're a prince, and I'm . . . me. The complexities of . . . our worlds are . . ." Her words trailed off as she saw a flash of disappointment pass over Louis's face.

Before she could complete her thought, he pulled her closer. "I don't care about complexities, Olivia," he said, his voice low and serious. His fingers brushed a loose lock of hair away from her face, tucking it behind her ear with a tender gesture that made her heart flutter. "All I care about is being here, with you. Can we try? Can we see where this . . . mushiness, as you say, leads us?"

Olivia searched his face for any signs of insincerity. But all she saw was hope, a desire to make this work, to fight for them. She was quiet, gathering her thoughts, her fingers tracing invisible patterns on his chest. Then, she nodded, a small smile finally reaching her lips.

"Yes, Louis," she murmured, feeling an unexpected rush of emotion, "we can see where this leads us."

A relieved smile spread across Louis's face,

his eyes lighting up with a joy Olivia hadn't seen before. It made her heart race and her mind fill with thoughts of their relationship's possibilities. There were hurdles, she knew. But looking at Louis now, she felt a glimmer of hope that perhaps they could overcome them together.

They stood close enough that she could pick out the black specks in his light blue eyes. All the swoon-worthy lyrics she sang alone in her bedroom during high school came flooding back, and Kelly Clarkson's voice singing "A Moment Like This" rushed through her mind. Yet she couldn't allow the emotions to overwhelm her. Not here. Not now. Not with this audience.

"Louis, the kids are watching. All of them. Besides, this is something we can discuss later. Right now, it's time to get serious." Olivia looked for a way out of this awkward situation and fixed her eyes on the slide. "It's time to race. Every one of us needs to get on a slide. The first one who makes it to the bottom wins."

Louis pointed to the long slides stretching to the hill's bottom. "You're not talking about those, are you? Are those what you call slides? They look more like death traps. I can already see myself sprawled out at the bottom of that thing with every bone broken. I am certain there is something in my father's rulebook against me riding down one of those."

Olivia opened her arms, spreading them wide.

"What are you talking about? Are you telling me that you have never been on a slide?"

"I have been on a slide when I was a child. On one of the small ones that are *safe*. But not a large demon slide such as these. Have you seen how the children have been flying off the end of them? I'd break my neck if I went down one."

"It sounds like you're a chicken." Olivia tucked her fists under her armpits and flapped her arms, clucking like a chicken.

"A chicken? That I understand." And with long strides, Louis made his way to the top of the hill where the second slide began, resting its start on the ground. Peering down, he assessed its steepness. Olivia saw her chance. Without hesitation, she hurled herself onto the slide, feet first. And then she immediately regretted it. The descent was steeper than she had anticipated, so her body lifted with every bump. Screams rose from her throat, and in the adjacent slide, Louis's echoed in kind.

Before she knew it, Olivia flew out of the slide. She hit the ground with her feet and then found herself propelled forward. She landed with a thud, partly on her stomach and partly on her side, with the wind knocked out of her.

Louis did the same and tucked into a tumbling somersault. Then he completed his unconventional performance with a flourish, landing firmly on his bottom. Even as he massaged his shoulder, Louis refused to allow any grimace of pain to cross his face. Without removing his eyes from Olivia, he rose. He picked up the baseball cap that had taken flight during his tumble then hit it against his leg to rid it of the dirt. Louis repositioned it on his head, pulling it low over his eyes to shield his smile.

The children around him erupted in a chorus of giggles and cheers, and he offered a regal bow. Louis then approached Olivia and offered his hand. She accepted it, letting him help her up.

"Do you do everything with such grace?" she asked.

A chuckle escaped from him. "That tumble was far from graceful."

Olivia was about to protest when the squeals of eager children filled the air as they raced up the hill toward the towering slide. When the kids reached the top of the hill, they jostled for the first turn.

"Don't worry," Louis called out after them. "We'll be there at the bottom to catch you!"

Olivia nodded in agreement, a sense of warmth spreading through her limbs. But before she had a chance to allow her thoughts to sweep her away, the first child shot out of the slide nearest to her, and another one spilled out from the slide closest to Louis.

"Whoa there!" Olivia called, catching the dark-haired boy. It took her full strength to make sure she didn't tumble over with him.

Twenty catches each later, the children tired of the slide and rushed the swings. It was only then that Olivia had the chance to turn her attention back to Louis. "Seriously, you even catch kids with grace," she spouted with a labored breath as she rubbed her aching arms.

A chuckle burst from his lips. "Catching these children tumbling from the slide is akin to a royal waltz. It's not unlike trying to sidestep single ladies at the palace ball. All the outstretched arms, giggles but with much less curtsying and far more grass stains."

"Are you trying to make me jealous?" She winked and tucked a strand of hair behind her ear. "I do hope the eager dancers never caused you to tumble like that—although I bet you *could* handle jumping up to your feet with a flourish, even in a tux. It looked like something from a movie." Olivia crossed her arms, narrowing her eyes. "You're going have to teach me that."

"Teach you what?"

"How to rise with grace after taking such a big tumble."

"Just imagine every moment with a teacup balanced on your head."

Olivia's jaw dropped open. "Seriously?"

His gaze stayed steady. "Of course. We lived with teacups on our heads as children."

He practiced a timid walk as if he were balancing a teacup. "My sister is much more graceful than I am. I'd love for you to meet her someday." He paused. "Maybe, well . . ."

"Maybe?"

"I would like you to meet her, but sometimes she gives a wrong first impression."

"You don't think she'll like me?"

Louis reached up to pluck blades of grass from her hair. "She'll love you once she gets to know you . . ."

Olivia brushed the dirt off his shoulder, moving her hand down his arm, thinking of what it felt like just moments before to have him hold her. She longed for it in a way she couldn't explain. Olivia pulled her mind back to the present. "But she might try to scare me off in getting to know me. Is that what you're saying?"

"Not you. You're strong." He smiled. "I'd like to see her reaction to your spunk."

"Spunk? That's a nice way to put it." Bored with their chatter, the children began to scatter again, and Olivia and Louis moved to the path that would take them back up the hillside to the rest of the playground.

"And what about you? Do you have family close by?" he asked.

"I have . . . family. No brothers or sisters. No family close, if you're measuring distance. My aunt Liz works in Naples. Well, she's my aunt by name only, not blood." Olivia paused, trying to decide if she should say more. *No, not today.* She didn't want to bring dark clouds over the day, sharing about her biological family members who she didn't know and who never wanted her to be born in the first place.

Olivia clapped her hands together. "How about we have the kids race and time them? That's one way to get their energy out, right?"

Louis looked at her, puzzled. "And this is not the time for this conversation, I see . . ." He smiled. "Yes, we can line them up. I can use my watch as a stopwatch."

Olivia was just about to line up the kids when her phone rang. *Sarah-Grace.* Finally!

"Can you line up the kids? This call is important. It's someone I've been trying to get in touch with since I've been back."

"I'd be happy to. Don't worry about me. I'm made of strong stock."

She smiled at his joke and then quickly answered the phone. "Sarah-Grace, hello. It's so good to hear from you."

"That's what you say now." Sarah-Grace's voice was grim. "Can you meet with me tonight? I talked to Miss Jan. She says it can't wait."

Olivia's stomach fell, and the joyful laughter of children made the hair on the back of her arms stand on end. "Does it have to do with the banquet?" Even as she asked, Olivia knew it was.

"Miss Jan says we should talk in person. Can you meet?" Sarah-Grace repeated.

Olivia looked at Louis, knowing she'd have to bail on dinner plans. "How about six o'clock? I'll see you then."

CHAPTER TWENTY-FIVE

Olivia sat in the coffee shop with Louis beside her. A few tables over, Sergio drank an iced coffee and read the *Arkansas Democrat* newspaper with such ease that it appeared like something he did every day. Even though Louis didn't like it, he conceded to having Sergio always near after the shooting at the laundromat. Olivia guessed that no one else in the room would believe that Sergio was a bodyguard or that Louis, who sat beside her wearing a red Razorback sweatshirt, was a European prince.

Miss Jan was seated next to Sarah-Grace, across from them. With her long blonde hair falling in waves over her shoulders and large hazel eyes framing her face, Sarah-Grace looked like one of those American Girl dolls that Olivia had always wanted as a child. Even so, the anxiousness in Sarah-Grace's gaze put Olivia on edge. Perhaps the reason Sarah-Grace ignored Olivia's calls had to do with something other than being away on her honeymoon.

Olivia sipped her coffee, telling herself that if she had to hear bad news, she could enjoy her favorite vanilla and caramel latte. Louis had insisted he join her and that they could go to dinner afterward. From the downcast look on

Sarah-Grace's face, though, Olivia questioned if she'd have an appetite after hearing whatever news her friend had to share.

Sarah-Grace crossed her leg and then uncrossed it. "I don't know how to say this, but when I took on this fundraiser, well, things were different. Then I met Jason, and it was such a whirlwind. We'd known each other years ago, and things clicked now."

Olivia's stomach tightened. She could tell by Sarah-Grace's face that there wouldn't be good news about the banquet plans. Olivia pushed her latte to the side.

"And now that you're married, you must cut back on volunteering?" Olivia lifted her eyebrows.

"No, uh, Jason got a new job," Sarah-Grace's words rushed out. "And we're moving to Topeka."

"Kansas?"

"Yes . . . in two weeks."

Olivia leaned forward and spread her hands open on the table. "But the big fundraising banquet is in three weeks. And you're in charge of it."

Sarah-Grace stroked her throat. "That's something else I needed to tell you." She moved her hands to her lap and folded them. "I—I, well, I let the ball drop . . ."

"On a few things?" Olivia's voice was no more

than a whisper. "On just a few things, right?"

Sarah-Grace glanced at Olivia then looked at the café window and shrugged. "I talked to Jason about the banquet last night, and he told me I needed to fess up."

Olivia waited. Miss Jan also sat silent, but her lips thinned into a tight line, and her eyebrows knit together.

"I haven't gotten anything done. Except I picked out linens for the tables. I was choosing things for my wedding and was there anyway." Tears filled her eyes. "I am so sorry, Olivia. I know I let you down. I just got caught up in the wedding planning, and December seemed so far away."

Leaning back in her seat, Olivia took a deep breath. She wanted to be nice but also needed Sarah-Grace to understand how serious this was. Not only did they need money for their basic expenses, but this year they needed more funds to replace everything they'd lost in the fire. An ache filled her at the idea of telling the young women they'd have to stop meeting. They had nothing to offer. After a few months, they'd have no space, let alone the materials needed to run their group.

Olivia folded her arms across her chest. She pushed down her emotions yet shook her head. "I know that everything happened in a whirlwind with Jason. I understand that. But we've had monthly meetings for the last six months, and you assured us everything was handled. We even asked if you needed help, and you said it was all taken care of."

"I know, and I did plan to have everything taken care of. But then Jason got this job offer, and we decided to move. So now I must focus on finding a new place in Kansas and . . . Are you mad at me?" Her eyebrows folded, and tears welled in her eyes.

Louis shifted beside her and touched her arm as if offering support. Olivia rubbed her brow. "No, I'm mad at myself. I shouldn't have given you so much responsibility. I should have followed up better." She tapped her foot. "I suppose we'll just have to figure it out."

"As I said, I'm so sorry. Maybe you could postpone—" Sarah-Grace started.

Olivia lifted her hands, halting Sarah-Grace's words. "We will figure it out." Her voice was more profound and gruffer than usual, even though she was trying to stay calm. She forced a smile. "Thank you for letting me know."

Sarah-Grace awkwardly stood. "Well, I should get going. I'm meeting Jason for dinner."

Olivia nodded. "Thanks for meeting with us today. And I hope your move goes well."

Sarah-Grace turned to walk away, and Miss Jan held up her hand. "Just one minute."

The younger woman paused and turned.

Miss Jan cleared her throat. "We love you,

sweetheart. And we know you have a good heart." Miss Jan reached forward and grasped Sarah-Grace's hand. "But I hope this will be a lesson to you. The smallest good action is better than the grandest intentions. If you want to be respected, Sarah-Grace, you must tell the truth. More than that, you need to follow through with your promises. You hurt us, but you hurt your-self . . . your reputation even more. I want you to think about that, will you?"

"Y . . . yes, Miss Jan." With a sad smile Sarah-Grace hurried away.

Olivia sipped her coffee, but even her favorite latte couldn't help the pain in her heart. What were they going to do? They needed to cancel the fundraiser, but doing so would mean stalling the program. This program wasn't just her purpose. It was her income. Even though she took as small of a salary as possible, she still needed it to survive. She lived from month to month and used almost all her savings on filming the documentary and extra expenses going to Kenya.

Miss Jan gave a pinched expression. "I was worried. I should have checked on her more when you were out of the country." Her lips pressed into a slash.

"We both believed Sarah-Grace was doing what she said." Olivia gave an exaggerated sigh. She crossed her arms, placed them on the table, and buried her face. "What am I going to do?"

Louis reached over and rubbed her back in wide circles. Slowly her shoulders relaxed. He moved his hand to the center of her back. A soft shiver ran down her spine. Olivia didn't even want to know what he thought of this. His family ran a country, and she couldn't even keep a small organization under wraps.

"You said that wrong," he said finally.

Olivia turned her head slightly. "What do you mean?"

"You said, 'What am I going to do?' The correct phrasing should be, 'What are *we* going to do?' "

A soft smile tipped up her lips. "This is not your problem."

"It's not my problem, but I can make it my concern, right? I've seen the wonderful work that you've done, and I believe in it. I would love to assist you in your event planning if you'll have me." He leaned closer so his nose was only inches from hers. "I'll repeat it, Olivia. I would love to assist, but you must let me help."

Her shoulders tightened, moving closer to her ears. She sat up straighter. "That's kind of you, but we cannot pull it off. The event is just three weeks away." Her gaze flickered to his lips. Was he smiling?

With a flourish, Louis pushed back his chair and stood at attention. A wink followed, and he offered her a bow and spoke just above a whisper. "During my lifetime, I've attended no less than a thousand royal functions. More than that, I have to approve everything for my father's upcoming Silver Jubilee. I know we can pull it off. Please trust me on this."

Across the table, Miss Jan clapped her hands together. "That sounds like a wonderful idea to me." She pulled out a notebook and started jotting down notes. "Let's keep the same date, and I'll start calling volunteers. When you figure out the venue, let me know." She closed her notebook, glanced at her watch, and rose. "But I need to go. You know how I am about driving at night."

Olivia looked between Miss Jan and Louis. "So, this is happening?"

Both nodded, and Miss Jan left with a quick hug and a wave.

Olivia's stomach growled, but she didn't want to think about eating.

"Relax a little . . ." Louis scooted his chair closer to her.

Olivia swallowed. "I want to trust you in this."

"Then do it." The muscles in his arms bunched and hardened as he grasped her hand, giving it a firm squeeze. "Get out your notebook, and we can start taking notes. But first, I'm going to order us some sandwiches." He craned his neck to look at the menu. "Do you have a favorite?"

"I'm not sure I can eat . . ." Olivia pulled out a notebook and pen and placed it on the table. His gaze narrowing on her told her he wouldn't listen to that excuse. "But if you insist, I'll take the chicken salad with chips on the side."

He nodded and approached the counter. Five minutes later, they had dinner and a list of empty spots.

Olivia nibbled on a chip. "I bet you have people at home that do all this work."

"I won't lie. I do, but I do not doubt I will find more satisfaction in this event than any I've attended." He took a large bite of his club sandwich.

"You didn't have to do this."

"I didn't have to, but I wanted to. Olivia, don't you understand that this brings me joy . . . that you bring me joy?"

"I'm sure glad because we need to raise a lot. The Character Club will fold if we can't raise enough money. But we don't even have a venue."

"Let's think about this wisely. It's the holidays, and so many places are already decorated. Since we are in what you call 'the Bible Belt,' I assume a church would be willing to give us free space or a discounted fee."

"Yes, there are some places that have helped us before."

"Perhaps we can start using whatever they already have for decorations and then bring in extras."

"Sounds good if we can find a place." Olivia made a note. "I can't believe we've come to this.

We have nothing. Nothing." She wanted to be grumpy, but Louis's smile was infectious.

"This is a good thing. We can start with a clean slate. What about a Chocolate Ball theme?"

"A Chocolate Ball?" Olivia took a bite of a chip.

"Let's focus on dessert instead of a full dinner—lots of desserts. People will be satisfied, and they will be much easier to prepare and serve. There are so many different types of chocolate desserts." His face brightened like he'd just won the lottery.

Olivia covered her mouth, and she tried to hold back a smile.

Louis peered at her, blinked slowly, and then looked over his shoulder. "What? Did I do something? Are you laughing at me?"

"I just think it's cute how excited you are about chocolate."

"Don't you love chocolate?"

"Yes, but not as much as you."

"That may be true, but we can visit local businesses to see what they can offer for free."

"Louis, I don't know how things work in your country, but people here aren't willing to give things for free."

"Unless they get something out of it. Remember the museum? The most important thing about negotiation is understanding your needs and understanding the needs of another. We need chocolate, and we can help with publicity for these businesses by honoring them with how they give back to the community. Twelve businesses can provide fifty desserts each if we plan for three hundred people. Then each attendee can choose two."

"That sounds reasonable."

"And we can have attendees vote on the desserts, and we'll give out awards."

Olivia jotted down notes as quickly as she could. "There is one church that has a wonderful women's group. They've helped us clean and sort items. They love what we're doing, and they love our community. Do you think I should ask if we can use their church? And what if different women sponsored a table to decorate any way they'd like?"

"Yes, and perhaps we can connect each of those women with one of your teens to buddy with that night. The women could help their teens find a dress. They can sit together, and the teens will be our special guests for the evening—the princesses of the ball. It will give the women the feeling that they are doing more than just setting up tables and setting out flatware. Hopefully, they will build connections with the teens, a friendship that will last into the future."

Olivia wrote down the ideas as quickly as possible, and excitement took over where dread had been moments before. She thought of local bakeries and caterers who she could reach out to. She was amazed by how quickly Louis had devised ideas that could work. "Should I start calling the bakeries to ask about donations?"

"Whoa, slow down," Louis interjected with a soft chuckle, an endearing light in his eyes. He gently closed her laptop. "Remember, Rome wasn't built in a day. And this, *my girl,* this will be our Rome."

The gentle warmth of the moniker made her heart flutter. It was a simple phrase, yet the weight of his words felt significant.

Olivia's heart fluttered at his words, the nickname rolling off his tongue like a sweet promise. She glanced at him, her eyes meeting his for a moment. There was a depth to his gaze, a warmth that ignited a rush of hope and a hint of fear. She was used to tackling challenges independently, but having him by her was different.

"Your girl?" she questioned, a playful tone to her voice to hide the thrill his words caused within her.

Louis nodded, his eyes never leaving hers. "Yes, my girl. And I want to stand by you through all of this. Through every hurdle, every success."

The sincerity in his words made her heart clench. She couldn't help but sigh softly, her gaze falling to her notes again. Could it be this simple? Could they truly make this work amidst all the chaos and complexity their worlds presented?

Louis gently lifted her chin, forcing her to meet his gaze again. His eyes held a promise, a reassurance that they could face anything as long as they were together.

"I mean it, Olivia. You have the passion, the determination, and the drive. Together, we can make this event a resounding success." His thumb brushed against her cheek, a simple gesture that sent shivers down her spine.

"You're not just saying this to boost my confidence, are you?" she asked, her voice barely above a whisper.

"I wouldn't do that," he replied huskily. "I believe in you, in us, and I know we can do this."

His unwavering faith in her gave Olivia the courage she needed. For the first time in a long while, she felt excitement for what lay ahead, a sense of anticipation amplified by the man beside her.

"Okay, let's do this," she said, locking eyes with him. "Together." And as she saw the smile on his face, Olivia realized that no matter what happened, she wouldn't want to be on this journey with anyone else but Louis.

Louis's excitement ebbed as he confronted Sergio's disapproval as he returned to the hotel.

"As much as you're enjoying this time, we need to head back," Sergio stated sternly, narrowing his gaze.

The room seemed to close around him, echoing Sergio's silent judgment. He felt his father's disapproval through the stern gaze of his loyal bodyguard. The walls of the lavish hotel room, a stark contrast to the vibrant community center he had just left, only heightened his sense of isolation.

The joyous bubble that had enveloped Louis when he'd been with Olivia began to deflate, replaced by an all too familiar tension that balled up in the pit of his stomach. His father's shadow extended even to this little corner of the world.

"I understand Father's concerns," Louis replied evenly, "but I have commitments here too. Olivia needs me. These kids need me."

"You also have commitments to your father, to your kingdom," Sergio responded, his voice unwavering. He paused, studying Louis with a seriousness that made him feel like a child being scolded. "And ignoring your father's voicemail won't make them disappear."

Louis felt a spark of frustration. "This is about more than just my duties as a prince, Sergio," he said, his voice firm but controlled. He moved to the window, staring out at the Little Rock skyline, so different from the towering spires and ancient walls of Alloria. "I care about what's happening here. I care about Olivia."

There was a heavy silence as if Sergio was

weighing his words. "Your father won't understand that, Louis."

"Maybe it's time he tried," Louis murmured, feeling a strange mix of resolve and uncertainty. He turned to face Sergio, his expression firm. "I will listen to his message, but I am not changing my plans. I am staying here with Olivia. I am going to help her. And nothing—no duty or responsibility—will stop me."

A flicker of surprise crossed Sergio's face, but it quickly melted into resigned acceptance.

As Louis continued to hold his gaze, a new tension enveloped the room—a tension not of looming expectations but of firm convictions. The kind of tension that signaled a shift, a change of currents. And as much as it made Louis uneasy, he knew it was a necessary step toward the path he wanted to carve for himself.

"And you think you'll be able to stay incognito indefinitely?" Sergio scoffed. "The papers have been asking about the missing prince. Some say you are in Tibet. Others believe you've joined a sailing crew at sea in hopes of healing your broken heart."

"No one thinks to look in America—in Little Rock." Louis grinned.

"Not yet." Sergio sank onto the sofa as if he had the world's weight on his shoulders. "And even though I never want to take sides, you must call your father back. Your father wasn't calling about the jubilee. It's something more—far more serious."

Louis sat on the edge of the leather chair situated by a small desk. "What do you mean more serious?"

"Why don't you listen to your phone messages and find out?"

Louis pulled out his cell phone and called his voicemail. His father's voice came across strongly.

"Louis, I hear you are having a wonderful time in America, but I hope you plan to return soon. Since the war concerning Russia broke out, we have had a refugee crisis. Cabinet meetings are planned, and everyone is asking if the future king will be there. Many believe you should have a voice on policies being put into place concerning the future of refugees entering our country." His father cleared his throat.

"But more than that, son, I have had some health struggles. Some of my recent tests point to a serious issue. Thankfully we caught it in time, but your aunt Regina has insisted I rest. I know this jubilee business has been an enormous burden on her. I was hoping you could assist— more than just attending video meetings. Believe it or not, you've always been a calming presence." There was a long pause. "Please return home soon if you can. You know I haven't asked much of you . . ." There was another long

363

silence, as if his father had wanted to say more but changed his mind. And then the call ended.

Health concerns? Fear lodged in his throat and refused to be swallowed down. His father had always been in excellent health. If Father had been ill, it had been reported to the press as "feeling unwell but quick to recover." Louis had always bought the story too. For his father to mention otherwise, the condition must be severe.

More than that, Father was right. He hadn't asked much of Louis . . . but his father hadn't cared much either. After his wife's death, Father had little to do with rearing his children. Father had done his work and retreated into his sorrow as if he were the only one suffering. Louis and Catina would have floundered if it hadn't been for Aunt Regina. Father getting involved could mean only one thing: This illness was more severe than he'd let on.

A heaviness fell over Louis, and he strode back into the living room area as if a ton of bricks rested on his shoulders.

"You listened to the message?"

Louis nodded. "He wants me to return."

"He's wanted that since you left." Sergio ran a hand through his dark hair. "I'm sure he didn't tell you over the message, but his cancer is back."

"Back? I didn't know it was that serious last time. Father told me if one had to get cancer, it was the best one could get—the most treatable."

"Cancer is still cancer, and there are no guarantees. As much as I've enjoyed watching you play 'ordinary citizen,' it's time to return to your real life—a life you can't put off or ignore."

"As much as I'd love to return, I've just committed to help Olivia. I'm staying to help her with the fundraising event. We only have three weeks. There is little time and much to do."

"And after that?"

"After that, I will go home." His heart sank even saying those words. "I have duties. I am certain Olivia will understand."

"And if she doesn't? It's easy for her to care for you when you have all day every day to devote to her. But Louis, we both know that's not who you are. You have a role. You have a responsibility. You have a life, one different from what you portray in Little Rock."

"Yes, I know. You don't have to tell me."

"But think of this. If she's falling in love with this version of Louis, is it falling in love when it's not who you are?" Sergio sighed. "I'm just afraid the longer you stay here—and try to become something you're not—you'll end up with yet another broken heart."

CHAPTER TWENTY-SIX

With the Chocolate Ball only a week away, Olivia needed to make a phone call. Rebecca had promised to come for the big event, and it was better for her to learn about Louis's presence before than at the event. As soon as Rebecca answered the phone, Olivia spilled everything that had been happening, from how he'd surprised her at the Character Club meeting to their time at the park with the kids and the planning of the Chocolate Ball. She left out that they'd almost gotten shot and that Olivia felt more comfortable in Louis's embrace every time he pulled her into his arms.

Rebecca's voice rose two octaves on the other end of the phone. "Wait. You have been hiding that Prince Louis has been there with you in Little Rock for more than a month?" Her gasp carried over the phone. "I thought we were friends. I thought you valued me. I feel incredibly sidelined right now." Humor frolicked with frustration in Rebecca's tone, making her words a mix of playful accusation and genuine disappointment.

Olivia cringed. "Maybe because I knew you'd make a big deal out of it?"

"And this isn't a big deal? A prince is pursuing you. A prince, Olivia." Her amused anger morphed into laughter. "And you, of all people—someone who's playing hard to get."

"I'm not playing hard to get. We've just been busy." Olivia sighed. She explained how they'd worked the Chocolate Ball together—how it had become their joint mission. From morning until evening, they'd worked side by side, and Olivia had been amazed by the response. "Just like Louis said, everything has fallen into place. We've gotten more than enough restaurants and caterers to donate desserts. We found a host church to take on most of the decorations. The women's ministry from that church is also reaching out to the teens to prepare for the event." Olivia smiled. "I don't know what I would have done without him."

"I'm amazed he's been able to stay so long. I hope his dad doesn't mind Louis not being around to run their country. Of course, doing this American fundraising is probably a novel idea to him, right?"

The thought of Louis not genuinely belonging, not being able to stay forever, made Olivia's heart constrict. It was a reality she was fully aware of yet chose to ignore for the precious moments they had now.

"He seems to be enjoying his time here, but you're right. I'm sure it's not what he's used to . . ." Olivia trailed off, her mind returning to the moments she'd spent with Louis. The way he laughed with the kids at the center, how he seemed genuinely interested in her work, and the softness in his eyes when he looked at her. It all felt so real and unpretentious, as though he was just Louis, the man, not Louis, the prince.

Suddenly, she was struck with a poignant realization that filled her with warmth and melancholy. In his efforts to help and be a part of her world, Louis offered his heart and sincerity without any shields. It was no wonder he blended in so well. He was simply himself, not a prince.

And Olivia was irrevocably drawn to this man. She wanted to be by his side, support him, and share these beautiful moments. But that constant whisper of reality reminded her of their different worlds. Could they maintain this romantic bubble forever?

A soft sigh escaped her lips as she placed the last stamp on an invitation. "I suppose it is strange in a way, Rebecca," she said slowly, each word echoing her internal struggle. "But it's also what makes him so special. He's just Louis here, and I . . ." She paused, grappling with the emotions in her chest, "I love him for it. I just hope our little world can last a bit longer."

Olivia's heart clenched as she admitted her feelings and hopes out loud. Louis was an integral part of her life now, and the thought of him leaving filled her with dread. It was an uncomfortable reality she would have to face, but not today. Today, she would immerse herself in the warmth of their shared dreams, bask in the comforting presence of Louis, and hope that their time together would not be fleeting.

"He is a prince, Olivia. He's probably wealthy. If he'd written a check for the Character Club's yearly expenses, it wouldn't have even put a dent in his pocket change."

Olivia's gut tightened. She rubbed the spot, but it stayed. "I would not have accepted that. Besides, doesn't it seem more special this way, knowing he could give us everything but instead choosing to work beside me?"

"Yes, well, I guess so. I don't know. While I've always been pro-Louis, the reality of the whole thing worries me." She sighed. "I'll come, but on one condition."

"What's that?"

"My parents bought a house there on the river in Little Rock. They're in Mexico all month, so why don't I come for the weekend, and we can stay there?"

"Sure, that sounds fun. I'd love to."

"By 'we,' I mean Louis, too. The place has five bedrooms—plenty of space for all of us. As your best friend, I must check out this guy. I can tell by the lilt in your voice that you're starting to care. Really care."

Olivia didn't answer right away. She couldn't lie. "Which means I'm in deep trouble," she confessed. "Because even though I feel I've been living in a bubble for the last month, this isn't reality. I know he's going to have to leave soon. In addition to helping me, he's had a lot of video meetings, helping to prepare for his father's Silver Jubilee."

"Let's worry about that later. This is your Chocolate Ball, and you'll be the princess for the night with your prince by your side. We never imagined this in Kenya, did we?"

Olivia sighed. She closed her eyes and let the slightest smile play on her lips. "No."

"And speaking of princesses, do you have any more news from Aunt Liz?"

"She's translated more of Alessandra's journal. I feel I'm getting to know her. And I can't wait until Alessandra's story is told." A sense of loss echoed through Olivia's chest. Getting to know Alessandra was like discovering a dear friend. One she'd never meet. The ache also reminded her of the loss of Louis, too. She knew, like Alessandra, he'd been raised with a sense of duty. He would fulfill his role to the best of his ability, meaning he wouldn't remain in Little Rock.

"Hey, listen, I have to run," Olivia said, hoping Rebecca couldn't hear the melancholy creeping into her voice. Pain pinged her heart—not physical pain but a sense of loss that balanced between what she'd discovered about Alessandra and the truth that Louis had a role to play outside of their growing relationship.

"All right. See you next week. I can't wait to meet your prince. I have a million questions."

Olivia touched the place on her heart where the ache was. "Yes, I'm sure you do."

* * * * *

Buchenwald Concentration Camp
Date Unknown

I have to admit I haven't had much sleep lately. I have so many questions. How could my Lord allow me to be in such a place when my only desire has been to serve Him all my life? Even though not everyone questions God, all my fellow prisoners question how they could end up in such a place.

Unlike the masses who live in shacks, which we see herded around like thin, sickly cattle, I am set apart. We are set apart. We live in a large house away from the camp and the prisoners' barracks. I sometimes feel guilty for not being with the people our family has served for so long—the Jews of Italy and the political prisoners—anyone who goes against Hitler's ideals or cause.

My bunkmates ruled governments and led armies only a decade ago, yet now they are under arrest. There are many conversations about Hitler, the Nazi party, and what could have been done differently to stop him sooner. I sit and listen but rarely contribute to the "what ifs." Nothing can change what happened, but we can change the future, even where we are.

Today, after many sleepless nights, I am choosing to rest in the arms of my Lord, even here. I prefer to hope and to love, even now. And as I lift my soul to God, He has given me a birdsong.

Outside my window, the skylark has appeared three mornings in a row. As I listened to the song again, I remembered the moment I walked past the gas chambers the first time I was taken in for questioning. I heard not weeping but songs. Voices—at least a dozen—voices lifted to Shema Yisroel. Their morning prayer was on their last morning. "Hear, O Israel: The LORD our God is one LORD . . ."

Their fear was gone, but their joy remained. May I find the same in this place? The memory reminded me that the most splendid defiance I can have against the Nazis is not to lose hope.

The Lord does not always give us what we want, but I trust He will work everything together for His good. I memorized this poem as a child, and it gave me comfort. A song is unseen.

To a Skylark by P. B. Shelley

In the golden lightning
Of the sunken sun,
O'er which clouds are bright'ning.
Thou dost float and run;
Like an unbodied joy whose race is
   just begun.

The pale purple even
Melts around thy flight;
Like a star of Heaven,
In the broad daylight
Thou art unseen, but yet I hear thy
   shrill delight.

Though I walk through the shadow of death . . . Today, I choose to rejoice in the shadow because for a shadow to be cast, that means there is light beyond. I must remember that light, and I must share it. For this season, I am where I do not belong, but even here, God reminds me to be a light as He is the Light—to sing a song unseen.

* * * * *

CHAPTER TWENTY-SEVEN

Little Rock, Arkansas
Present Day

"Three weeks from start to finish. I never would have believed it." Olivia stood in the front lobby area of the Summit Church, where no fewer than fifty volunteers had gathered to set up for the Character Club's Chocolate Ball.

Tall windows rose to the ceiling in the large square foyer of the church. Where attendees usually mingled on Sunday mornings, forty round tables were set up, each covered with a forest green tablecloth.

At each table, at least two women worked to set up their dishes and decorations. Olivia tried to picture how it would look tonight with low lights and flickering candlelight. It would impress the guests, but she was most excited for the teens to see the elegance and to know that all the work was for them.

Louis, standing beside her, seemed lost in thought. She watched as he glanced over his shoulder, curious if memories of the fine events he'd attended in Alloria ran through his mind. She suspected this was far different.

"A penny for your thoughts," she said.

He lifted his eyebrows, his blue eyes peering down at her. "Another American idiom?"

"Yes. But from that far-off look in your gaze, I may need to pay more than a penny for your thoughts."

"I was just thinking how much my mother would love this."

Olivia laughed. "Your mother was a queen. This would not have impressed her, but thank you for the smile."

"I'm not joking. Of course, we had grand events back home, but the staff organized them. The staff always did a fine job, but there wasn't the same passion. Everyone here is helping because they care for others. These people are giving of themselves because they want to make the world a better place. They aren't simply trying to live up to high standards and impress their friends."

Olivia gazed at the numerous volunteers around them, moving like busy ants around an ant hill—everyone with a purpose.

"God has brought amazing people around me to support this vision. I suppose I forget that sometimes. Even when I was in Kenya, I knew things would keep running. And then, after we lost everything, I knew my friends would come around us to help. I didn't know how much help we'd need at the last minute."

"It's a blessing to have friends like that. I suppose that no matter who I'm around, I always wonder if they want to be friends with me or the crown."

Olivia's jaw dropped slightly.

His finger curled under her chin. "Exactly."

"I didn't know who you were when we met," she confessed. "And I'm sort of glad I didn't."

"If you would have known, we would have never had that wonderful day out on the Masai Mara."

She pointed a finger into the air. "That is correct."

"You know, you're the first person I've met who considers it a disadvantage that I am the heir to the throne," Louis remarked, a playful glint in his eyes.

Olivia chuckled, "Surely not the first."

Louis leaned in, "And would you believe I also play the violin?"

Her eyes widened in mock surprise, "Really? A prince and a violinist?"

He smirked, "Are you going to hold that against me too?"

She laughed, "Maybe. It might just be a little too much royalty and sophistication for one person."

He leaned his forehead against hers. Louis's eyes fluttered shut, and he wrapped his arms around her, pulling her into a gentle hug. "It was wrong that I deceived you. I had a feeling that my status would push you away. It's not as if I want to hold back so much. I'm just afraid."

The hairs on the back of her neck rose at the moment's intimacy. She basked in his scent and placed her hands on his forearms, sliding them slowly to his wrists as if memorizing every muscle.

"Olivia, about the first time I saw you . . ." The tremble to his words frightened her.

Panic gripped her heart. "Louis, what is it?"

Instead of answering her, Louis turned his attention to the commotion around them. Chatter filled the room from the ladies decorating the tables.

Thirty-five women had each signed up to host a table. Since this morning, they'd been bringing in their linens, dishes, and centerpieces. Most of them had chosen a Christmas theme. Olivia's favorite was an African-themed table with fresh plants as centerpieces, beautifully patterned linens, and white and gold dishes with little wood-carved animals for the table place cards.

Anxiety crept into Olivia's heart as the chatter and festive atmosphere surrounded them. She held her breath, waiting for Louis to reveal what troubled him. His warm embrace provided a false sense of security, making facing the impending conversation harder.

"Surely not the first," she repeated the thought to herself, desperately seeking reassurance that her secret wasn't the cause of his distress. But deep down, she couldn't shake off the uneasiness within her.

Louis pulled away slightly, his eyes searching hers with concern and determination. The weight of his unspoken words hung heavily in the air as if the room had quieted, offering them a moment of privacy amidst the bustling activities.

Gently brushing his thumb against her cheek, he took a deep breath before speaking. "Olivia . . . I had been researching and stumbled upon a documentary that caught my attention. It was about Africa, and the voice narrating it . . . it drew me in."

Olivia's heart skipped a beat, her mind racing to find the right words. There were dozens of times she'd considered telling Louis about the documentary. Yet she always told herself she had plenty of time to tell him if she could figure out what to say.

I'm sorry, Louis, but I don't want anyone to connect my documentary with your royal status. I don't want anyone to think I'm dating you to grow my ratings.

Olivia had wished for her messages to come from a place of authenticity. The trouble was that she had to keep an essential part of herself hidden from Louis to do that.

Believing keeping this secret was the best course of action, she'd changed the subject every time Louis brought up her work in Africa. And now, confronted with the possibility that Louis had discovered her secret, Olivia struggled to maintain her composure.

Attempting to divert his attention, she gently withdrew from his embrace, her hands falling to her sides. "Louis, can we talk about this tomorrow? Tonight is about the event, and I don't want anything to spoil it for you or anyone else. I promise we'll discuss it then."

A flicker of disappointment crossed his face. "All right, Olivia, if that's what you want. But please, remember that I care for you and want honesty between us."

She forced a smile, her heart aching at the thought of losing the trust they had built. "I care for you too, Louis. Tomorrow, we'll have all the time we need to talk."

Olivia turned her attention back to the joyous surroundings. The familiar sights and sounds of the holiday season provided a comforting distraction, at least for now. Yet, deep down, she knew that their conversation the following day would be pivotal in their relationship, which could either strengthen their bond or push them apart.

Stepping back from Louis's grasp, Olivia smiled up at him. "This wouldn't be possible without you, you know. None of it." Her hand found his. "I need you . . . ." She opened her eyes wide and batted her eyelashes as she peered at him.

Louis opened his mouth to speak. "Need me? How—"

"Shh, don't say anything." She winked and placed a finger over his lips. "I need you to help me fold the programs. Are you game?"

Laughter spilled from Louis's lips. "Well, you got me there." He placed his hand on his heart. "Although I will always treasure those words, even if you simply need my help with folding programs."

Olivia pulled out a box and took it to a free table. Together they began folding the evening's programs, which included information about the Character Club and a significant ask for their financial needs. Too large of an ask for her comfort, but Miss Jan had sided with Louis.

"We can't expect people to open their pocketbooks wide if we can't tell them what we need," her older friend had said.

Louis sat by her side, and they began folding the programs together. She folded quickly while Louis ensured the edges lined up perfectly.

"I bet you never imagined yourself doing this." She pointed to where Sergio was helping an older lady carrying a cardboard box of dishes. She pointed. "I bet *he* never imagined it."

Louis glanced around at the hive of activity. "I can't speak for Sergio, but I love it. Mom wanted my sister and me to know real life, real people.

She'd often take us on humanitarian efforts with her, but it wasn't the same. The 'real-life' she offered us was still protected, sanctioned off, cleaned up, and protected."

"And if you weren't a prince, what would you have chosen to be?" Every day since his arrival, Olivia had become more comfortable asking Louis what she was curious about.

"I used to think maybe an outdoor guide. I love hiking with friends and imagined that taking people into the mountains would be thrilling. Or a treasure hunter. That always sounded adventurous. But, between us, I've always been partial to the strings. I'd enjoy learning new pieces and playing my violin. There's something special about connecting with an audience through music. So perhaps, a professional violinist."

"You play the violin? Why didn't you lead with that? It would've made for a much more fascinating introduction," she teased.

He chuckled, "Well, I like to keep some of my talents under wraps. Adds a touch of mystery, don't you think?"

Olivia feigned surprise, "Oh, you play the violin? I had no idea!" then winked.

He laughed, "Very funny. You caught me."

She grinned, "I aim to please. But, seriously, I'd love to hear you play. Can you imagine the girls' faces when they see all this? And then to hear you play . . ."

He straightened the stack of programs. "You love those teens, don't you?"

"I want them to see a bigger world out there than they know. They live in a place where daily survival is key. But they're smart. They're resourceful. I want to do for them what my aunt Liz did for me. Then maybe they'll see that instead of just thinking about surviving today, God has even more for them than they ever imagined."

Louis swept his hand around the room. "I love what you're doing here, Olivia. But have you ever thought of what you could do beyond Little Rock?"

"What do you mean beyond Little Rock?"

Louis's eyes studied hers intensely. "Have you ever considered the impact you could have on a larger world stage? You could be a voice. For the teen girls here. For the orphanages in Africa." He pushed aside the programs and took her hand. "You have so much to share. Stories people need to hear."

Olivia thought about Alessandra's journal. Liz wanted people to know about this amazing woman who sacrificed her life for others. Who went from a throne room to a concentration camp. Olivia's brow furrowed. She'd yet to tell Louis about her work, yet here he was, stating precisely what Aunt Liz had told her. *Your words matter. Your stories can make a difference.* Goose bumps rose on her arms.

Louis was helping her see that very thing in small ways here in Little Rock. A simple press release had gotten them museum passes. And the promotion of restaurants and caterers made this Chocolate Ball possible.

Since being here, Louis had shown Olivia that her words could benefit those in need—and those who gave—yet she was only one person. More than that, her heart was tied to these young women. She enjoyed getting to know them and spending time with them. And Miss Jan . . . Olivia's heart ached at the thought of abandoning her dear friend to do this work alone.

"I can't imagine not being here for the girls," she confessed. "They need someone to do for them what Liz did for me. I didn't know what it was like to grow up in a home with books. Yet with Liz, knowledge was valued. She praised my efforts. She gave me a sense of purpose. She introduced me to so much life to be lived beyond the inner-city streets I was used to."

Louis touched her arm, and Olivia paused, biting her lip.

"I promise to let this go, but I just have to say one more thing. And you don't even have to respond. It's just something to think about."

Olivia crossed her arms over her chest. "Okay, what is it?"

Louis sucked in a deep breath as if trying to get the courage to speak. "Perhaps, Olivia, the best way to help the teens is to show them how to live the life God has called them to. And to love and be loved in real ways. Can you imagine what an example that would be?"

Olivia allowed his words to sink in. To love and be loved? Is this what these feelings were? Or at least were they on the way there?

She opened her mouth to respond but didn't know what to say. How could she argue with his statement? She didn't know what life God had called her to.

"Can we talk about this later? I—" Olivia's words were cut short as the squeal of teen girls filled the air. Olivia turned to see Trinity, Destiny, and Leandra hurrying toward her. Each of them carried a garment bag.

While Olivia expected to see excitement and joy on their faces, nervousness and dread creased the girls' foreheads and dulled the sparkles from their eyes.

Olivia took a step in their direction. "It looks like you went shopping, but is something wrong?"

The teens looked at each other, and finally, Leandra spoke up. "After shopping, we stopped for gas and bought something inside the station. Uh . . ." Leandra looked at Trinity. "She took a test. A pregnancy test. And it's positive. Trinity is pregnant."

The world seemed to still as Olivia processed

the words. The joyful sound of the girls' laughter from moments ago seemed to hang like an unfinished melody, abruptly silenced. Her gaze darted to Trinity, who stood frozen, her gaze locked onto the ground.

The merriment that had earlier been evident in Trinity's bright eyes had vanished, replaced with a deep, hollow despair that Olivia found startling. The sight of the usually vibrant, resilient teen reduced to such a state struck a chord deep within Olivia's heart, and her breath hitched.

Louis, standing off to the side, shifted, eyes wide with surprise and lips pressed into a thin line. He appeared torn, wanting to step forward and offer comfort or support yet hesitating, perhaps trying to respect boundaries.

Undeniable tension filled the air. Olivia turned to the other girls, Destiny and Leandra, who stared at Trinity with mixed expressions of shock and concern.

Olivia's chest tightened. This was a significant turn of events, a new challenge to navigate. They had to talk, make plans, and offer Trinity support. But that would come later. Right now, Trinity needed comfort and understanding.

Taking a deep breath, Olivia crossed the distance between them and gently placed her hand on Trinity's trembling arm. Her eyes held a silent promise, an unspoken pledge to be there for her, to help her navigate this new reality. The path ahead would be difficult, but Olivia was sure of one thing: They would face it together.

Olivia remembered something that Miss Jan had taught her years ago. "No matter what news you hear, don't get emotional. And watch your words. Problems are problems, but people matter."

"God has a plan," Olivia heard herself saying. She offered Trinity a smile. And with that smile, big tears welled in Trinity's eyes.

"What am I gonna do?"

"We don't have to worry about that today, all right? We love you, and we're here for you. That's what family does." Then Olivia opened her arms, and Trinity fell into her embrace. Soon the other two teens joined in, their garment bags dropping to the floor. "It'll be all right. Everything will be okay. This baby—all babies—are a gift." Olivia patted Trinity's back and shushed her as if she were shushing a child. "I'm here. I'm here for you. You won't have to go through this alone." These girls were important. This night was necessary, even more so now.

CHAPTER TWENTY-EIGHT

After talking and praying with Trinity, the girls and Olivia changed in one of the church bathrooms. Over the years, other young women had become pregnant, and she and Miss Jan had done their best to keep them connected. The needs of being a teenager didn't change when a young woman became a mom.

As the time of the event neared, Olivia moved to the stage to check the microphone on the podium. She scanned the room. Louis was right. The addition of thousands of sparkly lights transformed everything about the room, converting it from a church foyer to a magical ballroom brimming with beauty.

Olivia smoothed down her simple black sheath dress that Rebecca had insisted she buy five years ago. Olivia was glad that she had listened. She wore it to almost every dressy occasion. It fit her curvy frame perfectly and looked good even with low heels and simple jewelry.

Footsteps sounded behind her. Olivia turned, and her breath caught. Louis stood there, his blond hair perfectly styled, crinkling his eyes into a smile. The navy blue suit covering his frame brought out the blue of his gaze. Even though the last three weeks had been a lot of work, she'd enjoyed this time of closeness. Their goal had been to pull off this event, yet spending time with Louis had kindled loving feelings toward him.

"Wow, you clean up well." Her words were no more than a whisper.

"And you, dear Olivia, are a feast for one's eyes."

Heat rose to Olivia's cheeks. She was about to brush off his words, but the appreciation in his eyes flipped her stomach. Even though she found it hard to believe, this remarkable man—this prince—found her beautiful.

She took another deep breath and averted her gaze lest she melt into a puddle on this stage. "The room looks nice, too, don't you think?"

"It's stunning. Everything is lovely."

She smiled. "I am certain this is nothing compared to your dinners at the palace. And I can't imagine the extravagance of larger events, but it looks rather nice." Her gaze moved from table to table, her heart warming at all the loving care that went into decorating each one.

While round tables had been set up in the center of the room, around the perimeter, long tables covered with gold cloth held delicious desserts. At least one representative from each restaurant or caterer waited with an eager expression to offer their treats to attendees.

Movement caught her attention, and Olivia

spotted volunteers opening the doors. "Well, here we go," Olivia said, watching as the first guests entered in gowns and suits.

"And your friend, Rebecca. Will she be joining us tonight?"

Olivia shook her head. "That was the plan, but no. Unfortunately, she had to work later today than scheduled because the maternity ward was hopping. Then she texted and said there was a big accident on 40. She may make it to the end, but don't expect her to."

"So after the ball?"

"She wants us to come to stay at her parents' new place. I have the address. She has a few days off and . . ."

Louis tilted his head. "And?"

"And I'm pretty sure she wants to check you out. Give you the third degree. Measure you up . . . you know, all the idioms that go with making sure you're good enough for her best friend."

Louis stroked his chin. "Yes, I see. I got your text. I packed a bag. Sergio isn't happy." Louis looked over to the door, and Olivia followed his gaze.

She chuckled to see Sergio keeping watch by the door. "At least he'll get a day off."

"Just don't tell my father." Louis ran a finger around his collar. "Speaking of my father, there's something I need to talk to you about. It has to do with what's happening back home. Back

389

in Alloria. I got a call from my father as I was changing."

She looked from Louis to the room, noting nearly every chair was filled. Then she checked her watch. "Now?" They had ten minutes left.

"No, later." He scanned the room with a hint of sadness she didn't understand. "Maybe tonight."

The Chocolate Ball flowed effortlessly, as if they had planned it for a year and not three weeks. After welcoming everyone, Olivia invited the guests to choose two desserts and to try as many samples as they liked. Every guest was given a sheet to vote for their favorite, promising that the winners would be highlighted in the *Arkansas Gazette*.

Olivia spoke about the Character Club and their work with Miss Jan by her side. Then, when they were called up, Desiree and Leandra shared what they learned—about job training, how to create a budget, and what they'd learned about the Bible and God.

As Desiree and Leandra talked, Trinity stood to the side. Olivia was about to thank the girls for speaking when Trinity approached the mic. "I wasn't going to say anything, but I have to tell you that my life is different because of these ladies. I thought I knew the meaning of family, but these ladies have shown me what it means. They love me when I do things right and when I mess up. And because they love me, I know that God loves me too. Thank you."

The girls hurried off the stage, but Louis approached and led them back up as everyone in the audience stood one by one. And then, as the teens clung to Olivia and cried, Miss Jan approached the stage. She thanked those who'd provided desserts, and the audience gave them a standing ovation.

With a beaming smile, Miss Jan announced those who had won for best desserts. The smiling owner of Cocoa Belle Chocolates rushed up to accept the award for her chocolate cherry croissant bread pudding. Then, after the photographer for the newspaper took photos, Louis picked up his violin.

Olivia hadn't asked what he would play, and the tune surprised her. She turned to Miss Jan. "This is 'True Colors' by Cyndi Lauper." The music filled the room with emotion and a sense of celebration.

Peace filled Olivia as she watched the scene in front of her. *And I see your true colors shining through. I see your true colors. And that's why I love you.*

She couldn't imagine a more perfect song. The violin picked up in tempo, and her heart soared. Yes, this was what she wanted these teens to know. That she saw them—saw their beauty. Their differences made them beautiful, and together they fit like a rainbow. She couldn't stop the tears from falling. And then, just as the last note faded and the audience rose to clap, Louis launched into a new song.

A captivating silence fell over the room as the final note echoed. The spellbinding performance had left a palpable stillness. Olivia found herself in a trance, lost in the resonance of the music and the mesmerizing display of talent before her.

Louis stood at the center with the violin still clutched in his hands. His eyes closed as if savoring the silence that followed the storm of his music. His hair was a bit disheveled, a testament to the passion and fervor with which he had played, making him look all the more enticing. A thin layer of sweat shone on his forehead, evidence of the intensity of the performance.

Olivia was captivated not just by the talent he possessed but by the passion and zeal with which he had played. She had always known Louis to be remarkable, but at this moment, he seemed almost ethereal.

His eyes fluttered open, and they instantly found hers in the crowd. There was a question in those blue depths, a silent inquiry if she had enjoyed the performance. Olivia felt a shiver run down her spine under his intense gaze. The air between them seemed to crackle with an electric tension that Olivia had come to associate exclusively with Louis.

A moment passed between them, unspoken words exchanged in a mere glance. And then, as if snapping back to reality, the room's silence broke into a wave of applause. The moment was gone, replaced by the tangible excitement of the audience.

The applause was thunderous. People stood clapping, their faces alight with awe and admiration. Yet, for Olivia, the sounds seemed distant, muted. All she could see, all she could hear was Louis. And at that moment, she realized how much she was entwined with him, not just by circumstances but by emotions growing stronger by the minute.

As if moved by the spirit, Miss Jan—who sat on the front row—jumped to her feet. "Thank you, Lord, for your music and your provision." She reached over and lifted a donation envelope from the table. "Don't you think if the good Lord can provide music like this tonight, He can provide all our needs? Yes, He can."

The room erupted into applause, and the crowd reached for the envelopes. Louis played softly in the background as guests filled the envelopes and passed them to the volunteers waiting for collection. Olivia had taken part in many fund-raising events, and although this part of such events was usually awkward, tonight's guests were filled with excitement and joy.

Tears filled Olivia's eyes as one of their

supporters, a local judge, stepped forward to the stage.

"I was supposed to urge you to give what you could before you prayed, but I think someone stole my thunder." Judge Leverett winked at Miss Jan. "I've been texting a few of my friends, and we decided to match whatever is given tonight." He waved a finger in the air. "So be generous, friends. It's almost the end of the year, and one of my friends thinks this is the perfect ministry to support an end-of-the-year write-off." Judge Leverett smiled. "Let's make him pay."

Laughter filled the room, and then a sweet peace as Judge Leverett ended the night in prayer. Olivia's heart felt as if it had expanded to nearly double the size within, and she couldn't have imagined a more beautiful evening if she'd tried.

As everyone rose to leave, Olivia stood as Louis strode toward her, violin in hand. She clasped her hands together. "What was that?"

"What?" He tilted his head with a mischievous grin.

"That second song." She placed her hand over her heart. "I've never experienced anything like it."

" 'Ciocarlia,' the Skylark." Louis set his violin and bow on the table, then squeezed her hands in his.

"Did you say Skylark?"

"Is that why it sounded like a bird chirping?" Desiree asked, rushing up.

"Yes. I had planned on playing something else. But when I was talking to Aunt Regina yesterday, she suggested it. It was my mother's favorite."

Louis released Olivia's hands and hugged Desiree. "You were wonderful. Simply wonderful—" His words were interrupted by a call from her friends, and Desiree quickly rushed off, her red gown with a tulle skirt bouncing as she did.

"It was amazing, unbelievable." Olivia took a step closer to Louis. "I had no idea you were so talented. And 'Skylark' . . ." She shook her head while the translated poem about the skylark that she'd just read filtered through her memory. Goose bumps rose on her arms. This was not a coincidence. God was in this. In all of it. If the purpose of her meeting Louis was only for this night, then their time together would have been worth it. Yet her heart told her it was for more.

"I'm thrilled you enjoyed it, but *you* were the queen of the ball." Moving as if he had walked off a movie set, he stepped forward and swept her into a hug, turning in a slow circle.

She laughed, imagining they had an audience for the display. She could almost see the teens from across the room laughing and pointing. In slow motion, Louis lowered her feet back to the ground.

"I feel like a queen at this moment. Or maybe a princess." She ran her fingers along the lapel of his suit.

Olivia felt a tap on her shoulder, and she turned. Rebecca stood there, arms wide. Olivia couldn't help but squeal as she opened her arms for a quick embrace.

"All right, you have to tell me what I missed." Rebecca pulled back and then eyed Louis. "The buzz as I walked in was this was the best event they'd ever attended, and I have to meet this violinist who everyone says must be smitten with the director from the pure look of affection in his eyes."

"Rebecca." Louis gave a low bow, then reached out his hand to shake. "It's an honor to meet you."

Rebecca eyed his hand and shook her head. "How about a hug instead? I deserve that. It was my tooth problem that brought you together, remember?" She laughed.

Louis chuckled, offered her a greeting hug, and stepped back. He cleared his throat. "Now, ladies, I've been ordered by Miss Jan to sweep you away." He offered both of his arms. "Olivia, under no circumstances are you supposed to stay to clean up. Let's be off, shall we? Olivia and Rebecca, if you join me, I have a car waiting outside to take us away from the ball."

"It's not a carriage, but it will do." She smiled

as she peered up at him. In her mind, she knew that Louis still had something to tell her about Alloria. And she had a few things to say to him, too. But for now, she would allow herself to be swept away by her prince, this time with her best friend.

As Olivia walked with Louis and Rebecca toward the exit, a reporter from the *Arkansas Gazette* rushed toward them, camera raised and a glint of excitement in her eyes. "Excuse me! I already took photos of the dessert winners. I'd love to get a photo of you?" she said, her voice tinged with anticipation.

Louis's face betrayed a moment of concern, and he turned to Olivia, his eyes searching hers for an answer. In the depths of those eyes, Olivia sensed his uncertainty and trust in her judgment. Gathering her thoughts, she replied with gentle firmness, "We really want the focus of the night to be on the program and the girls."

"Photos of smiling attendees are always a hit." The reporter shrugged. "It helps future donors to know that others enjoyed the event, although it's even doubtful the photo will make the paper, you know?" The reporter's voice stumbled over her words as she hurriedly explained. "Breaking news always jumps in and takes space from community events like this."

Olivia opened her mouth to protest again, and Louis touched the small of her back. His smile broke through, warm and reassuring, his words a soothing balm. "Well, in that case, how can we refuse a fleeting moment of fame?" He positioned himself between Olivia and Rebecca, but instead of looking at the camera, he turned to look into Olivia's face, offering a gentle smile. Olivia returned the focus as the reporter took the shot.

Smart. Olivia's smile grew. Just another handsome man attending the event—no one would ever tell it was Prince Louis from Alloria at that angle.

As they moved to leave, the reporter's voice followed them once more, a haunting echo. "You know, Olivia, your voice sounds familiar."

Louis's gaze, filled with curiosity and a hint of concern, weighed on Olivia. With a prayer for guidance, she summoned a light smile. "Some people have 'one of those faces,' and I suppose I have one of those voices."

As they left the venue, stepping into the cool embrace of the night, Rebecca's soft whisper reached Olivia's ear. "What do you think she meant by that? Do you think she knows?"

Olivia shook her head, her voice barely above a whisper. "It didn't seem like it. After all, I do have one of those voices."

"Yes, but she knew your name. She called you Olivia."

"I believe my name was in the program along

with Miss Jan's. Please, don't get me over-thinking this." Still, the reporter did mention her voice—the only thing distinguishable from the documentary.

Olivia breathed in a prayer of peace as Louis opened the car door for her. She wouldn't allow a pushy reporter to disrupt the night's memories and the growing affection for Louis that lingered in her heart. They were friends, but Olivia sensed it was growing into something more—a delicate dance of love, understanding, and increasing trust. She wanted Louis to know the full her. And she had a feeling tonight might be a good night to begin sharing her story.

But could she? Could she ever truly share all the broken pieces of her past?

CHAPTER TWENTY-NINE

From the look of their new house, Rebecca's parents had done well selling their business. The two-story dwelling had been built on a hillside overlooking the Arkansas River in one of the most sought-after neighborhoods in Little Rock.

Rebecca welcomed Louis and Olivia into the spacious living room with a view of the lighted Big Dam Bridge dancing in red and green lights for the Christmas season. Blues and whites adorned the space, and a fire glowed in the fireplace.

"I'm so glad you're here. It's only been a little over a month since I've seen you, but it seems like forever." Rebecca hugged Olivia again and squeezed tightly before turning to Louis. "So, you are the man my best friend speaks of with fond favor?" she asked with a flourish in her best English accent.

"Well, that is quite the sentence." His lips curled up slightly as they always did when he was humored.

Rebecca squealed and bounced on her toes, brushing her curls over her shoulder. "I'd say my pleasure, but it was the pits. I've told everyone I'd never want to relive the pain again or the stress of getting my tooth pulled in a dentist's office that also served as a taxi station. But now that you say that, I'm glad it happened. It was worth it for Olivia's sake, wasn't it?"

Rebecca stepped closer and elbowed Olivia. Her bony elbow jabbed into Olivia's rib.

Olivia winced. "Ow! Why do you always do that?"

"Bad habit, but you'll forgive me when you see this." Rebecca waved her hand to the large dining room table. "You two sit because I have a gift for Olivia—something she's going to love if I say so myself."

"Sure, but I'm still wearing this dress. Can I ditch it after this?" Olivia called after her friend, who'd disappeared down the hall. Not thirty seconds later, Rebecca returned with a small blue-and-white-striped gift bag in hand.

Olivia eyed the offering. "Hey, isn't that the bag I put your last birthday gift in?"

"Yes, and aren't you glad I saved it? It makes the surprise so much better." Rebecca gently laid the gift bag on the table. With eager movements, Olivia pulled the tissue paper out of the bag and peered in. She gasped when she saw the yellow princess Cinderella coach tucked inside.

Olivia burst into tears. "This is impossible." She lifted the lid and saw the mirror intact, and then she turned it over and noticed the turn key. "This can't be . . ." She slowly turned the key.

Tears pricked her eyes as the music played.

"What's going on?" Louis looked from Rebecca to Olivia, back to Rebecca again.

Rebecca shrugged. "Olivia's Cinderella music box broke during her last move. It had been one of her favorite things as a child, and I rescued it from the trash can. It took me a few years to find spare pieces and someone to fix it."

"This is amazing. Thank you!" Olivia placed the music box on the table and offered Rebecca another hug. "What did I do to deserve a friend like you?"

"Yes, well, you'll thank me in the morning," Rebecca whispered.

Olivia frowned as Rebecca pulled back and glanced at her buzzing smartwatch. She released a soft moan. "Ugh. One of my friends has been dealing with a bad break up. I have to talk to her." Rebecca rubbed her eyes and yawned, even though she didn't look the least bit tired. "Why don't you two enjoy the fire and relax? The fridge is filled with snacks and drinks." Rebecca stretched. "After this chat, I will call it a night."

Olivia eyed her friend. It was too convenient that she'd gotten a phone call right now. Rebecca must have set a timer on her phone when she'd gone for the gift bag, but Olivia wouldn't argue. Having time to talk with Louis in front of a fire sounded like the perfect end to the evening.

After Rebecca showed them their rooms, they

emerged in T-shirts and sweatpants ten minutes later. Olivia made them hot cocoa, and she settled onto one of the sofas while Louis stretched out on the floor before the fireplace.

"I was hoping you'd tell me about the jewelry box," Louis said before Olivia had a chance to ask more about his violin performances—a safe topic, in her opinion.

Olivia took a sip of her cocoa and shrugged. "I'm not sure you want to hear the whole story. It's not pretty."

"Each of our lives has high points and low points. But I understand if you aren't ready to tell me yet."

Olivia's brow furrowed at his words. Every day she woke up expecting Louis to decide that he wouldn't stick around, that she wasn't worth it. Yet phrases like *"I understand if you aren't ready to tell me"* showed her that wasn't true.

I need to trust him. More than that, he needs to know what he's getting into if he sticks around.

Olivia set the mug on a coaster on the side table, knit her hands together, and set them on her lap. She wanted to meet the deep blue of his eyes but was afraid she'd start to cry if she did.

"Things were difficult for my mother. She had me when she was eighteen, and I've never known my father. The only thing my mom ever told me was that his name was Robert, and he died in a car accident shortly after she found out she was pregnant." Olivia shrugged. "I'm not sure if that's the truth, but I've decided to leave it at that."

Louis nodded, urging her to go on. His eyes shone with sincerity.

"We never had much. Wait, let me rephrase that. We never had enough. I knew I was hungry more than full. My clothes . . . well, I'm embarrassed by what we wore. My mom tried, but the other shoe would drop as soon as something good happened, and we'd lose it all. Once, we were staying with a nice friend, and the woman died in a car accident. Another time the mobile home we were living in caught on fire. I was sure we weren't meant to have nice things."

"That's so difficult." Louis reached over and took her hand. "It's hard to believe all that happened to one person."

"It's what we knew. It's how life went for us. What would have seemed like a big trauma was just another part of life to us. How sad is that? From the time I was little, I had to be responsible. My mom struggled. She had a hard time keeping a job, and we never had a place to live. At the most, it was a few months.

"Then there were the guys. I can remember some of their names, but not all of them. She had a type—those who liked to make promises. Who'd give her money for bills or gas. Who'd invite her to move in but would treat her—us—like a burden after a few weeks." An involuntary shudder ran down her spine. "Maybe she thought living with guys like that was better than being homeless, but with each place we went, she changed, evolving into who she thought they wanted her to be so they'd let us stay."

"Did things ever get better?" He studied her with his blue eyes fixed on hers. So full of compassion and tenderness.

Olivia swallowed hard. She closed her eyes momentarily and pressed two fingers to her lips. She hadn't expected a surge of emotions to rise with his question. How could she tell him that things only got better after she lost her mom? Afterward, she was able to make her own choices. She only had to think of herself. She sucked in a deep breath, released it slowly, and blinked back moisture. She refused to allow herself to be pulled into the sorrow she'd been pushing aside for over a decade. She wanted to tell this story and share her loss.

"I lost her to an overdose. It was ruled a suicide, although some believe her boyfriend at the time gave her bad drugs. She died just a month after my tenth birthday. The jewelry box was the last present she gave me. After that, I moved in with a foster family. I took out my anger over losing my mom on them. Sharon and Dewayne live in Dallas. We keep in touch, but I'm closer to Sharon's younger sister. Liz is nearer to my age than Sharon."

Olivia wished she could confide in Louis about Princess Alessandra, but she'd made a promise to Liz to keep it a secret for now. Given his royal background, Louis might understand the princess's situation better than most.

"And what about other family members?" Louis inquired, leaning in.

"Grandparents, but I only remember seeing them once." Olivia's eyes darted from his gaze back to her hands. "They lived a few hours away from our Dallas home. I was too young to recall the exact place. We drove to their house.

"I didn't understand when she pulled into the driveway. It wasn't a castle, but it seemed like it to me." Olivia offered a sad smile and relaxed even more. "But there were three or four garages and a large covered porch in the front with a porch swing and flowers. My mom sat silently in the car for what seemed like hours, staring at the front door as if she expected someone to walk out. No one did."

"What happened?" His voice was soft.

"My mom took out her brush and brushed out her long blonde hair. I hadn't realized how long it was until she did. She usually wore it up, twisted around her head. But it was beautiful, long, and thick. She grabbed a pink sweater and put it on over her T-shirt, and I was amazed at how different she looked, almost as if she belonged in this house. Maybe I'd overheard her talking about it. Or deep down, I knew that she didn't belong in the types of places we'd been living.

"A woman came to the door first, and they talked for a minute, and then a man came outside and talked on the porch. They seemed to know each other. At one point, the man looked at the car as if eyeing me, and then he simply shook his head and walked back inside.

"My mother sat on the front porch step and cried. She looked so defeated, and that night we drove to a community park and slept in our car. I remember being hungry but didn't want to upset her even more."

"So those were your grandparents?"

"Yes, and from the looks of it, they had everything, yet they sent us away. I knew then that what I'd once heard in a backyard Bible club was correct: Money is the root of evil. To have more than enough and then keep it to yourself . . ." She shrugged. "It didn't seem right. I believed the only good riches were in heaven, pearly gates, mansions, and streets of gold. Only later I realized the true treasure of heaven is people. They are what's eternal. They are what we will find the most joy in. For the rich, what they have now is the best they'll ever have. But for those who believe in Jesus, we can look forward to so much more."

"But surely how your grandparents treated you

didn't make you think that all people with wealth are that way, did it?"

"Aren't they, at least to some degree?" Her brow furrowed. "It's not as if the needs of this world are hidden. Sure, the rich can stay out of the inner city, but homeless men and women are everywhere. Then there are the commercials on television asking for support. People must choose whether to make a difference or look away. There are a million reasons to cover your eyes, but in the end, it's easier to do so when you have money as a distraction."

The fire crackled, and the energy in the room did too. The peaceful moments of before were gone, and heat moved up Olivia's arms.

"But maybe they just don't understand—not truly," Louis said gently. "Maybe they need someone like you to tell them this in a new way they can relate to."

Olivia knew what he was doing, attempting to tell her again that God had a bigger purpose for her than the one she was living. She waited for Louis to bring up the generosity of those tonight, and she was glad he didn't. What she'd just experienced hours before proved that giving wasn't as black and white as she sometimes told herself it was.

"You're missing the point. The people who should have been loving us best turned their backs on us. They had everything, and we had nothing. All we needed was a little help . . .” She shook her head and glanced at the music box on the table. “I just don’t understand. That’s all.”

“Have you seen them since?”

“Not once. Why wouldn’t someone want to know their granddaughter?”

The fire spit and then settled. She stretched her arms along the sofa cushions, telling herself to relax. Without a word, Louis rose from his place on the carpet and settled beside her. With his closeness, she pulled her arms in tight again.

Instead of arguing, he wrapped a soft arm around her shoulders. Olivia’s back remained stiff, and her shoulders rigid, refusing to relax into his embrace. Her mind screamed at her to run. Louis, after all, represented what she’d grown up resenting.

With the gentlest movements, Louis’s thumb moved in small, tender, and delicate circles. The tension in her chest loosened with each circular motion.

Olivia couldn’t help but allow her shoulders to ease. Then her back slumped, and she leaned into him. Louis scooted straighter, allowing her room to tuck her head under his chin. They sat there in silence, everything else forgotten. And then he placed the softest kiss on her head. First, one followed by another, almost like a father would do to his little girl. A trickle of tears came then. This time they refused to be held back.

Conviction ran through her. Olivia had to tell him everything. If they couldn't be together, he at least had to know the real reasons why.

"I could have had a family, but I refused," she admitted. "Sharon and Dewayne were thinking about adopting me. To do that, they had to read the disclosure papers. Dewayne kept them in his closet, but it was an easy lock to pick. One night when they were sleeping, I got in there and read my file. I wrote down my grandparents' names. Then I searched for my grandfather on the Internet. He was some type of business tycoon."

"And why don't you think he helped your mother?"

"Bad PR for business is my guess. You see, he had a lot of ties with Christian organizations. What would it have looked like if people knew the truth about his daughter? About how she had a child so young?" Tears rimmed Olivia's eyes. "I always thought it was my fault. My mother could have lived that wonderful life if I hadn't been born."

"Olivia . . ."

Her throat tightened, and her eyes misted over at his compassion.

"How can any child be responsible for her birth?"

"I know that. At least now. But my heart sometimes tells me differently. And that's the thing about children. Their thinking is so limited. In one of my psychology classes, I learned what happened doesn't matter nearly as much as how someone perceives it."

"And what about the adoption?"

"I told them I didn't want to be adopted. Since I was older than eleven by that time, I was given the decision. I thought I'd hurt my mom if I let them adopt me." Olivia held up her hands. "I know, perception, remember? She was gone, but it was almost as if I was giving up on her too." There was more than that, but it was too much to explain. She had too many regrets.

"Sharon and Dewayne let me live there until I went to college. I went back sometimes for holidays until I met Rebecca, and she became more like a sister to me than a friend. And Aunt Liz never has allowed me to get away with blocking her out."

Olivia leaned back farther into the cushions. She surprised herself. Only once had she ever opened up like this, and that was with Rebecca. She hoped Louis could see now why they could never be together. The media would dig up every part of her past, bringing shame to Louis—to his kingdom.

Then again, what if he didn't know what was good for him? What if this didn't scare him away? When she looked into Louis's eyes, she knew he wanted more. The fact that he had come to Little Rock and spent all this time with her proved that. But he didn't know what he was getting into. Louis liked the idea of her. She was different from the other young women he was around. But different wasn't always good.

CHAPTER THIRTY

L ouis and Olivia sat quietly, their presence enveloped by the warm embrace of the living room. Soft rays of moonlight filtered through the sheer curtains, casting a gentle glow over the space. The delicate chimes of the mantel clock provided a comforting soundtrack. Olivia leaned against Louis's chest, finding solace in the rhythmic beating of his heart, a steady reminder of the love that bound them together.

Just as Olivia wondered if Louis had fallen asleep, his voice broke the serene silence. "I lost my mom too. I understand."

A wave of compassion washed over Olivia. She sat up, angling herself on the cushion to peer into Louis's face. Tears rimmed his eyes.

"Oh, Louis, I'm so sorry." She wanted to know more, to uncover the depths of his experiences and the memories that lingered within his heart.

"We used to joke that she was the party and Dad was the duty." Louis's voice was tinged with a bittersweet reminiscence. "We still haven't learned how to celebrate again. That's why tonight was so special. And that's why everyone is working so hard back home for my father's jubilee. I think everyone's trying to capture what was lost." Louis paused, his gaze lingering upon

Olivia. She shifted slightly on the couch cushion, still unaccustomed to the intensity of someone's gaze, especially one filled with tenderness and care. The living room, once a space filled with mere furniture and decor, transformed into a sanctuary of shared vulnerability and healing.

"What was she like?" Olivia dared to ask. "She must have been someone special to catch the attention of a prince."

Louis squeezed her shoulder. "Yes, she was." He paused, filling his eyes with her.

"I don't talk about my mother much, but I miss her daily. If my father is steadfast, she is life, light. She'd grown up in the mountains, and she loved them. No matter how beautiful it was, staying cooped up in an old castle wasn't for her. She loved to ski, to hike. The mountains were her second home. I was supposed to go with her the day she disappeared."

"Disappeared?"

"She'd gone out for a hike with a friend yet didn't come home that evening. Dinner came then bedtime. If my mother was anything, she was consistent. My father sent out search parties right away, and within hours the news received wasn't good. The body of my mother's friend was found on the trail. It appeared she'd suffered a heart attack. Like my mother, she was in her fifties, so it was a shock. From what they found on the scene, it was clear my mother had tried to help her. Everyone assumed she'd gone for help, but that doesn't explain why she disappeared."

Olivia lifted trembling fingers to her mouth. "I can't imagine. I'm so sorry . . ."

An echo of her words hung in the air. Louis's gaze fixed on her. His blue eyes harbored a profound sadness. For a fleeting moment, they were bound by an invisible thread of shared grief and the struggle to move beyond it.

Louis reached out, taking her hand in his. His touch was warm, a lifeline grounding her. She gave his hand a gentle squeeze.

Silence fell between them again. The silence spoke of shared understanding and comfort in each other's presence amid the storm of emotions.

As she looked into Louis's eyes, she saw more than the prince who had walked into her life unexpectedly. She saw a man battling with his past yet yearning to move forward. And in that moment, she realized they weren't so different after all. Their pasts chained both of them, their hearts bearing the scars of painful losses. Yet, here they were, holding on to each other amidst the whirlwind of emotions, finding solace and understanding in their shared pain.

"Hikers in that area that day had reported a solitary male hiker that no one could locate," Louis continued. "Some worried he was somehow involved in my mother's disappearance, but we discovered that wasn't the case two days later."

Louis's brow folded, and his eyebrows pinched with emotion. Tears filled his eyes, and he tried to brush them away with his thumbs.

"It's okay to cry if you don't want to share."

"No." The word slipped from his lips. "I do not mind. I have told the story to others. I am not sure why it is bothering me now."

Olivia waited, knowing the feeling of wanting to be strong yet failing.

"They found her body two days later at the bottom of a ravine," he stated. "She'd been running down the mountain for help when she tripped and fell. It was a horrible accident, and the only thing that makes me feel a little better is that she spent her last day in the mountains that she loved."

"And your father? How did he handle it?"

"Truthfully, he's made work his bride. He rules the country with wisdom, power, and dedication, but few realize the dedication is hiding a broken heart." Louis sighed. "When I was young, Aunt Regina told me that I could see our position as tasks, or I could see it as joy. She told me not to worry so much about work that I miss out on life. As responsible people, we will handle those things when they come. She told me we miss the beautiful moments of life if we're always looking ahead at what needs to be accomplished."

"Or looking back." The words slipped out of

Olivia's mouth before she had time to filter them.

"I suppose that can be the case. We often don't enjoy the moments God gives us because our mind is on something else, somewhere else, or even the past. A past we never can change."

The hour was late, so Olivia scooted forward on the sofa and stood. "I can't believe how long we've been talking." She shifted slightly, wishing she knew what to say. She'd poured out her life story, which was both freeing and scary. Would Louis see her differently now?

Louis stood, too, and reached for their mugs on the side table. "Here, let me get these."

He hurried to the kitchen and rinsed out the mugs, placing them in the dishwasher as if doing so was the most natural thing in the world. A longing grew within Olivia. If she opened her heart to Louis, it would be possible for evenings like tonight to be part of her everyday life. She wanted to tell herself that this growing relationship with Louis would lead to the ultimate heartbreak. But now and then, little lights of hope poked through her heart. And for the first time, she didn't want to snuff them out.

Suddenly, a sense of gratitude washed over her. Gratitude for Louis, his vulnerability, his strength, and his persistent presence in her life. This shared moment of emotion, of acknowledging their past and seeking a way toward the future, was a testament to the depth of their

417

connection. This connection was becoming more profound with every passing day.

As she watched, Louis moved with comfortable familiarity. Olivia couldn't help but marvel at the strange dichotomy of their worlds colliding. Here was a man, a prince, who belonged in the grandeur of castles and was accustomed to royal ceremonies, doing something as mundane as rinsing mugs in a kitchen sink. His graceful demeanor in such a humble setting spoke volumes about the man he was—kind, humble, and deeply compassionate.

Louis had shared a significant part of his life with her, laid bare the deep-seated pain and vulnerability he hid beneath the polished exterior. It touched her in a way she hadn't anticipated. His strength in confronting the past and his desire to embrace the present was inspiring and endearing.

Their eyes met as he turned, and a moment of understanding passed between them. A soft smile curved Olivia's lips. It was as though the barriers between them had been torn down, replaced by a newfound sense of intimacy. He was no longer just a prince. He was Louis, a man as real and complex as anyone else, bearing the scars of his past yet hopeful for the future.

With a sigh, she allowed herself to entertain the thought she'd been warding off since Louis had come into her life. *What if?*

What if she let him in? What if she opened

herself to the possibility of a future with him? As the thought blossomed, Olivia found herself surprisingly unafraid of the answer. Their journey through the night had seemed effortless, from formal wear and violin solos to sweatpants and cocoa. Could their journey together be the same, with grandeur and daily life ebbing and flowing from a common desire to serve God and others?

Louis turned and smiled, meeting her gaze. "Well, someone's lost in thought. What are you thinking about?"

"I was thinking about tonight—the Chocolate Ball, listening to you play the violin, pouring out my heart in the firelight." She laughed. "I didn't see that one coming."

Louis tilted his chin and lifted his arm as if holding up an imaginary violin. He moved his other hand to grasp the imaginary bow, and his right foot began to tap a lively tune. "You didn't know I had that in me, did you?"

"Not at all. That was the last thing I expected."

"I like that I surprised you. I like to see your smile. And hear your laugh. It's one of the most beautiful sounds I've ever heard."

"You make me laugh so easily, Louis."

Louis closed the dishwasher and then walked toward her. "Good, that means I'll hear more of it. A lot more."

Something, *hope,* brimmed in the blue depths

of his eyes. Did he also wonder if they could have ordinary days just like this?

Louis's posture was subtly relaxed as he leaned against the counter beside her. He rested his arm on the counter, reaching forward to rest a hand on her back.

"I'm glad we had this time, Olivia. Thank you for opening your heart, for trusting me, and . . ."

She tilted her head in his direction. "And?"

"I have to admit I'm falling in love with you. And if I don't kiss you this moment, I think I may burst. Do I have your permission?"

Olivia's heart skittered. Heat rose to her cheeks. Out of all the times someone had kissed her, no one had ever asked for permission. And no one had ever looked at her with such love in his eyes.

Louis's lips parted slightly. His intense eyes never left hers.

"Yes, you have permission," she whispered.

Instead of directing his lips to hers, he leaned down, kissed her just under her jaw, and moved first to one cheek then the other. He then pressed his lips to hers gently, tenderly.

Olivia wrapped her arms around Louis's neck. The softness of his skin and the curls of hair that touched his collar caressed her fingers. He spread his hands on her back, pulling her close, and the thrum of his heart permeated through his shirt. It was then, in his arms, the kiss deepened. His eager lips found hers. He tasted like chocolate. Sweet chocolate.

There was no place she'd rather be than with Louis.

And just when she thought she could get lost in his kisses, Louis released her and pulled back. Olivia released her clasped hands and dared to open her eyes.

Was something wrong? She wanted to ask, but from the look in Louis's eyes, nothing was wrong. Everything seemed right, too right. As she swallowed, attempting to control her emotions, Olivia understood.

Louis peered down at her with a smile. "I only asked permission for one kiss." His voice was husky. "I want to honor you. And I'm . . . afraid of myself."

"Thank you." It was all she could manage to say as she stepped away. She understood what he meant. She wanted the kisses to continue, which surprised and delighted her.

"See you in the morning?" She offered an awkward wave.

"There is nothing I'd love more." A hint of sadness touched Louis's smile, and she thought about asking about it but didn't want to break the spell.

Then, without looking over her shoulder, Olivia hurried to her room and quickly shut the door. She was falling hard for him, and for the first time, she wouldn't question what that would mean for her future. Tonight she wanted to fall asleep with the joy that filled her, knowing God had a plan. And for tonight, she dared to trust Him in that.

CHAPTER THIRTY-ONE

The buzz from her cell phone woke Olivia from a deep sleep. She opened one eye to read the text. Girl, you're dating a prince?

A gasp escaped Olivia's lips. She rubbed her eyes, blinked twice, and looked closer. The text was from Desiree.

Olivia wiped her left eye with the palm of her hand and then sat upright, adjusting herself on the bed. She smacked her dry lips together, noting her mouth tasted like chocolate. She tried to make sense of the text. *The Chocolate Ball . . . the prince of the ball, of course.* That had to be it. Surely Desiree hadn't figured out the truth.

The searing red numerals on the bedside clock of the guest room pierced through the early morning gloom, boldly declaring it six o'clock. Too early to get up by her standards. Olivia groaned, turning away from the accusatory glare of the digits, seeking solace in the muted gray light filtering in through the curtains.

Louis was like the prince of the ball. She texted back. Wasn't the violin music beautiful? What are you doing?

Haven't slept. Trinity stayed over.

A baby emoji filled her screen.

People magazine got photos of the ball. 2 of you.

Olivia gasped then opened the browser on her phone and went to *People*'s site. On the home page was a photo of Louis twirling her around with twinkling lights in the background. The image had been cropped to look like they were having a private moment rather than attending a significant fundraising event. There was a second photo of Louis playing the violin and Olivia watching him with a smile, sitting just off the stage. Then, finally, the photo that had been taken as they'd been leaving. Louis peering down into Olivia's face with a look of love and Rebecca cropped out.

A sinking feeling settled in her gut. She recognized the name on the photo credits—the reporter for the local paper. The reporter must have recognized Louis and sent the photos to *People* magazine.

"You spotted something more interesting than the winning bread pudding, didn't you?" Olivia mumbled to herself.

How foolish she'd been. Louis too. They'd moved around Little Rock for more than a month without concern. Other than a few intense looks, they had lived without Louis being recognized. But now their luck had run out.

Louis, she guessed, had not heard about their leaked photos. Yet instead of the anger that had been there the first time Olivia saw her picture in the press, a sad ache stirred within. The content life they'd been living in Little Rock for the last month would be no more. Now that the press was here, things wouldn't be the same.

Olivia dressed and brushed her teeth. Then, following the sounds of someone moving in the kitchen, she rushed out.

"Louis, our luck is up," she called down the hall. "Would you believe that you've been recognized?" Olivia rounded the corner and stopped to see Rebecca standing by the coffee maker.

Lines of sadness were etched on Rebecca's forehead. She pointed toward a piece of paper on the dining room table. "I'm so sorry, Olivia. He left a note."

Olivia rushed forward, reading the neat script.

Dear Olivia,

I am so sorry to leave in such a manner. Sergio came to inform me that a private plane was waiting for me at the Little Rock airport. My father suffered a stroke during one of his cancer treatments. My presence is required at home. I didn't want to wake you. I will be in touch soon.

Love,
Louis

Olivia absently traced her finger over the precise strokes of Louis's handwriting. Her heart throbbed at the stark words. His sudden departure

425

sent ripples of unease through her. Worries filled her mind about Louis's distressed state and, more grievously, his ailing father.

The word "stroke" stood out starkly amidst the cursive script. A few weeks ago, Louis had told her his father was a cancer survivor. Had the cancer returned? Olivia could almost picture Louis now, on the transatlantic flight back to his homeland, his face a mask of concern, his mind a whirl of worry. More than anything, she wished she could be with him to support him. He didn't know that. Louis only knew Olivia had wanted nothing to do with his life, even though he'd fully engaged with hers.

No wonder Louis didn't wake me.

The ghost of their shared kiss lingered. Last night, Louis was not the heir to a throne but simply a man who held her close. Olivia's fingers lightly traced her lips, remembering the soft pressure of his against hers. Now Louis was gone, and she was left to grapple with the uncertainty of what lay ahead. For him. For them. For the future they might have had together.

Disappointment washed over her, followed closely by a tide of sadness. Anger simmered at the edges. A lump of dread remained, lodged uncomfortably in her throat. She cared for Louis, and now his pain was hers to share.

Olivia's trembling fingers folded the letter. All she could do was wait for news from him. Her knees softened, and she reached for the chair back. Pulling out the dining room chair, she sat hard. She hoped Louis's father would be all right. But what if he wasn't?

Rebecca rushed forward. "I'm so sorry you awoke to such terrible news after a wonderful night."

"I can't believe they found him." Olivia rubbed a knot forming at the back of her neck. Had Louis seen the photos in *People*? Did it even matter?

Rebecca straightened. Her eyes widened. "Didn't you read the article? They found you *both*."

"No, that's not possible." She returned to the magazine's homepage.

"Yes." Rebecca's voice reached Olivia's brain like a distant echo. "Olivia, they know everything."

Olivia clicked on the photo and read the caption: *Prince Louis of Alloria's Royal Romance: Unveiling the Mysterious Love Story with Humanitarian Worker and YouTube Sensation Olivia Garza.*

Olivia's stomach lurched as she read the subtitle: *Fact or Fiction? In My Mother's Steps Documentary Captivates Hearts and Attracts the Attention of the World's Most Eligible Bachelor.*

Feeling her mouth grow dry, Olivia moved on to the article.

In an unexpected turn of events, Prince Louis of Alloria, the dashing heir to the throne, has captured the heart of not only his subjects but also that of a remarkable woman who is making waves both as a humanitarian worker and as an anonymous YouTube star. Prepare to be enthralled by the intriguing tale of their blossoming romance.

Meet Olivia Garza, the enigmatic lady who has stolen the prince's heart. While her identity as the woman behind the poignant documentary *In My Mother's Steps* has remained shrouded in mystery, her impact on audiences worldwide is undeniable. The original series, which delves into Garza's journey and her mother's extraordinary life, has left viewers questioning its authenticity. Is it a true account or a carefully crafted work of fiction?

Despite the lingering speculation, *In My Mother's Steps* has garnered sympathy, praise, and attention. The documentary highlights the struggles and triumphs of an ordinary woman who overcame immense obstacles, drawing viewers into raw emotions and thought-provoking storytelling. The fact that Prince Louis, one of the world's most eligible bachelors, has been captivated by Garza's creation only adds to its allure.

The prince, known for his charming demeanor and philanthropic endeavors, has long been an object of fascination for the public. His connection with Garza has ignited a new fervor of speculation and curiosity. As their relationship blossoms behind closed doors, royal watchers and fans eagerly await glimpses of their public outings, longing for a glimpse into their fairy tale-like romance.

"They think it's fiction? That I made it up?" Olivia gasped.

Rebecca threw up her arms. Her eyebrows furrowed. "Seriously? Is that what matters here?" She shook her head. "Louis needs you. He loves you, Olivia. His dad is in the hospital. You need to go to him."

"Wait, what? Go to him?" Olivia's chest felt heavy, and she moved to the kitchen chair to sit. "I want to go, but exactly what I was afraid of is happening. They figured out I'm the one behind *In My Mother's Steps*. Everyone's going to think I sparked this romance to gain viewers."

"So what?"

Olivia ran a hand through her hair. "So what?

That's easy for you to say. You're not in *People* magazine."

Rebecca opened her phone and began to scroll. "Just so you know, it's gone farther than *People*. It's all over." She held up the phone for Olivia to see one of the other celebrity websites.

Olivia's limbs felt numb—her whole body did. How could Rebecca act as if this was no big deal?

"Listen to this headline," Rebecca's voice rose. "*The Prince Is on a Roll Here in Little Rock.*" Rebecca held up a hand. "Wait, isn't that a Collin Raye song?"

"Clever, isn't it?" Olivia scoffed. "But this is my life."

"Isn't there a line in that song about not being me without you?" Rebecca said with a twang.

"What?" Olivia narrowed her gaze and crossed her arms, pulling them close.

"It's a line from the song. It's a sign, don't you see? You need to go to him. Go after Louis. Go to Europe. I've never seen you more *you* than when you're with him."

"You're talking nonsense."

Rebecca jutted out her chin. "I'm telling you the truth."

Olivia lowered her head onto the table, wishing she could return to yesterday, hoping this was just a bad dream.

"I know you won't listen to me. But why

don't you talk to Miss Jan? See what she says." Rebecca's eyebrows lifted in a challenge.

"Oh, you're hitting low," Olivia mumbled, pressing her hand to her forehead.

Olivia's phone buzzed. *No way.* But a niggling settled into her midsection. Sure enough, it was a text from Miss Jan.

I saw the magazine. Do you have time to meet for breakfast?

A cold chill traveled down Olivia's spine. Sure, she had the time. To do whatever she wanted to do. Alone.

Yes. Just tell me when, and I'll be there.

Olivia wondered how Miss Jan heard so soon. She guessed that Desiree had texted her too.

More than anything, Olivia wanted to return to bed again and escape into sleep. Yet the truth was, she also needed someone to talk to. Someone who'd met Louis. Someone who could guide her through letting go and attempting to put together all the broken pieces of her heart.

* * * * *

Buchenwald Concentration Camp
Date Unknown

I had to seek the Lord's forgiveness today. For so long, I allowed the darkness to overtake me. I longed for my husband and children until I could think of nothing else. And then, one day, a new thought broke through my fog. I knew I could do no good for them where I was. I also felt an urge in my soul to offer what I had. Yet what could it be? I had nothing. Less than nothing. I had rags for clothes and little food. My journal was tucked away, but it was written in my native tongue and would do no good to anyone.

"In your weakness, my strength is complete," my Lord whispered to my heart. And with the words of Scripture filling my mind, I knew what I had to offer. When I sat on my mother's knee, she taught me Scripture. It became a game between my sister and me, who could memorize more. Hope swelled within me at that thought. I had done the same with my children. Even though they did not have me, they had God's Word. They had God himself, and I had work to do until we could meet again.

Retaliation filled my heart, but that would lead only to my destruction. If I had anything to offer, it had to come from within.

An image of a grand banquet occupied my mind. The hunger of the men and women imprisoned with me was more than physical. How could I carry a banquet within my soul and have nothing to offer? And so I decided to provide what I had within me. Even though it seemed so little, it would be everything for some.

* * * * *

CHAPTER THIRTY-TWO

Alloria
Present Day

Even though Louis had walked the halls of Castle Alloria a thousand times, unfamiliarity wove through them after he'd been away for so long. When Louis arrived at his room, his suitcase had been unpacked. His things had been put away, and his laundry taken. Louis's heart pinched, and an ache filled him.

He scanned his room, noting his violin had been put in its familiar spot. And then his gaze fell upon a folded piece of paper on the coffee table in front of his sofa. The *Chocolate Ball* program. His fists balled at his side, and an overwhelming sense of loss filled him.

Glancing at his watch, Louis checked the time and then hit the one number he had programmed into the speed dial on his phone. It rang once, then went straight to voicemail.

"Hello, this is Olivia. I, uh, never mind. You know what to do."

Louis smiled, hearing her voice and her unassuming message. Not that he had time to talk to her anyway. His aunt, ever punctual, would arrive any moment.

Louis sat in the high-back chair in his private quarters, the air still and silent. Even though dozens of servants worked in this wing, their role was to be neither seen nor heard until requested. Still, something seemed off. The staff knew he'd just returned from the hospital, where he'd seen his father. The stroke had been severe, and his father had lost an extensive range of motion on the left side of his body. Yet the doctor had assured Louis that with intense physical therapy, the king might be able to walk again with a cane or walker. Undoubtedly, this had the staff worrying about their plans for the upcoming jubilee.

He picked up his phone and tried to call Olivia again, but it went straight to voicemail. Had it been a mistake not waking her, not saying goodbye? Sergio had urged him to leave a note, saying it would be easier. More than that, with his father's condition, they didn't have time to explain. Louis realized the seriousness of the situation when he'd boarded the plane to find a black suit hanging in the wardrobe, packed just in case his father passed away and he had to disembark in mourning clothes.

Still, Louis wished now he would have taken a few moments to say goodbye, to let Olivia know he still loved her, and this brief parting was no indication that he was giving up on their relationship.

As he waited for a meeting with his aunt, he missed the sounds of traffic from Hwy 630, which had been outside his hotel room. He missed the sounds of televisions, children running up and down the halls, and shouting. Lots of shouting. Americans were a rowdy bunch. Whether it was a misplaced phone, being cut off in traffic, or a funny TikTok video, you'd think they needed the whole world to know what they were pleased or displeased about. Well, except for Olivia. She was calm in the storm. She watched from a distance without being pulled in. Constantly aware, Olivia noted who was being vocal and needed a listening ear and a warm hug.

Footsteps sounded coming down the hall, and Louis perked up. He knew his aunt's steps primarily because the footsteps of the staff were rarely heard. The sound paused outside his ajar door.

"Come in, Aunt," he called before she could knock.

The door pushed open, and his aunt stepped into the room. She wore a patterned floral dress and low heels. Her hair was styled in a bun at the base of her neck. Although Louis hadn't thought much of her attire beforehand, it seemed so formal now. Did she ever tire of it? Louis rose as she entered, as he'd always been taught to do.

Aunt Regina entered the room with a smile and walked toward him with an outstretched hand.

"Louis." The way she said his name held so much meaning.

Louis approached Aunt Regina, and for the first time, he wished she'd pull him into a warm embrace, just like Miss Jan used to do in Little Rock. Instead, he extended his hand, which his aunt grasped, squeezed, then released. He considered going in for a hug for the briefest moment but changed his mind. His aunt cared—always had—and that was enough.

Aunt Regina sat on the plush sofa, and Louis returned to his chair. She offered him a sad smile, and he almost wished she'd asked him about Olivia. Of course, she was a woman of culture and never would until he brought it up.

"There are so many things to discuss, but I told Sergio we'd not bother you with your schedule yet. Although there is one thing we must discuss. It cannot wait."

Louis knew what it was. His birthday was coming up right before Christmas, yet to his aunt, it always received more attention and fanfare.

"Please, Aunt, can we forgo my birthday celebration just once? We do not need to celebrate, not with the condition Father is in."

"Certainly not. Everyone expects it. They set aside time in their schedules. This celebration is as much a part of the holiday season as anything else. Besides, the country needs to know that things are not as serious with your father as some fear."

He cleared his throat. "But they are serious."

Aunt Regina settled herself in a chair across from him. "Yes, but we do not need to raise the alarm."

Louis nodded his agreement, knowing it wouldn't be any use to argue. "Yes, of course."

Then, she clasped her hands together, allowing a soft smile to relax her rigid face. "We're going to celebrate you, sour face and all, whether you like it or not."

He couldn't help but force a smile in return. "By that evening, I'll ensure my face is no longer sour. I'm a royal, after all." He didn't mean for the harsh edges of his tone.

"It will be painless, I promise." She clasped her hands together. "I only have one request. Please choose a lovely song to play, nothing too sad. Think of something your mother would have liked. That will lighten everyone's mood."

Louis knew it was no use to respond.

Aunt Regina rose. "I have already been making plans. I'll send Ida around with the full schedule."

Louis rose and ran a hand through his hair, amazed at how his aunt was ready to move on as if he hadn't been living in America for the last month. "Yes, that will be fine." He considered talking about Olivia, but doing so would be futile. Not yet. He needed to figure out what he wanted for his future before he tried to explain it to his aunt.

Aunt Regina strode out of the room without a parting glance, and Louis moved to his violin. As requested, his fingers started a lively tune, but nothing felt right. Instead, with the emotion welling up from deep in his soul, Louis began a haunting melody. It rose and fell with the pain coursing through his heart.

He finished the melody just as he heard the tea cart coming down the hall. Then there was a knock. At his response, Beatrice entered. The tears in Beatrice's eyes alarmed him, and Louis approached her with quickened steps. "Is everything all right?"

"Excuse me if I'm talking out of turn, Your Royal Highness, but if you play that at your birthday, someone's going to keel over from her heart being broken in two, if not the lot of us." She set down the tray at the table.

Louis nodded once and returned his violin to its case. "Don't worry, Beatrice. That was just for me. I'll be certain to choose a piece appropriate for the environment."

He'd just settled for tea when a firm knock sounded at his door. *Ida.* One of his aunt's most dedicated staff members. Frustration rose within him. This life he'd always known no longer fit. He missed his independence in Little Rock, yet he'd have to do it sometime if he didn't deal with Ida now. The woman was persistent.

"May I speak with you, Your Royal Highness?"

"Yes, Ida." He poured them a cup of tea as Ida sat across from him. She perched her reading glasses on the tip of her nose and eyed him.

"Sir, I've mailed the invitations this morning, and we're working on the final seating arrangements. As for the menu, a light salad and ravioli stuffed with foie gras for a starter followed by broad beans with jamón and mashed potatoes."

"That will suit me fine," Louis said, even though the menu had been the same since he announced the foods as his favorite as a teen. An uneasiness stirred within him. He'd told his aunt he'd return for the holidays but never agreed to be home before his birthday. And still, the event had been planned. They probably knew him to be the dutiful prince who would always show up and do the right thing.

"And for dessert, sir, the chef insisted on something different this year. What do you think of Crema Alloria?" Her voice rose slightly as the words came off as almost a purr.

"Custard on my birthday? Is the chef mad? I always have chocolate cake."

"Yes, sir. But the chef thought you'd rather have a more traditional dish due to the circumstances."

Louis's teacup stopped midair. He brushed a strand of hair back from his forehead. "And what circumstances would that be?"

"Why, chocolate cake is an American dessert, sir. He just didn't want to stir up any uncertain memories on the night of your birthday dinner."

A spit of laughter burst from Louis's lips. "Let me get this straight. My birthday dinner will be ruined if the chocolate cake is served because it will bring up too many memories of the love of my life I left back in America?"

"Well, yes, I suppose that's the reasoning."

Louis set down his teacup. "Tell the chef I insist on chocolate cake. I need to celebrate my love for Olivia, not hide from it."

Ida nodded once and wrote a note.

Louis pressed his fingertips into his eyes and released a sigh. He couldn't return to Arkansas, but staying here without Olivia was impossible.

Ida released a sigh, and she placed her notebook on the side table.

"It's not just chocolate cake, sir," Ida started, her voice soft yet steady as she chose her words. "It's about letting go . . . for the good of the kingdom and, more importantly, for yourself."

Louis looked at Ida, his gaze falling on her aged face etched with wisdom and understanding.

"I'm not letting Olivia go, Ida," he confessed, his voice almost a whisper. "We're going to work this out." Yet even to Louis, his words didn't sound convincing.

"Of course, sir. But as things work out with your relationship, others need you too. Please remember that," she advised. "Alloria—this place, these people—it needs you. Your people need their prince, strong and committed."

Ida rose from her seat and walked toward the window, opening the heavy velvet curtains. The view was breathtaking—the palace gardens under a thin layer of snow, the bustling city beyond the palace walls, the sun setting over the horizon, painting the sky in hues of pink and orange.

"Look at all this." Ida beckoned, motioning for him to join her. "This is your world. And it's waiting for you to lead it, to shape it. Olivia may be in America, but you belong here."

Louis followed her gaze, taking in the sight before him. He felt the silent call from his kingdom, the sense of duty and responsibility.

As he stood by Ida, warmth for his country filled him. "You're right, Ida," he murmured, his gaze still fixed on the view outside the window. "And that's why I need to pray. It seems impossible to find the right answer for the sake of my kingdom and my heart."

Ida glanced up at him and smiled, her eyes filling with pride. "Indeed, sir. It's not about for-getting America. It's about remembering Alloria." She paused before adding, "And the chocolate cake will be arranged as per your request." She smiled, her eyes twinkling with subtle humor. And just like that, she returned to being a loyal staff member, dutifully fulfilling her prince's requests.

CHAPTER THIRTY-THREE

Little Rock, Arkansas

Olivia walked into the small café she'd eaten at with Miss Jan dozens of times, yet this time it felt different. She wasn't with Louis and couldn't look forward to seeing him later that day. He'd tried to call, and she hadn't picked up. She didn't know what to say to him. She also was afraid to hear his explanation for leaving. Telling her he loved her but still left would hurt as much as telling her he felt they needed time apart.

Olivia's favorite latte was waiting, and she guessed Miss Jan had already ordered breakfast for her too. The gesture would be wasted. She had no appetite.

Miss Jan offered a tender smile as Olivia sat across from her. "You know me well enough to know I love you and that I'm gonna tell you the truth, right?" Miss Jan, direct as always. Olivia expected nothing less.

"Yes, I know. And I'm almost afraid to hear it. You always tell the truth. I heard you talking to Trinity at the Chocolate Ball about how it was time for her to grow up and get away from Marcus since he doesn't treat her right. I'd never be able to get away with saying those things.

That's what I appreciate about you. You never hold back."

"That's because Trinity knows I love her. And Trinity knows she deserves better than someone who pushes her around. I just had to remind her of that. And what I'm gonna tell you, well, you know too. But you're not gonna like to hear it."

"Thanks for the warning."

"You know I've heard some of the stories about your mama. You tell the girls you want to help them because no one helped her."

Olivia nodded.

"Well, hon. The people God brings you to help ain't your mama. Nothing you can do will change things in the past. Bring her back."

"Yes, I know that."

Miss Jan cocked an eyebrow. "So you say." Miss Jan tapped her temple. "You know it up here, maybe." Two of her dark fingers patted her chest right above her heart. "But you don't know right here. And don't tell me you don't know what I'm talking about."

Miss Jan sighed, then leaned closer, focusing on Olivia's face. "God is going to bring lots of people into your life. Some people you might be able to help, and some you might not be able to. You know that. They get inspired and vow to make changes. But it's a hard world out there. It takes courage to go against the way everyone's living—to say no to the little feelings of happiness today, hoping things *might* be different tomorrow. But trying to do things differently is hard, especially when there are no guarantees."

Olivia wondered if Miss Jan was talking about the teen girls or her. Probably both.

"Then why are we even trying to make a difference?" Olivia asked. "Isn't it pointless?"

"We're doing it because folks need to hear that things *can* be different. Even small steps in the right direction are better than being stuck. More than that, we're here to tell them about Jesus. Let them know they can call out to Him even in the middle of a bad decision. Jesus loves them, and we must show them what that looks like."

Miss Jan pinched the skin of her arm. "This flesh here is Jesus on earth to them, and they need to feel his embrace. They need to see his love in my eyes, your eyes."

Tears filled Olivia's eyes. "Yes, and I need that reminder. Even when it doesn't seem like anyone is paying attention or trying to make good changes, I can be Jesus's love."

Miss Jan sat quietly as Olivia wrapped her mind around that message.

"It's funny, though, that you're reminding me that I'm here to be Jesus's love with flesh on to these girls. I thought you were in the Prince Louis camp."

"Wait a minute." The slightest smile curled up

on Miss Jan's lips. "No one said I was talking about our girls."

"Of course, you were."

"Listen now. Listen to what I said. I said, 'Some of the folks God brings you might be helped, but some might not be.' I said, 'They need to hear that things can be different, and you have a chance—in your flesh—to show them what Jesus's love looks like.'"

Miss Jan released a heavy sigh. "Don't you think those with status and wealth need it too, Olivia? Just as those with nothing need to know how much God loves them for who they are. Don't you think those with everything need to know the same?"

Olivia nodded, and as much as she didn't want to hear it, she knew Jesus's love was for them too.

"Okay, I get what you're saying, but I'm here to help these teens and tell their stories to a world that needs to hear and help. Look what happened last night. So many people have more compassion on the plight of our teens in the inner city than they had before."

"Yes, ma'am, you can stay here and do that, and I have no doubt God will use you. Yet why do you want to fight for a two-minute segment on local radio when God has offered the world as your stage?"

Olivia leaned back in her chair, pressing against the cool metal. "I suppose Louis knows what he's getting himself into by loving me, but something still holds me back."

"It's a different fear, isn't it?"

"To be in the spotlight . . ." Olivia let her words trail off.

"Then your grandparents will find you. Is that what you're worried about?"

Olivia gasped and remembered she had told Miss Jan part of her story once. It was an old pain. One Olivia had nursed over many years, kept dormant, yet never forgotten. The wound her grandparents had inflicted upon her was a scar now, healed over but still visible, still aching at times like phantom pains of the past.

"I can't face them after what they did," she said. "What if they reach out to me? Find me?"

"You let God deal with them. How they act or feel isn't your responsibility, is it?" Miss Jan soothed, imbued with the wisdom of years and the comforting certainty of faith. "One day, they'll have to stand before God and face how they treated their child and you. I guarantee the good Lord will have something to say about that. Do you know what forgiveness is?"

"I know forgiving someone is easier said than done. I know God asks me to forgive as I've been forgiven."

"Ah, but most people forget there's a word *'give'* right in the middle of forgiveness," came Miss Jan's quiet reply.

The words landed softly, nestling into Olivia's soul like a seed in fertile earth. "It's not saying what someone else did is right—because we all know what they did wasn't. Instead, it's giving what they did to God and letting Him deal with it. He is a God of mercy, but He's also a God of justice. I don't have to figure out what He's going to do, but I know He will do something, and I don't have to carry that burden around anymore."

Miss Jan reached over and took Olivia's hand in hers. Tears filled Olivia's eyes.

"It's okay, sweetheart." Miss Jan smiled. "You can give it to Jesus right here, right now. Nothing is stopping you."

Olivia swallowed down her emotion. She dropped her head slowly and closed her eyes. "Lord, help me to forgive," Olivia said softly. "It's a part of my story that I've clung to because I want them to pay, but the thorns are hurting me, not them." She swallowed again, breathing deeply. "Lord, I give it to you."

Miss Jan squeezed Olivia's hand and then patted it. Olivia opened her eyes and watched Miss Jan take a sip from her coffee as if Olivia's inner world hadn't just shifted on its axis. Conversations still flowed around them, but something within Olivia stilled.

A sense of solace wrapped around Olivia's heart, an enveloping comfort, much like the warmth of her worn sweater. She felt God's peace seep into her, calming the jitters and soothing the scars.

A quiet acceptance started to flicker within, like the first rays of dawn breaking through the darkness. God knew, and God would take it from here. Olivia's heart felt lighter, less burdened by the echoes of her past. She blinked, allowing a tear to roll down her cheek. Then she wiped it away quickly, smiling.

"I needed that. Needed to forgive." Olivia sighed. "You're so wise. Before I can step into what God has for me, I must let go of the baggage holding me back."

"And now, here is the fun part." Miss Jan winked. "You don't need to figure out the next twenty years or even twenty days. You just need to let someone know you love him and are willing to be by him. Poor guy, can you imagine him laying on those silk sheets with all those maids, butlers, and things with the woman he loves so far away?" A low chuckle emerged from Miss Jan's lips.

Laughter spilled from Olivia's lips, too, and as it did, out flew many burdens that Olivia had been carrying.

"Are you telling me I need to go to him?"

A smile filled Miss Jan's face. "Of course. I'm surprised you're still here."

"Yes, but it's easier said than done."

"Not really." Miss Jan pointed to Olivia's

phone. "Sergio texted me this morning. He told me to have you look at your email."

"My email?"

Olivia opened the email on her phone. Her eyes widened, and she gasped. "There's an email from Princess Regina."

Miss Jan sat straighter. "And what does it say?"

Olivia read quickly. "The princess is inviting me to Louis's birthday in a few days. She is asking me to come to Alloria as her guest. She wishes it to be a surprise for Louis. She already arranged my flight and is asking for my measurements." Olivia looked up, her eyes meeting Miss Jan's. "She asked if I would mind if she picked out some gowns for me to try on."

Miss Jan jumped from her chair and clapped her hands. "You're going to Louis's birthday party in Europe?"

Olivia nodded. "I have a flight that leaves tonight." Olivia rose and offered Miss Jan a quick hug.

"You better hurry." Miss Jan chuckled. "And I better get an invitation to visit you one of these days. I've always dreamed of going to a ball!"

CHAPTER THIRTY-FOUR

Alloria

Never in her life would Olivia have guessed she'd be picked up by a private jet and whisked off to Alloria to surprise a prince for his birthday. She hadn't even known a country named Alloria existed until a few months ago.

She'd been greeted at the car by a staff member named Ida, who led her to her sleeping quarters. Olivia entered the room, which appeared more like an apartment. Light blue wallpaper highlighted vines, leaves, birds, and orchid-like flowers. Colorful throw pillows sat perfectly arranged on a white sofa. A gilded mirror hung over the couch. Two sconce shelves adorned each side. A glimmering teal vase rested on each.

A polished wooden table sat in front of the sofa, and a crystal chandelier hung over it, its image reflected on the table's surface. Heavy, fringed drapes framed a tall window. Olivia tried to keep from gasping as she looked around. She spotted a bedroom suite between two double doors and noted fresh flowers on the nightstand.

"I hope you find everything to your liking." The woman stood with a ramrod straight back inside the doorway.

"I can't imagine anything better." Olivia's words were released with a sigh.

"Today and tomorrow, your meals will be brought to your room for breakfast and lunch. Prince Louis's birthday dinner is tomorrow at 7:30 p.m., and Her Royal Highness wishes your presence to be a surprise. I've been informed to ask if you need help dressing for tomorrow's dinner."

"Dressing for dinner?"

Ida eyed Olivia curiously. "Miss, did you bring formal wear?"

"I have a cute dress and sweater set. But I don't have heels. I did bring sandals. I suppose that's not what you're talking about?"

"Her Royal Highness guessed as much. She had some gowns brought to your room. I can assist."

Olivia nodded. "I don't know how to ask this, but are there rules for knives, forks, and things?"

Ida lifted an eyebrow. "Dinner etiquette?"

"Yes, that. I have no clue. Although, if you're busy, I'm sure there must be some YouTube videos to teach me the basics."

The woman's lips pressed into a thin line. She glanced at her watch. "We have a lot of work to do."

Olivia folded her hands over her stomach, and a sudden vulnerability washed over her, leaving her feeling exposed as if the world could see right through her. "Are you saying that YouTube won't cut it?" she asked, her voice dancing between jest and uncertainty. Her hands moved almost involuntarily, tucking a stray strand of hair behind her ear.

Ida frowned and then unbuttoned her cuff sleeves. "We will get started today and work tomorrow too. I think we can do it. I just hope you're a quick learner."

As Ida rang for a tea table and two service sets to be brought to Olivia's quarters, Olivia nodded and twisted her hair up in a bun. She thought of Miss Jan as she did. Miss Jan had told Olivia more than once that she always knew that things were getting serious when she twisted her hair up.

"I'm not sure where to start." The woman sat straight-backed in the chair, for a moment looking uncertain.

Olivia nibbled on her lower lip. "Let's talk about the bathroom. I've heard it said that no matter where you are, figure out where the bathroom is if you need it. And if you're in a foreign country, you must know how to ask for one."

"It would be impossible to point out all the facilities, miss. The good news is that someone will assist you once you walk out either door to the dining room." The woman leaned forward and smiled as if speaking to a child. "If you must use the restroom, simply say, 'Excuse me' without further explanation. Before you do, cross your fork and knife over your plate. This signals to the staff that you are not done." Ida positioned her utensils as so, and Olivia made a mental note.

"And when I am done eating?"

"Point the handles of your forks and knives to the bottom right of the plate."

Olivia nodded and then reached for her phone. The older woman cocked an eyebrow.

"I'm taking notes. I'm not texting, I promise." Olivia spoke into her voice-to-text. "Point handles of forks and knives to the bottom right of the plate when done eating. And that's forks, with an s, which freaks me out."

The woman tilted her head as if she were amused and surprised. Olivia had seen that expression on both Louis's and Sergio's faces.

Not only was she an American—she knew this woman thought of her as uncivilized. If Louis were set on stirring things up around the kingdom, this would do it. Olivia wanted to do this for the first time instead of questioning why she was there. She wanted to succeed. She wanted to make Louis proud.

"Now, for your napkin. It will be folded in half, and you will place it on your lap." Ida, whose back remained straight as a board, placed the folded napkin horizontally across her cream-colored linen skirt. "Then, when you have to use it, use the inside to wipe your face clean of food.

Then refold it. With the mess inside, it will keep your dress clean."

With the graceful movements of a ballerina, Ida lifted the napkin, opened it slightly, dabbed the corners of her lips, refolded it, then returned it to her lap. As she did, Olivia pictured herself sitting at the plastic tables with the teen girls and walking through the etiquette she'd learned.

An ache of longing filled her heart. She wondered what Miss Jan had planned for this week's meeting and made a mental note to recheck the time zone difference and video call the teens during the meeting if she could. A smile tugged at the corners of Olivia's lips, and then Ida clearing her throat reminded her where she was.

Olivia's mind raced back to Ida, and she looked from the napkin spread on her lap to the woman sitting next to her. "I'm so sorry. I let my mind wander, thinking about the teens I know back home. I need to teach them these things."

The woman gave a slight nod. "Yes, I suppose it needs to start somewhere."

Uncivilized Americans. Olivia straightened her back, mimicking the woman's posture and imagining her thoughts. *Deplorable manners, the whole lot of you.*

"And by whom will I sit at dinner?" Olivia asked. She didn't know if that was correct grammar, but it sounded good.

"The Office of the Marshall of the Court sets seating."

"There's someone whose job is just seating people at dinner?"

"This is a prestigious role. It's important that everyone is in the official spots at dinner and no one ends up out of place."

"Can I sit by Louis?" she dared to ask.

"I believe that is the current arrangement."

Olivia sighed. "Oh good, at least I will have someone to talk to."

"For the first course, yes."

"Wait, for the first course only?"

"It is commonly known that he speaks to the person on his right for the first course. For the second course, he speaks to the person on his left."

"That knowledge is not so common in Little Rock." Olivia broke into a smile. She waited a moment and was happy to see that Ida did so.

"No, that would not be common knowledge in Little Rock, Arkansas."

Olivia grinned. "And it is common knowledge that it's pronounced Ar-kan-saw, not Ar-Kansas."

"But that makes no sense."

Tucking a strand of hair behind her ear, Olivia shrugged. "You're right, and only talking to the person on your right doesn't either, unless you're used to it."

Ida nodded once.

"Okay, what else do I need to know? I'm sure there are many things, but the top of the top."

"When His Royal Highness, Prince Louis, is finished eating, everyone is done."

"What if I have food on my fork and am about to put it in my mouth?"

"You do not. You cross your fork and knife over each other, signaling you are done."

"Not that I should worry. My stomach is in knots. I don't know if I can eat anything. Unless . . . that isn't allowed."

"Eat what you can. It is better not to draw any attention. Knives go in the right hand, forks in the left, with the fork facing toward the plate. Also, use your knife to scoop food onto the back of your fork and then balance that food to your mouth."

"It's just too much."

"If you forget which fork to use or which way to sit, take a subtle peek at His Royal Highness and go from there." She returned her napkin to the table and folded it to the side of the plate. Olivia did the same. "And finally, royals enter the room in the order they ascend the throne and then the order of noble title."

"Which means I will enter last?" Olivia pressed her hands to her forehead. "I'm going to fail. It's going to be a complete mess. Everyone is going to mock me—even the servants."

"Quite the contrary. We finally have something

interesting to do around here." Ida smiled. "Now, let's look at those gowns, shall we?"

They walked through the bedroom and entered the largest closet Olivia had ever seen.

"No cleavage is important," Ida said. "Everyone is to be dressed modestly at all times."

"I like that rule."

Ida pulled out a gown. "I simply love this off-shoulder cream gown with gold embellishments. It reminds me of the one Princess Margaret wore for her birthday portrait in 1951."

"You mean Queen Elizabeth's sister?"

"Yes, one of my favorite royals. You sort of remind me of her."

"Really? How?"

"Well, she never really fit in. She marched to the beat of her drum."

"Should I take that as a compliment?"

Ida winked. "If you're around all the stodgy people I see, then you would take that as a compliment."

Ida showed her two other gowns that were both simple and beautiful. But then Ida pulled out something different. It was a white, floral ruffled gown. A yellow, burnt orange and green floral print decorated the sheer chiffon. It was accented with shadows of flowers and had a V-neckline that scooped low but not too low.

"This is breathtaking. Is it formal enough?"

"It is rather understated until we embellish it."

"Please don't tell me you'll take me to a jewel room."

Ida smiled. "No. We brought the jewels to you." Ida walked to the back of the cabinet and opened a drawer. Inside, three stunning necklaces had been laid out on velvet.

Olivia's mouth circled into an O. "This has to be a dream. Things like this don't happen to people like me."

Ida sighed. "Obviously, they do because it is."

Olivia eyed the pieces. "Are they silver?"

"Platinum." Ida motioned to the dress. "This bright hue looks prettiest with platinum or silver pieces, but of course, why wear silver when you can wear platinum?"

"Then you knew what dress I would pick?"

"Let's just say that I have been doing this job for a while."

"Wait." Olivia slumped onto the velvet couch in the closet. "I saw this on a magician show. It's the power of suggestion."

She padded over the lush carpet to the bedroom and pointed to the vase of flowers at the bedside. "Those flowers match the dress." Then she moved back to the living room area. "And so do the throw pillows. I guess there are numerous pillow arrangements, and you chose this one for a reason."

Olivia pulled a strand of her dark hair forward over her shoulder and then twisted it around her finger. She hoped she wasn't rude but knew she was right.

With a grin she couldn't hold back, Olivia looked at the coffee table at the display of photo books. One was gardening with a cluster of white flowers. The other displayed a woman walking through a field, wearing a similar dress.

Olivia turned, placing her hands on her hips. "You set me up." She couldn't help but laugh.

This time it was Ida who wore the surprise on her face. "I-I do not know how to respond."

Cocking her head, Olivia took a step forward. "Tell me I'm right."

"Of course you are, but out of all my years—"

"No one has figured you out? You are brilliant. You know what is best—looks best—but you also believe it's important for people to make decisions for themselves."

Ida clasped her hands and then pressed them tightly to her chest. She looked down, attempting to hide her pleased expression, and then she looked up into Olivia's eyes again. "No one has figured me out. Not once. Not Her Majesty herself when she was alive." She straightened her shoulders. "I do what I do to help."

"Yes, of course. I don't doubt that for a moment."

Unable to hold back her wide grin, Olivia strode through the bedroom area to the closet with the jewels. She leaned closer and eyed each one. "And this . . . you have something else going on with these." She tucked her lip under her teeth. "There is one that is huge, elaborate. It's worth a lot of money. Someone who values money will choose that one."

Olivia reached back and moved the chair closer. The blue velvet sank under her weight while she eyed the other two pieces. "There is also a piece of high design. It's so intricate and complicated. Someone has fine taste if they choose that." She rested her elbow on her knee and leaned closer to look at the third piece. It was simple yet beautiful. One single green gem was surrounded by a dozen smaller ones in the lightest blue.

"Louis's favorite color is green, and this blue is the same color as his eyes. I think it would look lovely against my olive skin, and I believe, Ida, you do too."

Olivia looked over her shoulder to find Ida standing just as straight as before, yet there was a new softness to her.

"I underestimated you, miss." Ida's voice was no more than a whisper. "I believe everyone has."

Olivia rose and blew a low breath before running her clammy palms down the front of her jeans. "I think most people do." But that was changing. Views on her documentary had tripled, and the response pleasantly surprised her. Instead of people accusing her of dating Louis to gain viewers, many said she was a breath of fresh air.

One commenter even called her a soaring eagle amidst a flock of sedate swans.

Olivia strolled around the room, taking in the wonder of the moment. *I'm really here. This is happening.*

Then she paused and wrinkled her nose. "That's what makes me good at my job, I suppose. I notice things that people often overlook."

"A unique gift for certain. Something your parents taught you? Your mother, perhaps?"

At the question, an ache pounced into Olivia's chest like a lioness creeping up and waiting and lurking until the moment it hit its mark. In her mind's eye, she saw herself as a little girl walking up and down the gas station aisle and noting what people bought—knowing who would be the best victim to whatever scheme her mother had drummed up that day. She didn't have long.

Olivia would only have seconds to decide upon entering the gas station, lest anyone become the wiser. Spotting the right person, she'd approach and ask them to point her to the bathroom. Her mother would get to work after Olivia hurried off in the right direction. Sometimes her mother would get them to fill her tank. A few times, a stranger even paid for a motel room with an all-you-can-eat breakfast. Her mother's stories constantly changed. It's as if she knew just what to say to gain sympathy.

"Excuse me. I was wondering if you could

help. We're going to see my mother, who just had a stroke. I think I left my wallet at the last gas station, but we're only fifty miles from home. Could you spare a few dollars for gas?" She always received more than a few dollars, of course.

Mom knew how to tell stories. Knowing she'd gotten these gifts from her mother had pained Olivia until she'd figured out how to harness them for good.

The sound of Ida clearing her throat startled her. Olivia jumped slightly and then dabbed the tears covering her lower eyelids. "I'm so sorry. I let my thoughts wander." She spread her arms wide. "I just can't believe any of this, you know. It's unbelievable."

Louis pressed his back against the leather seat of the chauffeured town car. A low breath escaped him. Sergio sat beside him in silence. Louis had already seen his father in the hospital and was pleased that he seemed to be making a slight improvement.

He was on his way to accepting an award in his father's place for opening a new wing of the children's hospital, yet standing in front of a sea of cameras and giving a meaningless speech written by another was the last thing he wanted to do today. Returning to America and trying to explain himself to Olivia was at the forefront of his mind. She'd sent him a brief text telling him she'd be willing to talk to him in a few days, and he just hoped he hadn't ruined all chances of being with her by the way he'd left.

Sergio turned from looking out the window toward Louis. "It's strange being back, isn't it, sir?" All morning Sergio had been going through the security protocol as if nothing were different. But his bodyguard had a distant look in his eyes as if he were trying to readjust to being back in this world of pomp and circumstance.

"I almost feel claustrophobic." Louis closed his eyes and leaned back against the seat. "In Little Rock, my schedule was not planned. I could wake up when I wished, eat what I wanted."

"Spend time with whomever you wished." There was a softness to Sergio's tone.

"Is it wrong that this morning I spent nearly all my time in the shower thinking of what it would be like to leave it all?"

"In the shower?"

"It's the only time I have to myself."

"Yes, well, the one thing I cannot get off my mind is the tacos," Sergio admitted. "It would almost be worth the flight back just to get some."

"Almost?" Louis grinned.

As they parked, an attendant approached. With a flourish, he reached for the door handle. He opened the door. "Your Royal Highness."

463

"Here we go," Louis mumbled only loud enough for Sergio to hear. Then Louis stood from the car, paused, and straightened his tie.

The attendant stepped to the side, and the hospital director approached. "Thank you for coming, Your Royal Highness. I hope your father is doing well."

"He is. You know my father. This is just a bump in the road," Louis assured him. "He apologizes for not being able to come himself."

"It is understandable. And I thank you again, sir. You will see the podium near the front," the man said, leading the way.

"I already placed your note cards for your speech. Then the president of the organization will come to the front. He will hand you the award. And afterward—"

Louis straightened his tie. "We will pause for a photo opportunity. Yes, my man, I know."

Beside him, the director flinched. "Forgive me, sir. I am required . . ."

"Required to go through protocol. I know." Louis softened his tone. "And I am the one who must seek forgiveness." He blinked. *Pull it together. It's not anyone's fault you left your heart in Little Rock.*

Louis considered using jet lag as an excuse but changed his mind. If he'd learned anything from being around Olivia and Miss Jan, it was that hiding the truth seemed like a wall of protection, but most of the time, it was locking yourself away in your web of lies.

"We had to call in even more security than typical, sir," the man confessed as they walked. "There are three times as many from the media as we typically see at this event. I believe your recent trip to America had something to do with that. And with the wedding not too long ago, I am truly sorry."

Louis followed the man, striding, to the secure area, with Sergio one step behind him.

He'd seen the photos and captions in the tabloids. When he'd returned home to Alloria without Olivia, everyone assumed Louis had been dumped and had a broken heart. He'd also seen that someone had figured out that Olivia was behind *In My Mother's Steps*.

A fierce pang of regret and longing twisted in Louis's heart. *She was right there, in front of me . . .*

Louis swallowed hard. His mind returned to a few days ago—the tenderness in Olivia's eyes. The warmth in her voice when she shared her stories of her mother and her hard childhood. Her stories were both a burden and a badge of honor. She had trusted him with her deepest secrets, yet why didn't she tell him about the documentary?

Was she afraid? Or did she just not trust me enough? His mind was a whirlpool of questions, even as he prepared to stand before the crowd in his father's stead. His presence would give his countrymen peace with the news of his father's hospitalization.

Of course, he could wonder why Olivia never told him, yet he'd never mentioned to her that he already knew—or that he'd sought her out that day in the courtyard.

The bitter pang of irony was not lost on him. Here he was, longing for a woman who hadn't been fully forthcoming and regretting a truth he'd hidden. He yearned for Olivia, for her fiery spirit, her compassionate heart. But the stark reality was that neither had truly trusted the other and now they only had missed opportunities.

As they approached the staging area, dozens of uniformed security officers blocked the growing crowd.

"Extra security, indeed," Louis said to the director. *They may think they know about the unlucky prince, but they don't know about the man who regrets, the man who longs, the man who misses.*

Spotting him, the crowd's voices filled the air, each syllable laced with curiosity and excitement. "Prince Louis! Over here!"

"What about your American girlfriend? Is it true?" one woman called.

Another, not so friendly, jeered, "How can you gallivant with an American when your father lies ill?"

The press of the crowd, the sharpness of their queries, felt like blows against his weary heart.

"Love or duty, Prince Louis? What is your choice?" A man's voice rang above the others, the question echoing in the sudden hush that descended upon the crowd.

The crowd seemed to collectively hold their breath, and Louis stared into the multitude of faces. Faces that didn't know his longing nor his deep-seated desire to be the author of the chapters of his life.

A pang struck his heart. His love for Olivia, his duty to his father. Each heavy with consequences, pulling him in different directions.

A tight smile graced his lips as Louis finally raised his hand, a quiet gesture that silenced the crowd. "The king's health is my priority. And as for my personal life," he paused, glancing around, "I would like it to remain personal, at least for now."

The crowd's voices rose again as soon as the words were out of his mouth.

The director stopped in the staging area, and Louis paused before him. The director cast an apologetic look. "They do love stories of romance, do they not?"

"The Unlucky-in-Love Prince sells papers. But even worse than facing the crowd is I miss her. I miss—" Olivia's name attempted to come forth, but Louis refused to let it slip off his tongue.

The man's mouth went slack. He leaned close and raised his voice so Louis could hear him over the crowd. "I am sorry to say I have read more than I should. Do you wish, sir, for me to give the organization's president your regards and tell them you cannot attend?"

"No, please put it out of your mind. It is not their fault I am unlucky in love." He blew out a breath. "We must be here for our people. To give honor where honor is due. To reward all good labor."

Another suited man stood at the side door to the press room and opened it. Louis strode through with a forced smile. Around him, the clicks of the shutters of cameras and the flashes of light tightened his stomach. This was his birthright. This was his duty and his role.

Louis moved to the podium, pausing behind it. He glanced at the note cards before him knowing he did not need them. As he'd been taught, he'd already memorized every word. He'd give this speech even though his mind was thousands of miles away.

CHAPTER THIRTY-FIVE

Olivia stepped into the ballroom, twirling a white rose between her fingers, almost oblivious to the clink of glasses ringing out in a toast and the curious whispers of onlookers who noticed the stranger in their midst. A quick breath escaped her lips as she eyed the tall pillars of flowers rising before her. The aroma of roses mixed with the scents of hors d'oeuvres carried by uniformed waiters. Finding a small vase on a nearby table, she placed the rose within, its petals standing out amidst the grandeur. Despite the room's allure, her pounding heart and tight stomach urged Olivia to refrain from taking a bite.

Seeing Louis ahead, Olivia's heartbeat quickened, and warmth flowed from her chest to her limbs. Men, draped in black tuxedos, escorted women adorned in a kaleidoscope of vibrant gowns. Yet amongst the colors and movements, Olivia's gaze never wavered from Louis. She moved toward him, her steps eager yet weighted with anticipation, hardly daring to believe that it had been less than two months since their paths had entwined beneath the warm, golden embrace of the Masai Mara savannah sun.

As she closed the distance, she paused at

Louis's side next to two towering bodyguards maintaining their vigilant watch. Sergio, noticing her first, let out a barely audible gasp. Capturing his reaction, Louis turned, and the glow of recognition in his eyes set her heart aflame. The world fell into a silent hush around them.

Not knowing what else to do, she offered a timid smile. Music wove around them, a soft symphony that matched the rising joy in her heart.

"Olivia. You're here?" Louis's voice was a whisper of surprise. He stepped aside, creating space for her at his side, and she felt a warmth spread across her skin.

"How did this happen? Just look at you." His gaze wandered, drinking in the sight of her. His eyes filled with such profound approval that it made her cheeks flush. "This dress. Wow, you look positively radiant."

"Your aunt Regina extended an invitation," she replied, her voice barely above a whisper. "Happy birthday, Louis."

With a tentative touch, her fingers grazed the intricate braid twisted and pinned at the nape of her neck. She hoped he liked it, wished he understood her efforts to fit into this world he inhabited. "I feel so, well, extravagant. It's unfamiliar. I'm not sure if I like it," she admitted.

Louis took her hand. Tenderness filled his gaze as he continued studying her. "You have nothing to worry about. You are the most beautiful woman in the room, and there is no one I'd rather have by my side." As if the fact that she was there fully hit him, a huge smile broke across his face. "I can't believe you're here. You came . . ." Emotion caught in his throat. "I have never been happier to see someone in my whole life."

"You think that now, but you haven't seen me trying to walk in these heels." She smirked.

He chuckled, a warm rumble of amusement that matched the sparkle in his eyes. "Did you get a photo to send to Miss Jan and the girls?"

"Yes." She nodded, her smile soft and nostalgic at the mention of those she left behind. "I wanted to video call them, but I was afraid I'd start crying if I did." She traced an arc around her face with her hand, the motion highlighting her painstakingly applied makeup. "And after hours of work on this face, the last thing I needed was smeared mascara."

She had barely finished her sentence when she noticed a shift in Louis's attention as his gaze darted across the room. His sudden detachment created a jarring pause in their intimate conversation, leaving Olivia's last words in the air.

Caught off guard, she followed his gaze, curiosity piquing. "Who are you looking for?"

"Aunt Regina. You haven't met her yet, have you?" he asked, his attention still split between their conversation and the sea of guests.

"No." Nerves covered Olivia's laugh. "But maybe we should wait until my stomach settles. All this is a little much."

"Nonsense. I can't wait for her to meet you. She's going to love you. I know it."

Emotion welled in Olivia's throat while she reminded herself to breathe.

Louis laughed again. "I finally understand why no one asked me to approve tonight's seating chart. Olivia, I can't wait to talk to you at dinner. To catch up. Honestly, I can't wait until we can be alone. I'd love to show you our family Christmas tree that the staff just finished erecting this morning. After dinner, I hope."

"I can't wait to talk to you too. For half of the meal, correct?"

Louis's eyes widened. "Yes. How did you know?"

"Ida has given me quite the education over the last two days. I just hope I'm a worthy student. I know that if I forget anything, I should just follow your lead."

"Well, it's about time." His smile stretched broadly as he adjusted his white collar and black bow tie.

"A tuxedo suits you."

"Yes, well, my collar is a bit too tight tonight." He ran his finger under the fabric covering his neck.

"Lou has been complaining about that since he

472

was a child." A woman's voice broke through. Olivia turned to see an older woman approaching. Aunt Regina was a bosomy woman with gray hair styled in a perfect knot at the base of her neck.

She paused and looked at Olivia, and immediately Olivia dipped in a curtsy just as she'd been taught. "Your Royal Highness."

Aunt Regina offered a quick nod. "So this is the young woman who has stolen Louis away?"

Olivia nodded, not confident about what she should say. "Thank you for inviting me . . ."

"She didn't steal me, Aunt. I ran away to her."

"Yes, I see. All is good now that you are home." She glanced from Louis to Olivia, scanned her from head to toe, and nodded her approval. "You are quite the lovely sight, aren't you? Now I know why Louis is smitten."

Heat again rose to Olivia's cheeks. "Thank you . . ."

"Speak up. You have a lot to offer, young lady." Princess Regina swept her hand around the room. "You are our special guest and the only birthday gift I knew my nephew would adore. You don't need to cower like a little mouse."

Louis touched his hand to the small of Olivia's back. "Thank you, Aunt. I'm sure Olivia appreciates your advice."

Olivia nodded. "Yes, thank you, ma'am," she said, even though she wasn't sure if Princess Regina's firm words were a sign that she liked her. Did she invite Olivia as a gift for her nephew or so she could evaluate the threat to their kingdom?

Then, with no more than a nod, Princess Regina moved toward two tall doors, which Olivia guessed led her to the dining room area.

After his aunt's departure, Louis's hand brushed her cheek as if she were the only person in the room. "Thank you for coming, darling Olivia. I cannot tell you how much this means to me." He stepped back. "It's time for dinner, and I must enter first. Wait here. I will ask Sergio to help you know when to enter the dining room. And from there, walk to me, and I will point out whether you are to my left or right."

Olivia nodded. "I can do that."

With a flutter of nerves in her chest, she crossed the threshold into the grand dining room. An ocean of eyes washed over her, curious and inspecting, like glistening pebbles on a sun-kissed shore. Each gaze was an arrow piercing through her armor of false confidence.

Just breathe, Olivia, breathe. Inhale courage, exhale fear. She reminded herself of her strength, coaxing her heart back from the precipice of panic, and approached Louis, who stood behind his chair.

"Welcome to dinner."

"Why do I feel I'm being eaten alive by everyone's gazes?" Olivia said, barely louder than a whisper. "I didn't realize I was the main course."

Surprised laughter exploded from Louis's lips, and even more heads turned in their direction.

"Shh," she hissed. "That isn't helping."

"Oh, just give them ten seconds, and they'll be fully absorbed in themselves again." Louis's laughter faded, but his smile remained.

Louis, her anchor in the storm, gestured to his left, lips twisting in an apologetic grimace. His soothing voice cut through the din of murmured conversations. "I can't wait to talk to you for the second half of the meal," he murmured just loud enough for her to hear.

Then, his voice grew louder, carrying over the simmering din of the room. "I'm sure my sister will provide lovely conversation."

Louis sat, and she followed.

The long grand table stretched from one end of the room to the other. Delicate china and silver utensils were perfectly arranged, and sweeping displays of flowers and candles decorated the center of the table. To Olivia's left sat a young, thin woman about her age. Her gaze fixed on Olivia's every move. Catina, Louis's sister. Olivia told herself to relax.

A young man in a white server's suit pulled out her chair, and she sat as gracefully as possible while he pushed it back in. Reaching to her plate, the staff took the cloth napkin and offered it to her, folded.

"Thank you," Olivia whispered as she placed it on her lap.

Louis cast her a wink, and a smile began tugging at one corner of her mouth. Only then was she fully able to give attention to the woman beside her.

Catina's light brown hair flowed to her shoulders, and she wore a stunning emerald green gown that complimented her hazel eyes. She looked similar to Louis, and Olivia guessed that the two would have the same smile if Catina dared to offer one.

"So, you are my brother's American interest?" Catina took a sip of water and cocked an eyebrow.

"I suppose you could say that. Have you ever been to the States?"

Catina nodded. "New York, once, but I'd rather talk about Louis than my time in the Big Apple." Catina paused as a salad was placed before each of them. "Listen, I love my brother. He is always quick to open his heart, which never leads to anything good. Did you know you are either the fifth or maybe the sixth woman he has fallen in love with? You'll find them all if you read past editions of the tabloids. He has a type, too. Petite, dark-haired, and mysterious. Although I admit, you're mysterious in a different way."

Olivia nodded, not knowing what to say.

Instead, she noted people around her were reaching for the outside fork, so she did the same.

"I saw the photos from Kenya. And my guess is you didn't know Louis was heir to our throne." Catina took a bite of salad that hardly counted toward her meal consumption.

"I had no idea." Olivia followed her cue.

"I believe you. I also believe if you did know, you would have never let your heart move in his direction. You're not the type of girl trying to win power and popularity. So why are you here?"

She pulled in a breath deciding what to say. It was obvious that Catina saw her as yet another one of Louis's girlfriends who'd play with his heart and then leave a crushed prince in the wake. Perhaps Catina would soften if she knew that Olivia did not see this as a game.

Olivia released a heavy sigh and then wondered if that was allowed. "That is something I've asked myself a million times," she confessed. "Part of me thinks that caring for someone like Louis is worth going out of my comfort zone, but the other part of me—"

"Would be correct," Catina cut in, speaking low. "Relationships are hard enough. I can't imagine how hard it would be to be opposite people from different worlds trying to make a relationship work. I mean, if you came here, what would happen then? You don't speak French or

Spanish. And then there's the Parliament. Would they even accept you?"

"Is that something I need to worry about?"

Catina cocked one eyebrow. "One of many things. Many people will have a lot to say about any relationship Louis tries to find himself in."

"Is that what happened in these other relationships? It was too hard to try to please everyone?"

A harsh laugh escaped Catina's lips. "If that were only the case."

"What do you mean?"

"Every young woman found something *more* to her liking. More status. More wealth. More popularity. You name it."

Olivia attempted to take a few more bites of her salad, but it did little good. Her heart ached for Louis—always being left behind after giving his heart.

"Do you know why Louis was in Africa?" Catina took her napkin from her lap, dabbed the corners of her mouth, and then refolded and returned the napkin. "Did you see it in the papers?"

Olivia had refused to look at the papers or buy those tabloids. She wouldn't put any money toward that type of reporting. But Louis had explained.

"Louis was in Africa because it was the wedding day of someone he was involved with." Olivia tried to keep her tone casual.

"Yes, and Constance was the love of his life."

Anxiety filled Olivia. She shifted her feet. Everything within her told her to run. Did she need someone to tell her she didn't fit in? Every ounce of her already declared that. "And what are you saying?"

"I am saying that you're a distraction."

"A distraction?"

Catina touched her long pearl necklace, rubbing the pearls between her fingers. "I think he needed the time away. He needed something different. I am sure the United States opened his eyes to a different world and let him get his mind off his lost love for a while. Or so I heard."

Olivia put down her salad fork and fiddled with the edge of her napkin. She didn't know what to say. Or what to do.

"I don't want to hurt you. If my brother is one thing, it's faithful. He's loyal to our father and aunt to a fault. And while everyone thinks you're charming, we all know nothing can come of this. There are certain expectations for royals and who they marry."

"Yes, but what about Harry and Meghan?" Once the words were out of her mouth, Olivia regretted it. Harry was not the heir. More than that, Harry had left royal life, his family, and his country. Olivia winced.

Catina lifted an eyebrow. "And we know how that has turned out, don't we? Harry stepped

479

down as a working royal. It's a tragedy. Yet their saving grace is that William has stepped up to fulfill his role. Harry was a spare. And my brother . . ."

"Your one and only prince?"

"Constance choosing someone else was a shock to all of us. They had dated for years. I liked her. She seemed to have a good head on her shoulders. But that's until she went to London for a holiday and met a man with ties to the British throne. Of course, the world knows and loves Great Britain's royal family. Why settle for a lesser-known prince when she could have so much more?"

"The relationship ended because this woman chose someone with a higher status?"

"Exactly. Goodbye, lesser royal. Hello, world stage. The wedding was broadcasted, you know, and Louis was invited."

"That's awful."

"I thought so too. So he went to Kenya instead."

"And met me?"

"And went on safari with you on the wedding day."

Olivia recoiled as if she'd been punched in the gut. Louis had told her that, but it sounded different coming from Catina, especially since the whole family—and maybe even their country—expected Louis and Constance to marry.

As her salad plate was swept away, Catina

continued speaking. "I wish I had different news for you."

Shooting pain throbbed in Olivia's heart. *And Louis goes for someone with no status this time. Why would I look above him when he's already out of my league?*

Olivia shifted in her seat, and she questioned Catina's motives. Was Louis's sister sympathetic to Olivia? Was she trying to protect Louis from another broken heart, or did she have other reasons altogether?

Tension tightened in Olivia's chest. *Lord, I need discernment here.* The prayer that filled her mind surprised her. She needed God's wisdom but often didn't remember to ask for it until after she crashed and burned.

The pounding of Olivia's heart softened as she witnessed sadness in the princess's gaze.

"You are a nice person, Olivia. I would just hate to see things go farther and not have them work out in the end." Catina offered a smile. "As I said, no matter how infatuated Louis seems now, there are simply too many other problems. He's a brother and a son but an heir too. It's sometimes difficult when there are so many people to answer to."

Olivia wanted to tell Catina that things were different between her and Louis, but she wasn't sure they were. Catina, more than anyone, had seen it all.

Catina's words hung heavily around Olivia, a pendulum of doubt swaying continuously. Olivia wrestled with her thoughts, trapped in the what ifs.

She'd flown across the sea, leaving the familiarity of her home behind for the alluring uncertainty of Alloria. Had she made the right choice?

The princess's words echoed Olivia's thoughts, *"No matter how infatuated Louis seems now, there are simply too many other problems."* The casual remark had struck Olivia like a hot blade. Olivia had barely scratched the surface of the complexities of royal life. And to continue the relationship meant she needed to accept this too.

Olivia longed to proclaim her unwavering faith in Louis, to reassure Catina that their bond was different, special, perhaps even immune to the pressure of the crown. Yet, she couldn't suppress the unease that stirred in her gut.

Her eyes met Catina's, and then Olivia quickly looked away. After the light salad, ravioli stuffed with foie gras arrived. Olivia did her best to eat it, even though she had no idea what it was. She thought she heard Catina saying something about goose liver, but she didn't want to ask. Instead, she questioned if she should just get up and leave before the main course was served. Did everyone here see her as Louis's distraction? Surely

Princess Regina wouldn't have invited her just to make a fool of her.

Then again, Aunt Regina could have asked Olivia to come to prove to her and Louis how much she did not fit into this world. Olivia's stomach tightened even more, and when the main course of potatoes, ham, and broad beans was served, Olivia questioned if she could eat a bite.

With eagerness in his gaze, Louis turned to her, and Olivia did her best to force a smile.

"I still cannot believe you are here. I could hardly sleep when you didn't return my calls." The words spouted out of him, and Olivia relaxed at the true joy on his face.

She released her breath, wishing to get out of this dress and slip into more comfortable clothes. Could she do this? Dress for dinner, be waited on by staff, face the judgment from everyone in Alloria? She moved her potatoes around on her plate with her fork.

Louis tilted his head slightly and eyed her. "Are you feeling well? Did you get some rest? Have you slept—"

"Maybe you've overheard. I've been chatting with your sister." Olivia blinked quickly, hoping the moisture she felt forming wouldn't turn into tears.

"I didn't hear." Compassion filled Louis's gaze. "But I fear what she had to say. I questioned this seating arrangement." The shadows beneath his eyes darkened. He cut a slice of his ham and took a bite.

"You didn't want me to talk to her?"

"I don't mind you talking to my sister. You are not the problem." He leaned close and spoke in no more than a whisper. "Catina has a good heart. She likes to think she has my best intentions in mind." He leaned ever closer. "And the truth is, she has always been jealous of me."

"Jealous? Why? Maybe she is realistic."

"Catina is only eighteen months younger than me. When we were children, we got along wonderfully. Often, she was my only playmate. It's not easy to organize play dates with friends from school. But as soon as I turned ten, things changed. I had special tutoring. I didn't have as much free time. I didn't have time for her. I was being prepared for my royal position."

"So, your friendship ended just like that?"

"It was a slow death. I was taken on trips and allowed to sit in on diplomatic meetings. The more training I received, the more she pulled away." He leaned close and spoke in a low tone. "And then, when our mother died, things worsened. I once overheard two men in the government saying that it was better for my father to lose his wife than his son, but no one mentioned he had a daughter. We both overheard them. Looking back, I understand they were speaking only about an heir. Even though the people care for her, she doesn't have much of a place."

"Unless something happens to you. Then wouldn't she be the heir? Shouldn't she have been prepared, too?"

A ghost of a smile touched Louis's lips. "It would require a vision that is yet to be embraced by all," he admitted, a thread of melancholy woven into his voice. "Unfortunately, some still frown upon the notion of a female heir, despite the powerful reign of Queen Elizabeth proving it can work."

"That's reasonable," Olivia conceded. "But there are aspects that your sister hasn't divulged, things I've discerned on my own."

Louis's gaze shifted back to her. "And what might that be?"

With a steadying breath, Olivia gathered the courage to speak. "You know I'm not drawn to status or wealth, Louis. You've adjusted your expectations to the point where you're not worried I'll forsake you for someone of higher stature."

Louis's eyes widened in shock. He bowed his head, and a rosy blush crept up his cheek. Olivia could almost taste the sting of her words. Immediately she wished she could take them back.

A feminine cough echoed from Louis's other side. Olivia's gaze flicked up to meet Aunt

485

Regina's steely eyes. A tidal wave of disapproval surged from Louis's aunt. Olivia quickly looked away. Now was not the time or the place for this conversation. She scooped up a small bite of potatoes and tried to push Catina's thoughts out of her mind. "This is a beautiful castle. Do you think tomorrow you can show me around?"

Louis's face brightened and then fell. "I would love to show you. But I have a speech on my schedule in the morning. I'd love for you to come if you can. It would be amazing to have you by my side."

"Yes, of course." She offered another smile, a genuine one this time. "I cannot wait to spend more time with you—to see your world." Olivia meant that. She really did. She just hoped she could get Catina's confessions off her mind. The upcoming days would reveal how well she could fit in here. At least she'd know—they'd both know. At least she'd be able to say she tried. Even Miss Jan couldn't argue with that.

* * * * *

Buchenwald Concentration Camp
Date Unknown

"Who shall separate us from the love of Christ? Shall tribulation, distress, persecution, famine, or nakedness, peril, or sword? As it is written, for thy sake we are killed all day long; we are accounted as sheep for the slaughter." Romans

8:35-36. Although outwardly I am confined, inwardly I have victory.

I woke again to the dream that I had been stripped down to nothing, just my last day in Rome before my transport. To stand naked before my captors in my dream was a replay of the humiliation, but it was more than that. In my dream, their hands were upon me, grabbing me, and I knew then they attempted to strip me of my soul.

I should have woken in fear, but instead, a new determination had welled in me—the desire to cling to life. To me, this is to consider beauty. To remember the concerts I had attended. To play with my fingers the songs I have known from youth. To reflect on the Bible stories the children asked me to read them repeatedly.

Oh, dear children, I know now that I confirmed my own in my efforts to build up your faith. As I remember the wonder of your wide-eyed gazes at the stories of Daniel's rescue from the lions or the three Hebrews in the fire, I am reminded that my faith will save me, too, although maybe not in the freedom I hope I will receive with my body, but indeed the freedom I know with my soul.

As the Hebrew boys proclaimed, "Our God can deliver us, but if not, be it known we will not worship your gods." Here, even on this dark day, I have hope. My God will deliver me by body or soul alone, yet I will praise Him. My heart believes in the reality of God's love as sure as the wickedness of men.

Oh, Lord, be with the children. Protect them in the shadow of Your high mountains. May they grow to know and love and follow You throughout their lives.

* * * * *

CHAPTER THIRTY-SIX

Alloria
Present Day

Six months ago, Olivia would have never imagined she'd be in Europe, being dressed by a lady's maid—with her hair and makeup perfectly styled—all to stand by her boyfriend's side as he performed his royal duties.

After emerging from the limo, Louis gave her a quick kiss before he was ushered away to give a speech for the tree lighting ceremony in the city center.

Olivia looked around, wondering if she should follow. Behind velvet ropes, the crowd chattered, many aiming their cameras and cell phones toward her. Olivia offered them a wave and a smile before she approached Sergio with tentative steps. "Does it say where I have to go?"

"Where do you have to go? What do you mean?"

"I know Louis's agenda is listed. Where to go. Where to stand."

"Yes, it's part of the security protocol."

Olivia smiled again as a young boy called out her name. "And I should be thankful that I don't need to be secure. But I would love someplace to sit." She pointed to her heels. Even though they weren't high, her feet were not used to them. "These things are killing me, and I see a place to sit in that tented area to the right of the stage." Olivia pointed with her chin, sure that pointing with her finger was unacceptable. "I think those teens are waiting to perform?"

Sergio gave a quick nod as he continued to scan the crowd. "They're a choir and will be singing in an hour."

"Do you think they will mind if I join them?"

"They won't mind, but I'm unsure if it's wise." Sergio furrowed his brows.

Wise or not, Olivia needed a place to sit. She could talk about it later with Louis, but she needed to get off her feet for now.

Olivia reached up and patted Sergio's arm. "I will be back there if you need me."

With quick steps, she hurried into the tented room, which was warm due to outdoor heaters. As expected, the teens sat around on their phones, showing each other videos and talking in low tones. Every eye lifted as she entered.

"Hey, guys, I hope you don't mind." With a flick of her foot, she kicked off one shoe and then the other.

"You're Olivia Garza, right?" One teen boy nudged his friend. "Look, it's really her."

Olivia laughed. "That's me, and my feet are killing me. You don't mind if I join you, do you?"

"Mind? Can I get your autograph?" one teen boy asked, eyes wide.

She shook her head and smiled. "What in the world would you want my autograph for?"

The teen threw up his hand in disbelief. "You are dating a prince."

"He likes you. Everyone can tell," one of the teen girls commented. Soft red curls fell around her face.

Heat rose to Olivia's cheeks at the sparkle in the young woman's eyes. Did Olivia also note a hint of jealousy? Many teen girls no doubt had a crush on the prince.

"We are good friends, yes." She winked.

"Do you think we can sing at the wedding?" another teen boy with white-blond hair asked. "Then we could be on television, which would be cool."

Olivia's mouth dropped open, and she held up her hands. "Hey, now. I think you're getting ahead of yourself."

"Are Americans always this friendly?" the red-headed girl asked.

"What do you mean?"

The blond boy flipped his bangs out of his face. "We do many of these events, and no one has talked to us before. I mean, no one."

"Well, don't tell anyone, but I'm pretty average. I work with teens where I live. I even live in an apartment."

"An apartment?" one girl asked.

"A flat," another voice corrected, laced with gentle amusement.

"Is the story of you two meeting in Africa true?" A bold voice broke through the surrounding murmur. Olivia turned to find its owner, a teenage boy standing behind the group seated at the table. He was subtly holding something behind him, acting nonchalantly.

Olivia's gaze met the teen's. Then she noticed a flicker of light reflecting off a sleek, black object in his hand. Her stomach sank as she realized he had his phone positioned on her, its lens unwaveringly fixed on her face.

"Wait, are you recording me?" Olivia's jaw dropped.

The boy shrugged nonchalantly. "Why wouldn't I?" he countered, a smirk pulling at the corners of his lips.

"Because it's against our policy." The voice that cut through the heated exchange was sharp, unyielding, like a steel blade. Sergio's words echoed in the spacious, tented room, the sharpness of his tone sending a ripple of hushed whispers around the gathering.

Startled by the sudden severity in the room, Olivia jumped slightly, her pulse racing as Sergio strode into the tent with a commanding presence. A mask of stern professionalism replaced his ordinarily calm exterior.

"I don't believe she was mentioned on the form." The red-headed girl shrugged. "She's not royal."

"She is nice, though." A teen girl with dark hair and a pixie cut leaned in. "I can almost see Olivia as someone I could be friends with."

Sergio's eyes remained fixed on the teen. "Delete it. Now."

"Sure, man."

Sergio narrowed his gaze.

"I mean, yes, sir." The teen fiddled with his phone.

Tension tightened in her chest. Olivia struggled for air. Heat rose to her cheeks, and she was afraid to meet Sergio's gaze. Had he seen how she'd kicked off her shoes as soon as she entered?

She slid her shoes back on as quickly as she could. Then, like a child caught with her hand in the cookie jar, she rose, smoothed her dress, and placed her hand on the teen girl beside her. "It was a pleasure to meet you." She scanned the faces of the others sitting around the table. "I'm looking forward to listening to your performance soon." She turned and approached Sergio's side.

Olivia cleared her throat. "Next time are you going to stop me?" she mumbled as they exited the tent.

He straightened his tie. "Would you have listened?"

"Probably not." She sighed. "But at least he deleted the video."

"He was streaming. On Instagram. It's already been downloaded and shared thousands of times. It will be millions by the end of the day."

Olivia placed a hand on her stomach. "I'm going to be sick."

"Yes, well, now the real work begins."

"What do you mean?"

"Now you need to act as if nothing happened. You're going to smile. You're not going to respond to any questions the media asks. You're not going to defend yourself."

"I understand."

Even though her shoes pinched her toes, Olivia pressed on a smile. She wasn't in Arkansas anymore. More than that, she represented the royal family of Alloria, whether she liked it or not.

"How bad will this be?"

"For yourself?"

"For Louis."

"Time will tell. This is the first time any of our royals has dated an American. It worked out well for Harry, didn't it?"

"Not really," she said, remembering her conversation with Catina the previous night. Her thoughts drifted to other examples, seeking solace in history. "What about Princess Grace? She was an ordinary American who married a prince." Her voice carried a wistfulness as she recalled the fairy-tale story of Grace Kelly, a Hollywood actress who became the Princess of

Monaco, navigating the delicate balance between royalty and her American roots with grace and dignity.

Sergio's face softened for a moment, acknowledging the romantic allure of the tale. "Yes, Grace's story was an exception. But remember, every romance has its challenges. Even Princess Grace had to adapt to a new world, learning new customs and a new language."

Olivia's chest tightened, the fairy tale losing some of its luster as reality intruded once more.

Sergio straightened his shoulders. "And that's why we'll have to wait and see. From the time that Louis agreed to go on that safari with you, everything changed."

The words hung in the air, a silent reminder that their path was uncharted, filled with unknowns. Olivia's heart trembled at the thought, but she also felt a spark of determination. If Grace could do it, then so could she. Even with pinched toes and a world watching, she would find her way.

* * * * *

Buchenwald Concentration Camp
17 July 1944

I cannot stop crying tears of joy. Though I was once again told I would not be able to see my children, I have been promised they are alive and safe. After so many lies, part of my mind worries that my captors are just telling me this, but as I pray, the Lord tells me it is true. Not just the children I birthed, but all I claim as my own now. I can see their faces, their dear, sweet faces.

Too many nightmares have visited me as I've worried they'd have to face what I see outside my window. Oh, my little ones, I cannot bear the thought of them knowing such pain or seeing such horrors. My greatest joy would be to see them again and whisper words of love. I hope they remember the feeling of being in my arms and my heartbeat in their ears as they leaned upon my chest.

I have told myself I do not want to turn my thoughts to how I ended up in this place lest I'm filled with hatred. I do not wish to have a hard heart like my enemies. When I heard my father had arrested Mussolini, I knew Hitler's wrath would find us. I knew it was only a matter of time before our defiance was discovered. Yet I dared to have hope when I was told I could be taken to Christian and that he would be freed upon my arrival. How foolish I was to trust the untrustworthy, but where is one without hope?

What is to become of me means little to me, for I know that to leave this earth is to be present with my Lord. Yet, to take me from my husband and children. They do not deserve that. I hope someday, all will realize that my sacrifice was worth the lives of many.

When I was first taken through these gates, I praised the Lord for allowing me to be His servant. It's always been in my heart.

Yet, being locked away in these isolation quarters made no sense. I did not deserve better because of the family I was born into. Why should I be given more even here when the men and women twenty yards beyond die of not enough?

Then God's message stirred as I paced my room, pleading and praying to either be sent into the camp or sent home. *Do you not see where I have placed you? Do you know the need for those who walk in the courtyard beside you? Do they not need hope, too? Do they not need my love?*

The tears came then, so heavy I was sure I'd collapse under their weight. People in need are all around us. The empty. The hopeless. The important men and women, all prisoners in solitary confinement within this same courtyard. Those with whom I now dine once knew great power, yet all has been stripped away. They rose high only to fall far. Yet they, too, need Christ's hope. Those who have everything and those who have nothing.

If any of us die, at least we can die with hope. May we live to share the hope our world will desperately need if any of us live.

* * * * *

CHAPTER THIRTY-SEVEN

Alloria
Present Day

Olivia tried to channel Kate Middleton as she stood in her heels, held her hands before her, and watched with an adoring smile as Louis participated in the Christmas tree lighting ceremony. As soon as the lights flipped on, a cheer arose from the crowd, and Olivia clapped her hands as elegantly as she could. Afterward, Louis strode around the group shaking hands. At one point, he looked at Olivia and waved her over.

Olivia did her best to walk straight and tall as she approached the older woman.

As she paused next to Louis, the woman reached for Olivia's hand. "I was just telling His Royal Highness that you are such a pretty thing." The woman's wrinkled face brightened with a smile. "And you remind me so much of Her Royal Highness, Prince Louis's mother. She was unsure and wide-eyed when she first started dating His Royal Highness, the King."

Olivia squeezed the woman's hand. "Please, are you telling me the truth? Because I think I felt a weight lift off my shoulders."

"Oh, please, child." The woman laughed. "No

one is comfortable around the royals right from the start." She patted Olivia's hand. "You're doing fine. Just fine."

Olivia looked at Louis, and he nodded his approval. "See, Olivia," he said as they walked away. "The people are going to love you."

"Are they?" She waved to a group of women as they passed. "Because I feel as if I'm messing everything up."

Louis led her in silence as they walked to the waiting car. It was only after they'd pulled away and offered last waves to the crowd that Louis turned to her. "I talked to Sergio briefly," Louis said. "He said he had to speak to some teens about a video."

"Louis, I'm so sorry. I wasn't thinking. This is all new to me. Are you upset?"

"Yes."

Olivia's stomach twisted, and she reached for his hand. "I wish I could take it back—"

"I am upset with myself, Olivia. I watched the video, and one of the teens was correct. They've sung for us yearly, but I have not spoken to any of them."

"I'm sure there is protocol," she responded, unsure if she should mention her aching feet.

"And that is the problem. We focus so much on being safe. We don't remember what it's like to be alive. How can we serve people when we don't know them?"

Louis ran his thumb over her hand, causing a shiver to race up Olivia's arm.

"My mother was more like you. She would step out of line, so to speak, to hug a young mother standing off to the side—just to encourage her. She would get to know the staff on a more personal level. My father always seemed frustrated with her, but I'm certain he missed it after she was gone. And I've been so focused on my duties, I've forgotten about the joy."

He paused for a moment. "One of the best things that happened to me was going to the laundromat, seeing that the crime problem is a fear problem. And going to the Character Club and seeing that it just takes a few women who care to change a generation."

"I'm unsure about the 'changing a generation' part." She chuckled.

"Do not discredit what you're doing. Each of those young women is different because of the time and love you and Miss Jan have given. I would love to bring her here and have her talk about how we can duplicate that good work here in Alloria."

"Bring Miss Jan here?" Olivia's voice floated on a hopeful note, the mere mention of her dear friend stirring a pang of longing within her.

"We will, hopefully, sooner rather than later," Louis assured her gently. "A nation built on principles of character and integrity will inevitably stand the test of time."

"This feels like a dream, being here," Olivia confessed. Out the car window, her gaze roamed across the medieval stone buildings and the newer buildings that displayed neon signs.

"And having you here is living the dream," Louis's fingertips brushing gently against her cheek, a featherlight caress that sent a current of electricity through her. "From the moment we met, when you shared the story of Promise, and how she was placed in your arms, I knew my life would change forever. Do you ever think of her?"

Olivia's breath hitched at the mention of the little girl who had touched her life so profoundly. "There isn't a day that goes by when I don't remember her, pray for her," Olivia admitted, her voice thick with emotion.

Louis's eyes held a surprising intensity as he nodded, a deep understanding reflected in them. "Me too."

"Really?" She looked up at him, taken aback by his confession.

"My heart has grown in ways I never anticipated. Falling in love with you has meant embracing and opening my heart to the world. Our shared compassion for Promise, for all the little souls like her, has enriched my life."

Louis's words wrapped around Olivia like a warm embrace, a promise of shared dreams, and a bond that went beyond mere romance. It was the kind of love that could stand the test of time. Yet could others in the royal family—in this nation—see that too?

Olivia held her breath as she walked alongside Louis down the gilded corridors during her tour of the castle. He smiled and swung his arm as he held her hand. "There is so much to see inside, but before we get to that, you must see the city as the sun sets."

Louis led her down the hall from her bedroom and walked through a parlor to tall glass doors. Louis paused at the door and opened it, waving her through.

With an anticipation that fluttered like the wings of a bird within her chest, Olivia gingerly stepped onto the long balcony, its surface covered with gleaming tiles. Wrought iron rails, masterfully crafted with intricate designs, encircled the space.

A breeze, laced with the crisp bite of early winter, brushed against her face, nipping her nose. Olivia pulled her sweater closer around her.

Stretched out on either side of the balcony, the castle stood majestic and unyielding against the backdrop of the clear sky. The castle's formidable stone walls reflected the sun, glimmering like molten gold. Set in the walls were windows accentuated by vibrant blue shutters.

Below them, the city unfurled like a storybook come to life. The cityscape, a miniature kingdom forgotten by time. Olivia's breath caught at the wonder of the medieval buildings nestled within a basin, cradled by towering, protective mountains.

"We're a microstate bestowed upon us by Charlemagne," Louis explained. "He rescued this land from the Moors, and his tales of valor are etched in our songs, our hearts. During the Spanish Civil War turmoil, we served as a sanctuary, a haven for many seeking refuge. Now, amidst the world's relentless pace, this place remains a harbor of serenity from the frenzied rhythm of life."

"It seems we're isolated, tucked away from the rest of the world."

"Our country's population is about the same as Little Rock's. We have our laws but feel the tugs and pulls of the larger nations around us. We have a small ceremonial army but do not have our armed forces because we don't have the infrastructure to support that."

"Doesn't that make you worry about being attacked?"

"If we are ever attacked, Spain and France will defend us. It's hard to stand up for our rights when our existence depends upon others. My father and grandfather have often said that being king is carrying the world's weight on your shoulders while still being forced to hold your head high."

"I can see that now." She pressed her lips together and then released a slow breath. "For so long, I thought being royal had everything to do with power and wealth. I really gave no mind to responsibilities." Her thoughts shifted, and she couldn't help but think of the news stories she'd read, the images she'd seen of desperate faces seeking refuge.

"There are things that keep me up at night, I will admit." Louis winced. "We have a smuggling problem. Since we're a natural route from France to Spain, it's been a problem from the beginning of our history."

Olivia's eyes widened, her heart pulling her toward the deeper issues that had seemed so distant before. "And the refugees," she whispered, her mind conjuring images of families torn apart, children lost and afraid, and entire communities moving in search of safety. "I've seen the reports. The crisis has reached even these borders."

"Yes." Louis's voice was filled with sorrow that reached Olivia's soul. "It's an overwhelming issue. The human suffering is immense, and it weighs on us all. We are doing what we can, but it's never enough. The world is watching, judging our every move, yet they do not understand the complexity."

A silence settled between them, filled with the unspoken pain of a world in turmoil. And in that moment, Olivia felt a connection to something far greater than herself. Being royal wasn't just about fancy clothes and elegant balls. It was about leadership, empathy, and making decisions that affected lives. The fairy tale was fading, replaced by a reality that was far more profound and far more demanding.

With determination, she looked at Louis. "I want to learn more, to understand. I want to help."

Louis's smile was gentle but proud. "And you will, Olivia. You have the heart for it."

Olivia's soul expanded with both ache and appreciation as he led her back inside, through the parlor and down a long, wide hallway lined with paintings and portraits, far more than in the Arkansas Museum of Fine Arts back home. Chandeliers cast golden circles on the gleaming marble floors.

"It's like a museum. I can't wait to see more."

"I can't wait to show you more, but I must insist on saving the best for last."

"The throne? Do you have one?"

"I will answer that later. But the best part is in the basement—something almost two thousand years old."

"Can I guess?"

"Do not worry, Olivia. I will show you. I finally have someone who's interested."

"Do you mean it's commonplace to most of your . . . friends?"

"Sadly, yes."

He led her into what appeared to be a former great room with an expansive fireplace adorned with marble statues. Suits of arms lined up against one wall, appearing so life-like that Olivia almost expected them to bow to Louis as they passed.

"The things in our home are collections built over the years. Books, paintings, engravings. We have a foundation that helps manage our collection."

She released his hand and playfully socked his arm. "So, we're not talking about some of grandma's things tucked into boxes in the attic. Ah, shucks. I was hoping to find an old whiskey bottle or two."

He chuckled. "No, nothing like that."

Louis led her down another long hall lined with beautiful furniture. Olivia paused at a large cabinet filled with blue and white porcelain pieces. The inlaid woodwork depicted a hunting scene, causing her to suck in a breath. She reached out a hand to touch it, then pulled it back.

"You can touch it. I promise that even if you do, it will be polished again by four o'clock."

Tapestries hung on the wall—more exquisite than anything Olivia had seen. "So many beautiful things."

"But my favorite happens to be the porcelains."

Louis paused before another cabinet that had floral porcelain dishes and figurines. He pointed to a small sculpture of three women in an open-air concert. One held a cello, the other a lute, and the third standing behind the other two a violin. They wore floaty, floral dresses, headdresses, and lush vegetation hung on their arched stage.

Olivia couldn't help but smile. "It's so beautiful and calm . . . and this is just one of many. I can see what you love so much."

"Lovely, yes, but remember, I told you I was going to save the best for last."

Louis took her hand and led her into an extensive library. He walked to the second section and grasped a book with a brown cover resembling thousands of others. He pulled it out slowly, emitting a scraping sound. As if sucked into the wall behind it, a portion of the bookcase opened, revealing a long, dim hallway on the other side.

"Please do not tell me it's a hidden passage-way."

Louis, looking bemused, ran his fingers through his hair. "Why don't you want me to spill the beans?" His eyes were filled with a playful curiosity that warmed her heart.

Her reply came out almost breathless. "You can't be serious." The realization struck her like a lightning bolt, making her heart race. Every childhood fantasy, every whimsical dream was materializing right before her eyes. "I feel like I'm caught within the pages of a Nancy Drew mystery." Her voice scaled the heights of her excitement. Her hands came together, fingers intertwining.

"I haven't uttered a word about it yet, but you look more excited than I've ever seen you." Louis's voice carried a note of affectionate amusement, and his lips curved into a tender smile that crinkled the corners of his eyes.

Unable to contain her delight, she leaped toward him, her feet barely touching the ground. She looped around his neck in a joyous embrace. "This is . . . it's amazing!" The words tumbled amid her giggles.

Then she stepped back.

Laughter poured out of Louis. "If I would have known such a thing would bring this reaction, I would have insisted we come here straight from Kenya." With another laugh, he tucked a strand of her hair behind her ear then leaned forward and kissed the top of her head.

The tenderness of the moment caused tears to fill Olivia's eyes. She wrapped her arms around his waist and squeezed again. Only then did Olivia step back and gaze through the open bookcase to the passageway hidden on the other side.

She peered down the long passage, slightly disappointed that it was lit by overhead lighting and not torchlight. With a sniffle, she wiped her nose with her sleeve.

"Are you crying?"

"I am not sure why, but yes. My favorite books growing up were mysteries, and more than anything—I mean anything—I always wanted to find a secret passageway. Especially one hidden behind a bookcase. I can't believe this is real and is happening to me."

"Well then, let me do the honors. It will take us to the next destination."

Olivia took Louis's hand, allowing him to lead the way.

Unlike the pristine rooms they'd just left, the rough stone walls lining the passageway hinted of dust. When they'd gotten ten feet from the entrance, Louis reached up and pushed against some type of switch. She heard the scrape of wood again as the bookcase slid into place.

"Some staff work for us for years before they even discover the passageway is here."

Doorways to other rooms stood out to Olivia as she and Louis walked down the passageway. They continued until they reached a stairway going downward. It was too narrow for them to walk side by side, so Louis led the way. Clinging to the handrail, Olivia descended multiple stories behind Louis. The sound of water dripping accompanied their descent. A musty smell wafted around them, and a breeze moved, coming from an unseen source.

Olivia ran her hand along the dusty wall while the scent of damp earth, dirt, and wet stone met her nose. They reached the bottom of the staircase, deep under the castle.

A small platform with a rail lay ahead of them.

"It is said that Charlemagne created Alloria to keep the Moors out of France," Louis explained. "Those who settled here often came for refuge. And they discovered a natural spring here and decided to stay."

A tingling sensation raced up Olivia's arms. "It all started right here. That's amazing."

Louis ascended the platform steps, extending a hand back to assist Olivia. She took it, allowing him to guide her beside him. Anticipating a covered well, she was taken aback to find a gaping expanse just beyond the protective rail. As she peered down, a gasp escaped her lips. The water below shimmered, casting an ethereal glow. To her astonishment, it seemed as if a constellation of stars danced just beneath the surface. Puzzled, she furrowed her brow and instinctively raised her gaze upward.

Momentarily disoriented, Olivia began to comprehend the architectural marvel they stood within. As they had descended, she hadn't grasped that they had entered a cylindrical tower, ingeniously designed to stretch high above them. Instead of the expected ceiling, the structure opened up to reveal the vast expanse of the night sky. The real stars above mirrored in the water below.

"Is that the night sky?" she whispered in wonder, her voice tinged with awe. "Are those actual stars reflecting in the water?"

Louis nodded with a proud smile, "Yes. The way they've integrated the heavens with this tower is nothing short of breathtaking, isn't it?"

"So, the entire castle has been built around this open tower?" Olivia's eyes widened as she took it all in.

"That's right. And we will always keep it open no matter how we expand," Louis affirmed, his voice echoing in the cavernous space.

"But why?" Olivia's voice softened, filled with reverence and a thirst for understanding.

Louis's gaze shifted upward, his eyes sparkling in the starlight as he replied, "It serves as a perpetual reminder for those who rule that we must always trust the maker of the stars. 'In the beginning, God created the heavens and the earth.' Even the mightiest rulers live under His divine authority. This is a belief held deep in the heart of our ancestors, one my father and I still honor. It forms the bedrock upon which our country stands. To see the stars is to acknowledge the presence of our Lord."

A sense of peace settled over her as she listened. "That's beautiful. I've never heard anything like it." Her gaze lingered on the twinkling constellations above, their reflections dancing on the water's surface. Her heart resonated with a divine song: *Yes, the Maker of the stars is here with me now.* The thought of her journey, her broken home, her history with her mother, her fears of relationships, her journey with Louis, everything was seen and known by Him. The idea that God, in His infinite wisdom, knew she would be here, even in her darkest hours, felt overwhelming. She found herself whispering, "I feel so seen. So known."

She also thought of Princess Alessandra. Even in a concentration camp, she'd found a purpose— to share God's love with those who'd fallen from the heights of power to being prisoners of the enemy.

A gust of cold wind whipped down the tower, causing Olivia to pull her sweater tighter around her.

Louis's smile warmed her further. "I knew you'd appreciate it. You're a gift, Olivia. Do you realize that?"

Before she could respond, Louis's arms enveloped her, drawing her closer. "There's so much more I want to share with you. About our people. About our land. But it's been a long day." He stepped back, his hand clasping hers. "Come, let's get you somewhere warm." He guided her back to the staircase, retracing their descended steps.

As she ascended the staircase following Louis, a sense of unease edged into her thoughts. He had shown her secrets she imagined were revealed to few. Some staff had worked there for years before discovering the secret passageway. As a newcomer, she had been introduced to it within days. He must believe that she was here to stay and that their relationship would only deepen from here. Part of Olivia yearned for this future, but another part was gripped with fear. Fear of the unknown, fear of love, and fear of the potential pain that could follow.

They made it to the top of the steps, and he led her back into the tunnel, shutting the door behind him. It was warmer here, yet a chill crept over Olivia. She should talk to Louis and help him to see that she still had questions and worries before things went too far.

He led her down the passageway a few steps ahead. "With Aunt Regina out of town, we don't have to dress for dinner tonight," Louis spoke over his shoulder. "But I must say, I find you more stunning each day."

Yes, this was the time to talk to him. She had to say something, to help him understand. Olivia paused and pulled her hand from his.

He turned, and worry filled his face. "Is everything all right?"

"I don't know, Louis. I don't know what to say. It's been fun to dress for dinner, but . . ." She nibbled her lower lip and then released her words with a sigh. "Just because I can dress the part doesn't mean I belong."

"Why would you say that?"

"You can dress in a flannel shirt and a baseball cap, but that doesn't mean you're a Southern boy. I can put on nice gowns and learn to curtsy, but that doesn't mean I'm meant to be a princess. Deep down, we are what we are."

"Do you believe that?" Louis ran a hand through his hair.

Olivia jutted out her chin. "I said it, didn't I?"

"If you believe that, Olivia, I have been fooled."

"What do you mean?" She took a deeper breath of dusty air and tried not to sneeze.

"If you truly believe that it's impossible to change and that we have to live with the lot we've been given, then what use is the Character Club? It doesn't matter if you help those teens stay in school, does it? It doesn't matter if you help them to get new clothes for job interviews or learn basic workplace skills. They are never going to be different from who they already are. Is that what you're saying?"

She crossed her arms over her chest. "That's different."

"I think you are scared. And you know what? I

am too. That's because it's not our pride we are most worried about. It's our hearts. Or at least it's mine. Going through this and losing you at the end hits me to the core." He tapped on his chest. "Each of us must decide if it is worth it." A sad smile joined his words.

"Louis." There was an appeal to her voice, but she didn't know what she wanted from him. What more could he say? Nothing. And still, her heart wasn't at ease.

Louis stepped forward, drawing her close to his chest. He leaned down to kiss her, grasping her shoulders as if he never wanted to let go. She melted into his embrace, the world fading away with their shared breath. When they finally broke apart, he gazed deeply into her eyes. Before he could speak, Olivia touched his lips. "Louis, I need to talk to you."

"Do we have to talk?"

Instead of answering, Olivia stretched so her lips reached his, trying to find an answer.

He wrapped one arm around her, capturing her.

She placed her hands upon his chest and rested them there. She stepped back again as her concerns fought for a place in her thoughts. "I need to say what I must say before changing my mind."

"Is something wrong?" Louis tipped her chin up so she could look at him.

"You mentioned the Character Club. I feel as

if I'm letting them down. It was a miracle that the Chocolate Ball brought in so much money. And amazingly, we have enough to cover over a year of expenses, but the problem is who will be there to ensure that happens? I cast a dream. I told those donating what they could expect. How can I leave?"

"That makes sense. I understand. I really do. But I need you to weigh something else." He wove his fingers between hers. "Olivia, I love you. I know my future. I know God has a plan for me, and I cannot imagine doing it without you by my side." He held her close, and she bent against him like a willow in the wind.

I love you. Had Louis said those words?

Olivia tucked her head under his chin, smelling cedar and pine. How could it feel so right in his arms and so wrong that she was leaving behind Miss Jan and the teens simultaneously?

She leaned back to look up at him. Hope and fear battled in his gaze too. Louis ran his finger over the hair above her ears, brushing the long strand back from her face. She closed her eyes as pleasure from the touch coursed through her.

"Louis, I want to say . . ."

"Shh. Don't feel like you have to respond. My 'I love you' can hang in this dusty air. I'm okay with that. I want you to be able to tell me when you know it to be true. Know it more than anything. Understand?"

516

She nodded slowly.

"I know this is hard. I also understand that it seems like it would be easier to walk away and go back to the life that you knew. It's a good life, a worthy life. But part of me dares to hope you could see this as a good life, too. That you could see what we could have together."

"You have so much confidence. I wish I had some of that. You've known your family members for centuries, and I don't even know my biological father."

"That doesn't matter to me . . ."

"I know it doesn't." She swept her hand in a wide arc. "But there's a whole world out there who it will matter to." She shrugged. "Can you give me time to think? Time to pray?"

"Yes, of course. Take all the time that you need. I'm not going anywhere." He smirked. "Just hanging out around here, exploring dusty passageways and hoping you'll see fit to join me."

Continuing down the passageway, they emerged back into the library, where Louis stood deep in thought. A few moments later, he took a deep breath and turned to her.

Louis pointed to the next door over. "Olivia, I have never shown anyone else this before, but would you like to see my mother's office?"

"Really? Are you sure?" Olivia searched Louis's eyes for confirmation. Stepping into the room was committing more than she'd ever done in any relationship. Louis opened his whole heart to her, and her answer was a promise.

Yes, I want to make this work. Despite the doubt of the media, the world, and even his sister.

"I am sure." There was no need for flowery language or grandiose gestures. Louis's voice alone was enough to convey the depths of his emotions.

"Yes," she'd answered. "I'd be honored."

With reverence, Louis opened the door, and together they stepped into an office that appeared to be an old-world Italian villa. Instead of intricately designed ceilings, a black iron chandelier hung from plain wooden paneling. Brick covered the back wall, and two inset bookshelves flanked a large portrait of Louis and Catina at ages six and seven. A simple desk and high-back chair sat in the middle of the room, and in one corner, a cozy couch held a pile of decorative pillows.

Louis pointed. "She used to read us stories on that sofa." Emotion caught in his throat. "The table in front of the sofa is a trunk filled with children's books." He walked in that direction and paused as if to open the trunk.

"She had work duties, of course, but she wanted to be a presence in my life. There was always staff, but nannies did not raise us."

"Do you mind if I look at the family photos on the desk?"

"Of course not. They are all as they were the

day she died." He sighed. "Well, except for the one Catina added a few years ago."

Olivia's eyes fixed on the newer photo of Catina, her husband, and two toddlers. "Your sister has a beautiful family. It must be hard for both of you not to have your mother around."

Louis nodded, then walked to the side of her high-back chair, putting a hand on it but not sitting.

Olivia leaned over and looked at a small cluster of photos. Their wedding photo with Louis's father in a regal dress. A baby photo of Louis and another of Catina. A gasp escaped Olivia's mouth as she noted a black-and-white image of a woman. An image that she'd seen dozens of times before in her research.

"Princess Alessandra." The name escaped Olivia's lips before she had time to stop it. She looked from the photo to Louis and pointed. "Why do you have that photo?"

He leaned forward, and his brow wrinkled. Louis squinted as if trying to recall a memory. "It's always been there. I believe I asked before." He straightened again and stroked his chin. "Mother told me that she was a dear friend of her grandmother. Yes, I think that's right."

"This is unbelievable." Olivia rubbed her brow, trying to remember if she'd told Aunt Liz about meeting Louis before she was sent information about the journal.

No, she had received the journal the day after she'd met Prince Louis, but this was something that her aunt had been working on for months prior. Her aunt could not have known about her connection with Louis. Yet, here they were together, in Alloria, looking at a photo of Princess Alessandra in a prominent place on the desk of Louis's deceased mother.

Chills traveled up Olivia's arms. She looked closer at the silver frame and saw that words had been engraved there. Instead of a name, it read Trust the Stars.

"Could we ask your aunt Regina what she knows about this woman?"

"Yes, of course, but my aunt has traveled out of town to be with a friend. She'll be gone for a few days. I do know someone else we can ask, though."

"Who?" Olivia's mind was racing. Her knees grew weak, and it took everything within her not to sink into the high-back chair.

"My father. If anyone knows about this princess, it will be my father. I am curious to know what you know about her. You seemed troubled. Or maybe excited." He tilted his head. "So much excitement in one day . . ."

"Princess Alessandra was a princess from Italy. She was arrested by the Nazis even though her husband was German. No one knows why the Nazis targeted her, but I believe she was a spy or maybe compassionate to the Jews. Her journal hints about lives worth sacrificing her freedom for."

"And yet her photo is on my mother's desk." Louis rubbed his brow. "Now I know we need to ask my father."

"How is your father doing?" she asked instead. "You said it's going to be a long road."

"Yes, but I talked to him this morning, and he was more talkative. He's been doing well in physical therapy. I can ask if he would mind if we visit tomorrow. He said he was eager to meet you."

"Eager or anxious?" Olivia cringed. She glanced at the photo of Princess Alessandra again, and butterflies danced in her stomach.

"He used the word *eagerly*. Unlike my sister, my father is being more open-minded about you. Maybe because he decided to marry the one person everyone agreed he should not be with."

"Now that's a story I want to hear," Olivia said. But more than anything, she had two questions: *How is Princess Alessandra of Italy tied to the former queen of Alloria? And why does this photo have a prominent place on her desk?*

Buchenwald Concentration Camp
24 August 1944

A cough racked Alessandra's body as she wrapped her thin sweater tight around her. Pain shot through her temples, yet she urged herself to enter the courtyard. A woman stood hunched over near the wall—starkly contrasting the barbed wire fenceposts that towered ominously, jutting into the sky.

Alessandra approached Josette, another political prisoner. The woman's face was drawn and haggard from their shared hardship. The ammunition factory's imposing form cast a shadow over them both. The air was thick with the scent of cold metal and gunpowder, a smell that had become all too familiar.

"Josette," Alessandra began, her voice soft yet firm. "Today is a new day. Didn't I tell you it would come?" She reached out and placed a gentle grip on Josette's shoulder. "We are still here. Do you know what that means? God still has a plan for us."

The woman didn't lift her head. "I don't know how long I can do this." Her chin trembled. "I close my eyes to see horrors and awake to nightmares."

"I know the situation is grim, but we mustn't lose hope."

Josette looked at her, confusion and despair etched in her tired eyes. "Hope, Alessandra? How can you speak of hope in a place like this?"

Alessandra gave her a gentle smile. "It's in places like this where hope is most crucial."

"It's hard to hope when I doubt we will make it

out." Josette gave a harsh laugh. "If I'd go back, I'd do things differently. We thought we would make a difference. It was foolish. We don't know if anyone we tried to help made it to safety. What if they are all dead, too? And yet look where we are."

"No." The word shot from Alessandra's mouth. "We must believe that they live, that all the rescued children live."

"But Alessandra, there seems to be no end to this. How can you still believe we'll make it out?" Josette's voice trembled.

Alessandra reached out and gently clasped Josette's hands in her own. They were cold, much like the reality they were living in. "Listen, Josette," she said, her voice carrying a subtle strength, "the world may seem to have forgotten us, but I assure you, God hasn't. If we are here, He has a plan for us. Each day we endure, we are a testament to the human spirit. We must believe that we are here for a reason."

When Josette didn't respond, Alessandra continued, her gaze unwavering. "Like you, I once questioned why God had placed me here. But then I realized, perhaps I was sent here to be a beacon for others. Let them know that even amid these horrors, we can hold on to our faith and believe this suffering will end. That's what gives me hope. God wants us to share this hope with others. After all, it's often in the darkest skies that we see the brightest stars."

Josette looked at her, something shifting in her eyes—perhaps a glimmer of the hope Alessandra spoke of.

"Remember," Alessandra added softly. "No night lasts forever. Dawn must come, and when it does, we must be ready to welcome it with open arms. For now, let our hope be our guiding light, burning brighter with each passing moment."

Alessandra turned her gaze upward, her eyes searching the overcast sky above as if her faith could tear through the clouds and call forth the stars. For a moment, under her steadfast gaze, the world around her seemed a little less daunting, a little more bearable.

She thought of her children. She also saw the face of the little girl, Leah. And she remembered when she handed the young girl over to the woman at the safe house.

I have a purpose for this girl and her family, God's Spirit had whispered to Alessandra's heart in that moment. Even now, goose bumps rose on Alessandra's arms, remembering.

Your next kingdom will be in heaven, His whisper spoke to her, *yet this girl will be part of a kingdom on earth. Her children will know Me and serve Me. Because of her, my light will go out. In a time of darkness to come, her descendants will shine.*

The words filtered through Alessandra's mind,

and she wondered why now—out of all times—she would remember that.

Then she saw it. The glimmer of the sun on the wings of an airplane, and Alessandra understood. This resurfaced memory was like stumbling upon a lost piece of a jigsaw puzzle. Finally, she saw the missing part that completed the picture of her life. And even as her heartbeat quickened, Alessandra prayed for Christian, her children, and Leah.

Lord, finish what you started in me and my family. Finish what you've begun in that girl and her descendants.

A shrill siren ripped through the stillness of dawn, followed by the hurried rush of feet and the urgent murmur of voices. Alessandra looked to the ammunition factory, and a deep knowing settled over her.

Glimmering figures appeared on the horizon, and a distant droning grew louder. Alessandra did not need to see the emblem on their wings to know what they were. *American bombers.*

A chill gripped her. The droning grew deafening, echoing off the stone walls surrounding the barracks and the factory, penetrating the grim silence of the morning. Alessandra grabbed Josette's arms and rushed her toward the trench that had been dug for moments such as these.

The first explosion hit the factory. Its destructive might tore through the iron and steel structure. With a sound that split her eardrums, a ball of fire rose into the sky. Then, like hundreds of soldiers firing at once, unexploded ammunition detonated, small explosions within the large ones.

Alessandra had no more tears to cry when the second wave of bombings came. The earth shook beneath the two huddled women as plumes of smoke and debris rose into the morning air. The metallic taste of fear filled her mouth as the world erupted into chaos.

"Our work is done!" Alessandra shouted to Josette, even though she knew her words would never reach the woman's ears over the explosions.

Alessandra closed her eyes, and before her was the image of a King. She breathed in a sweet aroma of the kingdom to come as the softest smile touched her lips.

Home.

CHAPTER THIRTY-EIGHT

Alloria
Present Day

Olivia expected something different from King Alfonso's hospital room. Two security guards stood outside the door, but once she and Louis stepped inside, the space looked like any other in the hospital.

Louis approached his father, who was lying in the bed. He bowed his head quickly, then took his hand. "Father, I brought someone to meet you."

He stepped to the side, and Olivia moved forward. She gave a perfect curtsy. "His Majesty the King." Olivia's eyes met the king's. The blue of his eyes matched his son's.

The aged monarch lifted a trembling hand to greet Olivia, his eyes shining with curiosity and warmth. "Finally, the woman who has captured my son's heart." His voice was barely above a whisper, akin to the soft whir of the respirator that aided his breaths. It hummed quietly, mirroring the king's tentative speech in the otherwise hushed chamber.

Louis perched himself on the edge of the hospital bed. The worry lines on his face deepened. "How are you feeling today?" he asked.

Olivia smiled. In this room, the grand titles of *King* and *Prince* were stripped away, revealing the raw, intimate relationship of father and son.

"I am doing better than your aunt. I told her today that we must postpone the jubilee," the king shared, his voice no stronger than the hushed humming of the heart monitors beside his bed. He shook his head slightly, the movement minimal, a mere suggestion. "She doesn't like when plans change, but there isn't much we can do."

"What matters is that you are well," Louis insisted. "Have the doctors had much to say?"

"Nothing worth blabbering about." He smiled at Olivia, then turned back to his son. "They say I will survive." King Alfonso smiled. "I walked twenty steps in physical therapy, which is something to be proud of."

They continued to talk about his health and essential meetings that Louis would attend in his father's place in the upcoming months. After twenty minutes of that conversation, Olivia smiled, realizing how much both men trusted her. They spoke of running a country, which included information she guessed few people were allowed to know.

As the conversation was dying down, Louis turned his attention to Olivia.

"Father, Olivia recognized a photo on Mother's desk today, and before we left, she wanted to ask you about it."

The king's eyes softened, a hint of melancholy deep within their blue depths. He inclined his head, his gaze moving to Louis, then Olivia. "Ah," he whispered, the quietness of his voice somehow enhancing the intimacy of the moment. "My wife's collection of memories. Which one caught your eye, my dear?"

Olivia held up the photo she'd brought. It was a black-and-white image of a youthful woman, her face alight with joy. King Alfonso reached out a shaky hand to take the photograph, his fingers brushing the edges reverently. His eyes filled with a mixture of joy and sorrow.

The monarch readjusted himself in his bed and looked at Louis. "Your mother wanted to tell you. She was waiting until you and Catina were older but never got that chance. Your mother's side of the family was from Rome. Your grandmother was brought to Alloria as a child in 1943."

Olivia took a step forward. "Was Alessandra Appiani involved? Princess Alessandra?"

King Alfonso's eyes opened wide. "How did you know?"

"You're never going to believe this, but my aunt works in a museum in Naples, and I have been helping her. My aunt is translating Princess Alessandra's journal into English. I've been reading it so that I can help create a documentary. As I read, I got the feeling that the princess was involved in helping Jews escape."

King Alfonso's eyebrows arched upwards in an unmistakable display of surprise. He studied her, his eyes probing as if trying to read an indecipherable code. "My sister told me about a journal a few months ago. She was informed about it. I'm sorry I grew too busy with my duties to remember to ask."

Louis looked at Olivia. "When did your aunt reach out to you about the journal?"

Olivia rubbed her brow. "I heard about it when I was leaving Nairobi. The day after we met. My aunt called me out of the blue and asked if I could help her with a documentary. I thought it strange that even she didn't know what I'd been working on."

"I knew." Louis's face brightened. He reached over and took Olivia's hand. "Don't be angry, but it wasn't a coincidence that we met in the courtyard."

Her mouth fell open. She stared at Louis, her mind scrambling to process his words. "You recognized my voice?" Olivia's voice wavered, the words barely audible over the crescendo of her beating heart.

"Yes, when you first arrived at the lodge," Louis admitted, a slight blush staining his cheeks. His gaze held hers, a genuine warmth radiating from his eyes. "I heard you on the phone. I couldn't mistake your voice. It has an enchanting quality, which was quite unforgettable from the documentary."

Her heart pounded, and she could not comprehend how her world was changing with his every word.

"Then in the courtyard . . ." he continued, breaking into her thoughts. His voice softened, his eyes squinting with boyish mischief that left her breathless. "I was watching you. I couldn't help but approach you when I saw you smiling at those monkeys."

Her mouth dropped open even farther. He knew who she was? A wave of heat rushed over her. "You were watching for me?" And all this time, Olivia had thought she'd been keeping that from him.

Louis shrugged. "Guilty as charged."

"So, did you have something to do with connecting me with this story?" Olivia pointed to the photo.

He shook his head. "I had no idea." Then his eyebrows lifted. "But I told Sergio about you, Olivia."

"And Sergio must have told your aunt I was behind *In Her Mother's Steps*." As the words slipped from her lips, Olivia turned to the king.

A silent understanding passed between them, her revelation acting as a bridge.

"Remarkable," he breathed, a frail hand resting over his heart. "It seems that once she'd heard about you, my sister didn't waste any time finding a way for us to share Alessandra's story."

The king's gaze flitted between her and the photograph as though he saw her in a new light. "Indeed, Princess Alessandra was very much involved in our story. My dear wife's grandmother was among those she helped to escape. That kind, brave woman risked everything to provide a haven for those in need."

He paused, a faraway look in his eyes as if the cobwebs of the past were being gently brushed away. Then he turned to Louis. "Your mother was proud of her Roman roots and her Jewish heritage. She wanted to pass on those stories to you and your sister."

"I'm Jewish?" Louis's eyes widened. "And my great-grandmother was rescued?"

King Alfonso's voice lowered. "It's truly amazing how paths cross, how stories intertwine. Olivia, your involvement with Alessandra's journal, your connection with my son, it's as if the threads of the past and present are weaving themselves into a tapestry of remarkable design. I'd say fate has a hand in this, but it seems to be my sister's doing instead." His eyes gleamed with an inner light. "Your coming here doesn't seem coincidental anymore. It feels like it was meant to be."

At that moment, standing next to the king felt less intimidating to Olivia. Instead, it felt like she was part of a larger narrative, a puzzle piece clicking into place. Her heart swelled with the realization, her emotions brimming over.

Princess Regina had a hand in all of this? Olivia's heart warmed.

King Alfonso smiled at Olivia. "You are a bright young woman. Ida—one of our most faithful staff members—told me so, but I'm discovering it for myself firsthand."

Then the king turned to Louis. "Your great-grandmother, Leah, was one of the children rescued from Rome during World War II. Although her family attended the Catholic church, all four of her grandparents were Jewish—and in the eyes of the Nazis, that alone deserved the death sentence.

"And her mother—your great-great-grandmother—was desperate for her daughter to go somewhere safe. There was a network, moving the children from village to village and country to country. Many children ended up here, traveling from Rome to Alloria, all with the help from Princess Alessandra."

"And what of the rest of the family?" Olivia asked.

"Every one of them died in a concentration camp. It's a hard story."

Louis sucked in a breath like the wind had just

knocked him out. "How could I not have known about this before?"

"Secrets once hidden are hard to reveal." The king's eyes fluttered. He was clearly growing tired. "Your mother knew much more than I, of course. But I remember one interesting fact. Each safe house was named after a celestial constellation. They moved the children from place to place like shooting stars across the sky."

"This should have been celebrated, not kept as a secret," Louis said.

"And what about Christian and the children?" Olivia asked.

"I met Christian years ago. He was not the illustrious figure the world knew him to be, but he became a friend. During the tumultuous times after the war, Christian was held by the Allies. He was part of the Nazi party after all. Christian was held on the island of Capri then later moved through a series of detention centers. By the time they released him in 1947, Christian had endured so much, but he bore it all with that characteristic stoicism. He never remarried, and he always spoke well of his wife."

Olivia released the breath she didn't know she'd been holding. "That's good news."

"Even now, I receive the occasional letter from Christian's children," the king continued. "They lead rather private lives, away from the glare and the clamor of the world. But their words, when they write, are always filled with memories of their father. And through them, Christian's legacy continues. As does their mother's."

"So they know?"

"Yes, they know the truth of all those their parents saved."

"And my mother knew all this—the connection with Christian and Alessandra?"

"Yes. She was thankful, but to her just knowing the truth was enough. Your mother loved me but did not love the attention," the king smiled. "She knew this event in her past was a part of her—a part that had shaped her into the person she was. But just as a precious gemstone can bring attention and scrutiny, she feared that revealing her secret would bring the unwanted glare of the media spotlight upon her toward our whole family.

"Your mother feared that if the truth was revealed, it could draw unwanted attention to her children. She worried about the scrutiny and judgment you both may face. You and your sister were too young to understand or handle such attention at the time. She also feared that whatever her past revealed would damage her reputation or credibility." His voice softened. "Your mother loved you both so very much. She wanted to keep you safe and protected. She believed that she could look into her past when she got older. Of course, that time never came."

Trust the stars. The words engraved on the picture frame replayed in Olivia's mind. And she thought of the well and what Louis had told her yesterday, *"Even those who rule must live under God's authority. To see the stars is to remember our Lord."* Warmth filled her chest, and despite all her doubt, she knew that God had brought her here, to the bedside of a king, for this moment, to learn the truth of Louis's heritage and Princess Alessandra's legacy.

"Father, did you say children?" Louis asked. "How many children did this princess save?"

King Alfonso nodded once as his eyes fluttered closed. "Twenty children. Your grandmother was one of twenty children saved by the princess."

* * * * *

Buchenwald Concentration Camp
Date Unknown
Found Among the Rubble

There will always be a *before* moment and an *after* moment when I realized how brave I could be. And *after,* I knew the joy of looking into a mother's eyes and giving her hope. I cannot save the world, but I did my best to protect those God asked me to . . .

* * * * *

Olivia had just sat down to eat breakfast in her quarters when her cell phone ringing caught her attention. She hadn't been able to sleep. Instead, she'd thought about the journal entries and all they meant. First, Princess Alessandra had no doubt come to the attention of Nazis due to her work in saving the lives of Jewish children, one of whom was Louis's grandmother.

Second, even in her captivity, the princess had realized she still had something to offer—this time to those imprisoned with her. The political prisoners she found herself with until her death. Olivia didn't want to think about that part.

Reaching her phone, Olivia saw Liz was calling and quickly answered. "Hello."

"Oh, good. I'm so glad you picked it up. We have a problem."

"A problem?"

"There has been a leak. I heard from a reporter friend that copies of some of the journal pages have gotten out. My boss agreed that we can't wait. I've booked a flight to Little Rock and scheduled a two-day press conference. There is one last journal entry, and I just emailed it to you. You should have everything you need now."

Olivia's mind raced, trying to keep up. "But I'm not in Little Rock."

"What do you mean you're not in Little Rock?"

"I'm in Alloria visiting a friend."

"Alloria, like the Alloria in Europe? Goodness gracious, Sharon was trying to tell me the other day that you were dating a European prince. I didn't give it any thought. You know how she exaggerates at times."

A heaviness settled on Olivia's chest. As hard as it was to come to grips with it, she was going to return to Little Rock. She'd been praying about whether to stay or go for the last few days, and she had her answer. Liz called from a layover in New York and was going to Little Rock. Soon Olivia would be too.

"I'll pack today and pray I can get a flight home." Olivia ran her hand down her face. "I'll finish the press release on the way. I've already learned so much." Olivia was already scripting the documentary in her mind. She knew that Liz, too, would be surprised about Alessandra's connection to the royal family of Alloria.

"But before you hang up, I have one question first," Olivia said. "Can you tell me where the journal was found? I think that's an important part of the story."

"It was found at the Vatican among the personal items of a priest. After more research, we discovered that the journal was found in Alessandra's barracks after her death. She died from injuries sustained during an Allied bombing. One of the political prisoners freed after liberation—a woman named Josette—returned the journal to Rome and gave it to a priest. When the priest died, it was packed away. Someone going through the archives found it."

"Amazing. All of it is amazing, isn't it? Wait until you hear how my European prince is tied into this story. I met Louis in the courtyard in Kenya and then found out his grandmother was one of the rescued children. He probably never would have known . . ."

An announcement blared through the phone, and Olivia wasn't sure how much of that Liz just heard.

"What are you talking about?" Liz asked. "Who is Louis? And did you say that someone was rescued?"

Olivia smiled. "I'll explain tomorrow. I'll do my best to meet you in Little Rock, and everything will be cleared up there."

Bean-bug,

Here is the last entry in the journal. Another wrote this last entry. It was not in Princess Alessandra's hand. Yet because of it, we know the rest of her story. I am eager for you to share this brave princess's story with the world.

Aunt Liz

* * * * *

I know these are the words of our Princess because I was imprisoned with her. I only write these words because I have heard that Hitler is dead. Yet I still worry that the Nazi rule will claim my body, for I am too weak to rise from this. Even though I may not rise, the deeds of my friend must live on.

Before I met Princess Alessandra in person, I'd heard of her piety and charity. When she wed a prince, they chose a simple ceremony to celebrate with villagers. The princess never was one to think of herself as better than others, and she always looked to the least of these, even until her death.

Her husband was the same, and many did not know about his generosity of heart. Though a German prince in his own right, he used his position and money for Jews and helped them escape to a place of refuge. A place of safety where the Nazis can neither find nor hurt them.

When faced with the plight of the children, our princess could have looked in the other direction. She could have lived out her days in relative safety with her children rather than within the walls of Buchenwald. As our princess told me, to refuse to speak against evil was to join it. And when she was told that she was needed to assist her arrested husband, she too was arrested.

Even though I faced more pain and horror than I could have imagined, I am thankful I was imprisoned, too, for I have this story to finish.

The Nazis tried to strip her name within the camp. They called her Frau Weber, yet they could never take her identity. The people knew their princess; she walked with care and grace, even in the darkest places. As a political prisoner, she had better food, yet she always shared. In the darkness, beams of hope shone through her eyes, making us vow to be stronger and fight to live another day.

I was there as they carried her broken body away on a stretcher. "Remember me not as your princess but as your sister," she spoke in her last conscious moments. And forever my sister she will be.

* * * * *

CHAPTER THIRTY-NINE

Alloria
Present Day

Clothes, trinkets, and souvenirs lay strewn about the room, evidence of Olivia's internal debate about what to pack. She moved from item to item, trying to decide what could fit into her suitcase and what had to be left behind. At the center of it all, a beautiful gown encased in a garment bag lay on the bed. Ida had placed it there, but Olivia knew she wouldn't take it. What need was there for such a gown in Little Rock?

Having spent most of the night drafting the press release and the morning making preparations for her departure, she was caught off guard when Louis entered her room, his eyes filled with worry.

"You're leaving?"

Her voice wavered slightly, and she took a shaky breath. "I don't want to have to leave you," she replied, her fingers absentmindedly twisting the hem of her shirt.

She was momentarily lost in the depths of his arresting eyes and every feature that highlighted his handsome appearance. The gentle curve of his jawline, the fullness of his lips, and the unwavering intensity of his gaze were almost too much to bear. The slightly tousled hair that framed his face showed the warmth of his eyes, and even in this tense moment, her heart swelled with an overwhelming affection for him. She loved him, more deeply than she'd ever imagined possible. That realization made their impending separation more painful.

His gaze, deepening with concern, pulled her back to the present. "But you are. For how long?"

"I don't want to give you an answer. I don't want to make another promise that I can't keep. I'm meeting Aunt Liz, and we'll share a short press release about what we're working on. Your aunt has given her approval for this, of course." Olivia smiled. "Although your family's part of the story won't be told until the documentary releases.

"I also want to ensure Miss Jan is doing well," she continued. "More women have stepped up to volunteer, and I think it'll be good for us to talk. I must let Miss Jan know we should look for someone to take my place."

Louis's eyebrows lifted at her words, and hope sparkled in his eyes.

"I care for you, Louis, I do. And I hope you know how hard this is."

Olivia tried to keep her tone casual but could only maintain it for so long. Overwhelmed with emotion, Olivia entered his embrace. She lifted her lips to his and relaxed into Louis's arms as the kiss deepened. Then, knowing the task before her, Olivia pulled back and stepped away.

"I am not leaving *you,*" she stated. "I thought about it through the night, what I wanted to say to you, and it's this." Olivia took a deep breath then released it. "You are the most amazing man I know. I used to think of your role as something I wanted to run from, but I couldn't be prouder of you. Alloria is in good hands with you as its prince. It will be in good hands with you as their king. I still don't know what the future holds for us, but now I'm not afraid to open my heart to you.

"With everything that's happened and the connection between your family and Princess Alessandra, I know God has had a plan for us from the start—and a reason for bringing us together. I love you, Louis. You told me not to say it until I knew I meant it. And that's why I'm saying it now. I love you."

He wrapped his arms around her, lifting and twirling her in a slow circle over the lush carpet as if she were Cinderella at the ball. "I'm just not sure how to think about waking up tomorrow without seeing you, being with you."

The moment hung between them, delicately wrapped in the warmth of their shared confession.

His expression softened, the usually confident prince reduced to a man in love. "Olivia," he whispered, his voice carrying a tremor. "Your words mean more to me than any crown or title ever could."

Louis lifted his hand to cup her cheek. His thumb traced her lower lip. His gaze held hers captive, reflecting the depth of his emotions. "There is an old saying in Alloria," he began, a tinge of solemnity coloring his tone. " 'He who finds love finds his castle.' And Olivia, you, my dear, are my castle. My haven."

His other hand encased hers, fingers intertwined, and he pressed a tender kiss to her forehead, breathing her in.

An hour later, they sat side-by-side as a limousine drove Olivia to the airport. When they arrived, Louis helped her out of the car and maintained a grasp of her hand. He brushed his thumb against the back of her hand ever so slowly. In a way, his touch was even more intimate than a kiss. She knew that no display of affection could happen because they were in a public place. But even now, his touch told her how much he loved her. How much he didn't want to let her go.

They walked through the airport doors, and Olivia paused her steps.

Before her, Princess Regina stood.

Olivia offered a curtsy. "Your Royal Highness."

The older woman walked toward her with quickening steps, and then she surprised Olivia with a warm embrace. Princess Regina planted a kiss on her cheek. "My brother called and told me about your work to honor the memory of Princess Alessandra. Just think—Louis would not be here if it were not for that wonderful woman. I am so proud of your work, and I look forward to seeing you again."

"Well, it seems there's a story of how all this came to be." Olivia grinned.

"A story for another time," Princess Regina said with a wink. Then she slipped her hand into her pocket and pulled out a thin, silver bracelet. "This is a gift that Louis's grandmother—my dear mentor—gave me years ago. Louis's maternal grandmother became a dear family member once her daughter married my brother. I want you to have it."

Princess Regina placed the bracelet on Olivia's wrist then released a satisfied sigh.

Glancing down, Olivia saw an inscription.

"The skies proclaim the work of his hands . . ." Louis translated.

"Trust the stars. Trust God," she whispered. "Yes, this was the hope I wanted to cling to."

Olivia saw Louis's surprised smile out of the corner of her eyes.

"It's an honor to do this work. I will treasure this gift. Thank you, Your Highness." Olivia didn't expect the tears to come, but it was impossible to hold them back. She hadn't cried this morning with Louis or on the drive over, but the tears were flowing freely at Princess Regina's words.

A surge of emotion momentarily took away Olivia's breath. The ache of years spent yearning for a family's acceptance and love welled up within her. The thought of belonging was overwhelming. Yet here she was, on the brink of something beautiful and profoundly life-changing.

Swallowing the lump in her throat, her voice was thick with emotion, "Your words, this gift, it's more than I ever hoped for." She hesitated for a brief moment, her eyes shining with sincerity. "Louis has captured my heart," she confessed, "and I'm so eager to build a relationship with you as well. To be part of a family like this, it's like a dream I never allowed myself to fully envision."

Princess Regina's eyes glistened, and the tremble in her lower lip betrayed her emotions. "There will be plenty of time for that, my dear. Just promise to come back to us soon. And when you do, call me Aunt Regina. It's what family does."

Little Rock, Arkansas

The sounds of Interstate 30 and the shouts of neighbors pulled Olivia from her sleep. She was home, but for the first time in years, it didn't feel like it. She had left her heart in Alloria.

The image of Louis, his face glowing with genuine delight at the sight of the baby elephant, swam in her mind. Memories of the playful sparkle in his eyes and the laughter lines etching deep into his cheeks made her heart ache. His wind-tousled hair on the savannah, and the twinkle in his eyes on his birthday, were images seared into her memory.

Now, lying in her bed, she understood the reality of the saying, "Home is where the heart is." Her heart was far away in Alloria with Louis.

Home was no longer a place for her. It was a person. It was Louis. It was his warm smiles, tender touch, and loving words.

Loneliness settled over Olivia. She thought about the events on Louis's schedule. She considered him attending them alone, which saddened her even more. She smiled softly, missing Princess Regina—*Aunt Regina,* too. The thin silver bracelet prickled the skin along her wrist, stirring her heart with a happy longing to spend more time with the older woman. She did not doubt that Aunt Regina would challenge her and cause her to see the world, and herself, in new ways.

Olivia sat up and stretched. She needed to text Miss Jan. Olivia had let her know yesterday that she was returning to Little Rock, and she wanted to invite her to today's press conference.

A knock on Olivia's front door surprised her. The sound belonged to her aunt Liz. Although Olivia recognized her aunt's knock, she didn't know what Aunt Liz was doing here so early in the morning. Olivia threw off the covers, put on her robe, and hurried to the door.

She opened the door to find Liz standing there—tall, thin, with short-cropped brown hair and sparkling green eyes. It was only the second time her aunt had been to her apartment, and this time urgency emanated from her. "Liz, what's wrong? Is there a problem with today's press conference?"

"No, not at all." Liz stepped inside the apartment as Olivia welcomed her in. "There's something I have to give you. I was going to wait until after the press conference, but I woke up with an urgency that I needed to do it today. This morning."

Olivia looked at her clock and rubbed her eyes. "At six o'clock in the morning?"

Instead of responding to the time, Liz continued, sitting on Olivia's sofa. Olivia followed suit.

"Sharon and Dewayne gave this letter to me a few years ago, but they told me to wait to give it to you until the time was right." Liz tilted her head as she studied Olivia. "There's something different about you, Bean-bug. I could tell when we talked on the phone yesterday.

You used to carry your pain around you like a suit of armor. You had a hard time letting in love and hope, too. But something's different now."

Olivia nodded. She knew what Liz was talking about. "It's Louis. He refused from the beginning to let me keep him at arm's length." A smile creased her face. "And it's Alessandra, too. She's shown me we can be strong even when we feel weak. We can depend on the Lord's strength."

"I'm glad you're saying that because what I have for you will bring back many hard memories. Your grandparents hired a private investigator to find you a few years ago. They got as far as Sharon and Dewayne."

Olivia's mind attempted to follow what Liz was saying. "My grandparents?" she whispered, a boulder building in her gut.

"They all met and agreed that your grandparents would write a letter, but we'd wait to give it to you until we felt you'd be open to it."

"And why would you think I'd be open to reading it now?" The words spat from Olivia's mouth, and a deep ache formed in her chest.

"Love changes things, sweetie. It's like food coloring dropped into water. Just a little of it spreads to every part."

Liz lifted her satchel onto her lap, unzipped the front pocket, and pulled out a long, white envelope. With a slight hesitation, she placed it on the scratched wooden coffee table, setting it before Olivia.

Fingers trembling, Olivia reached her hand forward, then pulled back. "This is so hard. I'm not sure I can read this. Not with everything that's happening today."

Liz sat in the chair opposite Olivia, tucking her shoulder-length brown hair behind her ear. "I know. I was going to wait until tomorrow night at the earliest, but God kept tapping me on the shoulder." She stretched out her hand and pushed the envelope closer. "I'm not sure why, but here you go. I'll be praying for you. Praying that the words will help and not bring more pain to your heart."

Staring at the envelope, Olivia glanced at Liz. Her aunt's tear-filled eyes reflected the morning light through the window. Her expression beseeched Olivia to consider the letter.

"I don't know what memories you have of your grandparents. I've never wanted to pry, but Sharon said they seemed concerned about you."

"Concerned?" Liz's words reignited the pain of abandonment and loss she'd tried to push down for a long time. How unfair they'd been to their daughter and granddaughter, not even caring that they were forced to sleep in their car, hungry and scared.

The hairs on the back of Olivia's neck rose in

her anger. "No good memories. But thanks for caring."

Liz nodded and rose. She reached out her hand to place it on Olivia's shoulder, then pulled it back, changing her mind. She walked to the door. "I'll see you at noon, Bean-bug. I can't wait to hear what you have to share." Without another word, Liz stepped out the front door.

Olivia sat in the echoing silence, her eyes drawn to the unopened letter lying on the table. Her heart pounded in her chest, and her breath seemed to catch in her throat. With trembling fingers, she reached for the envelope.

Slowly, carefully, she broke the seal, the sound of tearing paper echoing in the room. Her fingers brushed over the words, inked in a simple script. Whatever the letter contained, it was a turning point, a step into a world she still struggled to understand.

Dear Olivia,

It's hard to know where to start this letter, but we will say that we hope you are well, and we are so sorry for the way things have worked out with your mother, our dear daughter. To say that Christine was the joy of our lives from the moment we knew she was coming was an understatement. The doctors told us a few months into our marriage that children would not be in our future. Imagine our surprise when we discovered your mother was on the way ten years later.

She was a sweet child, outgoing. She always looked out for others. She would cry whenever she saw someone in need, especially when we couldn't find a way to help them. We had to stop watching the news for years because it was too hard. Yet when she wanted to do service work in Kibera after high school, we knew we couldn't protect her from the world forever.

When Christine returned from that trip, we knew something wasn't right. She was distant and aloof. And then we found out she was expecting you. Things went from bad to worse when Christine heard that your father had been killed in an accident. After you were born, we tried to help. Later we discovered our lovely daughter had turned to substances to deal with the pain of her loss and the stress of being a young mom. Even though we tried to show her our love, she believed all eyes were on her, judging her. One night she left, believing it was better to be with those who accepted her than those she believed judged.

We tried to get custody of you. We

helped so many times during those first few years. But things went from bad to worse. Our daughter robbed us of money and stole items from our home. We demanded that she go. It was the hardest decision we had to make.

We told her that you could stay, of course. We wanted you to stay. But Christine refused. She said that you were her daughter. She said that if we wanted to get to you, we'd need to help her. She left, and we hadn't heard from her in years. No parent should have to wonder if their child is dead or alive. And when she came to us years later, we told her she was welcome to move back. We told her that we wanted to help care for her. She refused. She said she needed money. That's all she wanted from us. She wouldn't even come in the house or let you come in. She made you sit in the car and refused to let us see you. We've never been so heartbroken in our lives.

Christine wouldn't budge, and we knew we couldn't either. Giving her money wouldn't help her. We knew it. We could tell just by talking to her that she was using drugs. We called social services hoping to find a way to help you, to provide a safe place for you, but she disappeared again like she always did. There is no heartache like being unable to help someone you genuinely love. To pray until you cannot pray anymore that they'll find a better way, only to have those prayers go unanswered.

We discovered Christine passed away a few years ago, and we've been looking for you ever since. We haven't been in your life but would like to be. We love you, Olivia. We always have. We know we haven't always done what was right by you. Will you forgive us? And maybe someday, we can see you—more than anything, we'd love to see you and perhaps even be part of your life.

Love,
Papa and Nana

Olivia didn't realize she was crying until she saw the wet spots on her paper. All those years ago, she'd seen her grandparents through her mother's eyes—as self-centered people who refused to help. Now she saw things differently. She'd worked side by side with Miss Jan for years. She knew things could be better for the teens she helped, yet she also knew it was impossible to help unless one wished to change.

Olivia looked into the mirror and peered into her dark eyes. Today she'd allow herself to see her mother there. "I have to let go of the past to discover a future . . . my future."

She closed her eyes and tried to remember when her mother's gaze had been soft and kind. Once upon a time it had been gentle. Then one dire situation after another hardened her look.

Yet even that hardness had been easier to see than what came next—only emptiness. "I am not her," she whispered. "I can miss and love her but choose a different path."

She wouldn't reach out to her grandparents today. In time she would. Perhaps Louis would go with her. Joy filled her heart at the thought of that. There would be much they could face together. She looked at her bracelet again. *Light in the darkness. Stars in the night.*

CHAPTER FORTY

As Olivia started her day in Little Rock, the warm morning sun streamed through her window, casting a gentle glow on the room. She sipped her coffee, and the familiar aroma of freshly brewed java enveloped her senses. The sounds of the bustling inner city drifted in through the window, a cacophony of distant car horns, chattering pedestrians, and the occasional rumble of a passing bus.

Outside, the urban landscape painted a stark contrast to the tranquility within her apartment. Olivia savored the rich, comforting taste of her coffee as it warmed her tongue. Her fingers traced the smooth surface of her favorite mug, its familiar texture grounding her in the present moment. But despite the familiar sights and sounds of the city, Little Rock no longer felt quite right to her.

As she contemplated this, her phone buzzed with a text message, disrupting the peaceful ambiance. Olivia glanced at her phone and noticed an email notification from Liz, prompting her to put her coffee down and delve into the message.

Bean-bug,
I know the press conference is in an hour, but I realized that I hadn't emailed

you the second to the last entry in Princess Alessandra's journal. I meant to mention it this morning, but then I forgot. I hope you're doing all right after that letter. I'm praying for you.

Nothing said here will change your writing, but you will appreciate it all. The princess had no idea these would be her last words written, yet they speak volumes about her life.

Thank you for all that you've given. I wouldn't be here without you.

Love,
Aunt Liz

Olivia took a slow sip of her coffee, the warmth spreading through her as she savored the bittersweet flavor. With a subtle click, she transitioned from Liz's email to the intriguing journal entry, her curiosity growing as she continued her morning ritual of discovery.

* * * * *

Buchenwald Concentration Camp
Date Unknown

Last night, I awoke with a line in my heart that I learned as a schoolgirl: "All of this is mine and thine." I memorized Tennyson's poem about the Earl of Burleigh because my tutor insisted I choose something, and this filled my heart with such romantic notions. The poem seems so simple, but its lines have so much truth.

Under the guise of a landscape painter, the earl won the heart of a simple village maiden. She married him out of love, not realizing his title. Love, she knew, was enough.

The maiden expected a simple cottage as their home, and she was confused when they passed the cottages one by one. And that's when he took her to a grand estate. His estate. He led her past all the fine dwellings to the greatest of all.

> And beneath the gate, she turns;
> Sees a mansion more majestic
> Than all those she saw before:
> Many a gallant gay domestic
> Bows before him at the door.
> And they speak in a gentle murmur,
> When they answer to his call,
> While he treads with footstep firmer,
> Leading on from hall to hall.
> And, while now she wonders blindly,
> Nor the meaning can divine,
> Proudly turns he round and kindly,
> "All of this is mine and thine."

All of this the Lord has given to me. So much my soul overflows. All that my groom—my Lord—has is at my disposal, and it took me coming to the pit of hell to realize this. While my physical eyes view the horrors unknown, my heart and soul touch heaven's edge, and no prison guard can strip this from me.

I no longer have a voice, but maybe I can shine. I have no speech, but my prayer is that my voice will go to the ends of the earth. I can speak against injustice, but perhaps the world needs to hear that God found us even in the deepest pit. He was seen by us even *here*.

When you are dying, you see things from a different perspective. To stand at the edge of eternity with those from every background shows how we're all the same. More than food or clothes, we need hope. I need hope. I've seen how a grain of hope can sustain a being for days. We're all the same, flesh and bones, soul and spirit, and the ranks we leave behind matter little.

Those who are greatest in this prison are not those who had wealth or honor in a previous life but those who give hope. A woman, a simple shopkeeper, somehow smuggled a Bible into this place. She sneaks away and reads it at my window—just a few lines daily to sustain me.

The one who had meant little and was over-looked means everything to us, everything to me. The hope she offers is food to my soul. It's all I have, but it is also all I need.

I will write of this place so the world may

know. If none of us survive, maybe my words can explain some of the hell we face on earth.

When we are stripped of everything, I realize the most important thing we possess is held within our hearts. Before coming here, I would have told you that the most crucial part of my life was the family I was born into and the family I worked to create.

Now I know differently. The essential part of me is that I am a child of God, not that I was a daughter of a king. The kingdoms of the earth could not protect me, yet God is here with me. And I will forever be with Him.

* * * * *

Olivia parked at the Arkansas State House, where the press conference was going to be held. Her nerves were on edge, and the large number of media vehicles parked out front pricked every one of them as more and more reporters exited the vans. Christmas decorations adorned the ornate, white historic building—or at least as historic as was possible in Arkansas. Yet the weather was far warmer than Alloria's. The bright sunshine, blue sky, and pansies waving in the breeze reminded her more of spring than winter.

Entering the building, Olivia saw Liz standing off to the side, talking to someone. His tall frame and the blond hair that curled over his jacket at the nape of his neck sparked recognition. "Louis?"

She must have said his name loudly enough for him to hear because Louis turned and strode toward her, a smile filling his face.

Olivia hurried to Louis, allowing herself to be washed away in the depths of the blue of his gaze. Propelling herself into his arms. "You came after me."

"You sound surprised."

"I had hope . . ." She didn't know what else to say.

His eyes lit with a knowing glint. "I don't mind going back and forth between my place and yours. And I even talked to my aunt about staying for Christmas." He shrugged. "Maybe she'll even join us. And then . . ." He let his voice trail off.

Olivia bit her lower lip. "And as much as I wish I could say that I want to leave with you right after that, I can't."

Louis's brows folded slightly, and he touched his heart. Yet like the gentleman he was, Louis didn't argue.

"Can you give me a few weeks? I talked to Miss Jan. She found an apartment for Trinity and her older sister, who will be helping with the baby when he or she comes. The apartment will be available in a week, and I'd like to help her set it up."

"Of course, I will wait." Deep contentment brightened his face. "I'm not asking about *when* you'll return, Olivia. I just ask that you do."

Olivia shrugged. "That's my plan. You can't get rid of me that easily."

Then Louis leaned down and offered the briefest kiss. She heard the murmurs behind them and the click of cameras, but she didn't care.

Olivia wasn't sure if it was the kiss that made her feel lightheaded or the idea that she was doing this. She was going to Alloria to be by Louis's side. She would be queen someday, Lord willing. Even though Alloria was a small kingdom, she could still make an impact there.

"There is just one more thing for us to settle on then." He winked. Just to the side of the stage where Olivia was about to read the press release of her life, Louis took both her hands in his.

"Olivia, this is no grand garden, and I have no eloquent speech memorized. But I offer this: to be by your side as we walk with God, to believe in your dreams and help you pursue God's call on your life, and to give you my heart."

Louis went down on one knee. He slid his hand into his pants pocket and pulled out a small velvet box. "I came to tell you that I love you with all of my heart, and I will do whatever it takes to give you a beautiful life." Louis cleared his throat and opened the box. "Olivia, will you marry me?"

She gasped at the ring. "Is that a pink diamond?"

"It belonged to my great-great-grandmother on

my father's side. She had a mind of her own, just like you . . . or so the story goes."

A tear trickled down Olivia's cheek. Instead of wiping it away, she leaned forward and touched Louis's face. The softest smile tipped his lips.

Seeing the love in his gaze allowed her to take off the suit of armor she'd built around the raw, tender parts of herself she'd attempted to protect for so long. Heavy and constricting armor had saved her, but it had also limited her ability to connect deeply with others, and—now she knew—God too.

Olivia sucked in a breath, and she knew more than anything this was her most significant act of strength and courage.

"Yes, Louis. I will marry you. I have no idea what that means for my life, but as long as you're in it . . . well, that matters most. I love you."

Olivia's heart seemed to double in size as she stepped into his embrace. And at that moment, it felt like stepping into the light, leaving the shadows of the past behind, and embracing a new beginning.

Although this wasn't an African savannah or a palace garden, it was the perfect place to accept Louis's love and to launch into the future God designed for her.

Olivia glanced over her shoulder. "I suppose we don't have to figure out when to release our news to the media." Then she took a step back.

"And as much as I want to talk about our future, I'm here because I have a job."

Louis lifted her hand and kissed her fingertips. "That's why I love you, Olivia. You want to change the world without letting anyone hold you back. While what we have together will undoubtedly be a positive influence, I hope that maybe what we have isn't just for the world but for us too. For me. For you. God loves us enough to see our hearts and will continue to bring us together, knowing how much we each need the other's love."

Olivia opened her mouth, wishing she were eloquent. Instead, four words squeaked out. "You need my love?"

"Like the air I breathe." He leaned down and kissed her, his lips gentle, tasting like honey and green tea. Her love for this man expanded in her heart until she was confident it would explode.

With a joy that filled her heart with the light of a thousand stars, Olivia walked up to the podium and told the beginning of the story that she couldn't wait to tell the world. Alessandra's story. Louis's story. And now her story too.

PRESS RELEASE

What would you sacrifice to give yourself entirely to the God you served, the cause you believed in, and the man you loved?

Have you ever heard about a princess in a concentration camp? Princess Alessandra Appiani was born to the king of Italy in 1902 and died within the walls of Buchenwald in 1944. How did one so noble end up imprisoned by the Nazis in a place of horror? Some say Alessandra was a spy. But the truth was, Princess Alessandra used her position to smuggle twenty Jewish children to safety. This princess gave her all to save those who had no hope.

Princess Alessandra could have survived the war. After her husband's arrest, she sought refuge for herself and her children within the walls of the Vatican, where she could have remained until the end of the war. Princess Alessandra chose to leave in hopes of securing her husband's release. Yet the German's request was just a ploy, and Princess Alessandra was soon arrested and transported to Buchenwald in East-Central Germany, where more than fifty-six thousand people died, including the princess herself.

Even in the midst of a great darkness, a great

light was found. Princess Alessandra Appiani trusted her Father—though not her earthly one, who proved to be fearful and weak-willed. She grew in trust to her heavenly one who never left her side, whether in the grandest palaces or in the darkest hell.

She could have chosen to live in safety within the walls of the Vatican, but building up our false sense of security does not ever guarantee our protection. Instead, Princess Alessandra threw herself into the arms of God and declared Him to be her safety.

Today a great gift is available to the public for the first time—some of the journal entries of Princess Alessandra—saved all these years by an unlikely protector.

The words within the journal are not only Alessandra's story. It is all of ours. We find ourselves in hard places even when we choose what is good and right. Our prisons may look different, but pain and conflict, hardship and hurt cage us just the same. Only when we step out of our safe place and risk everything do we discover who we are to the core.

Princess Alessandra did not allow the prison to change her. Instead, she let her strength of character change the prison—or, more accurately, the other prisoners. May we read her story and discover the truth that she learned. Each of us can give what matters most to those around us, whether they may be rich or poor. We each can provide love within our hearts, knowing that this love changes everything. And that, in the end, we are changed too.

Center Point Large Print
600 Brooks Road / PO Box 1
Thorndike, ME 04986-0001 USA

(207) 568-3717

US & Canada:
1 800 929-9108
www.centerpointlargeprint.com